Ex-army officer, mountaineer, payment security consultant and Internet entrepreneur, Duncan's writing draws on his adventures in his personal and professional life, supplemented by extensive research. He has worked and operated in over forty countries, spending much time in the Middle East, The Gulf, South East Asia and the Indian subcontinent. Duncan now lives in the Northern Fells of Cumbria, close to the Lake District, where he can indulge his passion for climbing and continue with his writing.

Dedication

For Ed, Hugo and Anna

and in memory of Sergeant John L Arthy:

for all the climbs we didn't do.

26th October 2021

Duncan Sperry

FAULT LINE

For Martin.

Remember, it is fiction!

Best Wishes

Duncan

AUSTIN MACAULEY PUBLISHERS™
LONDON • CAMBRIDGE • NEW YORK • SHARJAH

Copyright © Duncan Sperry (2018)

The right of Duncan Sperry to be identified as author of this work has been asserted by him in accordance with section 77 and 78 of the Copyright, Designs and Patents Act 1988.

All rights reserved. No part of this publication may be reproduced, stored in a retrieval system, or transmitted in any form or by any means, electronic, mechanical, photocopying, recording, or otherwise, without the prior permission of the publishers.

Any person who commits any unauthorised act in relation to this publication may be liable to criminal prosecution and civil claims for damages.

A CIP catalogue record for this title is available from the British Library.

ISBN 9781788780766 (Paperback)
ISBN 9781788780773 (Hardback)
ISBN 9781788780780 (E-Book)

www.austinmacauley.com

First Published (2018)
Austin Macauley Publishers Ltd™
25 Canada Square
Canary Wharf
London
E14 5LQ

All characters and companies in this publication are fictitious and any resemblance to real persons, living or dead, is purely coincidental.

Acknowledgements

This book would not have been written without the assistance, support and advice of my family, friends, supporters and mentors. I would like to thank my manuscript editors, Rosie Smith and Elaine Thornton; my old friends, Jim Askew, Jeremy Beswick and Mark Laycock, for putting me right on military matters – and also Jim, for the Arabic dialect translation; Will Aaltonen, for his mentorship, editorial input and support over many years; John Porter, for the cover photo; Richard Boyd, for his insights and unwavering enthusiasm; Diana and Matt Horner at e-book partnership, for the original digital publication; my regular climbing partners, Jim Fotheringham and Colin Downer, for keeping me marginally sane through this whole process; and especially Caroline, for being a wonderful mother to our children. To these and all others who have supported me, a heartfelt thank you.

Preface

Idris Morgan monitored the oscillating green lines dancing across computer screens, just as he had for the past ten days, fourteen hours a day. The daily business of moving large volumes of credit card payments internationally between banks was essentially a recurring and predictable business; just what investors had liked about CyberX when it was floated on the London Stock Exchange. However, for the last couple of weeks it had become unpredictable. Now and then a large spike, far larger than the usual flow, indicated abnormally high credit card payments transacting through an intermediary. Morgan knew what was happening: credit card fraud on a huge scale. He just hadn't been able to pin down the source – until now. It was his senior analyst, Abdul Shahid, who had initially picked up on the irregular flow of money and alerted him. The same analyst was now walking over to Morgan with a slip of paper.

Morgan took it from him and peered at the scribbled note: *Prague hub: Internet Payments Bureau.* 'Who the hell certified this service bureau from Prague?'

The question was rhetorical. He knew that it was either stupidity or collusion from within CyberX's Prague office that had allowed this fraud to be let loose. 'Thanks, Abdul. Top man. Good job. Have we got a full audit trail?'

'Of course we have, Idris,' Shahid replied. He prided himself on the integrity of his operations and he took this breach personally. Morgan looked at the screen for a full, long minute, weighing up the risks to the business, balancing his integrity and reputation against the need to trace and eliminate the source of the fraud. Eventually his solid, rugby-player's frame shook itself, and he walked over to the window looking out over the South Oxford Business Park. 'Kill it, Abdul! Switch off the third party payments bureau. Switch off the fraud.'

'Are you sure, Idris? Shouldn't we contact the authorities first? This is a criminal activity, isn't it?'

'What, and have our operations suspended? No, I'm positive. Just kill it. Pull the plug on them!'

'Consider it done,' replied Shahid with finality.

Chapter One

Two Weeks Later: Sunday, 22nd April

The blade swung upwards in an elegant arc. Anyone who knew about these things would have registered an element of ritual in the smooth, ruthless efficiency of the act. But no one saw it, not least the jogger deep in the Oxfordshire woods who took the full impact of the razor edge. There was simply no time: no time to observe the sweep of the blade dispassionately or intimately, no time to contemplate death, and certainly no time to pose the question: 'Why?'

***

Within the white tent pitched over the victim's remains, the Scenes of Crime Officer (SOCO) puzzled over the lack of ground disturbance around the body. The whole context conveyed a sense of supreme stealth. It was as though the perpetrator, if there was but one, had feline qualities. There was no discernible impression in the leaf litter; *as though they had carefully replaced the disturbed leaf-litter before they left*, SOCO recorded. Others present at the crime scene whose professional life was spent largely in grisly contemplation were surprised that a single blow to the throat could almost sever a man's head in such a well, smooth, elegant and efficient way.

SOCO had nothing tangible to show for several hours of microscopic investigation. With a mixture of admiration and professional frustration, he was just about to terminate the close-quarter search when he was handed something by one of the search officers that grabbed his attention: what looked like a miniature knife about an inch long with an equally small highly-polished handle. He popped it into an evidence bag for investigation. If the police at the scene were surprised, the pathologist was oddly enthusiastic. His initial irritation at having been requested to attend the crime scene on a Sunday had given way to professional admiration. 'Pure elegance. Any of our aristocrats up for the chop in the past would have paid handsomely to have their execution done as well as that.' Dr Andrew MacAllister hadn't quite got over the fact that in choosing this particular branch of the medical profession, he had somehow disappointed his parents. As a result, he always tried to find glamour in his chosen field.

Detective Chief Inspector Beckwith of Thames Valley CID nailed the pathologist with his unblinking gaze. 'Did you say "execution"?'

MacAllister paused, reflected, and drew himself up to deliver his verdict. 'Yes, execution. This, in my opinion, was not a random or opportunist act. Whoever did this was skilled, trained and purposeful.'

'Time of death?'

'Between six and nine this morning.'

'That's not much use,' replied Beckwith's young colleague. 'He left his house at six to go for a run. His wife called the alarm when he didn't return home. He wasn't found until midday.'

'Was this run routine?'

'According to his wife, he ran his life like a Swiss Railways timetable.' Detective Chief Inspector Beckwith spoke to his deputy. 'OK, Sergeant Lowe, you liaise with SOCO. I'm going to find the victim's boss.' He turned back to MacAllister. 'Thank you, Andrew. Anything interesting, give me a ring.' He eyeballed the pathologist. 'You say whoever did this was skilled? Like, say, a butcher?'

'This isn't the act of a butcher, Chief Inspector. It's more like the work of a trained slaughterman!'

**

Monday, 23rd April

Philip Dunstan left the gates of Green Park, central London, and turned right onto Piccadilly. He had enjoyed the walk across the park from his *pied-a-terre* in Belgravia. It was his favourite time of year. Spring: the season of renewal, and the end of his ritual three winter months in a workaholic stupor. It had been the same for the past nine years; work-yer-bollocks-off through the long, dark days and nights, then relax with a weekend retreat in London, followed by a week abroad pursuing his passion. To the casual observer viewing Dunstan's athletic, indeed languid, stride across the park, he might have appeared arrogant – spoilt, even. But this air of self-assurance and detachment belied the complexity of a man who had in the past forced himself to compensate for his natural insecurities by pushing himself beyond normal human limits of endurance, and who often retreated into his sensitive inner shell to reflect and contemplate before emerging with a clearer vision and sense of purpose.

For his leisure time, he rejected outright what he considered to be the stupefying rituals of golf, watching major ball games, shooting, or even the canned excitement of the early spring skiing trip. Going up and down a snow slope all day on a set of expensive planks was not his idea of fun. Nor indeed golf: *useless pastime*. The fact that he was useless at it, and was not inclined to lose gracefully, had of course no bearing on his prejudice against the game. As for blasting pheasants out of the sky with a shotgun, he had lost interest in that many years ago, if he had ever possessed it in the first place, although every other year he did hone an old skill with a few days of winter deer-stalking, preferably in the arctic depths of a particularly cold Scottish winter.

No, it would require a keen, trained observer to extrapolate how Dunstan spent his active leisure time, and the clue lay in his hands, which were muscular and veined to an extraordinary degree. *His* passion was a world of tiny edges of rock, of thick fingers stuffed into thin, overhanging cracks, of hands jammed awkwardly into rough fissures, of physical struggle juxtaposed with smooth-flowing upward motion: a world of verticality, of jagged peaks and soaring pinnacles. He had been a climber since his school days. It had defined him as boy and man. In short, it was in his soul.

However, he was by no means fuelled by adrenaline alone. In a life of thrills, spills and unheralded change, Dunstan treasured his few oases of constancy. One such oasis was his shirt maker, located at Jermyn Street, St James. New and Lingwood has been in existence since 1865, but Dunstan had only used their services for twenty-seven years, since his father had taken him there at the age of fifteen. The ownership had changed in that time but some of the staff hadn't, and neither had the quality of the cotton. Their shirts were still as good as new years after certain other Jermyn Street shirts had been consigned to the bin; a timeless quality in a changing world. 'Ah, young Master Dunstan. Been a while since we've seen you. Busy, no doubt. Put on a bit round the neck and midriff, have we?' To Mr Burdon, he was still the gangly schoolboy.

'Over winter, or since I was fifteen, Mr Burdon?'

Burdon ignored the question, peering at him over half-rim spectacles.

'Looks like you're in your usual hurry, young man. That will be ready-made then. Follow me.'

What followed was a well-worn ritual. Dunstan selected a bold red chalk-stripe. 'Doesn't really comply with your father's dictum, God rest his soul, of "never draw attention to yourself", does it, Master Dunstan? Understated elegance is what we're trying to achieve, sir, is it not?' The dialogue hadn't changed in twenty-odd years.

Dunstan replaced the shirt and selected a light blue number woven in ultra-fine herringbone. It gained immediate approval from the rheumy eyes. Dunstan imagined he saw a twinkle. 'Ah, much better. On account, sir?'

'Certainly, Mr Burdon.'

'Are you still in that funny-money business, sir?'

'If you mean the noble business of authorising and settling bank card payments, then yes, I am.'

'The business may be noble to you, sir, but they tell me the Internet attracts some pretty unsavoury characters. You don't know who you're dealing with. Not like face-to-face service. You be careful now, sir.'

'Technology has taken care of all that, Mr Burdon. The anti-money-laundering laws that came in after nine-eleven make it much harder for the fraudsters to operate.'

Burdon looked unconvinced.

As he left the store, Dunstan's mobile signalled an incoming SMS message. It was his Chief Financial Officer sending over a summary of the previous day's business: *>>>Daily report: Total Transaction Value $32,434,836>>>*. Thirty-two million dollars' worth of credit and debit card transactions from all over the world duly authorised and switched to the retailer's designated bank through Dunstan's company computer systems. *That's over ten billion dollars per annum*, mused Dunstan. *Eight years of hard graft and I've broken the ten billion dollar barrier.* Of course, his fees was relatively miniscule at an average of 0.5% of transaction face value. All the same, a small percentage of a very big pie still gave his company nearly fifty million dollars revenue a year. Not bad for a total of seventy-two employees worldwide.

Now, as he rejoined Piccadilly, his relaxed, some would say laconic gait belied an intensity of purpose. Two attractive women of mature age and predatory nature awarded him more than a passing glance and a compliment as he eased around them on the crowded pavement. He didn't register either the women or the body language. It certainly wasn't because he didn't like women. Far from it, he loved women: he had a family and adored Faith, his wife of fifteen years. It was just that he didn't know how to communicate with them on acquaintance other than on a gentlemanly or professional basis. In the chat-up game, he was an innocent abroad. He could never make the first move, let alone register a woman's passing interest, and all his past passionate encounters had been the consequence of a blindingly obvious frisson, a build-up of tension to a mutually unbearable pitch where something had to give, and there was only one way to dissipate it. Finding his soul mate – his wife, Faith – had come as something of a relief to him. No, 'The Chase' was not a game that he pursued. He was more interested in another game, 'The Great Game', a game of cerebral rather than lustful pursuit. And he was a man with a mission.

As he crossed the road onto the north side, his antennae, little used in recent years but not fully out of commission, picked up a slow-moving Metropolitan Police car in his peripheral vision, slightly over his right shoulder. It appeared to be keeping pace with him. He headed east for four blocks before turning left into Sackville Street. On entering Henry Southeran Limited, Fine and Rare Antiquarian Booksellers, Specialists in Travel and Exploration, a wonderful smell invaded his nostrils. He paused for a moment to scan his eye over the calf and goat-skin spines that contained much of the recorded history of man's exploratory endeavours: Burton, Hunt, Shackleton, Scott, Livingstone, Thesiger, Ross and many other boyhood heroes were enshrined here. Dunstan's speciality was 'The Great Game', that period of British colonial history when all the frontier lands adjoining the Greater Himalaya, from the uplands of Burma through the Nepal Himalaya, the Karakorum and beyond to the Hindu Kush were in dispute, and Russia and Britain used exploration as a political weapon in a game of transcontinental jousting.

'I got your call about the Henry Savage Landor book, Sidney.'

Sidney Greathead raised his heavy eyes from the listings on his computer screen; even archivists have to move with the times. 'Ah, Mr Dunstan. A pleasure to see you.' Greathead spoke in a high-pitched wheeze, the result of years of breathing in fine dust. '*Across Coveted Lands*, MacMillan and Company 1902, first edition, original red cloth, original gilt titles to the spine. A good copy and good value at five hundred pounds.'

Dunstan reflected that he could buy a copy at half that price at auction, but he had neither the time nor the inclination to rummage through auction lists. Besides, just visiting Southerans was worth the premium. 'So what's the gist of it, Sidney?'

'Not dissimilar to other Landor escapades, Mr Dunstan. A privately-funded expedition like all of his. He sets off into troubled regions with all the arrogance and insouciance that was typical of the man and of the age. Takes off from Teheran across the contested borderlands to Afghanistan and into Quetta, which I believe is now in Pakistan.'

'Al-Qaeda country, Sidney.' What has been deleted: can't see it?

'I'm sorry, sir?'

'Er, nothing. What's the read like?'

'Well, Mr Dunstan, one might say it's a gung-ho narrative that conveys the excitement of the times, together with the cut-and-thrust of the Great Game. Fine read, especially as I gather it was your old playing field, sir?'

Dunstan ignored the rhetorical question and let Sidney Greathead continue with his pitch. He was enjoying it.

'Good anthropological research material on ancient peoples and tribes, and quite an insight into the geopolitical contest of the time. A perfect addition to your library, if I may suggest.'

Closure. *What a salesman*, thought Dunstan. But he couldn't decide whether Greathead actually admired or despised Savage Landor. 'Wrap it up, Sidney. By the way, any sight of the account of Savage Landor's expedition to Tibet?'

'The one where he heads into Tibet on his own from Baltistan, treats his porters and the locals abominably, gets captured, and whilst in prison gets his backside a well-deserved frying on a red-hot griddle? Not yet, I'm afraid, sir.'

Despises. Definitely despises.

'I didn't realise the Tibetans were so brutal with their fellow men.' Dunstan queried.

'That was the state of their society. Their monks rooted them in a medieval culture, didn't let them move on. No Age of Enlightenment for them.' He paused. 'Highly resourceful lot, though. The warrior monks put up a damn good fight against Younghusband's 1904-5 incursion. They were out-gunned, though. If they had the chance to fight with modern technology, I'd say they would be pretty formidable.'

How a nation-in-exile with their homeland an Autonomous Region of China could fight back effectively against overwhelming odds, with or without modern technology, Philip Dunstan didn't know. He entered his PIN into the machine – even Southerans had embraced new technology – and eased out of the comfortable gloom of the shop into the spring sunshine. As he did so, an old Leyland Sherpa van pulled into the street and parked on a yellow line. Fleetingly, and from deep within his psyche, the word 'surveillance' popped into his head.

***

He had three missed calls, all from the office. He chose to ignore them for the moment. After all, it was his first day off in months. He retraced his steps west along Piccadilly. Next stop, lunch at his club. Ten minutes later, as he turned south into St James's Street, he became aware of a silver BMW Metropolitan Police saloon car pulling onto the pavement about five metres ahead of him. There were two uniformed officers in the front and a large man in civilian clothes seated behind them. Thinking nothing of it, Dunstan set out to cross the road. The rear window of the BMW rolled down. 'Mr Philip Henry Brooke Dunstan? I wonder if you wouldn't mind hopping in for a quick chat, sir.'

The casual nature of the offer made a sharp contrast with the precise use of his name. If he did decline, perhaps things might become yet more 'precise'.

He profiled the man who had made the offer. 'To whom am I talking, officer?' Dunstan asked.

'Oh sorry, sir. Detective Sergeant Wylie. New Scotland Yard.' He flashed an ID card. 'Now *do* please get in, Mr Dunstan. It looks a bit as if we're lost and asking for directions. Wouldn't want to embarrass my officers, now, would we?' The officers in question, Dunstan noted as he opened the rear door, wouldn't have been embarrassed if their dear old mothers had caught them masturbating.

'To what do I owe the pleasure, Detective Sergeant?'

'We thought you might be able to help us with a little something that's just come up, Mr Dunstan. Only rather than hauling you into the Yard or', he chuckled mirthlessly, 'Paddington Green, we thought you might be more comfortable in a facility just across the Park here... belongs to some of our friends.'

Friends, thought Dunstan. *Is that with a lower case or capital F?*

They skirted past Buckingham Palace on the other side of St James's Park, moved east along Bird Cage Walk then turned right into Queen Anne's Gate. Parking on the left-hand side of the street, the driver sprung out and opened the door for Dunstan. The main entrance to New Scotland Yard was directly ahead of them but his escort ushered him in the opposite direction, through a large black door set in one of the handsome Queen Anne façades that lined the street. They stepped through into a lofty, panelled drawing room studded with high-quality period furniture.

'Please take a seat, sir. I'll order some sandwiches, as we have probably hijacked your lunch.' Wylie trudged out, leaving Dunstan to his own reflections. He scanned the walls for hidden cameras, didn't see any, but wouldn't have expected to. *Too damn small these days. Do I do a runner? And what would I be running away from? And how far would I get before having to replay the whole scene again in less inviting circumstances? Might as well enjoy the picnic lunch.*

Wylie returned carrying a plate of sandwiches. Another man followed him in. Dunstan assessed this addition: young-looking, mid to late thirties, fit, well-dressed, urbane and purposeful. Tailor too close to Savile Row for a policeman.

The new man held out his hand. 'Freshfield, Graham Freshfield. Special Branch.'

Special Branch, Special Operations Group, or some other less-well-known Special? Special Needs? No, this is Establishment, capital E, Dunstan mused. They shook hands and exchanged pleasantries whilst Dunstan eased into the sandwiches. *The condemned man ate a hearty meal... Soft northern accent with very precise diction, possibly Cumbrian or North Lancashire – settle for South Lakes. One of a new breed: top northern grammar school, or maybe Sedbergh, nestling in the Howgills and famous for producing England rugby players and hard,* fit, self-assured characters like Freshfield. University? Leeds, Durham or maybe Oxbridge, at a push.

'Could you give us a precise account of your movements this morning, sir?' This was Wylie, transformed from the downbeat, put-upon detective sergeant into a seasoned enquirer.

Dunstan raised an eyebrow; the pause let Freshfield in. 'Just the basic timings please, Mr Dunstan.'

Dunstan ticked off his movements that morning.

'And can I assume that the people you mention will vouch for your movements?'

'Unless they've all met with a sticky end in the past couple of hours, yes,' Dunstan laughed sardonically.

Freshfield didn't. 'Have you been in contact with your office this morning?' he enquired.

Dunstan hesitated. A question he had certainly not been expecting. *Three missed calls. Why on earth would the police and the intelligence services be interested in my business?*

The tiny camera clipped to the sideboard zoomed into Dunstan's face. The operators in the control room upstairs studied the taut lines for any sign of deception.

'Seems pretty innocent to me,' said the well-dressed woman standing behind them.

'Not necessarily, Miss Lovat,' declared the senior policeman to her immediate left. 'I've seen lots of innocent-looking murderers. Could be he's a psychopath, ma'am.'

'Agreed, the two are not mutually exclusive, are they, Detective Chief Inspector?' Rebecca Lovat responded. 'All right, let's go down and talk to him.'

The miniature receiver attached to Freshfield's ear signalled his colleagues' imminent arrival. Dunstan had just decided he'd had enough of playing the mystery game when two new people came in through the oak doors. Freshfield made the introductions: 'Miss Rebecca Lovat and Detective Chief Inspector Beckwith of Thames Valley CID.' Alarm scurried through Dunstan's fibre for the first time. Whatever the hell was going on here, it was serious.

Beckwith spoke first. 'For the sake of formality, sir, could I just confirm you are Philip Henry Brooke Dunstan of Charlbury, Oxfordshire, and Belgravia, London, and that you are the Chief Executive Officer of CyberX plc?'

Dunstan took stock of his new interrogators. First the man: middle-aged; blue worsted twist suit, white shirt, collar slightly too small, dark blue tie; bristly red moustache, receding hair, badly groomed. A hard life – or had seen too much of other peoples' hard lives. Accent... what do they call it nowadays... that's it, *Estuary*. Dunstan wondered if he had done the long or short Estuary course. Beckwith's question sounded to Dunstan like the precursor to an arrest. 'That's correct, Detective Chief Inspector. May I ask what this is all about?'

Off to the side, the woman's ice-cold eyes held their steady gaze; legs together, hands crossed on knees, she maintained an upright posture with a gap between her back and the chair back, body turned slightly side-on to her audience, skirt pulled down below the knee. Expensive education. No rank, no explanation, no rings, no jewellery. Just a good body squeezed into a classic grey suit that could have been styled in the 1950s, but had clearly been made to measure much more recently, and by a first-class tailor at that. Crisp, white, slightly mannish blouse. A uniform of sorts, set off by close-cut hair of the silkiest black. Blue, no, *violet* eyes, friendly enough on the face of it, but strangely devoid of any feeling when you looked close. Over thirty-five and the better for it.

The ice maiden joined the conversation for the first time. 'Mr Dunstan.' This was like pass-the-parcel. He didn't know what was coming but he braced himself for it anyway. Whatever it represented, the power in the room lay with this woman.

'Fifteen years ago, you were in military intelligence and you were security cleared to "Top Secret: UK Eyes Alpha only". You have not been positively vetted since then, but shall we say that any discussions that might take place here, or beyond, are within the bounds of that original vetting and the Official Secrets Act?' Not a question; a statement couched as a question. 'Step outside those bounds, and you, as much as anyone present, must be aware of the consequences.'

Dunstan waited. He'd be damned if he'd blink before she did.

'Good. Now just so that we *really* understand, what does your business actually do, and how does it work?'

Play the game, thought Dunstan. *We'll find out the rules later.* He sat back, unbuttoned his jacket and crossed his feet. Be blowed if he'd let her make him feel uncomfortable. He hadn't broken the law – at least not knowingly – and there was no reason for him to feel afraid. And yet... a small worm of doubt was burrowing hard at the base of his skull.

'It's quite straightforward. I founded CyberX at the end of 2001. In simple terms, we use the Internet to transact bank card and other payments securely, specifically credit card payments, business-to-business money transfers and some multi-currency payments. Our customers are primarily multi-national retailers and companies that wish to settle their online sales and purchases daily in the currency of their choice, in the country of their choice. In other words, we've created a global marketplace where any company can run their financial operations "virtually" from anywhere in the world, from different countries if they wish, by means of a single agreement with CyberX.'

'Where are your operations based? Geographically?'

'We have a network of computers operating from purpose-built secure facilities. Our worldwide HQ, as I'm beginning to suspect you know, is just outside Oxford. Our main computer is hosted at a secure facility in London Docklands, with regional centres – or hubs – in Bermuda for the Americas; Prague for Europe; Poona, India for North Asia and Southern Africa; and Melbourne, Australia for South Asia.'

'And how do you vet the retailers who use your services? How do you *know* that the retail clients have actually gone through the correct KYC vetting procedure and been certified as genuine?' she asked.

The question seemed to confirm what Dunstan was beginning to suspect, that this was something to do with money laundering. *Where was this woman from? SOCA? MI5?*

In the aftermath of 9/11, security services worldwide, especially those of the USA, UK and Pakistan, had homed in on the means by which terrorists were financing their operations. They began to monitor the interbank movement of all and any funds suspected of having links to terrorism. They also set up programmes to identify and track sources of laundered money gained from terrorist or criminal activity.

A key strategy in this financial war on terror was the introduction of 'KYC' – Know Your Customer – into the banking industry. This relies upon authentication, the process of verification that can be stated simply as

'Are you the person you say you are?' As a part of these efforts, all individuals and companies holding, or wishing to open, bank accounts, and all retailers wishing to process card payments, are authenticated by a strict ID check that includes passport and utilities bill verification for individuals, together with Companies House or other registration checks for companies according to their country of residence.

Dunstan engaged the violet eyes. He was on secure ground. 'Because we insist on seeing the bank's KYC approvals as a precondition of service for all of the companies we do business with.'

'I see,' she said in her best headmistress voice. 'Of course, that assumes that any given bank is acting in a legitimate manner in conducting its KYC checks, doesn't it?'

Again, more of a statement than a question. And one to which Dunstan could make no response. The truth was that no amount of legal checks and balances could thwart a really resourceful and determined criminal.

'You see, Mr Dunstan, friends of ours have reported tracking and tracing unusual sums of money. Millions of dollars. These sums were paid into an account in an Islamabad bank. By following the money trail backwards, we've traced these payments to the account of a certain third party payments service provider, one under contract to a British-based company.' She paused, her violet eyes penetrating. 'Your company, Mr Dunstan, CyberX plc.'

A small hollow opened in the pit of Dunstan's stomach. 'What? When?'

'So are we to understand you know nothing about this?'

Dunstan did not reply immediately. The violet eyes rested on his for what felt like a very long time. Dunstan knew there was no way in which this woman would reveal anything about how her department had come by the knowledge. But to Dunstan's mind, she had to have some kind of human asset working for her inside the Islamabad bank.

'What would you like me to do?' Dunstan wanted out of it. This was a shock; his brain was racing. He needed answers to questions he hadn't yet thought of.

'We'd like to know this money's origin. We'd like your organisation to conduct a track-and-trace, an audit trail. If you find out anything of interest, please phone this number.'

Lovat glanced across at Freshfield who picked up the thread. He handed Dunstan a card. 'Ask for "Redmond", key "hash", and someone will phone you back on your mobile number.' He handed Dunstan a small, square, transparent envelope. 'We'd like you to use another SIM card. It's with your current network provider, but it includes an encryption key devised by our friends at GCHQ. Chief Inspector Beckwith has kindly offered to drive you back to Oxford, sir. If that suits your present circumstances, of course?' His tone once again suggested very subtly that Dunstan had better fall in with the arrangement – or else.

As Dunstan moved towards the door, Lovat, Freshfield and DCI Beckwith exchanged glances, as though they had been waiting for something that had not yet materialised. Dunstan caught it. As he turned back towards them, Freshfield nonchalantly delivered the thunderbolt. 'By the way, Mr Dunstan, when did you last see Idris Morgan?'

Dunstan reflected. Besides being one of his closest friends, and the man who had helped him set up CyberX in the first place, they met when they had to, which was only a couple of times a week. Out of sheer necessity, most of their business was conducted by email. *What was this question getting at?*

'I spoke to Idris on Saturday night. Why?' he responded.

'Saturday? Was there some kind of company emergency?' It sounded like an innocent query.

'Not at all. He wanted to give me the weekly operational summary. I'd been out earlier that day.' Dunstan smiled. 'More time off. Obviously something that has to stop.'

'Did Mr Morgan seem, er, normal, when you last spoke with him?'

'Perfectly normal. Why do you ask?'

'You stuck to business?'

'I'm sorry – dragging me in here to quiz me on a potentially illicit transaction and soliciting my help is one thing. Grilling me about my staff is another. Care to tell me what's going on?' Dunstan was visibly irritated.

'Still...?' Freshfield pressed.

Dunstan sighed. 'He helped me set up the company. Idris is one of my oldest professional friends. I'd be lost without him.'

Freshfield drew a deep breath. 'Mr Morgan was found dead yesterday morning in a stretch of woodland on Boars Hill in Oxfordshire. Detective Chief Inspector Beckwith here is in charge of the murder enquiry.'

Dunstan felt as if he were falling. As if someone had just kicked a prop out from under his legs. 'My God! Idris! How did it happen?'

Eyes steady, DCI Beckwith looked directly into Dunstan's eyes, looking for any weakness. 'Your colleague's head was severed from his body, Mr Dunstan.' Dunstan said nothing. His friend's open, smiling face flashed into his mind. This information was so shocking that he balked, denying it. There was a long pause. Dunstan gathered himself. 'What are you telling me, Inspector? That Idris was, what... *executed*?'

The use of the word caused Beckwith's gaze to harden further. 'You could put it that way. As a matter of fact, that's the very word the pathologist used this morning. Except...'

'Except what?'

'The stroke was delivered from the front by means of a long, sharp-edged instrument. Like a samurai sword, or something similar. We think the killer may have been waiting out of sight behind a tree. He stepped out into Mr Morgan's path, and...'

Dunstan reeled. 'But... I don't understand. Everybody liked Idris. He was... he was a good man.' A fresh and terrible thought struck him. 'He has a wife and a sixteen-year-old daughter. How are they coping?' His voice tailed away.

'They're being looked after by our bereavement counsellors. Were you familiar with Mr Morgan's habits?'

Dunstan shook his head. 'I'm sorry, his habits? What are you asking me, Chief Inspector?'

'You knew he liked to keep fit, and you knew his daily routines.'

There was a slightly harder note in the policeman's voice, so that Dunstan stared at him, and his jaw set. 'Well, in his prime he was a top rugby player. I know he liked to run when he could. When time permitted, I mean. Why?'

'We think the killer must have known Mr Morgan's routine.'

Dunstan had had enough, and he rallied. 'I need to get back to Oxfordshire. I need to pick up the pieces. Now, if you please, Detective Chief Inspector.' Rebecca Lovat had the final word. 'Don't forget the audit trail, will you Mr Dunstan? Phone the number as soon as you find anything.'

Dunstan merely stared at her. *You hard-nosed bint*, he thought, and, still in a daze, headed for the open door to the waiting transport. As he did so, something else occurred to him. *She knows a lot more than she's admitting to. Is this 'request' for an audit trail just a way of testing me and my organisation?*

Chapter Two

In the rear of the unmarked police car, Dunstan made his calls, turning the volume to minimum. 'Kate, Philip here. Are you guys okay?'

Kate Cross was his long-suffering Executive Assistant, who made the working lives of the Board and the Executive Team efficient. There wasn't a personal assistant or secretary to be found at CyberX.

'Philip, where have you been? We've been trying to get hold of you for ages!' Despite her best efforts to expunge it, a slight Birmingham accent remained in her voice.

'I've been helping the police with their enquiries, Kate. How's morale?'

'We're all in shock. Everybody is just going through the motions.'

'I'll be with you in about ninety minutes. Let the staff know that I'll speak to all of them when I arrive. Oh, and please ask Vernon Hamill to get to the office ASAP and review staff security. Double his fees if necessary.' Hamill was an ex-Special Forces security consultant retained by CyberX for the physical security of its systems and the personal security of its staff.

He was about to dial home when Beckwith butted in. 'I realise this is all a bit of a shock, Mr Dunstan, but I need you to tell me everything you know about Idris Morgan.'

For the next hour, all the way up the M40 in heavy traffic, Dunstan told Beckwith everything he knew about the dead man. Fresh out of the army, Dunstan's main purpose in life had been to forget the past and invent a future for himself – a process in which Morgan, a workaholic firebrand, had been key. Brilliant at designing and implementing large-scale computing projects, Morgan had employed Dunstan at First Transaction Data Inc, where he was vice-president of operations. He had mentored Dunstan through the complicated business of international computerised transactions in a way that had made it seem both creative and fun. Then Dunstan had wanted a sabbatical and left, only to resurface and demand

Morgan join him in starting a new global payment services company. Morgan had been the first person he'd contacted, and Dunstan's passion and persuasion had won him over. Eight years later, they were poised to put some of the biggest players in the market out of business.

Or had been, until now.

'Did Mr Morgan have any problems you knew of? Financial, domestic, work, old enemies coming back to take revenge for something he might have done or said?'

'None that I know of, and I saw more of him than probably anyone else, including his wife.' It was true; for several years now, Morgan had become something of a recluse, devoted to work, Welsh rugby and his wine cellar, in that order.

Beckwith was firing questions now. 'He was a past member of Plaid Cymru – did you know that? Was he connected in any way with some of the more radical elements of Welsh nationalism?'

Dunstan shook his head. 'You mean the home burners? They hardly exist anymore, do they? I'd be very surprised. Idris was an intelligent pragmatist, first and last.'

The exhaustive questioning continued until they lapsed into silence as they approached Oxford. Chief Inspector Beckwith worked on his case notes, Dunstan tried to make sense of the morning's events. But there was one that would never make sense to him for as long as he lived: the idea that someone might have taken Morgan's head off with the sweep of a sword.

'Tomorrow morning, Mr Dunstan, I should like my officers to start interviewing your staff on an individual basis. Purely routine, you understand. We'll try to cause as little disruption as possible. Could you please ensure that all members of your staff are available for our officers to interview?'

'Of course – apart from those who are sick or travelling overseas. I'd like to keep the operation going. We have a 24/7 obligation to our customers, Detective Chief Inspector. Please ask Kate – Kate Cross, my assistant – to schedule the interviews as you wish.'

***

The architecture of South Oxford Business Park pays homage to the state-of-the-art technology companies that operate from it. At Dunstan's suggestion, the police dropped him off outside the Park. He lifted his parcels from the boot, set off up the drive, walked past the fountains and 'installations' that passed for art at the beginning of the 21st Century, and showed his pass to the duty security man.

The office was almost silent; everyone was staring intently at their computer terminals. Kate's face reflected the collective shock. He went over to her and gave her arm a gentle squeeze. She gave him a wan smile. 'Marc's waiting for you in the closed session room.'

The office was open plan. It was normally a high-energy environment, noisy and busy, everyone an expert in their own field. Dunstan was accessible and, when he was in the office, all staff understood that they could wander over to 'the Boss' and engage him on any matter. When he was not in the office, they could phone or email him, in any time zone, at any time. He made a point of it.

Above all, they all knew he cared about every one of them. CyberX was still small enough for him to think of it as a family unit. Now, as he surveyed the floor, he knew he had a fight on his hands to keep it together.

CyberX had recently been admitted to the AIM market of the London Stock Exchange. With Morgan's help, Dunstan had raised £30 million from the flotation and they still had most of it in the bank. Being a listed company meant that information that might affect the share price had to be kept within a tight circle of named people, who were restricted as to when they could buy and sell CyberX shares. The world had changed since CyberX was three guys in a room, so Dunstan had built the closed session room, which was more like a small flat. It had a suite of desks with computers on their own separate, secure network, with completely different email addresses and passwords to the rest of the company for the authorised users. There was a large but not overly ostentatious Board table and computerised presentation facilities. This was his very own intelligence cell. His staff called it 'the Bunker'.

'Is everyone OK for seventeen hundred hours, Kate?'

'Of course, Philip.' He was different, she could tell. Something had changed – his blood was up. She found herself lingering slightly longer than usual by his desk. Dunstan looked up. Kate was sharp, from the tips of her fashionable shoes to the collar of her tailored blouse. It wasn't like her to hang around but then, like everyone, she had suffered a profound shock.

'I won't keep them long, Kate, ten minutes tops.'

He gave them a minute to settle down and then strode in. Marc Tysoe, his finance director, was waiting. Tysoe was a short and wiry Lancastrian who was assertive with a fierce, dispassionate intellect. Above all, though, he was practical.

'Hi, Marc.' Dunstan's gaze narrowed. 'I have to ask you this: do you know anything about Idris's death? I mean, can you think of any reason why anyone might want to kill him?'

Tysoe shook his head. 'The whole thing's bloody incredible.'

'What about these rogue transactions? Have we uncovered the agent of origin, the point of origin, worked out how they got in under our radar, and found out where the money's gone?'

'I don't know, but I've got the key members of the team investigating now. Five of them have volunteered to work through the night. I'll let you know as soon as we have any news.'

Dunstan pressed his palms hard together, an old habit he'd picked up from long, cold nights in the backwoods and hedgerows of Northern Ireland. 'All right, let's get back to business. For now, Marc, I want you to take over the day-to-day running of operations, and make sure the wheels don't come off. Any anomalies get reported to me, personally, immediately. I need you to help me get to the bottom of this. CyberX has got to be the common thread between the laundering – if that's what it is – and Idris's murder. Now, we need to draft an announcement for the Stock Market. Express deep regrets about Idris, but try to keep the whole thing bland. Put the release on an embargo until after the markets close this evening. If they want me to comment in person, I will.'

Tysoe knew exactly what he had to do. As CFO and Company Secretary, it fell to him to draft releases to the Stock Exchange on behalf of the Chairman and CEO. Dunstan hadn't yet got round to appointing a non-executive Chairman but he had two non-executive Directors, Henry Stanton and George Jackson, both 'old sweats' who had made their money in banking and heavy industry respectively and whom he respected for their business acumen and sound judgement.

He called Kate in. 'Kate, please call an emergency Board meeting for seven a.m. tomorrow in this room. I need you to take minutes, please.'

She turned to go but he stopped her. 'Also, please arrange for taxis home or to the nearest station for any employees who are on public transport. And hire five cars for senior staff – include yourself in that. They are not to use their own cars. And get the hire company to change the cars for tomorrow, regardless of cost. Make sure I have a pool car to travel home in this evening. Oh, and Kate, please ask Vernon to make sure the company personal security plan is raised to another level of alert.' Kate stared at him for a moment, nonplussed by all these security measures, then turned on her heels.

Dunstan left the Bunker, perched himself on an island desk in the middle of the room and watched as the thirty staff in the Oxford office gathered in front of him. He had never seen so many pinched, worried faces since his days as a platoon commander in the Bogside. The key thing was to keep it relaxed, make sure the tension didn't turn into something worse. He told them what he could and asked for their continuing support and commitment in the business. He took questions and passed them over to Vernon Hamill, his security consultant, for a briefing on their personal safety. Then he went back into the Bunker.

There was a knock at the door. Kate entered with Abdul Shahid, closing the door behind them. Dunstan was about to continue a pretence of normality when a look on their faces pulled him up short.

'What is it?' he demanded.

Shahid spoke. Small, yet with a proud bearing that served to increase his physical and moral stature, he was the technical expert. 'Philip, we're under cyber attack. It started thirty minutes ago. Spam, Virus, Trojan Horses. It's a sustained assault directed at the heart of our operations.'

'How bad is it, worst case?' Tysoe wanted to know the bottom line.

'We're doing our best, but...' Shahid's voice trailed off.

'How long have we got, if you can't stop it?'

'This is one of the worst attacks I've ever seen. Right now, we're struggling to process any transactions at all. If things go on as they are, it's only a matter of time before the firewalls are breached and the proxy servers, the sentry servers – everything comes down. Then – '

Dunstan wrapped it up. 'Thank you, Abdul. Please keep fighting. If it overwhelms us, we'll just have to close down, clean and repair, and then reset the operation. How long would that take? Worst case...?'

'At least five days, probably a week,' Shahid responded weakly.

They all looked at him aghast: a week with no transactions? Their entire customer base would have upped sticks and moved elsewhere. It meant defeat, annihilation, the end of CyberX as a going concern. All they had collectively sweated and worked for, all these years, would be blown apart in a matter of a few days.

As they turned to go, Abdul Shahid paused and opened his mouth as if to speak. He looked at Tysoe, then at the retreating back of Kate Cross, seemed to change his mind, dropped his gaze, turned and left the room.

Dunstan registered this at some subconscious level. Consciously he was thinking fast to save his company and himself. 'Marc, I want you to go to Bermuda immediately and start a full forensic trace on these rogue transactions.'

'Bermuda?'

'Yes. On the face of it, you're going to Bermuda to support the staff there to carry out a transaction audit that has been scheduled for some time. That is precisely what everyone, and I mean *everyone*, in this company except you and I, will understand. Okay?'

'Yes, Boss.' Tysoe was watching him intently. It was now six o'clock.

Dunstan softened his tone.

'Now listen. I want you to consider this place burned. Terminated. Fatally compromised.'

'What?'

'Just as I said, consider it burned! Go to Bermuda and create a clone from the clean back-up servers. Run it in tandem for a short time to make sure it's not under cyber attack, and then switch systems. Kill the worldwide hub here other than for local UK bank stuff, and make the Bermuda operation the main global operations hub. Then replace this operation here in Oxford lock, stock and barrel with the one you've set up in Bermuda.'

'Fuck! That would normally take weeks. And it's taking a big risk.'

'We have to embrace the risk. Use it as a weapon to our own advantage. I would prefer you not to take anyone from here to help. I've arranged for access to the reserve account. Try not to go over a million in direct costs. Tickets will be with you in a couple of hours – pick them up at Heathrow. Oh, and Marc…'

'What, mate?' came the flat northern response.

'Nothing, my friend. Just look after yourself, won't you?'

***

Dunstan had one final job to do that evening before heading home – to call on Gwyneth Morgan. Above all else, he was dreading this.

First, though, he phoned his wife, Faith. 'Hi, darling. You sound tired. Tough day shopping?'

'Very funny. You need to try doing some real work sometime. Like looking after four children.'

She doesn't know, Dunstan thought. *But then there's no reason why she should.* 'I don't need picking up from the station. I'll be home about eight-thirty.'

'Supper?'

'Lovely. See you soon.'

As Dunstan left the Bunker, Abdul Shahid came up to him. A devout Sunni Muslim as well as a top systems engineer, there was something 'Old World' about Shahid that Dunstan found very engaging. Cerebral, deferential, but possessed by a rare moral fortitude, he looked as if he would have been perfectly at home on the wild mountain slopes of the Khyber Pass. Dunstan judged him to be a loyal and highly-valued member of CyberX.

Indeed, so had Idris Morgan. Any sideways glances, or the slightest hint of an unfunny joke, and Morgan had stamped it out in a flash.

'Could I have a word, please, Philip? In private, if possible.'

Dunstan looked in at the Bunker and decided that a walk with Shahid in the grounds of the Business Park was the better option. They went out the back way. A glorious Oxfordshire spring evening greeted them.

'It's about Idris, Philip, a thousand blessings upon his soul. I believe he had discovered something.'

'Go on.'

'About two weeks ago, Idris started to stay late, to run statistics on certain transaction volumes and sources. I was staying late as well, and he asked me to help with some systems checks after work. While I was running these checks, I noticed large peaks in transaction volumes for very short bursts.'

'Why didn't we pick them up on the daily reports?'

'That was the point.' Shahid's face was grave. 'Overall, they increased the mean daily transaction value by a relatively small amount, and their duration was also very short. But if you were to examine the volume of transactions within this duration it was extraordinarily high: about one hundred per second. In other words, it was lots of small value payments being processed.'

They were well away from the building now, and in the crisp Oxfordshire spring air a male blackbird was singing at the top of his voice. This air of serenity was not reflected in Dunstan's soul, where a deep chill was settling. 'All from one retailer?' he asked sharply.

'No, that was the point. They were from a broad range of merchant types, different retailer sources. However, having satisfied myself of a recurring pattern, I looked at the detail behind them.'

'And...' the answer came to Dunstan, even as he formed the question. 'They all had the same retailer payment identification number, didn't they? Hundreds of false retailers. And we were the idiots that were processing their transactions, weren't we?'

Shahid's expression said he was right. 'So why didn't we pick this up?'

'If I may say so, in our recent runaway success, we may not have been as diligent as we might have been in certain areas. The devil always lurks in the detail.'

'Which transaction gateway?'

'Prague.' Again, the answer didn't surprise Dunstan. But the chill he now felt was new and unwelcome.

'So who the hell in our organisation set them up, and which bank issued the merchant IDs?'

'No one. They came to us through a third party processor, a payment service bureau.'

'Are you telling me we didn't check the merchant ID validity for hundreds of merchants?'

'I didn't think that was possible either, under the security systems we have in place. But this bureau had a large block of merchant ID numbers available to it that it could issue on its own account.'

'So we're dealing with a crooked third party bureau?'

'Possibly, or collusion between crooked people within a bank who issued the licence in the first place...' He didn't finish the sentence.

And someone in CyberX? mused Dunstan. He checked the long burst of expletives that rose to his lips. The London Stock Exchange would be reacting to the announcement in the morning. If things went to form, the market makers would stalk the company like a bunch of ambulance chasers. If 'CyberX', 'money laundering' and 'credit card fraud' were to be mentioned in the same breath, the vultures would soon be picking over his carcass.

He forced his attention back to Shahid. 'I presume you've taken measures to stop any transactions from these delinquent merchants passing through the gateway?'

Shahid nodded. 'One of the first things Idris did on identifying the originator…'

'Was to cut them off summarily, wasn't it?' Dunstan didn't wait for the answer before continuing. 'Which bank is behind the bureau?'

'We don't know, Philip. That information was never asked for at the set-up stage.' Shahid looked at Dunstan gravely. 'Please take all precautions to look after yourself. I shall pray for you.'

'Thanks, Abdul, I might need it. One last thing: Who the hell – forgive me – signed up this bureau within CyberX? Did you and Idris verify that?' 'Indeed, we did. It was one of the very early signings. I'm afraid to tell you that it was you, Philip. It was done by telephone and fax application from Prague to the UK. No due diligence, either, I'm afraid to say.' Dunstan stared into a bottomless black pit.

***

The drive to Boars Hill, five miles away from the office, seemed like five hundred. Seeing Gwyneth was going to be emotional. She and Idris had been childhood sweethearts. A bereavement specialist woman police officer had been posted full-time to look after her. He followed Gwyneth into the kitchen as she put the kettle on. She turned to him, speaking softly and urgently.

'He was onto something, you know. He was like a bloody terrier this last month.'

'I know he was. Gwyneth, I have to ask if you've told the police that I was supposed to be out running with Idris…that we ran together most Sundays?'

'No. Why? Oh My God! You think that you were the intended victim?' Gwyneth Morgan's face contorted.

'Or both of us. I don't know, Gwyneth. What I do know, or feel, is that there's a lot more to this. Idris found out that the company was being hit by a major money laundering operation, probably using stolen or false cards. It could be straight fraud but I have a feeling there's more to it. I have to find out who's behind this, Gwyneth, and I can't do that from behind bars. Look, I'll see you soon. Kate is on standby to fix anything you need. She'll phone you tomorrow.'

They hugged each other as he left. She squeezed him extra hard and long, and whispered in his ear, 'Find out what it was, Philip. And nail his bloody killer.'

With that instruction ringing in his head, he set off home to Wychwood Forest.

***

In the north-west corner of Oxfordshire, in an area known as the Cotswolds, nestles a beautiful valley, the Evenlode. It was once covered by the Wychwood Forest, little of which now remains, most of the trees having been cut down in the nineteenth century. What is left is a patchwork of small farms, thriving villages and fields surrounded by well-maintained Cotswold dry stone walls. It was now eight o'clock and, away to the west, the base of the sun was just touching the Wold. Dunstan stopped the car at the same spot he often did before descending the hill to his family, leaving his work behind him.

'Never take work home, boy,' Morgan had advised Dunstan early in the latter's marriage, when he couldn't understand why he and Faith were not getting on as well as they should. 'Imagine that you're going through an airlock from one world to another, leaving the stress behind.'

As he surveyed the scene before him, his valley, Dunstan knew he had to get help, fast, but who could he turn to? Who could he *trust*? He dug deep into his briefcase and retrieved a tiny, battered red leather book, together with an equally battered mobile phone containing an unregistered pay-as-you-go SIM card. After the inquisition in London, he now assumed that his contract mobile was being monitored.

He dialled a number in the Elan Valley, in the heart of Central Wales. There was a pause, clicking noises, but no voice. Dunstan spoke first. 'Monk, it's Sherpa. Can you meet me?'

Still no immediate response, then – 'Why?'

'For a dance on a spring evening.' Dunstan could almost see the wry smile on the other end of the line.

'When?'

'Soon, probably within forty-eight hours. Please be on standby.' No response; the line went dead. Dunstan was going for a dance, and his prospective partner was certainly someone he could trust. 'Dance' – as in 'Fan Dance' – was the code between them to meet up if the shit hit the fan. He got out of the car. A brisk, cold north wind cut into him. The local farmers called this seasonal wind that came straight from the Arctic at this time of year a 'thin wind', in that it 'went through you, not round you'. But Dunstan was indifferent to it. As he stood facing north, surveying miles of open countryside, the big orange disk of the sun halfway along its journey below the horizon, the scream started in his insides, the scream he had locked and chained since hearing the news at lunch-time. It welled up through every fibre of his soul until his whole body was one prolonged cry. All grief, frustration and anger was channelled into a single primaeval scream.

He stood looking at the sun making its final descent, then began his own descent off the top of the wold.

Chapter Three

He wound his way up the long, chipped-stone drive to the old farmhouse and the sanctuary of his family. Its location and lack of pretension followed the Dunstan family dictum of 'never draw attention to yourself'. His father would certainly have approved. *Oh, and so would old Burdon*, mused Dunstan as he parked up and remembered his shirt and book in the boot of the car.

But for how much longer will this be our sanctuary? he thought, as he surveyed the ancient buildings. One of the outbuilding doors opened and Faith strode across the yard to greet him.

'Hi darling!' His usual greeting. He pulled her to him, but as he looked into the deep blue eyes, he knew that she knew. 'When did you find out?'

'It was on the local radio this afternoon, Philip. The police have only just made his identity public.' She looked at him hard and observed a barely discernible but significant change in her man: a hardening of the features, a defensiveness in the set of his jaw. She could see that he was grinding his teeth slightly. Momentarily, she lifted the mood: 'All the kids are here and can't wait to see you. I told them to stay inside for a while. You must be hungry. Supper first, then we can talk.'

The little ones were in bed but the two elder children were up and about. Both boys were back from their respective boarding schools for the long Easter holidays. The two girls were still at the local primary school and didn't enjoy such long breaks.

Number One Son, James, now fourteen, had to remain cool. As determined by the somewhat esoteric mores that governed his age group, he wasn't allowed to greet his father in a 'civilised' manner. Instead, he gave Dunstan a big hug round the waist, half dislocating his spine in the process. Dunstan wriggled free and got James in a headlock before Faith called a truce.

'Stop it, you two! James, leave your father alone.'

'But he's got me in a headlock!'

'Precisely. Put him down.'

'It's called women's logic, James,' said Dunstan, releasing his grip.

Dunstan continued through to the sitting-room where a small animal in human form, not to be outdone by his elder brother, launched a flying tackle at him.

'Harry, you twit!'

Grunting and straining noises came from beneath a mop of shaggy blond hair as Harry tried to wrestle Dunstan to the ground. Harry had gotten a lot stronger and bigger this last term, observed Dunstan, as he tried to wrestle him off. Then another small shaggy thing joined in: the terrier, 'Pull-Through', so called by Dunstan because it was just about the right size and furriness to be an effective cleaning rag for a Chieftain tank barrel. Harry gave up the tackle and smothered Dunstan in kisses. He wasn't a teenager yet, so he was still allowed to demonstrate affection.

Over supper, all the talk was of heroics on the school rugby field; work and school reports didn't come into it. At about nine-thirty, Faith packed the boys off to bed. There was a half-hearted protest, but both boys were happily exhausted.

'Go!' said Faith, and off they went, each knowing better than to argue.

Faith Donnington-Drax, as she had been before she met Dunstan, could trace her family back to pre-Norman times. For most of the last thousand years her family had been in the service of the Crown. John Drax had been a sergeant-at-arms to Henry V at Agincourt. The Draxes had married the Donningtons to boost the family coffers in the seventeenth century, and their offspring had played a significant part in adding bits of empire to the world atlas in the subsequent two centuries. Faith saw her role in life as breeding and nurturing a new generation of adventurers, and she was proud of what she had achieved so far. But if anyone merely saw her as a housewife sitting in the back seat of life behind a husband they would be sorely mistaken. She was intelligent, perceptive and very straightforward. Above all, she was unflappable. Her grandfather, observing her as an eight-year-old, had declared, 'If an Impi of Zulus were about to overrun the place, that girl would insist on having tea.'

Deciding against alcohol, they sat down with a cup of tea. 'What's been happening, Philip? You look awful. Tell me everything. And no bullshit.'

Dunstan's large, rough hands gripped the mug of tea tight as he told her everything he knew. As she listened, the blue eyes grew colder and harder. She knew it was serious. Her instinct told her this was much wider and bigger than Morgan's execution. 'Somewhere along the line, I'd say you've made a bad enemy, Philip.'

This remark stopped Dunstan. 'You think this is personal? Not just some outfit trying to use CyberX to launder money?'

'The sword thing says it's personal. Loud and clear. Would you lop someone's head off with a samurai sword? Or even pay to have that done? And the cyber attack? Personal. And you usually go running with Morgan on Sundays, don't you? So who have you upset, Philip?'

Dunstan racked his brains. He had no real enemies he could think of, at least not in that kind of league. But Faith was right and it irked him that he hadn't thought about it in quite those terms.

'If you're right, Faith – and I'm not too sure you are – Idris's murder could be retaliation to him switching off the fraud. And if you are, then I'm even less happy about the security situation here for you and the kids. In fact, I'm bloody worried.' They were facing each other across the kitchen table; her hand reached out and took his as he continued airing his thoughts. 'You know, if I'm going to save the company and really find out what's going on, I may have to travel. You and the kids will be exposed here.'

'I'm sure we could go to Ellie's place. I'll phone her now. We'll be well out of the way up there.' Her sister Ellie's 'place' was sixteen thousand remote acres in the Scottish Highlands with a tumbledown Victorian shooting lodge to go with it. It was a family tradition to head up there for a long weekend in early spring when the Highlands were at their loveliest. A deer-stalking estate that had been in Ellie's husband's family for generations, it was now used by the extended family for recreation and for renting out to stalking parties. The kids loved it.

'Do it, Faith, just do it. There won't be any stalking going on at this time of year. Make up some excuse. Pull the kids out of school.'

***

Tuesday, 24th April

Dunstan was up at dawn to get into the office. As he was leaving, he handed his wife two long keys. 'Here are the keys to the gun cabinet. Whatever happens, Faith, remember, I love you!'

'Just don't do anything bloody stupid, Philip.' Faith smiled. It was her way of returning the endearment.

Reverting to old habits, Dunstan checked underneath and all around the company Golf for improvised explosive devices before opening the door and turning the ignition key. He varied his route from the previous night by going down the back roads to Oxford through Charlbury, skirting the rear quarters of the Blenheim Palace estate and barrelling on down through Woodstock. On the way, he placed a call to Henry Stanton, his non-executive Chairman. He drove into the business park at six-thirty and parked as far as he could from the office. He sat for a while pretending to examine some papers, watching for any unusual movement: there was none. He got out of the car, walked up the grass bank and made another casual 360-degree scan. Seeing nothing out of the ordinary, he entered the building via the service bay at the back. On arrival, he found George Jackson, Henry Stanton and Kate Cross already in the Bunker. Kate was bringing them up to date with what she knew.

'Morning, Henry; morning, George. Thank you for responding so quickly. Sorry to drag you out of bed so early. Hi, Kate. Did Marc get away okay?'

'He got the last flight out from Heathrow.'

They moved to the big oval table and sat down. 'Kate will take the minutes.'

'Gentlemen,' Dunstan said, addressing his Board. 'This meeting has been convened to discuss the recent tragic events, the actual and potential impact of those events on the company, and to plan remedial action. Marc Tysoe sends his apologies, as he's now en route to Bermuda. The London Stock Exchange announcement you have in front of you is under embargo until seven a.m. this morning, so, by my watch, it's just about to go public. It states that we are taking practical steps to remain operationally effective in the face of extraordinary circumstances.'

Dunstan leaned back in the leather and chrome chair, wondering how they would take his next statement.

'George, I'd like you to take over as Chief Operating Officer with immediate effect. Take over the day-to-day running of the business. Henry, I'd like you to take on the role of Chief Executive Officer, acting in tandem with George in my absence.'

They stared at him. 'Your absence? What do you mean? Where are you going?' asked the newly appointed COO.

'I'm going to find out who killed Idris. And who is trying to destroy this company. And for that, I'm going to need time and space. Can you hack it?'

Jackson was not one to rush into things. 'Can we have a day or two to think it over? CyberX is under attack. I'm not certain…'

This wasn't anything like what Dunstan wanted to hear. 'How about two minutes, George, while we have our coffee?'

'What about Henry? He needs to think about it, too!' He looked across at Stanton but got a very different impression to that of a surprised man.

'You knew about this already, didn't you? I've been bloody well ambushed.' His voice dropped to a near-whisper. 'What if I refuse?'

Dunstan looked at him evenly, a look that brooked no doubt. 'Then I'm afraid, George, that the necessary reconstitution of the Board would be wider than planned.'

'Fired?'

'Yes.'

'Just like that?' He looked at Stanton, whose vote would be needed to oust him from the Board. Stanton merely gave the slightest hint of a nod.

Jackson was stumped. 'Well, I can't think of any other bugger better than me to do it, so the appointment as Chief Operating Officer is accepted.'

'Excellent!' said Dunstan. 'Now let's take a break before "Any Other Business" and draft yet another Stock Exchange announcement for release just before the markets close this evening. Timings okay, Henry?'

Stanton was looking over Dunstan's shoulder, his gaze glued to a large computer screen linked to a live London Stock Exchange price feed.

Dunstan knew what he was looking at. He didn't turn round to look himself.

'Damage, Henry?' Dunstan enquired with as much sangfroid as he could muster. Stanton looked over his gold-rimmed spectacles:

'Down 70% in early trading and still falling.' Dunstan went stock-still. He was shocked to the core. The drop was catastrophic. He realised that he had been naive to think that the announcement would support the share price. If it went down any further the company would have virtually no value, nicely complementing the void in his soul.

There was a sharp knock at the door, and the receptionist came into the room. 'Excuse me, Philip, but the police are here. Earlier than they said they'd be.'

'Could you ask them to wait, please, Susi?'

'Er, I did, Philip, but they insisted they wanted to see you. Now.' Susi looked around the room and shifted uncomfortably. 'Er, they showed me an arrest warrant. For you, Philip.'

Chapter Four

'Are you arresting me for the murder of Idris Morgan, Chief Inspector?'

'*Detective* Chief Inspector,' said Beckwith, setting the tone for the rest of the day. 'No, we're not arresting you for murder, not yet anyway. We're merely inviting you down to the police station as a witness to help with our enquiries.'

'Gentlemen, I have matters to attend to here. If I were to decline your, er, request to attend, then what?'

'Then we'll arrest you on a holding charge. Conspiracy to murder will do for a start, then we'll look at fraud, and then money laundering using your company as a front,' retorted Beckwith.

'And on what flimsy basis would those charges be levelled?'

'On the very solid basis that you normally go out running with Mr Idris Morgan every Sunday, and that he found out there was a fraud going on in your company.' Beckwith enjoyed delivering that one.

'And how did such rumours come to your attention, *Detective* Chief Inspector?'

'From Mrs Morgan, Mr Dunstan. She opened up a lot to our specialist bereavement officer last night.' Beckwith was positively gloating at this information coup.

But Dunstan was using this exchange to think how he could buy some precious time. 'Given these developments, I shall have to relinquish my role here and hand over formally to the Board. This is a public company after all, and we wouldn't want to breach Financial Services Authority and Stock Exchange Regulations, would we now?'

Beckwith hesitated, unsure of the 'Regulations' of such 'Authorities' and their legal standing or, indeed, the implications of being cited as the reason for Dunstan breaking them. A grudging nod gave Dunstan the signal to go back into the Bunker where he brought the others up to speed, formally ended the meeting and summarily relinquished his role as CEO.

He pulled Kate to one side. 'Kate, take this phone. If I'm not back by ten-thirty, call this number and ask for "Redmond". Press hash and his office will call you back. When they get back to you, please explain that I've been unavoidably detained on suspicion of Idris Morgan's murder – yes, I know it's not technically true, but it might well come to that. He might ask you some questions. Please be open. No questions now, thank you, Kate. And, most importantly, get through to Vernon Hamill and tell him to raise the security status to "Bikini Black". Got it?'

'Bikini Black?' she asked.

'Hamill will understand,' replied Dunstan sharply.

'Got it,' said Kate.

While Kate was preoccupied with the Board, Sergeant Lowe had taken the liberty of leafing through her corporate diary and noted with interest that Dunstan was booked on a flight to Bermuda leaving at 1520 hours.

Dunstan breezed back into the room, to face his inquisitor. 'Now, Detective Chief Inspector, I'm all yours.'

***

Interview Room 2 at Kidlington police station was airless and stuffy. Dunstan inspected his interrogation chamber. His one psychological advantage over his interrogators was that he knew they were wasting their time – they didn't. He had considered replying to every pedantic question with a monotone *I'm sorry, I cannot answer that question* as per his training, but winding up the police would do him no favours now. Besides, the last thing he wanted was to be held for several days on circumstantial evidence while they laid spurious charges of 'conspiracy to murder' or worse at his door. Moreover, he wanted to be out of there as quickly as possible.

Dunstan knew that he needed an alternative focus, something to latch onto, however small, which allowed his conscious brain to answer questions intelligently yet mechanically whilst his subconscious was on another plane. It was a technique he had perfected as a child; *Planet Dunstan* his mother had called it. Planet Dunstan had served him well over the years. It had to serve him well now.

The high walls around him were coated in layers of green gloss paint, mute testament to years of turgid interviews, frustration and anguish. Or was it mute? As he waited, Dunstan mused on 'Stone Tape Theory', the notion that certain materials, like quartz and silica, have the properties to absorb energies and 'replay' them later under certain conditions. How many interviews were stored in these walls? How many confessions, real or concocted? As he drifted away into a separate reality, DCI Beckwith and Sergeant Lowe entered the room.

'Detective Sergeant Lowe will be sitting in on this interview, Mr Dunstan. If you're comfortable, sir, we'll start now.' If there was any irony in Beckwith's voice, Dunstan missed it.

Lowe started the tape recorder, made the usual noises of time, place and people, and looked across the desk. 'So, let's start by recounting your movements last Sunday, shall we, Mr Dunstan?'

The questioning dragged on and on. The minutes and hours ticked by, with Dunstan straining to be polite and helpful. He had assumed they would focus on the days around Morgan's death, but Beckwith and his team went back over the whole of the past year with a fine-tooth comb.

At ten o'clock they took a fifteen-minute break, then resumed with their joker question: 'We were just wondering, Mr Dunstan, why you failed to mention that you were in the habit of running with the deceased, Mr Idris Morgan, on Sunday mornings?'

Dunstan knew he was in for the long haul.

***

At ten-thirty exactly, an anxious but ever-dutiful Kate Cross picked up the mobile phone Dunstan had given her just before he left and dialled the number on the screen. A woman answered, making no attempt to engage the caller.

'Redmond, please,' Kate said.

There was a pause on the other end of the phone, she keyed hash and the line went dead. At ten thirty-five precisely, the phone rang.

'Yes?' Kate tried and failed to keep the nervousness out of her voice.

The line seemed to go dead for a few seconds. Then an educated English voice said, 'This is Redmond. May I ask who you are?'

'I'm calling about Mr Philip Dunstan.'

'I assume your boss asked you to make this call to me. How might I help?'

Kate tried to control her nervousness. 'The police arrested him at eight o'clock this morning.'

'The policemen he went with, did he seem to know them?' came the unexpected response.

'Yes.'

'So we can assume they're real policemen, can we?'

An odd and alarming question. 'Yes, I recognised one of them. He'd been here before.'

'Were they local policemen?'

'Again, yes. From Kidlington, I think.'

'Leave it with me. Thank you, Kate.' The line went dead, which was just as well; Kate had dropped the phone when she heard her name.

***

As 'Redmond' terminated the call to Kate, Freshfield picked up the internal phone. 'Ah, good morning, ma'am. Our man Dunstan has been picked up by the boys in raincoats from Thames Valley Constabulary on suspicion of murder. Been in there for at least two hours with no fresh air, ma'am. I'm not over-sensitive to his grilling, but the longer he stays there, the more chance of his detention becoming public, which isn't what we want at this juncture. I think, with respect, we need him under our control.'

Celia Fanshawe, Director of International Counter-Terrorism, MI5, thought for a moment. 'I need the full picture. Convene a meeting for eleven-thirty. I need Rebecca Lovat and her team of SOCA analysts ready with the detail. I know it's short notice, Graham, but we don't have the luxury of time, or of making an ill-informed decision.'

After another moment of reflection, she went through to the anteroom of her office. 'Jane, could you please get through to the office of the Deputy Assistant Commissioner, Counter Terrorism Command, Metropolitan Police, and ask if he would kindly take a call from me at twelve-fifteen. Also, I want to freeze the personal bank accounts of Mr Philip Dunstan. Type up the warrant for me to sign and then get it to the duty judge, quickly, please!'

***

Dunstan had been in the green room for over three hours now and was becoming seriously bored. They had analysed the last two months in detail again and again. *No, he hadn't noticed anything odd in Morgan's behaviour recently. No, he couldn't think of anyone who would want to kill him. Yes, he had a genuine reason for going to London. And no, he hadn't had anything to do with it.* His interrogators had gone out of the room and left him to stew, to view him through the CCTV and look for any signs of his guard dropping. His boredom was cut short when a pleasant young constable came in with a tray of tea. 'Thank you,' Dunstan said.

The constable eyed him in a way that invited something further. 'The Chief thought you might like to look at these, sir. While you eat.' He placed a buff-coloured folder on the battered table and left. Dunstan swallowed. Without opening the folder, he knew what was in it. If they had played their joker, this was the *coup-de-grace* as far as they were concerned. Slowly, he unfastened the cord ties and lifted the flap: the scene-of-crime photographs. Morgan, his old friend and ally, lay where he had fallen, among the familiar leaf litter of the Boars Hill Woods, his head hanging from his body by the slenderest of cords. The blood had spilled around him in a dark stain. Beckwith's idea of an interrogation ploy, intended to shock him into telling the truth. But Dunstan had been interrogated by people far more skilled than Beckwith and his team.

As he gazed at the gruesome photographs, he felt the creep of cold and intense anger, an anger directed at Beckwith, Lovat and Freshfield, but above all at the person or persons who had done this to a friend and a good man. Whatever it took, and however long it took, his mind was now made up. He would hunt them down to the ends of the earth. And make sure they paid in blood for what they'd done.

***

At 1115 hours, in an acoustically secure meeting room overlooking the Thames on Victoria Embankment, Lovat was waiting for her team to arrive. Her analysts entered the room one by one: Vince Fleming, a shaggy-haired Scot with a Masters Degree from the School of Oriental and African Studies; Elizabeth Hamilton, a couple of years out of Cambridge and fluent in Urdu from her childhood in Pakistan, in the days when her father ran the British Council there; and Ratty, one of MI5's technical wizards who in another life would have been a top computer hacker, a specialist in penetrating international banking systems.

'Are you sure this isn't premature, Boss?' Fleming looked concerned. What he really meant was that he didn't want Lovat to look a complete idiot in front of a woman with a razor-sharp mind and a finely-tuned intuition that could spot the flaws when you were only halfway through a sentence. 'I mean we haven't really got a firm audit trail on this one. And we're not at all sure of Dunstan's role. It's so full of holes you could fall through to another universe.'

'Precisely, Vince. That's why we're here.'

There was a sharp drop in temperature as Celia Fanshawe entered the room with the Head of UK Counter-Terrorism, Freshfield, in tow. They fell silent.

'All right, Rebecca and Graham, the floor's yours. I've only got forty-five minutes, so don't make it War and Peace.'

It was Lovat who led off. 'Right, ma'am. To recap quickly, for the last two months we've been tracking and tracing substantial funds that have been fraudulently acquired, laundered through a UK-based electronic payments company – Philip Dunstan's company, CyberX – and deposited in an Islamic Bank in Islamabad for purposes unknown at this moment.' She looked across at Fanshawe, who had clearly engaged her considerable intellect and appeared to be processing thoughts on multiple levels.

'I know all this. Get to the point. Where is it going and for what purpose? That's what we need to know in order to identify and quantify the terrorist risk.'

'That's the problem, ma'am. We don't know the ultimate destination of the money or the purpose for which it is intended. That's what we're trying to find out. If I might submit, the fast track is to harness Dunstan's resources in CyberX to find the origin, while engaging Six's assets on the ground in Islamabad in order to identify the demand end of the money flow...'

'I think we'll keep Six out of this until we're sure of our ground here, thank you,' Fanshawe interrupted sharply. 'Go on, please.' Only Fanshawe could manage to make 'please' feel like the thrust of a rapier into the heart of the recipient.

'However, we also have to consider the murder of one of the key employees of the UK Company concerned, which, er, *complicates* our ability to harness CyberX's resources.'

Fanshawe looked across at her Head of UK Counter-Terrorism. Freshfield nodded in agreement. 'I agree with the principle that we should get under CyberX's skin but Rebecca and I differ on the methods; I favour a less co-operative approach. We should sweat Dunstan. He must have known this was going on.'

Lovat's violet eyes flashed at Freshfield. Fanshawe didn't miss it. 'And you, Rebecca. How would you play this?'

Lovat was unfazed. She knew what she wanted. 'We need CyberX as a whole: its resources, systems, operations; its wholesale co-operation, lock, stock and barrel. Without having any on-the-ground intelligence at the demand end, we need their resources to enable us to track and trace the flow of funds electronically and find the source of the fraud.'

Fanshawe went silent, ruminating. They were both right. Both had equal seniority and she valued their respective expertise and incisiveness. But Freshfield was the operational generalist, Lovat the anti-money-laundering specialist, heading up the Financial Terrorist Investigation Section. They had their own separate agendas: Lovat to track and trace the money, Freshfield to work out where the money was heading operationally and if the destination posed a threat to the UK or its allies. Fanshawe's intuition told her it most certainly did, directly or indirectly. This man Dunstan was an unknown quantity and it was by no means certain he was not involved in either the fraud or the murder. In some way though, he had to be a key into this. Which way did she go? Could she satisfy all ends? She let her thoughts process and switched her tack. 'How much money are we talking about now? How much has been laundered into this account?'

'Fleming has the figure, ma'am.' So had Lovat, but she needed a bit of mental space to deal with the intellectual broadside that was inevitably coming her way.

Ratty passed a slip of paper to Fleming whilst trying to look very small indeed. Fleming took a deep breath. 'Can't be exact, ma'am, but we estimate in excess of forty million dollars.' Fleming had a pained expression. He lived for exactitude and he knew 'in excess of' did not qualify as a proper answer. *What was Lovat doing presenting this pile of bones to Celia Fanshawe?*

Ms Fanshawe wrinkled her nose in displeasure. '*In excess of... about so much...* what does that mean? Eighty million, four hundred million? How can you be so vague?'

Lovat had anticipated her. 'We can't get in on the ground, ma'am. We've been tracking movements electronically for the last two months and have identified what looks like the principal recipient bank account, but there may be others. We don't know if there have been deposits before that time, but there have been significant withdrawals over the period. We can only identify *electronic* transfers in, and they are *in* only, which seems to indicate that huge amounts of money are being withdrawn in cash, ma'am. Our estimate is based on the deposits we've identified, which were made during the period in question. Furthermore, we don't know who or which organization is initiating the fraud or, indeed, who the ultimate beneficiary is.'

'Inside job from CyberX?' Fanshawe shot back.

'We don't believe so, ma'am, although we're obviously keeping an open mind on that score. If it's someone inside the company, it's very deep and hidden.'

Celia Fanshawe set her half-moon spectacles onto the end of her nose, raised her head, and peered through them. It was her pose for focusing her mind on what was relevant and discarding the rest.

What to do? She could drill down into the UK situation but she suspected Freshfield was on top of that, as far as he could be. It was the demand end that interested her. If huge amounts were going out of the account in cash, the chances were that, if this was a terrorist-related plan, it had already been initiated. 'You say you've identified a recipient bank account. Does it have a name? Do we know at this moment in time *exactly* how much is in it?'

Fleming shifted slightly in his seat, as though establishing himself on firmer ground. 'Yes ma'am; as of this morning, thirty-eight million, five hundred and thirty-three thousand, four hundred and fifty-three dollars and forty-six pence to be precise when we last, er, took a look at the account two hours ago. That's exactly five million dollars less than last week when the last electronic funds transfer was made.'

'Cash withdrawal of five million dollars?'

'We can only assume so, ma'am.'

'Any idea why the transfers stopped two weeks ago?'

Lovat looked at Ratty, who had an answer. 'It was because the fraud stopped, ma'am. Suddenly, in mid-flow. As though someone, somewhere, had thrown a switch. Ma'am.'

To Celia Fanshawe this was a vital piece of information. 'And a few days later, Mr Idris Morgan was ritually murdered...hmm. And the name on the account in question?'

Fleming shot a glance at Lovat, who nodded imperceptibly. 'The Greater Himalaya Education Foundation.'

Fanshawe looked at each of them around the table in turn. 'The Greater Himalaya Education Foundation: hardly sounds like Al-Qaeda core, does it? And why would there be an account with such a name in an Islamic Bank?'

There was an uncomfortable silence. It was Hamilton, speaking for the first time, who broke the pregnant pause. 'Probably because it's not an Islamic Bank.'

'What?' Fanshawe was staring at Lovat, who in turn stared at Hamilton as if she held the keys to her future career.

Don't screw up, Elizabeth, she willed her.

'It's the Commercial Bank of Pakistan ma'am. It's not a bank run on Islamic principles. It's just like any other international commercial bank, but small, and one that operates only inside the borders of Pakistan.'

'How are you sure of this?' Fanshawe never took anything for granted – one of the reasons she had risen near to the top.

'Because my father had an account with CBP when he was with the British Council in Pakistan.' There was a momentary silence as this fact was digested.

'So how did this fraud work?' Fanshawe continued.

'We're not totally sure,' responded Lovat. 'The best scenario is that stolen credit card details were automatically fed into false retail merchants, set up by someone in the corrupt payment service provider in Prague, and then processed through CyberX to settle with the card issuing banks. Several transactions per card, small individual amounts so they didn't attract too much attention. But then somebody, somewhere, switched off the operation.' Fanshawe reflected. 'But if the individual card payment amounts were small, you would need hundreds of thousands of stolen card details to generate forty million dollars of fraud, wouldn't you?'

'Yes, you would,' said Lovat, confident on home turf, 'but these are readily available and can be bought over the Internet. As to the possible source of all these card details, well, for example, one of the largest retailers in the USA had their database hacked into last year and were relieved of some *one hundred million* customer card details which they were holding against recognised best practice.' She looked pointedly at Ratty who had a *don't look at me* look on his face.

'This fraud,' said Fanshawe, 'could it be switched back on?'

'Indeed it could, ma'am. If the stolen card details are still held in a database…and with the full co-operation of CyberX.'

'I thought that was where you were heading,' smiled the Director of International Counter-Terrorism, who now had a very clear view of how she wished to proceed. She looked across the table at Lovat and Freshfield. 'Now this is what we're going to do. We're going to make Dunstan sweat for two or three days in Paddington Green and then, depending on what he has to say, make him an offer to co-operate – on a very short leash only. And I mean short! I've already taken the trouble to freeze his bank accounts. Graham, I want you to make arrangements for a very thorough series of interviews, please.'

It was 1210 hours as she ended the meeting to make her phone call to Counter Terrorism Command.

***

Shortly after 12:30, a policewoman stuck her head around the door of Interview Room 2. Beckwith went outside and was absent for a few minutes. When he came back into the room, his face was puce, as though he had been arguing with someone senior and for his assertions had received a senior bollocking.

He held Dunstan's look with a sardonic smirk. 'This interview is terminated, Mr Dunstan. Now don't look too relieved. The "powers that be" want you to be grilled by the Professional Grillers, Sir. Capital P, Capital G.'

'So what does that mean in the Queen's English?' Dunstan was not going to be fazed by mind games.

'Well, Mr Dunstan, you're being transferred to Paddington Green High Security Police Station *with immediate effect*, as it says on the transfer warrant.' Beckwith was now enjoying himself.

Dunstan was shocked and couldn't hide it. His bowels churned, a legacy from too many bouts of dysentery from his travels. *Which 'grillers' are these 'professional grillers'?* All he could think was that if he went into Paddington Green High Security, he might not come out of the system for a long, long time. And he had to, for all those people depending on him.

Beckwith was determined to make the most of it. 'You know, the secure unit for terrorists and other nasties. I reckon you might last longer than most, sir, before they crack you open. All psychological, of course. Very clever people, they tell me, with very clever methods, I believe. Two days at the very most, I reckon, that's all you'll last.' The grin was still in place. 'Shall I phone your family or your solicitor on your behalf, sir, to let them know your destination? Or do you want to tell them yourself?' His tone was now irritating Dunstan.

Dunstan stared at him, fighting to maintain control. *Revenge is best served on a cold platter. I'll get you back, you bastard, and make you look such an idiot you'll want to crawl away and commit professional suicide.*

'I believe I *am* allowed one phone call, Detective Chief Inspector. I should like to make that now. My office is my preferred call. My business is my main priority,' Dunstan replied pleasantly.

You mercenary bastard thought Beckwith, as Lowe passed the phone over.

'Kate? Listen. They appear to have finished with me here... No, it's not necessarily good news, I'm afraid. Some people in London now wish to interview me... Yes, I'm being taken to London. Please get onto Herbert and Gornall in Oxford and tell my solicitor I'm going to Paddington Green... Yes, Kate, it *is* somewhere near to Paddington Station. Now Kate, please listen. I haven't much time, and I'm very concerned about the safety of the staff and that of my family. Could you please get onto Faith and suggest very strongly that she prepares to head off to Scotland sooner rather than later? She'll understand... No, just say to her that I'm being routinely interviewed by the police and that I'll be in touch. Now, most important, before you do that, please tell Vernon Hamill to raise the anti-kidnap alert for "A"-list staff to "Bikini Black Alpha" with immediate notice to move.

Thanks, Kate. Please look after yourself. Tell everyone to keep their spirits up. Got to go now.'

As Kate put down the phone and prepared to call Hamill, she chewed the end of her pen and mused that the anti-kidnap 'A'-list comprised of one person only: Dunstan himself.

'You're a cold fish, Dunstan,' said Beckwith, eyeing him oddly. 'Do you always keep your wife in the dark about your activities?'

'Don't need to, Inspector – telepathy normally suffices.' Dunstan stood and stretched to his full height. As he made his way to the door, Beckwith stepped in front of him. He reached into his pocket and pulled out a small, sealed plastic bag.

'One last thing. Do you know what this is, and what its origins might be?

It was found at the scene of the crime.'

Dunstan took the bag and held it up to the light. Inside was a tiny knife with a rough-looking blade about an inch long and a triangular-shaped handle of the same length. The handle of the knife wasn't plastic. It was shiny black bone. Dunstan knew perfectly well what it was, and what it was used for. It was a *chakma,* and it was the sharpening tool for a weapon belonging to a very special warrior. But from his reaction, no one would ever have known that he knew.

'Are you asking me because you don't know what it is, or because you think I do?' He handed it back.

'Personally, I suspect you do know… *sir*!' responded Beckwith, allowing his professional cool to drop.

Dunstan merely gave a curt nod and moved past him.

With that, Dunstan was escorted outside via the covered rear entrance and into a car, with Lowe driving and Dunstan in the back next to a thick-set constable with the size, shape and demeanour of a fully mature mountain gorilla. With Dunstan under orders to keep his head down, they drove slowly out of the car park. Once they had left the confines of Kidlington, they joined the A34 to Junction 11 of the M40 and wound up the supercharged engine of the unmarked white Volvo V70 estate.

As it was approximately fifty miles to London, Beckwith was in no particular rush as he kept up his line of questioning, which Dunstan refused point blank to answer. As they saw the one-mile sign for Wendlebury Services, Dunstan spoke up.

'I need the lavatory, Detective Chief Inspector. At the next services if you would be so kind.'

'You can wait until London for a pee,' replied Beckwith brusquely. 'It's not that I need, if you don't mind.'

'You can still wait, Dunstan.'

'The consequences of that, Detective Chief Inspector Beckwith, do not bear thinking about. I came back from my last trip to Asia with a particularly vile form of dysentery called Tropical Sprue. The effects are still with me and I reckon in about three minutes max I'll have foul-smelling diseased crap running down my legs, staining your car seat and floor permanently.' Dunstan noticed the Gorilla sitting next to him was retreating as far as he could into his corner of the rear seat. 'If *you* chaps don't mind, then I certainly don't. I've had to put up with worse things in life, but you and the reception committee at Paddington Green may well not have. It's up to you!' Beckwith wrinkled his nose and nodded to Lowe. He wasn't going to take a risk on having to deliver Dunstan to Counter Terrorism Command in a foul-smelling state. They pulled off the motorway and parked in the far recesses of the service station car park. Beckwith pulled rank so that Lowe and the Gorilla were designated to escort Dunstan over to the lavatories. There was a brief discussion on the pros and cons of using handcuffs in a public place. Beckwith's instinct was to go low-profile, no handcuffs, so with the vice-like grip of the Gorilla on Dunstan's left tricep, they proceeded to escort Dunstan, who smiled inwardly at what was about to unfold, towards the toilets. Beckwith followed alongside. This odd threesome hadn't gone fifty yards when a blue, high-powered motorbike screamed round the corner at close range and headed straight at the Gorilla. Before he could react it screeched to a halt and he found himself staring down the barrel of a 9mm Browning handgun. Simultaneously, Dunstan's elbow crashed into Lowe's face and a well-aimed kick knocked the detective's knee sideways in a direction that nature hadn't intended it to travel. Dunstan leapt onto the pillion seat of the motorbike just as the Gorilla tried to grab the handlebars. The rider was prepared: a short metal bar crashed onto exposed knuckles, eliciting a heartfelt scream. It was over in seconds. As the motorbike headed out of the services, Beckwith sped over in the Volvo and screamed at the others to get in. 'Where to, Lowe?'

A very sore Lowe pointed south and said 'Heafrow' through a bloody mouth and nose. 'He'shh got a flight to Bermuda at fif'een-t'enty hourshh.' The Gorilla cursed through gritted teeth. Beckwith, driving, wound up the engine and blasted onto the M40.

Vernon Hamill, ex-Mobility Troop, D Squadron 22 SAS Regiment, was comfortably in charge of the safe extraction of his boss from the unwanted and doubtless unwarranted attentions of the law. As Hamill headed south on his Yamaha XT1200Z at a somewhat sedate seventy-five miles per hour, continually looking in his mirrors for the Volvo, he was willing his pursuers to get within sight of him. He hoped he had timed his deception plan just right.

At the approach of the gap where the M40 motorway cuts through the chalk of the Chiltern Hills up a steep climb, Hamill caught sight of his pursuers. He always chose the tools of his trade carefully: they had to be fit for purpose and his choice of motorbike was no exception. With a big, powerful 1200cc engine, the Yamaha has a low centre of gravity for light, agile handling, from walking pace on wooded tracks and rocky trails to high-attack velocity in twists and turns. It's a tough machine and it's also very fast: as Hamill opened up the throttle, it shot forward and soon hit 130mph, giving Dunstan a much-welcome adrenaline surge.

Over the crest of the hill at the Stokenchurch Junction, Hamill braked hard, swept off the junction and turned back north into the cover of the woods. The back-up team was waiting: an identical bike, two-up with identical clothing and the same registration plate, but this time legitimately registered to the bike. The two hired Hells Angels from the Oxford Chapter, retained by Hamill for such an eventuality, had been paid five thousand pounds in cash each to have a police car chase them at a hundred and thirty miles per hour down the motorway to Heathrow. Half the cash up front, the other half if they did the job well and got arrested in the right place. For that amount of money, they didn't care if they lost their licences for a while. They pulled out onto the M40 and accelerated fast just as the white police Volvo crested the hill. For them, it would be a fast, furious and fun chase to Heathrow.

***

Hamill set off down the tight tracks in the dense woods of the Chilterns escarpment. Kate Cross was waiting for them at the bottom in a nondescript Golf.

'Your wife's trying to get hold of you. She says it's urgent. I didn't tell her where you were.'

As Dunstan jumped into the passenger seat, Kate threw the mobile phone into his lap. It was a moment before he caught up. 'Did you contact "Redmond"?'

'Yes. Didn't seem to do any good though, did it?'

Privately, Dunstan agreed. He stored that thought for later retrieval.

By now, a fierce April shower was hammering down. Kate peered anxiously through the windscreen. 'Which bloody way now?'

'North through Thame and across side roads to the Cotswolds. Not too fast so we don't draw attention to ourselves.' Dunstan paused and phoned home. 'Hi Faith, it's me,' he said, trying to sound nonchalant.

'Philip! Where the hell have you been? I've been trying to get hold of you all bloody morning. I need to talk to you!'

Dunstan reflected that wherever he was at any given moment, he didn't seem to be in the right place for a lot of people.

'I was unavoidably detained.'

'What? Where?' came the sharp retort.

'At Stalag Luft Kidlington, answering a few questions for the police.' Kate shot him a glance as if to say *Don't say anymore!*

'They didn't charge you, did they? Sorry, that sounds awful. You know what I mean – are you all right?'

The voice had softened, but to Dunstan there was clearly something amiss. 'I'm fine, Faith, it was just a preliminary chat. Kate picked me up. What's the problem?'

'A couple of things I thought you should know about. First, our joint bank accounts have been locked down. The bank manager says it was a court order. You might want to check your personal account. My building society account in my maiden name is still accessible, though.'

'Shit!' said Dunstan with feeling. 'What's the second thing?'

'We had had a visit this morning.'

'What? From whom?'

'Two men. We were out at the time. Jenny next door told me. She said they were a bit like Jehovah's Witnesses but "foreign looking", dressed smartly in blazer, shirt and tie. They looked around for about ten minutes around the outside of the house, up the steps of the barn, poked their nose into the garage, and then drove off.'

Alarm bells sounded in Dunstan's mind. 'Listen to me, Faith. I want you to get out of there right now. Pack and leave ...'

'What, *now*? Are you serious? The girls are in school,' she interrupted.

'Pull the girls out of school, get the boys to start packing and head out for Scotland as soon as you can. I'm deadly serious. I might see you briefly, I might not. Pack the small Sat phone – it's in my den. I'll call you on it at twenty three hundred hours BST every other day. Please, darling, just do it. Love you; now please get going! Oh, and leave the keys to the gun cabinet.'

If there were strangers snooping around the property, he wanted to be ready for them.

Dunstan watched the rain driving against the windscreen. 'So the question is, Kate, how long have I got before Beckwith realises he's chasing a decoy?'

'Well, they'll have to go all the way to Heathrow first.' 'Why Heathrow?'

'Because I left the corporate diary open at today's date with an entry in bold that you are booked onto flight BA2233 to Bermuda, leaving from Heathrow at fifteen twenty hours. The detectives can't have missed it."

Dunstan smiled. 'You know, you'll be in trouble for this, Kate. Wasting police time, perverting the course of justice…'

Kate ignored him. 'You've probably got a couple of hours at the very most, Philip. Take care.' With that, she stopped the car near Glympton and without a backward glance in case he saw the tears streaming down her face, she transferred to another of Hamill's pre-arranged car swaps.

Dunstan took to the tiny roads around the back of Blenheim Palace estate, then onto off-road green lane through the outlying woods of another Cotswolds Estate, Cornbury Park. It was bumpy but manageable in the sturdy little Golf. The lane brought him out on single-track roads close to home.

***

The tyres of the Golf scrunched the stone chippings of the drive as he pulled up in front of the house. He'd made it in time, his family were just about to leave. It seemed to Dunstan as if half a football team had descended on him. Freya and Laura, just picked up from school, were squealing with delight and Pull-Through, in his overexcitement, was jumping up and trying to attach himself to any part of his master he could. It was a surreal moment of normality. 'Come on guys, we need to get you on the road if you're to make it past Birmingham before the rush hour. Let's go. Have you all packed?' A rhetorical question if ever there was one. Faith would have done all the packing in her usual supremely efficient style.

His wife was in the doorway, watching him intensely and issuing orders. 'Harry, put that bloody dog down. James, help the little ones to get comfortable in the back and then programme the satnav thing so that if we hit traffic, we can find another route. Oh, and turn off the voice – I don't want to be told where to go by some electronic backseat driver.'

James winked at his father and mouthed the word 'Ozzy'. Dunstan suppressed a laugh. His son had downloaded the 'voice' of Ozzy Osbourne onto the satnav. He imagined the scene as the Prince of Darkness and Living Rock Legend gave his first directions, Faith swearing at the device and all the kids in hysterics. He wished he could be there to witness the moment.

Dunstan crunched over the drive to his wife and whispered sharply in her ear, 'Keys to the gun cabinet, now please, darling.'

He took the keys from her and went through the house to a small, purpose-built room off the boot room, and to the custom-built, steel-lined gun cabinet which housed his shotguns. Two four-lever mortice locks top and bottom, with different keys, unlocked the safe. He opened another locked compartment in the base of the cabinet and withdrew his Browning 9mm handgun and two full clips of ammunition, a 'trophy' from one of his travels and kept quite illegally for a day he thought would never come. It had just arrived.

Feeling marginally more able to protect his family, he went outside to see the final packing taking place. Within ten minutes they were loaded and ready to go; it was now just after two o' clock. Dunstan looked at his wife. She had a wonderful ability to create space and time in the middle of confusion and chaos. She caught his eye. 'I've got something for you in the kitchen before we go. Stay there you lot!' The kids all knew better than to move. She turned to the house and Dunstan followed.

'When are you flying out?'

'It's supposed be fifteen twenty.'

'What? You can't make that. You'll kill yourself, and probably others, trying.'

'I know. I'm not going to Bermuda. I'm staying right here. I've called The Monk.'

'Ah,' said Faith with complete understanding and agreement. '*He*'ll look after you.'

He put his arms around her waist, before sliding them slowly down to her buttocks. She melted.

'Come on, you two. You're not *snogging* are you?' The cries of protest came from the car.

She pulled away and held his gaze for a moment. 'Work out who your friends are, Philip.' With a final hot kiss, she turned on her heels. Within seconds the Land Rover Discovery surged and his family receded rapidly into the distance, arms waving and Pull-Through barking manically at the window.

He stood in the drive of the empty house staring after his departing family. A profound feeling of desolation crept over him and he fought a welling-up of emotion.

Focus, Philip, focus! Appreciate, evaluate, plan! His rational, military mind prodded him out of his gloom. Immediately it was countered by his intuitive side: *This is still a game of shadows, Philip. Shape-changers abound. Forget a rational approach. Follow your instinct!* For the moment, his intuitive side won the internal battle.

Chapter Five

Dunstan turned towards the house but instead of heading for the open kitchen door, he made for the barn, bounded up the outside stone steps to the old granary and opened the door into his den. He slumped into his old, battered arm-chair and, for a moment, stared into space. Thoughts and images tumbled through his head. He knew better than to fight them.

But he had to get going.

He moved over to his desk and poured a shot of Laphroaig from his great-grandfather's whisky decanter. He viewed the world through the dark peaty liquid then knocked it back in a single, satisfying gulp. He rarely drank spirits but on this occasion he was prepared to make an exception. With his family gone, he felt exhaustion creeping over him, like a slow succumbing to hypothermia before accepting death from cold, but he knew it was now that he had to dig deep; deep into reserves he hadn't called upon for a long time. He didn't know where he was going, what he was doing, and where all this would finish. He had no idea where to turn, or even what he was going to do in the next hour before the police worked out he wasn't catching the flight to Heathrow and all hell was let loose. He didn't have much time, yet he had to be methodical and purposeful.

He tried to review his situation but all he had was questions crashing around in his brain with no answers. As he sifted through the margins of his mind in a futile attempt to match and rationalise the unfolding events, he formed no conclusions. His immediate feeling was one of intense frustration, but he knew he couldn't afford the luxury of frustration. He was under pressure from all sides: from a potential enemy he could not see, but who was capable of extreme ruthless violence; from the police; and from the potential destruction of the very pillars of his existence – his family and his business. And all this set against a backdrop of spooks and international subterfuge. He was in the middle of a jungle.

He moved over to his beloved book collection, and pulled out a hardback with a fading, pale beige spine. He flicked through the familiar pages.

Dunstan had read *The Jungle Is Neutral* by Freddie Spencer Chapman many times. As the Japanese were heading down through Malaysia sweeping all before them, Spencer Chapman was heading towards them in, of all things, a scarlet Ford V8 pickup packed with explosives and ammunition to conduct guerrilla warfare behind enemy lines. For three and a half years, he endured hardship and irregular combat against the Japanese Army, and even Chinese bandits operating deep behind enemy lines, for which he was awarded a DSO. He was helped by rubber planters, hardy men who had chosen to stay behind, and Chinese communists who had traitors in their midst. Little wonder the book, published in 1949, later became a handbook for the Special Air Service Regiment in developing their jungle skills and operations against Communist insurgents in Malaya in the late fifties.

If the jungle is neutral, reflected Dunstan, *then providing I have no expectations of it, it shouldn't mind me living in it. And if that's the case, then providing I use all resources available to me, and yet more which the jungle provides for me as I move through it, I have to assume that I'm not at an overall disadvantage to the others playing in this jungle. And, like Freddie, I need to work out who my friends are and recruit as I go along.* He snapped out of his reverie. 'Work out who your friends are.' The last thing Faith had said to him. *Easy for her to say, hard as hell to do!*

Dunstan stood with the book in his hand for a few more moments, then headed over the courtyard to the kitchen, where he opened a drawer full of tangled phone chargers and old phones. He picked up an envelope which contained five pay-as-you-go SIM cards from different carriers, pre-loaded with fifty pounds each. He also picked up two new handsets plus two chargers and a very old handset that looked like a brick (not flash, but effective and less likely to be lost or stolen). He also picked up water, energy bars and soluble energy powder.

Returning to the den, he walked over to an ancient pine coffer and opened the lid. Out of it he pulled a Berghaus Centurion dark green Bergen, vintage 1988. It was a curiosity both in respect of its age and its modifications: extra padding made of foam, camouflaged insulating tape around the shoulder straps and waist band and extra padding at the base of the pack which rested against the lower spine. Taped to each shoulder strap were pieces of Velcro with a small water bottle attached to one and a torch to the other, each well camouflaged.

He had checked the contents the previous night: ultra-down sleeping bag, spare dry clothes, lightweight merino layers and a cashmere vest, Swiss Army knife, large water bottle and camouflage waterproofs, which he now swapped for Goretex salopettes and a thermo-fleece top. He added spare pairs of expedition socks and, just for good measure, a black wool balaclava. He went to his desk and pulled out a prismatic compass and several 1:50,000 scale maps of South and Mid Wales. He also picked up a much more robust expedition jacket made out of double cotton ventile with full face protection. Next, a pair of Goretex and reversed leather boots, and a pair of lightweight trail shoes, spare underclothes and wash kit went into a small holdall. A multi-fuel stove and a fuel bottle went into the top of his sack, along with concentrated energy bars and mountain food in a waterproof stuff-sack. Finally, into the front compartment of a large leather Targus computer bag went Dunstan's laptop with a 4G international roaming wireless card and the spare handsets and SIM card. Into the rear compartment went an ultra-lightweight Sat phone that no one other than Faith knew he had. The Sat phones had been purchased in advance of a 'final' expedition to the Nyenchen Tanglha Range in remote Central Tibet, which he had been planning with his oldest climbing friends. But Al Scott's premature death in an avalanche while climbing the Super Couloir on the side of Mont Blanc had put paid to that. He glanced up to see Al's grinning countenance looking down at him from the wall. 'OK, Al, this trip's for you!' Finally, in went a polythene-wrapped 'stash' of money: ten thousand pounds equivalent in multiple currencies and denominations.

Dunstan shouldered the Bergen and was about to pick up his bags when he suddenly thought, *Chakma!* Dropping the Bergen, he moved over to his desk and unlocked the second drawer down. From it, he picked up a pair of curved knives sheathed in dulled buffalo leather. Inserted into the top of each sheath was a tiny rough blade, each with a small buffalo horn handle

– chakmas for sharpening the blade of the kukhris, one of which he now drew out of its sheath, running his finger along the ultra-sharp edge of the eight-inch-long blade. He hadn't picked this fight, but there was nothing like fighting fire with fire.

A lot of kukhris are manufactured for tourists. These were different – a matched pair of British Army-issue Gurkha kukhris issued to him personally at Pokhara, the Gurkha depot in the Himalayan foothills. He knew for sure that it was one of these types of weapons that had killed Morgan. He also knew that within the next few hours, the police might discover the same thing. The key issue was this: would they be able to work out how an eight-inch-long blade could sever a man's head in a single blow? Because he, Captain Philip Dunstan, late Platoon Commander Queen's Gurkha Engineers, knew exactly how. And in that knowledge, he also understood that the assassin was a very special kind of warrior with an unusual level of skill. He put the pair of kukhris into the holdall, followed by his 9mm Browning with three spare magazines of ammo.

Dunstan pressed the key fob that triggered the automatic garage door, locked the den and went down the granary steps to the house. In the sitting room, he picked up all the framed photos of Faith and the kids and locked them in the gun cabinet. He didn't want to add to the threat by allowing their faces to be 'out there'. He then secured the place and set the alarm, little knowing that this was a futile gesture. A last look around. He consciously hoped it wasn't going to be his last ever view of his beloved home. Sadly, his hopes were misplaced.

***

When Dunstan first floated CyberX on the London Stock Exchange, Faith had said that he should buy himself a 'boy's toy' by way of celebration. *After all, you've earned it.* But Dunstan had been too absorbed in business. Then, the previous September, the boys had persuaded him to go to the International Land Rover show at Malvern.

'I want that old SAS Pink Panther,' said Harry, pointing, 'with the Vickers machine guns on the back so we can drive around shooting people who get in our way.'

'In your dreams, Harry, in your dreams,' Dunstan had replied.

The show had been a revelation to Dunstan, a mixture of nostalgia and high tech, but it wasn't until they got to the Land Rover G4 Challenge stand with its bright orange vehicles specially prepared to perform in the most extreme terrain that Dunstan felt a spark of interest. He headed straight for the supercharged G4 Range Rover Sport. Within twenty minutes he had made an appointment to see the special vehicles section of Land Rover in Solihull the following week. He ordered a custom version, not in bright orange but in dark green, with an Overfinch modified engine producing 530 bhp, full satellite navigation and video communication, and extra under-floor compartments for maximum stowage of expedition gear, water, and a reserve power unit for long-range battery power. He and two very excited boys had picked it up from Solihull only three months previously. With the money, he could have bought nearly two Aston Martins, but this bespoke beast said more about Dunstan than any sports car: function over form, substance over style.

There was one other peculiarity of the G4 which arose from the fact that he had bought an old Berber house in the foothills of the Atlas Mountains as a retreat. From this base, he and Faith had planned to cross the Atlas and travel down through Mauritania, Niger and Mali. He had, therefore, decided to spec his G4 as a left-hand drive, to ship it straight out to Morocco as an expedition vehicle, and not to use it in the UK. The upshot was that the G4 was registered at DVLA Swansea on a temporary export licence only; for the purposes of the standard DVLA driver and car search, the G4 and Dunstan were 'off radar'.

Dunstan threw his Bergen into the back and the holdall and leather Targus into the front footwell. He placed his own mobile with the 'spook' SIM card, together with one spare pay-as-you-go SIM card and an old handset, into the centre console, turned the key and gunned the engine.

The 21-inch wheels with All Terrain tyres crunched the gravel as he headed out of the drive. The time was just 1530 hours. He headed west through the Wychwoods, then up onto the ridgeline that divides the Evenlode and Windrush valleys.

As he crested the rise, the police car containing Beckwith and Lowe skidded into the driveway of Dunstan's house, throwing a spray of gravel over the grass verge. Beckwith, especially, had been steaming with rage since the road-block just outside Terminal 4 at London Heathrow. The Metropolitan Police, with consummate professionalism, had boxed in and run down the speeding Yamaha. They were less than amused when the helmets were removed and instead of Dunstan and his 'rescuer', the battle-scarred countenances of a couple of unsavoury reprobates grinned back at them. Having been made a laughing stock in front of the Met, together with having to explain the non-arrival of a highly valued suspect at Paddington Green Station, the Thames Valley police officers now issued a stream of invective as they surveyed the empty courtyard and buildings. Their sense of humour failure was complete. *Revenge is best served on a cold platter.*

If Detective Sergeant Lowe thought that his boss couldn't look and sound any wearier and resigned, he was wrong.

'Okay, Lowe, go through the motions, check the place out. Look for any signs of life and do a once-over on the Golf.' He picked up the comms handset and got through to the team at HQ.

'Is Dunstan at his office?'

'No, sir,' came the succinct reply.

'Do any of us or any of his colleagues have any idea where he is, or indeed where his family might be?'

'No, sir.'

'Somebody knows. Let's start with that secretary of his, Kate Cross. Run a check with DVLA on all cars registered to Dunstan or CyberX and set up a call triangulation service for his mobile just in case he's daft enough to use it, which I very much doubt. Also, request a comprehensive block on all UK exit points.'

'That's Divisional Commander level authorisation at least, sir.'

'That's right – assume it's approved, I'll do all the paperwork afterwards. We're on our way back to the station now. As soon as you have anything to report, phone me.' Beckwith looked like a bullfrog that had just been denied its conjugal overtures. 'What would you do now if you were Dunstan, Lowe?'

'I'd try and find some intelligent help with the right level of resources, which probably means money, equipment and the necessary skills. All provided by someone I could trust.'

'And where would you find the kind of help that fits that shopping list, Sergeant Lowe?'

'With old friends, sir.'

'Ah. Good thought…where? How do we get to them?'

'According to the initial profile we have on him, Dunstan is ex-army. Why don't we take a shufti at some of his old forces chums?'

'Lowe, when is your promotion board to inspector due?' Lowe brightened. 'September, sir!'

'Well, it's cancelled. You're much too valuable as my detective sergeant.' Lowe watched his boss climb into the Volvo. He couldn't work out whether he had just improved his chances of promotion to inspector or been sentenced to career death.

***

If the police had missed Dunstan, someone else hadn't. On a hill above the Evenlode, the occupants of a well-disguised demilitarised Land Rover monitored his progress through powerful binoculars.

Dunstan stopped the G4 next to the old Rissington airfield. *I have to embrace risk. Take the battle to the enemy. Remember, the jungle is neutral...* He made his first critical decision and placed a call to 'Redmond'. Freshfield was looking out of his Thameside office window when the phone rang.

'Dunstan. Why am I not surprised to hear from you? Where are you now? Not in Bermuda, after all, eh?'

'Shut up and listen.' Dunstan's confidence came from a clear insight. His rapid, staccato voice rattled down the phone at Freshfield. 'Very shortly, GCHQ will have me pegged to within ten metres of this location. I've got about thirty seconds, so let's not play any games. Who ordered my transfer to Paddington Green and closed down my personal bank accounts?'

'No idea. Not my department.'

'You're a useless liar. We've got a common enemy, even if we are on parallel tracks. For different reasons, we both need to find out who is doing this, and why. Mine is very personal, yours a probable threat to national security that you can't afford to ignore. To neutralise the threat, we run our operations in tandem and share resources; call it mutually parasitic.'

There was a pause before Freshfield responded, 'What you're asking is outside my remit.'

An alarm bell started going off in Dunstan's head. 'Bollocks. Either help me out or stay off my back. Make a clear decision – there's no halfway house. I'll phone you on this number in the next twenty-four hours for a decision – not from this phone, so assume open line.'

The line went dead as Dunstan killed the call. He looked at his watch. Thirty-five-second call, better get going. With that, Philip Dunstan *Fugitive at Large* took a very rural but direct way through the upper Windrush Valley via The Guitings and down off the North Cotswold escarpment to the M5. To make sure that he wasn't recorded on the motorway traffic monitors, he cut out the motorway and headed across country on minor roads, staying just within the speed limit. Not only did he not want to draw any undue attention to himself, but he had taken the gamble that Freshfield had more to lose by mobilising the police to find him and chase him. Only two hours to the Brecon Beacons, and then, with any luck, he could go to ground with someone he *knew* he could trust.

Graham Freshfield, aka 'Redmond', stood looking out over the river Thames from the window of his MI5 office. There was so much that was flaky and risky in this project. The international aspect disturbed him, since his was a UK remit. But forty million dollars plus change, potentially made available to train terrorist operators in Pakistan for attacks on the UK mainland, *was* in his bailiwick. Even if that money was destined for other countries, from Europe to Asia and Australia, he had a responsibility to follow the money, find the source of the fraud operation and quantify the threat. In the absence of on-the-ground assets and intelligence in Pakistan, the only people who were in a strong position to do that were Dunstan and his team. He picked up the phone, called Rebecca Lovat and brought her up to speed on events.

Lovat was quietly impressed with Dunstan's initiative and would have liked to have known more from Freshfield, but something else needed attention.

'Graham, another two million dollars was taken out of the account this morning in Pakistan.'

'Transferred to where?'

'It wasn't. There was no electronic transfer on the bank's systems. We have to assume it was taken out in cash.'

'Our options, Rebecca? You're the fraud expert. Get some assets on the street in Islamabad for physical track and trace? Or …'

'Or harness CyberX, meaning Dunstan. Or both. Am I right?'

'You're right. We need to see the Headmistress ASAP. I'll place the call.'

***

'Good afternoon, ma'am. Reason for the call is a key development in our card fraud project. I would appreciate a meeting with you, Miss Lovat, and the analysts on the case.'

'When?'

'Now?'

Celia Fanshawe looked at her diary. She was scheduled to take her daughter to The Globe this evening to see *The Comedy of Errors*. She was not superstitious but she sincerely hoped that the choice of play was not in some way prophetic. 'I take it this key development warrants rescheduling my diary?'

Freshfield took a deep breath. 'Firstly, ma'am, Dunstan escaped his escort on the way to London. I can explain how at the meeting.'

'No need, I know. I've been waiting for you to tell me,' Fanshawe replied sharply.

He ploughed on as though he hadn't heard the rebuke. 'We have to make a key policy decision, ma'am. Or rather, I think you need to make it.'

'You're the Head of UK Counter-Terrorism. Not trying to cover yourself, are you, by any chance?'

Freshfield ignored the jibe. 'Two million dollars has gone from the Greater Himalayan Education Foundation Account today without electronic record. We can only assume in cash. This isn't about my behind, ma'am, it's about the fact that my department's operational remit doesn't cover the international dimension that needs tackling and Rebecca's team only has access to the account, not the chain. We need other resources.'

Two million in cash would fund a huge amount of terrorist activity, Fanshawe reflected. 'What resources?'

'We need to close the supply and demand loop. Find out who's behind it, why, and what for. In order to do that, we need much deeper intelligence at either end. At the bare minimum, we need feet on the ground, direct intelligence from Pakistan. It may even be a job for Six.'

'Aren't you over-reaching your remit here, recommending we go across the river to provide the resource?'

'Indeed, ma'am. But what I can say is that the people who are best placed to track and trace the fraud are those with the best resources. I am therefore formally requesting that we engage Dunstan as a person of interest to the Service.'

'Risky, isn't it?'

'On the contrary, ma'am. I submit that the biggest risk is inertia. If we want to get to the bottom of this, and stop a terrorist funding operation or a potential outrage, then some risks are inevitable. Dunstan is a known quantity. We can keep him close to us once he's on board.'

'Sixteen thirty hours then, for one hour only. It had better be succinct. And it had better be good!'

***

'What do we know about him?'

Lovat slid the brief on Dunstan over to Fanshawe and gave her a synopsis. Three generations of army on his father's side. After Sandhurst, Dunstan was commissioned into the Royal Engineers. He served for two years in the UK with the Queen's Gurkha Engineers, then went out to Hong Kong with his Gurkha Engineer Squadron, finishing that tour in Nepal, where he climbed the South Face of a 7,000m Himalayan peak, without oxygen. Then, posted to 59 Commando Squadron Royal Engineers, passed commando training with flying colours. Posted to Ireland, South Armagh 'bandit country', where he applied to go into military intelligence, and then on to Special Forces. Passed selection for 14 Intelligence and Security. Served for a year on operations in Fermanagh, where he was credited with stifling movement of arms and IRA and INLA operatives through wide-scale deployment of eavesdropping equipment… received a General Officer Commanding Commendation for his efforts. Volunteered for SAS selection but *failed*. Left the Army shortly afterwards.

'Quite a career until the last bit,' mused Lovat.

'Failed? Why?' Fanshawe was not one to leave a stone unturned. 'Seems like he failed the endurance test. The notes say that he stopped to rescue a fellow Selection candidate in poor weather. He was invited to come back on another Selection, a rare occurrence, but failed to turn up and left the army shortly afterwards.'

'Straight away?'

'Not quite, ma'am. He went on another Himalayan expedition and then served for six months at the Joint Service Survival Centre in Bavaria before resigning his commission.'

People who owe Dunstan, that's who he'll head for. Fanshawe had any number of questions but restricted herself to one. 'For whom did Dunstan fail SAS Selection? Whom did he rescue?'

Hamilton scanned the notes. 'I'm afraid it doesn't say, ma'am. It just says "a foreign national".'

'No nationality?'

'No, ma'am.'

'Commonwealth citizens are eligible for Selection, ma'am,' Freshfield said. 'There have been, and are, quite a number of Fijians in the SAS. Could explain the "foreign national" bit.'

'Hmm, find out for our next meeting who it was, will you, Graham? Also, I want more research. Something is missing. Dunstan has secrets and I want to know what they are. In the meantime, take it from me that you have leave to engage Dunstan as a temporary and deniable asset on a very tight rein indeed.'

Deniable, thought Freshfield, *means expendable.*

'And also to requisition the use of his company's systems and resources, with the sole proviso that Dunstan works with us on the supply side only, and does not under any circumstances leave UK territory. You are to know his physical whereabouts at all times. If he is complicit in any way, we don't want him slipping the net. After all, he's still a possible murder suspect on Thames Valley Constabulary's list. Where is Dunstan now?'

It was the question he'd seen coming. He knew he had to play it straight. 'At this moment, we don't know. He contacted us at sixteen hundred hours and is scheduled to phone back before the same time tomorrow. I'll need to offer him protection from the attentions of the police, ma'am.'

Freshfield was waiting for the broadside but it never came.

'Take that as read; I'll handle the police. Let's set the next meeting for tomorrow, fourteen hundred hours in this room. That should be enough time to allow Dunstan to come in from the cold. In the meantime, I'll also talk to our Foreign Service to see if we can get the ball rolling in Pakistan. That's all for now. Thank you.'

Fanshawe went back to her office. She looked at her phone and thought of calling her counterpart in SIS across the river. After a moment's reflection, she changed her mind and instead put through a call to the Directorate of Special Forces. Her MI5 rank was difficult to translate into an army equivalent, but it was somewhere around the Major General level. She spoke to the staff colonel on duty and requested a meeting with the Director himself at 0800 hours the following morning. Whatever her rank, Fanshawe had the knack of getting what she wanted.

Chapter Six

Dunstan had made reasonable time along the old A40 through Brecon.

He parked his Range Rover at the Storey Arms car park in the shadow of the Brecon Beacons. It was 1800 hours, and there were still two hours of daylight left. After ten minutes a nondescript ten-year-old Toyota drew slowly into the car park and parked near the hedge. The man in the car checked his mirror and looked around him before switching off the engine. He eased himself out of the car. To the casual observer, he looked like any middle-aged walker: hiker's trousers and jacket, a rucksack that had seen better years, and a well-worn pair of mountain boots. His gait was slightly awkward, as if he were compensating for an old leg injury, and his woollen hat hid his shaved head. The trained observer, however, would have seen him walk not across the car park but around the edge, tucked into the shadow of the privet. Dunstan didn't see him until it was too late.

The door of the Range Rover was flung open and a gnarled hand gripped Dunstan's throat from behind like a vice, temporarily paralyzing him. He tried to wrestle clear but it was no good. He wanted to scream, but it was all he could do to keep breathing. He grabbed the hand in a jujitsu hold and wrenched it away from his neck. As he did, it squeezed harder momentarily, then relaxed. He half turned, holding his throat. He was staring into a pair of flat black eyes.

'You're dead, Sherpa. You call a rendezvous under the code, clearly under pressure, travel in an ostentatious monster with an odd number plate, park up and switch off not only the engine but also your brain. Did you see me arrive? No! Did you see me hard-target around the car park perimeter? No! Did you see my final approach to the car? No! Have you forgotten everything you learned in the Det and what I taught you? Yes! Tosser!' The Monk had arrived.

The Det, now incorporated into the Special Reconnaissance Regiment, is the insider's name for 14 Intelligence and Security Company, whose members are all on 'detachment' from their parent regiments.

'Jesus, I thought I was coming to meet a friend,' Dunstan gasped.

'Who are your friends, Dunstan?' The Monk's eyes bored into him.

Dunstan rubbed his neck. 'Point made – if a bit more effectively than I would have liked.'

'Lock up this heap of metal, then let's walk,' The Monk ordered.

Dunstan got his pack out and locked the car. All the time, The Monk's coal-black eyes scanned the car park, then the road, the surrounding hills, and back again.

***

The Monk had abandoned his original name. After his nearly twenty-five years in 22 Special Air Service Regiment (or simply 'the Regiment'), even other seasoned campaigners were in awe of his Trappist existence. When he left the Regiment as a senior non-commissioned officer, he had no possessions other than a single large rucksack filled with what was needed to live off the land. He had no known friends and had never sought them, and he had no family. Illegitimate, The Monk was half-Maltese, the product of a post-war assignation between an RAF NCO stationed in Malta and a local girl that had lasted barely a few weeks.

He had assumed that his grandfather, who had brought him up, was being fair when he beat him with a camel whip for his frequent misdemeanours. It had hardened The Monk and he bore the old man no grudges. There was one vital gift his grandfather had bequeathed to him: the Arabic language, and with it the ability to think in a different time and space. On the back of his father's nationality he had joined the British Army as a boy soldier.

Throughout his service career, he had invested all his money wisely, mostly in blue chip companies on the London Stock Exchange. Twenty-odd years of capital growth and re-invested dividends had produced a nice 'stash', as he called it. With some of this, he had bought an old Welsh farmhouse high above the Elan Valley, which he'd chosen for its back-to-the-mountain position, its commanding views to the front and a small courtyard with stables and cattle stalls to either side to protect his flanks.

Earlier in his career, as a staff sergeant, The Monk had been seconded as senior instructor to the Joint Service Combat Survival Unit in Bavaria. This special unit near Garmisch Partenkirchen at the base of the Alps had started its life as a survival training centre for RAF nuclear bomber pilots. If you were flying a Vulcan bomber during the Cold War, the chances of you making it back in your aircraft, having dropped your bombs, were slim to say the least. But pilots were valuable: the unit's sole purpose was to teach them to maximise their chances to escape and evade all the way back home.

The Monk had met Dunstan during his second month at Garmisch and for some reason they had hit it off. In the tented mess one night shortly after Dunstan's arrival, a fellow instructor asked him if he had climbed Everest. Dunstan explained that he had no desire to climb Everest, as he considered himself unable to climb it without the aid of artificial oxygen, and he couldn't see the point of climbing with it. Besides which, the logistical effort involved in an Everest expedition was a disincentive in its own right. He much preferred climbing steep, technically difficult smaller peaks, up to 7,000m in height, alpine style, without oxygen and with just a few companions or, in one memorable instance, solo without ropes or back-up. For those who didn't understand the sport, this was dismissed as being crazy. For The Monk, it marked Dunstan out as a soul mate, and he took him under his wing, teaming up with him for most of the courses. Theirs was a curious partnership, but one that worked: each was a self-contained and self-assured unit, and neither sought nor expected anything from the other. Over six months working together they had developed a strong unstated bond based on mutual respect and trust. Though neither sought to describe the relationship as such, they had become firm friends.

As they crossed the stream at the bottom of Pen y Fan and started up the well-worn path that led to the summit, they automatically slid into a brisk, rhythmic step. Dunstan's lately underused muscles protested and creaked. 'You didn't bring me here to do the Fan Dance, did you, Sherpa?' The 'Fan Dance' was part of the first stage of SAS Selection, a march across the summit of Pen y Fan several times in a seemingly futile and random pattern with full equipment. The majority of potential candidates dropped out at this stage or shortly afterwards. Dunstan had loved the exercise during Selection and had been one of the first back to the transport trucks.

It was during their time together in Bavaria that The Monk had dissuaded Dunstan from returning to the UK for another go at SAS selection. In a number of late-night conversations, as they directed Hunter Force searches for 'escapees', The Monk had peeled back Dunstan's veneer to get to his true motives. What he found was not so much a professional soldier as someone who used soldiering as a means to challenge himself beyond normal human limits, as he did in the mountains. For the SAS, it was the wrong motive and one that carried with it the danger of overreaching, putting not just himself at risk, but also his team. He made Dunstan confront his real self, and in doing so had saved both the Regiment and Dunstan much wasted time.

As they hit their old rhythm, Dunstan gave The Monk a short summary of recent events. When he finished, there was a long silence, which lasted until they reached the summit. Then the dark eyes looked into his. 'What's your plan?'

'For now, I was wondering if I could doss at your place tonight. It might give me enough time to persuade you.'

'Persuade me to do what?' The Monk managed to sound both sceptical and intrigued.

'To come with me. Let's go back via the Plantation.'

As they descended the familiar north-east shoulder of Pen y Fan, Dunstan's memory took him back to the howling blizzard when he had come upon another Selection candidate in real trouble, exhausted and in the final stages of hypothermia. He had wrapped the man up in his emergency bivouac gear and then, much to the other chap's surprise, wriggled into the sleeping bag with him. It was the best and safest method of treating a hypothermia victim. The freezing gale had battered them for eighteen hours before it started to subside. It had been one of the very rare times when the endurance March phase of SAS Selection had to be abandoned and all personnel called off the mountain.

Dunstan and his charge, trapped near the summit, had been left on the Fan; the Training Major wouldn't risk anyone in a rescue attempt. Almost twenty hours later a team of seasoned SAS instructors was dispatched to find the missing candidates. After a short while, they saw a huge figure emerging out of the still swirling snow. It was Dunstan, with a big grin on his face and the other Selection candidate draped over his shoulders. He had carried him down the mountain through the tail end of a blizzard with winds still gusting at forty knots. One of the Selection staff had commented, 'You must have legs like a fuckin' Sherpa's'. The nickname 'Sherpa' had stuck.

The Monk broke into Dunstan's reverie. 'Whoever they are, they're out to destroy your business. But why kill Morgan?'

'Because he was close to finding out who was behind it.'

'Let's assume that's correct. Why kill him in that way? Whoever did it is either insane or he bears some kind of personal grudge. Which direction did the chop come from?'

'I don't think it was a chopping action: I think it was a single slice inflicted from Morgan's left side.'

'Don't be daft, you don't get through all that muscle and spinal cord from the side in one hit – especially on an ex-rugby-playing Welshman's thick neck.'

'It takes a special kind of knowledge and honed technique.' Dunstan had been fingering the chakma in his pocket. Now he brought it out and showed it to The Monk. His companion eyed it knowingly.

'A chakma. Are you saying a kukhri killed Morgan in a single swipe? Because if you are, you really have lost the plot.'

'I *am* saying that, and I haven't lost the plot. There are only a few people alive in the world who could possibly do it, and every one of them has to be a serving or retired Gurkha soldier. Or, as an outside bet, an ethnic Gurkha who hasn't served in the British Army.'

'I still find it hard to believe. The kukhri's a small weapon. Have you ever seen it done with your own eyes?' The Monk was both sceptical and incredulous.

Dunstan paused, his mind reliving the moment. 'Years ago, when I was seconded from the Queen's Gurkha Engineers to help select new recruits in Nepal, I visited one of the Indian Gurkha regiments. It was Dussehra, the most important Hindu festival of the year. The regiment was celebrating it in the old way, with a ritual sacrifice. On the first evening, one of the Indian Gurkhas led a huge billy goat out into the centre of the square and tethered it to a post by tightening the rope around its neck through a hole. The Brahmin priest recited prayers and sprinkled the goat with holy water from the Ganges. Then the Gurkha executioner came out. He had bare legs and feet, and he was wearing a white vest. In his right hand he was swinging a gigantic ceremonial kukhri about thirty inches long. He strode up to the goat and felt its neck to find where the vertebrae were. Then he stood legs apart and waited. After about a minute, a horn blew high on a hill as the edge of the moon appeared over the surrounding mountains. In one smooth movement, the goat's head was on the floor with its arteries pumping blood. The whole parade ground burst into cheers – a single stroke ensures good fortune.'

'A nice yarn, but a long way from executing a running man with a standard issue kukhri.'

Dunstan continued as though he had not heard The Monk. 'The next morning, each company of the regiment made their own sacrifices. Most chose goats but one company chose to sacrifice a buffalo. The bigger the sacrifice, the more good fortune for the company – assuming the execution is efficient.'

'And if it isn't?'

'General gloom and doom all round. And the executioner is run out of the regiment. He often dies of shame.'

'No pressure, then! And you say you've seen this done to a buffalo?' The Monk questioned.

'The buffalo was tethered just like the goat. The Brahmin did his bit and the executioner strode onto the square dressed the same as the other chap the previous day, except that he wasn't carrying a giant ceremonial kukhri, only the standard size one.'

'I had a feeling you were going to say that. What happened next?'

'The one thing you noticed about this guy was that although he was of average height for a Gurkha soldier he was about twice the average width. Really powerfully built. He didn't even feel the neck to find the vertebrae. He just strode up to the tethered buffalo and stood looking at its neck for what seemed like an age. It was hard to see what happened next, because it happened so quickly. All I remember is this guy raising his kukhri two-handed over his head and bringing his arms down and through the neck of the buffalo, using his body weight and momentum to propel the stroke, ending up in a squat position. The buffalo's head came off in one. The whole place erupted.'

The Monk eyeballed Dunstan. 'What's his name?' 'Whose name?'

'The name of the bloke who killed Idris Morgan. The logical conclusion of your story is that there are only a couple of people in the world capable of killing him that way. So who is he?'

'How am I supposed to know that?'

'This isn't Mad Dog McFlynn, or any of the other people you upset in Fermanagh. This has to be the work of a Gurkha. Most likely someone you served with. Did you upset any of them?'

'No, we got on great. I thought they were some of the best blokes I'd ever served with. Still think that.'

'Okay,' The Monk said, 'first things first – your family. Good thing they're out of the way. Who else knows their whereabouts?'

'No one.'

'Good!'

'Except Kate Cross.'

'Who the hell is Kate Cross?'

'She's my Executive Assistant. I'd trust her with my life.' 'How about your children's lives? Where is this woman?' 'What do you mean?'

'I mean, there's every chance "they" are going to come looking for her, my friend. Shove her in a hole and exert a bit of pressure on her.'

Dunstan's blood ran cold and his scalp contracted. The Monk always took the worst possible view of given circumstances. What if he was right in this case?

'Next,' continued The Monk, 'we need to work out who's frozen your personal accounts. Are our old friends in Box playing games with you?'

'Box' was Regiment slang for the Intelligence services.

'I don't know. They hauled me in for a little chat. I've been trying to work it out since I left home.' Dunstan stared at his boots. He could see, and yet he couldn't see. It was all so disorientating – and horrible. The Monk was visibly exasperated.

'Have you really thought any of this through? Have you made any kind of plan?'

'I have got a plan. Of sorts,' Dunstan said, defensively. 'If I can get out of the country and link up to my guys who are currently in Bermuda, we might be able to trace the fraud to its source and find out who's behind this. They've got the systems to do it. Then we neutralise them. I need twenty-four hours to go hull-down before we move.'

'We? *We* move? *We* neutralise this unknown, unidentified, un-fucking-quantified enemy?'

'Yes. We. You're coming with me, aren't you, Monk?'

'Oh, I'd better cancel the bloody milk delivery then,' he replied sarcastically. 'How and where are we going? And who's going to fund this wild goose chase?'

'I've got enough money in cash to keep us going for as long as it takes to get out of the country. And I've got a substantial seven figure slush fund in Bermuda. And beyond that, I've got a scheme to fund the "search and destroy". I'll look after the search element; you, my old friend, are going to look after the 'destroy' bit. If you're willing, that is.'

'And if you don't find these people?' They were nearing the car park now. 'I'm stuffed.'

The Monk didn't respond. He stood with his blank gaze fixed beyond several horizons, then, seemingly satisfied with what he had seen, or not seen, in his mind's eye, he turned. 'Follow me, Sherpa. And don't make it look like a bloody convoy. What are you using to communicate with the world? We don't want any more cock-ups.'

Dunstan listed his mobile and satellite options. The Monk was grudgingly impressed.

'OK, but one call only on each of the pay-as-you-go cards, then throw them away. Agreed?'

'Agreed.'

They ran the last few hundred metres to the car park. It was 2015 hours and almost dark. The Monk took out a road map and pointed to a high wooded area of the Elan Valley. Then, using a blade of grass to point so as not to leave a trace on the map (for old habits die hard), he pointed to the exact location on a 1:50,000 Ordnance Survey map and gave Dunstan a grid reference, which Dunstan programmed in to his satnav.

'We take different routes, Sherpa. I'll go first. Leave a gap of at least fifteen minutes before you set off. And go slowly. No point in arriving before me.'

The Monk looked at his old friend and laughed. 'What's so bloody funny, Monk Face?' asked Dunstan.

'Just remember – no matter how they much they screw you, they can't make you pregnant!' It was an old joke, but for a moment, it lightened the burden.

Chapter Seven

Dunstan left the Storey Arms car park and headed towards Brecon. About half a mile into his journey, he glanced to the left. Around three hundred feet up the hillside, he could just make out a military Land Rover. It had three large aerials, which were definitely not standard fit. *The army on a night exercise?* He couldn't see the registration plate. And if it was on exercise, then why was it out on its own? He concentrated on the journey up to the Elan Valley, dismissing the vehicle from his mind.

He turned off the Brecon road into Sennybridge. Home to the most famous of the army's live firing ranges, this was where the backbone of the British Army – non-commissioned officers – were tested to the limits in battle simulation exercises. From Sennybridge he cut north over B roads and into the heart of the Cambrian mountains where many years ago he and his team of Queen's Gurkha Engineers had won the annual Cambrian Marches, a gruelling two-day patrolling competition, where eight-man teams have to march a distance of forty miles, carrying full kit weighing up to 60lb, and engage in realistic scenarios against enemy patrols. Navigating by day and night and linking up with friendly agents en route, they faced specialist challenges, including covert observation and reconnaissance, cold river crossings in full kit without access to boats, and defensive shooting under attack.

He settled back into the leather of the Range Rover as it ate up the miles. After about an hour he reached the 'old country' around Plynlimon Mountain, the last bastion of the original Ancient Britons. Distinguished by their narrow heads, brown curly hair and prominent eyebrows bearing witness to an unbroken genetic heritage over several thousand years, Idris Morgan had most definitely been one of them.

Dunstan pulled into a rocky farm track. There was a wooden tractor shed to one side. Jumping out, he peered through the cracks: the Toyota. The Monk must have swapped cars here for something more agricultural. It was beginning to chill now and as he started out again he put the heating up and pressed a button on the console. The vehicle's suspension rose four and a half inches to its maximum height. No way was he going to let his oil sump and differential be ripped out by boulders. He dropped into low gear and gunned the engine. The big car ground its way up the mountain, heading straight towards the remote homestead nestling against the shoulder of the hills. He caught a glimpse in the rear mirror of a Land Rover bouncing along in the distance. *Pity that poor bugger, up all night in an old Land Rover*, thought Dunstan.

'*Shit!*'

Dunstan braked hard; sweat started to run down his spine, adrenaline and fear mingling together. He could smell it. He stopped, controlled himself and double-checked the thought that had just hit him. He was not mistaken, he knew now where he had seen that old military Land Rover before. It had been in his peripheral vision in a field as he had exited from the track in Cornbury Park Woods on his way home. *But it couldn't have followed me by line of sight, I would have seen it. So how the...* The horrible implication of the only alternative hit him. He leapt from the car. It wasn't just himself he had compromised by failing to check his car, it was The Monk, and his own family as well. *Stupid twat, idiot, you stupid bloody idiot!* he cursed himself. In dread, and fuelled by adrenaline, he raced up the track to be greeted by a smiling Monk who stood in front of the farmhouse, calmly watching the silhouette of a running man against a huge setting sun slowly descending into the Irish Sea.

'What's the matter, Sherpa? That useless machine of yours couldn't make it, or did you need more exercise?' The Monk saw the horror in his friend's eyes. 'What? What is it?' he said slowly and deliberately. Dunstan's face contorted in an anguished mixture of embarrassment, fear and apology. The answer, when it eventually crawled from the tangle of his emotions, gasping its way to the surface, hit The Monk like a bolt between the eyes.

'I think my car's bugged. A Land Rover's been following me. Old style, most likely Army surplus. At least two guys in it. Maybe more. I thought they were on an exercise.' The Monk's eyes rested on his friend for a couple of seconds and then he ran back into the house. After what felt to Dunstan like an eternity, he came back clutching a black miniature brief case.

They ran back down the hill. Dunstan flung open the door and The Monk passed him the briefcase. Three seconds later, they were watching a signal peaking on the hand-held display. It was coming from under the front wheel arch. *It must have been planted by the 'visitors' to the house this morning*, thought Dunstan. The Monk passed him a torch. Its narrow beam picked out the tracking device at once, the size and shape of a large spider squatting. Both men understood the importance of leaving it in place.

Trying his best to sound normal, Dunstan kicked off a brief and innocuous exchange: 'Cheers for coming down to meet me. Didn't quite know the best line up this track.'

'No worries, mate, I'll hop in and show you the way. I've got a brew going and there's plenty of hot water. You get sorted out while I knock up some grub.'

***

If you had to find a good place from which to defend yourself against seen or unseen enemies, Bwlch-y-Ddu would be up there with the front runners. When The Monk had bought the old farm, it had no electricity and the household water had come directly from the fast-flowing stream cascading down the mountain behind. It now had electricity – not from the national grid but from a small hydro-electric power plant that The Monk had installed himself. The household water came straight from the stream, with the drinking water passing through a charcoal filtration system. Solar panels and a couple of small wind generators helped make the place entirely self-sufficient.

Bwlch-y-Ddu itself was built around three sides of a slate-flagged courtyard, facing out from the mountain-side. With its back to the mountain, its three-foot-thick stone walls to protect it from the northerly storms, and panoramic views to the front, it was as good a stronghold as you could wish for in a domestic house. The Monk, being The Monk, had not been content to settle for that. Surrounding the house was an interlocking mesh of ground sensors, including infra-red cameras and trip wires linked to flares that extended in a five-hundred-metre perimeter. They were all controlled from a central panel in the house and linked to a bank of remote monitors in The Monk's study. He also had a remote device for activating and deactivating the defensive web from outside the boundary. His final defence was a psychological one. Above the door that led from the courtyard into the main body of the house he had painted a spoof Coat of Arms: a monk's cowl with the words 'Only the Paranoid Survive' scrolled beneath.

***

Dunstan reversed the Range Rover into the courtyard and the two men dismounted, leaving the engine running and the CD player on. Silently they entered the sanctuary of the house. The Monk signalled to Dunstan to remain quiet. He then took the bug detector and did a complete sweep of the house. The place was clean. From his study he switched on the defensive ring main and the bank of remote monitors, checking they were all working. He checked the log and confirmed there had been no recorded intrusions over the past twenty-four hours other than the odd rabbit and an inquisitive polecat. The sun had by now set over the Irish Sea and dark clouds were rolling across the mountain from the South East, reducing visibility to a few hundred metres. A dark, moonless night was in prospect.

Dunstan came back to the sitting room looking subdued. He gazed at the images from the infrared cameras trained on the mountain-side. The Monk said, 'Stop dreaming and start thinking. Someone is prepared to kill one of your best friends and then hunt you down to a Welsh mountainside. Who and why?'

Dunstan shook his head, 'I honestly have no idea.'

The Monk made an impatient sweep of the arm at the screens. 'Sit here and watch for movement. The bug is still on the car, so with any luck our friends still think we're unaware. Actions on: if they come for us, we crush the bug and pack the kit in the car. As soon as that bug goes dead, the clock's ticking. We have to be ready to abandon this place at a moment's notice, by car or on foot if necessary. I'll pack the right kit for either eventuality. In case we have to crash on foot for any reason, I'll give you a map, grid reference and bearings to an emergency RV about fifteen miles from here. You've got your crash kit?'

'In the car, in the Bergan and the leather Targus bag with the Sat phone and mobiles in it,' Dunstan informed him.

The Monk went to the car, whistling tunelessly. He came back in with the bags, dumped them on the floor and disappeared again. Dunstan unpacked his gear and camouflage Goretex top and changed into it. Then he opened up the leather bag, took out the Sat phone and mobiles, and switched them on. He was confident that none of them could be traced by any means other than very powerful and sophisticated satellite equipment. He switched on the Sat phone and tuned into a Norwegian satellite service provider. He dialled the first number, a landline in Scotland. 'Hi Faith, how's it going?'

'Philip! Where are you? Are you okay? Are you safe?'

'Well and good. I'm with The Monk. I have to ring off in less than thirty seconds. How are the kids?'

'We only arrived about half an hour ago. Bloody awful traffic.'

'When those guys came to visit yesterday, were the doors to the garage open?'

'Yes. I'd taken the Discovery. We never lock up the garage for local runs. Why?'

'Have you been aware of anyone following you?'

'I'm pretty sure not, but I'm not an expert at that sort of thing. God, are we bugged?'

'Just a thought, Faith. Please go over the car with a fine-tooth comb, the kids can help you. If you see anything the size of a large black spider, or even a small black spider, kill it. Crush it. Then beep me on the Sat. Sorry for the news, darling. I have to go now. I'll call again tomorrow as arranged, plus or minus forty minutes unless and until I hear from you earlier. If you're bugged, I'll get some protection in place for you. Keep your antenna up for any suspicious vehicles or people around the place – and keep the shotgun handy. Love you, darling. Bye for now.'

'Philip! What the hell have you done?' Faith shouted down the empty line to nobody.

Driven by an overriding concern for his family, Dunstan picked up the 'Redmond' mobile phone and switched it on. The incoming text tone sounded. The Monk leapt through the door at the sound. 'Who the hell is that?'

'Spooks,' Dunstan replied. He scrolled to his in-box. 'Here we go ...'

>>>*Your wish granted by Fairy Godmother. Conditional upon your not leaving the UK. Contact ASAP for co-ordinating instructions. Redmond.* >>>

Dunstan turned the screen so The Monk could read it, then killed the call. The Monk's only reaction was a raised eyebrow. He signalled to Dunstan to follow him. He turned into the hall and unlocked a large cellar door set into the floor. They went down a set of stone steps into a temperature-controlled room which The Monk had built under the house with his own hands. Dunstan saw that he was standing in a well-stocked cellar but, instead of wine, the walls were lined with state-of-the-art weaponry. Dunstan let out a long, slow whistle. The Monk began packing his weapons and ammunition into strong Mountain Equipment duffle bags. Up in the study, Dunstan pulled out his laptop and connected it to a mobile phone via a data cable. He dialled into his Internet service provider. He had about thirty emails waiting, all work related except for one. It was from Detective Chief Inspector Beckwith at Thames Valley Constabulary. It read:

Come in Dunstan. Your time is up.

It was 2200 hours. The Monk had finished packing the bags and was ready to load them into the car. He sealed the cellar, and went through to the study. Dunstan was in front of the screens, doodling on a pad on his knee.

'OK, Sherpa, ready to move. Gear packed?' Dunstan nodded.

'Then let's eat. Anything happening out there? Any foreign bodies lurking?'

'Sweet Fanny Adams. A couple of sheep. Otherwise, nothing,' Dunstan responded.

The Monk went through to the kitchen to get the food. As Dunstan's eyes followed him out of the room, the outline of something moved on the monitor screen. Larger than a sheep, it was taking a particular and intelligent interest in The Monk's security arrangements.

***

They had just finished eating when the missile hit. The whole farmhouse shook to its foundations. The shockwave threw them to the floor, momentarily disorientating them. The Monk screamed, 'Go! Go! Go!' Adrenaline and fear combined to propel Dunstan through the door and into the courtyard, rolling as he reached the cold mountain air. The second missile hit the back wall, this time higher, blowing out the whole of the upper part of the house. Dunstan ran to the Rover, ripping the tracking bug and crushing it underfoot. He then ran back into the house, grabbed his Sat phone and the mobiles and threw them in with the rest of his stuff. Both men tensed for the next explosion. The Monk was holding an M-13 rifle with underslung grenade launcher. As he made the weapon ready, a machine gun opened fire on them from the hillside at the back of the house. Without thinking, Dunstan jumped behind the wheel of the Land Rover. The Monk flung himself into the passenger seat. Dunstan gunned the engine, and the big vehicle shot out of the courtyard into the night.

'Right, right, right!' screamed The Monk.

Dunstan swung the vehicle right onto a narrow, stony miners' track that had once brought slate down from a small mine on the mountainside. As the Range Rover blasted its way up the track, they came into full view of the machine-gunner on the hillside. It took the gunner an instant to reposition his weapon and lay down a blast of fire. Firing downhill at a moving target, he had not quite got his range and trajectory right. The tracer floated in a flat arc above and to the right of them, in a beautiful but deadly light show. It gave The Monk and Dunstan a momentary breathing space.

The Monk yelled 'Faster!' and then an instant later, 'Stop!' Dunstan slammed the brakes on and the vehicle fishtailed to a barely-controlled halt. The Monk had stopped them in a cutting that had been blasted by miners through a small rock outcrop some twenty feet high. Rounds exploded over their heads as the gunners, now with the right aim and trajectory, laid down a withering fire. The noise was deafening as the volcanic rock shattered over their heads but, for the moment, they were safe.

'Seven point six two mil machine gun,' shouted The Monk above the din. Both men were frantically calculating how they could move from their position without getting blasted.

'Lights out!' Dunstan shouted. He turned all the lights off and pressed a button on the console above his head. A hidden compartment in the passenger footwell opened, revealing two infra-red night goggles still in their shrink-wrap packaging. The Monk ripped them out, but then had an idea.

'Wait a second. Don't move!' He reached into the back and grabbed one of the kit bags. Shards of rock and debris hammered on the roof. The Monk pulled out a small, round object and grinned at his companion. 'Fragmentation grenade. Should give them something to think about.'

'I need about thirty seconds,' replied Dunstan, pressing a button and looking at a small dial on the dashboard.

'What the hell for?' The firing had stopped. They both knew why: the gunners were tabbing to a better position.

'Automatic tyre decompression. I had it fitted for moving in soft sand, but with squidgy tyres we can get straight out onto the mountainside and move across boggy ground.' Another burst of tracer fire came at them, the rounds swiping in from their right side.

'Then bloody hurry up. We'll have rounds up our arses soon.'

'OK, do your stuff, Monk.' Dunstan readied the infrared goggles. The Monk opened the door and threw himself against the wall of the cutting. 'Eyes shut!' he yelled. He stuffed the grenade into the M-13's underslung launcher, aimed the weapon and pulled the trigger. There was a flat crump, followed by a blinding flash of light from the hillside above. The machine gun fell silent. The Monk jumped back into the vehicle. Just before he slammed the door, they could hear the sound of a man screaming.

'Now or never,' shouted Dunstan as he gunned the engine. 'Goggles on, let's go!'

Hitting sixty miles per hour in less than twenty seconds, in spite of the rough ground, they shot out of the cutting and bounced cross-country towards the shoulder of the mountain. The terrain was peaty ground covered in coarse grass, heather and occasional clumps of spring flowers, mostly gentians and saxifrage. The main hazard, apart from any deep unseen bogs, was the boulders, all shapes and sizes, left as they were from the last Ice Age.

Dunstan concentrated hard, the landscape glowing a strange ghostly green through the NVGs. The Monk scanned behind for any sign of pursuit but saw nothing. Soon, they began climbing more steeply up the side of the great rocky shoulder that buttressed the mountain. They had to slow down and Dunstan dropped the drive to the lowest ratio. They were crawling now, the mixture of engine noise and the sound of the tyres clawing their way over loose rocks and boulders certain to give away their rough position. 'Shit, how steep does this get before we're over the other side?'

'Walking, it doesn't seem more than 45 degrees.' The Monk was as laconic as ever, seemingly unfazed by the mayhem they had just survived, not to mention the destruction of his lovingly constructed redoubt. The only sign that he had been under fire was in his eyes: his pupils were dilated to their fullest extent. 'From the screaming, I reckon one of those fuckers got a piece of shrapnel in him. Looking after him ought to keep them busy.'

The big car was now ascending a gradient that was steeper than its designed capability. He was having difficulty making the power stick. He was just considering trying to reverse a little and attempting a stretch that was farther to their left when a new burst of tracer ripped past them, followed by the harsh, staccato bark of machine gun fire.

'Stuff this!' shouted The Monk. 'Maybe it's time we gave them something else to think about.' Scrabbling in the weapons sack, he brought out a camouflaged L96 sniper rifle, loaded it, and made ready. 'There's another miners' cutting up ahead – put the car in there, take a weapon and give me support if you can, okay?'

Dunstan grinned. Suddenly, the blinding fear that had been gripping him evaporated. That could happen under fire. 'Just like old times,' he said. The Monk nodded, and was gone into the night, head low and running.

Dunstan gunned the engine again. There was a horrible grinding sound as the chassis hit an unseen boulder that scraped against the aluminium protection plates. Dunstan was more worried about tipping over backwards, but there was hope: through his infrareds he could see the crest of the ridge. The front wheels went over the edge; it was so steep that for a moment the car hung in space, its rear wheels churning wildly to get traction. A burst of machine gun fire clipped the back of the roof. As if the impact had made the critical difference the vehicle lurched forward, dropped into dead ground and began a head-long charge down the other side of the mountain. It bounced wildly, sliding over the wet heather and careered to the right with Dunstan struggling to regain control. Shooting over a glacis of rock, the nose of the car lurched vertically down and into a small crevasse, embedding itself with a tortured crunch in the volcanic cleft.

Dunstan grabbed the weapons bag. As he did so, he heard the sharp crack of the sniper rifle reverberate in the night air. Any minute now, the police were going to be on their way up here. Somebody, somewhere in the vicinity, had to have noticed the small war going on in these ice-quiet hills. The rifle barked again, and then a third time. The Monk was not an enemy

Dunstan, personally, would like to be facing, especially when he was on his home turf.

From nowhere, his ally reappeared. 'All right?'

'Bearing up. You?'

The Monk patted the rifle. 'Pretty sure I hit one of the bastards.' He reached down and hauled the pieces of a 5.56mm Light Support Weapon and a belt of ammunition from the weapons sack. 'Only be a moment,' he said to no one in particular, clipping the machine gun together in the space of a few seconds.

Dunstan tried to assess the damage to the car. A General Purpose Machine Gun can rip a man to shreds at a kilometre. The effect on the roof of the Range Rover was awesome. It hadn't just left holes in the roof, it had ripped open the back end like a tin of sardines and then continued down and through the reinforced underbody, fortunately just missing the drive shaft and rear differential. The Land Rover was now stuck, nose down in the landscape. The Monk followed the direction of his gaze. 'Looks like our transport's buggered,' he observed drily.

'No way! The bull bars at the front have taken most of the impact. Tyres are all okay. I'll need five to ten minutes to get her out.' The Monk looked at the Range Rover's peppered back end, sticking almost vertically out of the cleft. 'Now I know you *are* mad Sherpa. What are you going to do, haul two tons of car out of a crevasse with your bare hands?'

'No, it's going to haul itself out. Now get back up to that ridgeline and keep those bastards busy while I sort this out.'

'Yes, sir!' He picked the LSW up by the handle, shouldered the L96 and scrambled back up to the crest. Just below the ridgeline he dropped the tripod, clipped in the ammunition feed and settled the weapon's butt into his right shoulder. In a straight exchange, the LSW was no match for the 3GPMG, but it would slow them down a bit. As he scanned the ground to his front for a target, The Monk got a rude shock. A burst of tracer came in from his left, from a position that was nearly on the ridge itself. 'Shit, the bastards are in enfilade,' he said out loud. 'How the hell did they get up there so quick?'

He dropped farther back down below the ridge and repositioned himself behind a large boulder. Placing the LSW on a ledge of rock he fired a quick initial burst, then picked the weapon up and ran as hard as he could to his right and slightly down the shoulder of the mountain. A hail of bullets chewed the area around the position he had just quit, leaving a stinking smell of cordite in the still air. This was going to be hard work; the bastards were well-trained, and despite at least one definite casualty, they weren't ready to give up.

Dunstan pulled a steel hawser and coupling device out of a compartment underneath the car. He ran up the hillside for about twenty yards and threw the hawser over a large boulder. Then he took the cable's looped ends and coupled them together with a three-way device. When it was fast, he raced back down to the car and started the motor on the Warn winch. When he'd had the car modified he hadn't quite been able to see the point of a rear winch as well as a front one, but as the old boy at Solihull had said, 'Yow'll very rare run off the rowd backwards, will yow?' Now he was blessing his foresight and cursing his fate.

Dunstan ran out the winch cable and coupled it to the hawser looped around the boulder. Praying the rig would hold, he cranked up the engine to full throttle. There was a hard, grinding sound of metal on rock as the winch took the strain and then bit. Slowly, the car began to rise out of the cleft. Watching from above through the NVGs, The Monk stared, amazed. Then he remembered where he was, let off another burst, and moved again. *Too bloody old for this game*, he thought. Another burst from the hillside ripped down along the ridge, showering him with rock shards. This time, he spotted them: two men, about two hundred yards away, down and up to his left. Even better, a thin shaft of moon broke through the cloud at that moment and he had them in silhouette. He ripped the sniper rifle off his shoulder, flipped up the NVGs and lined up on the figure beside the gun.

He put the luminous circle on the target's chest, took up the first pressure and then squeezed. The report cracked around the hills and the figure fell back. Good. This time The Monk didn't try to move position. Instead, expecting the gunner to attend to – or at least look at – his mate, he was lined up for the next shot. The man came into vision and The Monk fired.

Now, he picked up the weapon and ran, tabbing hard and fast, and down to his right. When he reached a clump of gorse he stopped, pulled the NVGs back on and looked back. He set up the machine gun again, fired a long burst at the hidden position to keep the man thinking, and then set out to rejoin Dunstan. *Mad bastard's only gone and got the car back out of the cleft.*

As The Monk ran down to meet him, Dunstan ran back up the hill to decouple the hawser. 'Ten seconds!' he shouted as The Monk let off another short burst of fire from his hip, aiming in the general direction. Dunstan raced back down the hill and switched the winch to haul in the loose cable. 'Get the gear in the back!' he screamed at The Monk. He started to check the underside for any signs of major damage, thought better of it, and jumped in. The machine gunner above heard the engine start and began firing at the sound. The hillside came alive with small glowing balls of tracer. Dunstan slammed the gear box into high ratio and let the clutch up. The big vehicle lurched forward and charged off down the slope like a rampaging bull.

Off the rough terrain, they hit a sheep drovers' track. 'Where to now?' asked Dunstan.

'North, through to Dolgellau then up to Blaenau Ffestiniog. I know an old slate mine we can drive straight into. Hole up there for a while.'

'You make us sound like the Dalton Gang!'

'Dickhead!' shot back The Monk. Dunstan laughed. A few seconds later they were both howling with laughter: an adrenaline-high, the pure release of screwed nerves.

As they travelled north, both men were concerned about being stopped by the police, even though there were probably only three mobile policemen in the hundred square miles of remote country they were crossing. It would be difficult to explain the presence and ownership of a left hand drive vehicle shot through with bullet holes when half the population of the Elan Valley would for sure be reporting the firefight they had just left. Dunstan had an idea. 'In case we get stopped, we'll go "Official".'

'What do you mean, "Official"?' replied The Monk, who was always unimpressed with bureaucratic methods.

Dunstan pulled into a lay-by and stopped. 'Pass me the log book folder from the glove compartment, will you?' The Monk handed it over. Dunstan opened the large leather-bound folder and took out a set of sticky-backed transparent 'Land Rover Experience' signs. Stepping out, he stuck two to the front door panels of the car and pasted a third – rather crookedly – over the damage to the tailgate.

'There you go, Monk. We're from the factory in Solihull, testing a special new version of the Range Rover Sport, and we've been on a rather long and testing night drive.'

The Monk snorted. 'Ever the optimist. But we might just get away with it if they don't look too close.'

A few miles north of Dolgellau, The Monk suddenly shouted, 'Stop! That old garage back there, reverse up to it.' Decaying slowly by the roadside, the old garage in question was 1950s vintage. The ancient Esso petrol pumps had been disconnected and the old giant Scammell tow vehicle parked on the grass verge looked as if it had towed its last wreck. But it sported a fine pair of trade licence plates. The Monk liberated them and covered the export plates. Feeling pleased with themselves, they headed north towards the hidden mine.

Chapter Eight

Celia Fanshawe had arrived early at Special Forces Headquarters, Regents Park. The staff sergeant on duty might be missing most of his fingers and one eye, but he had just made her one of the best cups of tea she had ever had. He had also procured for her that morning's edition of the Daily Telegraph. 'Taylors of Harrogate Yorkshire Tea, ma'am. Best there is. The Quartermaster's a Yorkshireman – short arms and deep pockets. Keeps it under lock and key, but I'm a better lock picker than he is a locksmith.' A grin split his battered face. 'Procurement' and 'liberation' of quality equipment and goods, in a just cause, of course, was a longstanding army tradition. The one area totally off limits for anyone bent on liberation was arms and ammunition.

Fanshawe thanked the sergeant and glanced through the newspaper. A short paragraph on page five caught her eye:

Royal Military Police in Hampshire are investigating the disappearance of weapons and ammunition from an arms depot. No official communiqué has been given but a source who did not wish to be named stated that anti-tank missiles, surface-to-air missiles, machine guns and ammunition are among the weapons rumoured to have been stolen. The police and the army suspect insider help.

Major General Christopher Gibbs, Director Special Forces, strode in through the door, in typical British fashion apologising profusely for being late, even though he knew he wasn't. A well set-up man just on the wrong side of fifty, he wore a civilian suit and could have been taken for a successful city businessman – provided it was one who ran ultra-distance desert marathons for fun. As a very young SAS troop commander fresh out of Selection, he had earned his Military Cross in the assault on South Georgia during the Falklands war. He followed this with a Distinguished

Service Order in the first Gulf War for leading his company on a series of daring raids deep behind Iraqi lines, harrying the Iraqis from their northern flank and recruiting Kurdistani 'irregulars' along the way. Fluent in three Arabic dialects, he had just taken up his new post on return from a stint as Defence Attaché in Saudi Arabia, but by his own admission he was a new kid on the block when it came to liaison with his security agency counterparts.

He held out a muscular arm. 'Miss Fanshawe. I am delighted to make your acquaintance. Clearly, you haven't come here just to sample our tea, good though it is. What can we do for you?'

She smiled. 'General, we have an emerging threat to our shores that originates overseas. Its source is fraud and money laundering on a significant scale. I need the use of one or more of your soldiers from Special Reconnaissance Regiment to conduct surveillance.'

'I see. But surely this is SOP; we're on standby to support your organisation anyway.'

'In the UK and Northern Ireland, yes. But we need this surveillance conducted overseas. Within Pakistan to be precise. And it will have to be deniable.' She held his eye. 'We both know what that means.'

Gibbs was taken aback at the baldness of the request but intrigued by the possibilities it held. 'Just to be clear, you want my soldiers to put their lives on the line – risk capture, torture and death – and have no official back-stop if things go wrong?'

'In a nutshell. It wouldn't be the first time, would it?' Fanshawe responded in her usual straightforward manner.

'Shouldn't SIS be making this request if the operation is on foreign soil, Miss Fanshawe?'

Fanshawe smiled sweetly. 'The lines do blur a little sometimes, don't they?'

Gibbs steepled his fingers. 'Before we go any further, Miss Fanshawe, you should know that you have my full support except where my men are unduly exposed or compromised through ill-thought-out or ill-conceived projects. We don't do ill-conceived operations with no back-up. In short, we don't do suicide missions.'

'I'm pleased to hear it!' declared Fanshawe, smiling. 'But this operation won't be for "men".' She looked across at Gibbs, who, she could see, was struggling to contain his rising curiosity and professional cool.

'Now let me explain,' she continued. 'It's imperative that we stop this money being channelled into funding terrorist activities. Do you have any women members of SRR who are of Muslim or at least Indian sub-continent background?'

The DSF looked through and beyond Celia Fanshawe for a moment.

Then he leant towards the intercom. 'Chief! Find out if SRR have any female soldiers of Muslim or Indian sub-continent origin, please. Include biographies.'

A knock at the door interrupted their continuing discussion. 'Morning, ma'am.' The Chief Clerk moved in short, staccato movements, as if powered by a coiled spring. He was one of the few people who travelled the London Underground late at night actually hoping that he would be mugged, preferably by three 'hoodies' with knives so that he had a real excuse for some legitimate self-defence. He slipped a piece of paper across the desk.

'Thank you, Chief. Right, Miss Fanshawe. We have two that fit the bill. A corporal born of a Sikh family, and a young captain.'

'What's the captain's parentage?'

'Kashmiri. Father, a doctor; mother, a nurse.'

'Religion?'

'Muslim.'

'And languages?'

'Colloquial Urdu, Kashmiri, Hindi and Spanish.'

'They sound ideal. Can we have them?'

'Subject to a full situation report four hours prior to departure, you can have them on standby. They will, of course, remain under this Directorate's ultimate command and control.'

'I suggest we set up a dedicated joint control centre from my office for the operation, General. My office will give you at least four hours' advance movement notice. Thank you for your co-operation and good day.'

Major General Gibbs escorted Celia Fanshawe to the door, and then called his Chief of Staff, a full colonel responsible for planning operations. He had a feeling there was more to this than just surveillance.

***

Wednesday, 25th April

The Monk's farmhouse was cordoned off. Lloyd, the detective inspector with local jurisdiction, was sure he was dealing with a terrorist bomb-making factory. His men had already tripped over the perimeter defences and ignited several flares, which had sent them scurrying for cover like chickens. Lloyd was convinced the place was booby-trapped and was waiting for Ordnance Disposal, Anti-Terrorist Branch and Firearms support. While they waited, one of his braver constables was taking a particular interest in a trail of spent 7.62mm ammunition, clip belts, freshly shattered shards of rock, and several exploded sheep scattered across the mountain-side.

***

At the old slate mine in the Moelwyn Mountains above Blaenau Ffestiniog, Dunstan and The Monk were stirring from a deep sleep. Ten years ago, when The Monk had discovered the place, it was still being worked on a freelance basis by two old miners. He had found the entrance high on the hillside when out hiking. A water company service track led past it to a nearby reservoir, but it was rarely used. His curiosity was aroused when an ancient flatbed truck with freshly cut slate on the back appeared out of the blue directly in front of him. Investigating later, he had discovered a hidden entrance to the mine down a short side track behind a curtain of rock. On a dedicated reconnaissance a few days later, he had established that the two men who had still been working the mine were about to give it up, as the slate near the surface was worked out.

Dunstan's phone beeped to signify an incoming message: >>>*Authenticated: (214) 017214*>>>

The string of numbers was a six-figure grid reference for a point just west of the south-east shoulder of Pen y Fan, close to the summit. It had no meaning to anyone other than the two parties who had set up this method of mutual authentication years ago.

>>>*Authenticated and acknowledged; is this my prime contact number for you?* >>>

>>>*For now. What is reason for contact?* >>>

Dunstan texted: >>>*HELP REQUIRED AND REQUESTED; URGENT. Will call in five.* >>>

As he prepared to move back up the mountain, he thought about sending a text to 'Redmond' but thought better of it; he didn't want his position to be known... yet.

Dunstan was perched out of sight above the mine to get a better signal on the Sat phone. The Monk was organising and cleaning gear in the main tunnel. Dunstan logged into his account with Telenor, the Norwegian satellite service provider, and called a number in the Gulf. The line at the other end answered but nobody spoke. Dunstan took a deep breath. 'This is Sherpa. I wish to speak to Dreadnought.'

Calling His Excellency Sheikh Suroor Al-Qurum "Dreadnought" was a privilege only he enjoyed. On leaving the army, Dunstan had stayed for several weeks with the man he had saved from death by hypothermia, enjoying his legendary hospitality, lavish entertainment, his thirst for adventure and not least, his mischievous sense of humour. They had lived as Bedu in the desert for two of those weeks, shaping ideas for combat training, Long Range Patrol exercises and survival courses for the Sheikh's fledgling Special Forces unit, Scimitar Force. Al-Qurum was astute enough to know that the defence of his tiny Emirate depended on a highly-trained rapid reaction force that was ready to counter any external, or internal, threats to national security.

As he was leaving, Al-Qurum had embraced him. 'Dunstan, my brother, as long as either of us is alive to see a desert sunset, your life is my life, my wealth is your wealth, my home is your home. Any time you are in danger, call me. We will use the names we have earned on the Fan. Yours will be Sherpa, and mine,' his face split into a huge grin, 'mine will be Dread-nought.' To Dunstan, this had had the ring of a childish game. He had never thought he would be playing the game, his very own Great Game, for real. The educated Arab voice on the end of the Sat phone was familiar, though indistinct. 'Sherpa, this is Dreadnought.' The tone was full of concern, almost protective.

'Dreadnought, I need your help.'

'What are your needs and instructions, my friend?'

'I require EXFIL from this country to yours. Circumstances are extreme. Timings, details of payload and location to follow, once only. If you can help, please text back.'

'Got it, Sherpa. Ready for your instructions.'

'Timings: 2200 hours for exfiltration...' Dunstan rapidly ran through the remaining instructions. 'Method...; Location...; Payload...; Co-ordinating instructions...'

Dunstan and The Monk reached the bottom of the track and paused. 'Where do we go now, and how?' queried The Monk.

Dunstan put the final digit into the GPS. 'Here,' he said, pointing.

The Monk leaned across and peered at the screen. 'Oxfordshire! We're going back to bloody Oxfordshire! What the hell for?'

'It's a mile into Gloucestershire, actually. Look again.'

The Monk looked. The fog in his mind lifted and he grinned at the audacity of the obvious plan. 'Have you got a contingency plan if it doesn't work?'

'No,' Dunstan replied emphatically. 'Nothing like being committed, eh? We've got ten hours to reach our RV over minor and unclassified roads and tracks, avoiding all towns en route. The bit on the lower ground between the Welsh Borders and the Cotswolds will be the trickiest. Once we're up onto the North Cotswold escarpment I can take us cross-country on tracks.'

'Talk about a bloody long shot.' With that acute observation, The Monk fired the engine into life and took the mountain road out of Blaenau towards mid-Wales. It was 1200 hours.

***

As Dunstan and The Monk picked their way over the mountain roads of Wales, several hours in front of them an ex-military Land Rover was heading east up the limestone escarpment that overlooks Cheltenham. The occupants were unhurried yet purposeful. As with any stalk, you have to anticipate your quarry. And sometimes, you have to put out bait and wait for your target to come to you.

***

Bermuda

Deep within the bunker of the Cable and Wireless hosting facility at the southern end of Bermuda, Marc Tysoe sat in front of three large racks of winking lights. He was now peering at the movement of bank card payment transactions switching across the CyberX worldwide network through to the Bermuda payment gateway. Working through the night since he had arrived, and with the help of the Network Service Manager and his team, he had taken control of the worldwide operations based in Oxford. He had prepared two new payment servers in the two racks provided by C&W and was now ready to switch all of CyberX's worldwide operations to the new system. He placed a call to Global Reach in London and confirmed that the new Internet Protocol (IP) addresses for re-routing the transactions were available to him. Another call to Network Transaction Systems (NTS) in New York confirmed that they were ready to recognise the new IPs on their transaction switching computers. Global Reach provided the 'rails' and NTS the 'trains' and 'stations', or transaction gateways, that allowed CyberX to authenticate, switch and settle bank card payments between any point-of-service in the world to any bank. Tysoe was in his element, channelling all his mathematical capabilities and hard-nosed practical application into making this happen.

As a fail-safe security measure, Idris Morgan had created a facility which split a given payment into two parts, added message identifier tags with individual routing instructions to each part, and then encrypted the whole. The benefit of this was that if anyone managed to hack into their networks across the Internet, and then subsequently managed to decrypt the encrypted transaction, they would only ever get half a transaction, which in and of itself was useless. As the individual transaction parts hit their pre-routed destination they were automatically decrypted, matched and paired again within CyberX's secure firewalled servers. From each of these they were rerouted on along a secure communications pipe – not the Internet – using asymmetric key encryption, into the bank card payment host systems.

If this stopped the hackers, it did not stop fraud originating from outside the secure network. So CyberX employed another defence, a sophisticated service provided by The Third Eye – a company specialising in behavioural software and analysis. Every transaction was screened by Third Eye software and profiled for lost and stolen cards, frequency of use, type of spend and other irregular spending patterns. What it did *not* do was profile transactions by volume and measure them against CyberX's normal pattern of business. The weakness in the system, Tysoe now realised, was that unusual volumes of apparently bona-fide payment card purchases – originating, albeit fraudulently, from an accredited Internet payments service bureau – would not be noticed in the normal course of business. It was only by intelligent human monitoring and diligence that Abdul Shahid had noticed the transaction spikes and reported them to Idris Morgan.

Tysoe logged into the core transaction log; with Abdul Shahid's log references to hand, he quickly found the spikes. He stared at the numbers on the screen. *How the hell did we miss those?* He picked up the print-out of the transaction logs together with details of the originating source and then logged into the central financial accounting system over CyberX's secure virtual private network. He then compared the transaction log with the financial accounts. The profile comparison was instant.

With the alternative CyberX system now ready to run, Tysoe was fired up to go hunting for the originators of the fraud. The question was: would the fraudsters restart when their payment gateways were switched on again?

***

Somewhere in the mountains of Mid Wales, near Bala Lake, a pay-as-you-go cell phone beeped to signal an incoming text.

Dunstan flipped the screen back: >>>*Exfil confirmed 2200*>>>. He then made another call from the same phone. In Bermuda, Tysoe's telephone shrilled on the desk.

'Philip! Where are you?... Yes, the gateway is switched and we have some, er, interesting results on the transaction audit trail. We've identified a single service provider: they're issuing their own merchant IDs provided to them by a licenced merchant acquiring bank. They've been running the payments, presumably using stolen cards, through our Prague gateway. We don't know yet which sponsoring bank they're using.'

'Thanks, Marc, keep at it. We *have* to locate the sponsoring bank to find the source and the perpetrators. Time to ring off. I'll contact you in twenty-four hours.'

Dunstan quickly finished the call and crunched the pay-as-you-go SIM card under the heel of his boot.

If Marc Tysoe had known the truth, his paranoia would have multiplied. Several thousand miles away in Cheltenham, the conversation had been taped and flagged for the analysts. But it wasn't Dunstan's pay-as-you go that was flagged for interception, it was Tysoe's company contract mobile. Tysoe's phone was roaming through a Bermuda telecoms provider. As a Crown colony and an international tax haven, communications into and out of Bermuda by satellite, cable or mobile networks were part of the GCHQ worldwide sweep.

Dunstan and The Monk covered another fifty miles in silence across single track roads, over mountains, taking the occasional short cut via green lanes – the ancient drovers' roads. The Monk let out a soft chuckle.

'What's so funny?'

'If someone had told me a week ago that within a few days I'd get a phone call from an old mate, which would lead to the loss of my home and the disintegration of the secure, quiet life that I've created for myself; that I'd get a couple of Javelin rounds up the arse, get strafed by a fucking machine gun fired at me from my own mountain by someone who clearly knows what he is doing, and be running to God-knows-where with my now *ex*-mate turned raving lunatic, all in the space of twenty-four hours, I'd have said they were barking mad, not just bloody crazy. Nothing, but nothing, would surprise me now!'

And on that note, The Monk slammed his foot to the floor.

***

In London, Celia Fanshawe was speed-reading through the contents of the courier package sent round the corner from Scotland Yard by Jim Hoskins, Commander Counter Terrorism Command, Metropolitan Police, which confirmed her research the previous evening. She phoned him.

'Jim, I have a meeting starting at fourteen hundred hours. We're going to have to act on your information.'

As she put the phone down, it immediately rang: it was Director Special Forces being patched through. 'Miss Fanshawe, you've got your reconnaissance team. Captain Dhar and Corporal Murria have been re-deployed and are now on four hours' standby to move at your discretion.'

'Thank you, General. Has anyone briefed them yet?'

'They've been briefed to pack kit for a possible covert reconnaissance and surveillance mission in an Islamic state – on volunteer basis pending a full operational briefing.'

'A bit too much information at this stage, don't you think, General?' She sounded brittle; the dissemination of information on a need-to-know basis was a fundamental part of Celia Fanshawe's fibre.

However, a self-assured DSF wasn't going to have a spook interfering in his operational domain. 'I considered that, but if we want them on true operational standby, we need them to think through their personal surveillance equipment in advance and, as time allows, procure it and pack it. Not least, their full formal burkhas need to be prepared and packed.'

'Ah, of course you're right. I'll arrange a full brief after our daily update meeting this afternoon. Your team will be backed up by our own watchers on the ground. Thank you for your timely response, General Gibbs.'

As she replaced the receiver, she wondered what she had let the two SRR soldiers in for.

Chapter Nine

The ex-military Land Rover had just passed the watershed between the upper Windrush and Evenlode valleys. It was heading south-east but before it reached its destination, its occupants had one small job to do. They meant it to be a Spectacular.

On a wooded escarpment high in the Cotswolds, the two occupants unpacked a number of heavy, dark green bags. Then one of them jumped behind the wheel of the Land Rover and drove it straight into the middle of a large bush. Working quickly, they covered it with more brushwood, shouldered the heavy equipment and moved stealthily to the perimeter of the woods, looking down over rolling farmland to the edge of a nearby village.

They had failed to execute their mission in Wales; one of their number was dead and another had a shrapnel wound to the arm. Their current orders were to destroy a new target, one that would increase the psychological pressure on their quarry. This time it was very personal.

Using powerful binoculars, they watched patiently for signs of life in the farmhouse a thousand yards away. At the end of two hours' surveillance, they were satisfied there was no-one in it. One of them unzipped a long green bag, lifted out the Javelin Medium Anti-Tank Weapon and made it ready. With a maximum range of 2,500m, the Javelin is very effective in the hands of an expert operator, and this operator was one of the best. A herd of fallow deer grazing nearby set off full pelt across the fields, leaping like springbok, as if they knew what was coming. Bird song seemed to fall silent. The gunner adopted his firing position, shifted his body until he was fully comfortable, slowed his breathing and waited for his heart rate to come down. This preparation was second nature to him and he knew that, barring a misfire, it guaranteed him a successful kill. When fully relaxed, he simply placed the sight mark on the base of the target, pressed the firing button and tracked the missile to its final destination.

The impact shattered the building. Dunstan's house lay in ruins. Smoke billowed up in a huge plume as the ancient internal wooden fabric caught fire. The men in the wood gave each other a brief grin of satisfaction, packed up their kit and walked back to the Land Rover, secure in the knowledge that it would take at least twenty minutes before the local emergency services arrived. One of them backed the vehicle out of its hiding place and they repacked the bags. Satisfied that all was in order, they powered up an HF military radio, sending a Morse code message in a single high-speed burst transmission. Once they had a response, they drove through and out of the dense wood, south towards Oxford, and their next objective.

***

At 1400 hours in Thames House, the team gathered for a council of war. Celia Fanshawe came into the acoustically screened meeting room. She positively breezed in. Her upbeat mood was in direct contrast to that of her team.

'Good afternoon, everyone. Your latest synopsis, please, Rebecca.'

Lovat referred to the report in front of her from the 'sniffer' computer programme, which the techies had attached to the suspect Islamabad bank account. 'Another two million dollars have been removed.'

'Who's on the end of it? Possibles?' Fanshawe demanded.

Elizabeth Hamilton, the analyst and regional expert, fielded the question. 'The main terrorist organisations operating out of Pakistan in addition to Al-Qaeda are: Jaish-e-Mohammad; Harkat-ul-Mujaheddin and Jama'at ud-Dawa – JUD – previously known as the Lashkar-e-Taiba, LET. Out of these, we consider JUD to be the most active and dangerous,' said Hamilton. 'We believe JUD is simply a new name for Lashkar-e-Taiba, which has been operational in India for a decade. In 1997 it began sending suicide-jihadists into Indian Kashmir to "free" the population. All these groups are classified as foreign terrorist organizations by the UK and the US State Department.'

'Okay. So we have some possible recipients. Thank you, Elizabeth. The next question is, where is Philip Dunstan now? Has he been in contact?'

Freshfield took in a deep breath. 'Dunstan hasn't contacted us, nor has he replied to our texts on his service-issue mobile. And we have no idea where he is, except...'

Fanshawe raised an eyebrow. 'Except?'

Freshfield held up a late edition of a daily newspaper. 'Last night, there seems to have been a full-scale shoot-out on a Welsh hillside. A very remote spot near the Elan Valley. In the course of this firefight, a farmhouse was partially destroyed – it's thought that at least two anti-tank missiles were fired.'

There was a short silence. Then Fanshawe said, 'And the relevance to Dunstan?'

'Locals' enquiries suggest this small-holding belongs to a reclusive supposed former Special Air Service warrant officer. He goes by the sobriquet of "The Monk".'

'What's his real name?'

'We haven't established that yet.'

'Well, well. So let us assume our friend Dunstan went to ground with an old pal in the Welsh hills. And someone came looking for him – with anti-tank rockets.'

'Not to mention 7.62 millimetre machine guns. It's a safe bet to assume he can't have gone far – these characters tend to have bolt-holes. My guess is that they're in one right now, lying very low.'

'So what's the real connection between Dunstan and The Monk?' Fanshawe posed the obvious question. She was greeted by blank faces. Then, clearly wanting to move the meeting on for her own reasons, she said, 'I've been doing a little homework of my own and I've come up with an interesting name.' The team looked at Fanshawe as if she was about to draw a prize lottery ticket. 'On SAS Selection, Dunstan saved the life of a very important man, Sheikh Suroor Al-Qurum.'

'Al-Qurum is one of the smallest of the Gulf Emirates,' said Lovat, 'and a staunch ally of this country.'

'Indeed, it is, Miss Lovat,' continued Fanshawe pleasantly. 'I thought to myself, could it be possible that Dunstan has contacted the man he saved and is calling in a favour? So, overnight, various agencies have been listening and trawling for any communications to do with Al-Qurum. Graham?'

Freshfield ostentatiously cleared his throat. 'As it happens, this morning we received a flight order via Counter Terrorism Command for a transport aircraft scheduled to land at RAF Brize Norton at 2200 hours. Military aircraft are often used by visiting foreign dignitaries instead of commercial airlines, especially if it's a low-key visit.'

'I think we all know that, Graham,' interrupted Fanshawe impatiently. 'This aircraft is registered to the Emirate of Al-Qurum and the purpose of the visit is ostensibly to pick up a new Warrior armoured personnel carrier for Al-Qurum's forces. Alvis Vickers, the manufacturers, have been contacted: no such order exists and they don't have any deliveries scheduled to Brize Norton in the next seventy-two hours, or to any other UK air facility for that matter. The aircraft in question is also of interest. It's a Lockheed MC130-E Combat Talon, basically a Special Forces version of the Hercules, designed for infiltration and exfiltration in hostile terrain, equipped with terrain-following and terrain-avoidance radar, extra long-range fuel tanks, and capable of hugging the ground in any weather at sub-two hundred feet. Now, why would they be using that aircraft when, according to Jane's, Al-Qurum has any number of ordinary Hercules transporters?'

The question was clearly rhetorical. Freshfield continued, 'Given the overall intelligence picture, it would be safe to assume that Philip Dunstan is somewhere between Mid Wales and RAF Brize Norton. *Supposing* he has a twenty-two hundred hours' deadline coinciding with the arrival of the Al-Qurum aircraft, he would have to be somewhere in Powys, Herefordshire, Worcestershire, Gloucestershire, or possibly Warwickshire if he's coming in from the north. His sidekick will know Powys and Herefordshire like the back of his hand, and Dunstan will know Gloucestershire and especially the Cotswolds, so I *reckon* they're now somewhere on back roads in the Welsh Marches. The only problem we have is that Thames Valley Constabulary has reacted to a request from Counter Terrorism Command, and roadblocks have been ordered to be put into place around Brize Norton. As if that wasn't enough, tactical firearms units are on standby to arrest or shoot – depending on Dunstan's and his friend's actions.'

Fanshawe's neck flushed from anger. This was not what she wanted. There was embarrassed silence in the room. No one knew how Fanshawe would react to being ambushed on her own turf. However, she knew that to go to the Home Office to argue against Counter Terrorism Command's initiative would be foolhardy. There were upwards of thirty potential UK mainland terrorist plots under investigation at that moment, and all required intimate co-operation between MI5, Counter Terrorism Command, the Anti-Terrorist Squad, SOCA, police forces across the UK and other services. There was a prolonged silence.

Freshfield sat for a while looking down at his briefing paper with his finger tips on his temples. He was thinking on a number of levels. Privately he was pleased that Dunstan had been located, if not yet too precisely, and was wondering how he himself could contact him before he hit Brize Norton. This was exactly what Rebecca Lovat was thinking, too.

'Right,' said Fanshawe with finality. 'Let's wrap this up for now. Keep the effort up, and be on standby for any developments and orders.'

***

At 1500 hours, Celia Fanshawe placed a call to the Chief of Staff, Special Forces Directorate. 'Colonel, we would like Captain Dhar and Corporal Murria to be available for a full briefing this evening at my location, with a view to an early morning departure to Islamabad via Karachi. How long will it take them to get here?'

The Colonel was unfazed. 'Good job, we have them ready to go then, Miss Fanshawe. They've now moved up to two hours' standby as you know, so let's say forty minutes to check their equipment and documentation, lodge their Last Will and Testament and so on; then let's say one and a half hours by Lynx helicopter from South Wales to Battersea Heliport then fifteen minutes across the river by flashing lights. That's two and a half hours minimum. I assume you've arranged transport from Battersea to Thames House, Miss Fanshawe?'

Neatly turned, thought Fanshawe. 'I'll have a car waiting. The briefing is fixed for twenty hundred hours. They can stay in one of our safe houses overnight.'

***

'Got it!' Detective Sergeant Lowe exclaimed. 'Dunstan has a brand new Range Rover Sport, left-hand drive, dark green, registered for export to Morocco!' He handed the transcript, together with the Home Office release authority, to Detective Chief Inspector Beckwith.

'Good work, Lowe. Get the call out to all constabularies. Identify, track and report *but absolutely no intercept and no bloody heroics*!'

'No intercept, sir?' repeated Lowe.

'No intercept, Lowe. We'll find out why, apparently, at a briefing with Counter Terrorism Command officers here at nineteen hundred hours. We've been asked to provide up to twenty officers and six unmarked cars on twenty minutes' notice to move from nineteen forty-five hours onwards.'

'Counter Terrorism Command? Move where, sir?'

'How the hell should I know, Lowe? Counter Terrorism Command has also asked, via the Assistant Chief Constable, that Thames Valley Tactical Fire Arms Unit should be on standby. Dunstan is attracting interest from some strange quarters. I'm beginning to feel like a mushroom: kept in the dark and fed on crap.'

***

South of Oxford, 1800 hours

Kate Cross left the offices of CyberX on her way home. Although untrained in any form of security, she diligently checked the car park and her car for threats, real or imagined, as Vernon Hamill had shown her, and set off round the Oxford ring road. Her limited 'training' did not extend to observing the dark green military Land Rover shadowing her.

***

By 1900 hours, Dunstan and The Monk had skirted the Malvern Hills, but they had to cross over Junction 9 of the M5 at Tewkesbury: they were unlucky. Two traffic officers of West Mercia Constabulary were patrolling the M5 about three hundred yards north of the junction. The co-driver had just received an all-cars alert for a high specification left-hand drive, green Range Rover Sport, registration unknown. 'Says here, *Report on sight. Under no circumstances attempt to intercept or arrest occupants.* What the hell do you make of that, Barney?'

His partner nodded at the speeding lanes of traffic. 'Funny you should say that. I could be wrong but I just spotted what looks like a vehicle

answering to that exact same description right above our heads about…
now.' He looked in the mirror as the green blob vanished. 'Back end looks
as if it had been in an argument with a tin opener.'

His colleague's eyes widened. 'Barney, we've got a customer.'

Barney checked his rear view mirror again, slammed on his brakes, pulled
onto the hard shoulder and performed a high speed reverse up the south-
bound slip road of Junction 9, spinning around at the top and cutting the
wrong way across the entrance to the roundabout to head east through
Ashchurch. They followed the Range Rover at a discreet distance for about
half a mile and reported to Control. The reply was clear: do not arouse
suspicion, back off.

Dunstan and The Monk watched the police car peel away in the rear view
mirrors and relaxed slightly. At that very same moment, a police helicopter
with long-range infrared camera and video link equipment lifted off from
Staverton Airport near Cheltenham, where it had been idling on standby.
Five minutes later, it had acquired its target.

Chapter Ten

Dunstan and The Monk were high in the Cotswolds, on the edge of woods alongside Campden Street, the ancient prehistoric drovers' track that skirts the perimeter of the North Cotswold limestone escarpment. The early spring sun was setting behind the Malvern Hills to the west; further west still, they could see the outlines of the Black Mountains in graded purple relief. Directly below them nestled the small market town of Winchcombe, the capital of the Kingdom of Mercia some thousand years ago, huddled under the bulky mass of Cleeve Cloud and surrounded by other high-topped hills. It had been chosen by the Saxons for its natural defences. On the steep pastures of the valley below the hills, Sir Walter Raleigh had successfully grown tobacco on the same slopes where the Romans had once planted vines in a warmer climate. Between here and Winchcombe, the monks of Hailes had built their abbey, and formed a religious community that thrived for four hundred years until a certain British monarch divorced his Queen. To the north and below, nestling in the Coscombe Woods, lies one of the great estates of the Cotswolds, Stanway, with its landscaped parkland of majestic oaks, natural fountains and dry stone walls crawling their way improbably up the landscape like giant stone caterpillars. Nearer still lay one of the last of the great medieval forests of England, Guiting Wood, with its woodpeckers, buzzards, kestrels, merlins and roe deer.

'Let's lay up here, Monk. We still have a couple of hours to RV and it's only twenty miles away.' The cell phone Freshfield had given him began to ring. Dunstan looked across at The Monk who had adopted his thousand-mile-stare out across the Vale of Tewkesbury. He let the phone ring out.

'We'll stag rest periods of twenty minutes,' said The Monk as he gazed ahead. 'My paranoia says that the police helicopter doing odd manoeuvres across the valley is looking for us.'

'As soon as I make this next call, Monk, GCHQ will pick it up, and MI5 will know our exact grid reference to the nearest sheep's arse.'

'Looks like you're damned if you do, Sherpa, and damned if you don't. All my senses tell me that the helicopter over there knows roughly or precisely where we are anyway. It's keeping us under obbo and relaying our location to God-knows-where. Place the call, you've nothing to lose.'

Before he could act, the phone rang again. There was a pause before Freshfield finally came on the line. 'Dunstan, can you hear me clearly?' Dunstan had placed it on speaker phone so The Monk could hear the conversation.

Freshfield sounds nervous, thought Dunstan. 'Yes.'

'Okay. First: do you have any plans to travel anywhere near Brize Norton this evening, possibly to make a rendezvous?'

The Monk just stared hard at Dunstan, who was thinking quickly, working out the implications of the question. In that single suspended moment both men appreciated that their future hung on Dunstan's response.

After a pause, Dunstan replied cautiously, 'Now where did you hear such a rumour?'

The Monk shot him a hard glance. Dunstan gave him a thumbs-up as if to signal *I know what I'm doing.*

'Well, if you are, and if I were you, I would expect the unexpected,' Redmond replied.

'Stop playing pathetic games. Are you saying there might be a reception committee waiting for us?'

'Something like that. Not too friendly, either.'

'So you know where we are then?'

'Within a couple of feet, yes, of course we know where you are. The helicopter in front of you has your heat signature square in its infrared camera screen.'

'So why don't you guys move in now and intercept us?'

'Because we don't want to or need to. My Service wants you working with us and given the events of the past forty-eight hours, the police, who consider you armed and dangerous and fully responsible for all this mayhem, don't want a full-scale gun battle in the idyllic streets of Bourton-on-the-Water. They want to nail you in a controlled area. The choice is yours. Come with us and you have a chance. Go to Brize Norton and attempt an exfiltration and you're stuffed: either in prison or, worse, your kids are fatherless.'

'It seems that a lot of people want my arse. So why the hell are you warning me off? How do I know I can trust you?'

'You have no choice.' Freshfield paused to let Dunstan absorb that one before launching his salvo. 'Look, Dunstan, I assume you're not yet aware that your secretary, Kate, has been abducted from her car on her way home from work this evening by a person – or persons – unknown. For extra measure, your house has been blown up. Your family weren't at home, but I assume you knew *that*. It's also reasonable to assume that your family is in clear and present danger. They need to be ring-fenced by professionals who know what they're doing, to protect them from whoever is trying to get you and yours. I can arrange that protection but I need your unconditional co-operation. And I need it now.'

Quick as a flash, The Monk slammed his gnarled hand over Dunstan's mouth and rammed him against the passenger door, knocking the breath out him. It was all he could think of doing to prevent him from making an inappropriate response to the dreadful news. Dunstan looked at him like a dog that had just been whipped. His mind did the splits. The bit that controlled his mouth stayed rational, the rest didn't. He was sure parts of his brain had fused together. His whole body pumped with adrenaline, his heartbeat soared and his pupils dilated. He composed himself and tried to focus on what Freshfield was driving at.

Freshfield, impressed at least with Dunstan's control, filled him in on the scant details as he knew them, stressing that nothing had been heard from Kate's abductors and nothing was known about her state of well-being. He didn't know much about the house either; Thames Valley Constabulary had teams at both sites. Dunstan was struggling to maintain his composure. Even though the evening was cool, sweat ran in rivers down his back and his guts were burning with the surge in his metabolic rate. Nevertheless, he managed to maintain an outward semblance of calm.

'So you're blackmailing me with the security of my family in order to get my co-operation, is that it?'

'You know more than anyone, Dunstan, you don't get what you deserve in life, you get what you negotiate. I'm merely being pragmatic. There's more than just you and your family's lives at stake here. My responsibilities are wider.'

'So what's the deal, then?'

'The deal is that you RV with me and my team before you reach Brize. We take you and your friend to a safe house, where we work until we drop on finding out what the hell is going on. We take the pressure off you from the police, and we deploy some of my organisation's precious resources into locating Kate and into putting full protection in place around your family.'

'I want one promise here and now,' responded Dunstan, knowing that he was hardly in a position to negotiate terms.

'What's that?'

'You put a team in to protect my family tonight. Without that, they're exposed and I'm worth nothing to you. I want to know they're secure and I want your word you'll do it, as much as I don't trust you or your service!'

'You've got it: a full close protection team will go in tonight.'

'And a wide area cordon!'

'I can't promise that. Wide area will be down to the local constabulary with a Counter Terrorism Command directive, but I'll try and boost the firepower of the CP team. Now *your* commitment, Dunstan!'

Dunstan chose his words carefully. 'I promise I will co-operate fully and unequivocally with your investigation into this matter.' *But I'll do it on my terms*, he thought to himself.

'Good. Now in terms of the RV, Dunstan, I defer to your wisdom, fieldcraft and local knowledge. When and where? You know the ground and travel times in these parts.'

Dunstan was still thinking. 'Are you travelling to Brize with the, er, reception committee?'

'No, we're to RV with them there.'

'Who's with you? I mean with you personally, not the whole shebang.'

'Rebecca Lovat and a three-man tactical team.'

'Armed?'

'Of course we're armed!' came the curt response. 'In one vehicle?'

'Yes.'

'Has it got four-wheel drive and good brakes?'

'Yes. Why all the questions?'

Dunstan now had a clear tactical plan. 'Good. You'll need it. This is what you do: continue to RAF Brize Norton so as not to arouse any unnecessary suspicion. Dump the tactical team. Somehow you need to get yourself to the west end of the runway, the Filkins end. I'll call you on this phone at 2140 hours precisely and give you a grid reference to go to from there for the RV. You'll have to reach that location within fifteen minutes or I'll be gone. On meeting up, you'll follow me and I'll lead us to a new Forming Up Point which I believe to be a safe place. I'll then hand myself over to you and your ice maiden. Absolutely no one else. Those are my terms. Agreed?'

'Agreed!'

'Now, my wife's location follows... I'll contact her shortly as scheduled and will let her know that babysitters are on the way.'

Well turned, and he's managed to keep his options open, thought The Monk as Dunstan read out the location and contact number.

Freshfield was not finished yet. 'By the way, Dunstan, the weapons that were fired at your friend's farmhouse in Wales, including the Javelin, were stolen from an armoury belonging to a Gurkha infantry battalion. Would that make sense to you?'

'It might,' replied Dunstan, non-committal.

'I thought it might. And my bet is that these are the self-same people who are responsible for your house going up in smoke and your secretary's abduction. And maybe even for Idris Morgan's demise. So who have you upset, Dunstan?'

'Not you as well!' Dunstan looked pointedly across at The Monk. 'Listen, I've hurt absolutely no one! Please just make sure the police are putting their efforts into finding Kate.'

'To the extent of my influence, I'll do that. Keep your communications line open. Keep your promise and I'll keep mine.' Freshfield was already scribbling a set of orders around the location and contact details Dunstan had just given him.

The line went dead and Dunstan stared ahead across the valley.

The Monk slapped a hand on his friend's shoulder as Dunstan stared into the void with moist eyes. He knew that his business, his home, and probably his whole life in the UK was down the pan. He had only one overriding question: *could he save his family?*

'Keys, please, my friend. I need to drive.' Dunstan held out his hand.

They swapped places. Dunstan gunned the engine, dumped the clutch and channelled all his frustration and anger into covering the ground in front of him. The helicopter manoeuvred to follow them. The Monk checked his watch. It was 2000 hours.

As he drove, Dunstan reflected on the state of his mind. He didn't yet know what was really going on, but he did know that without the right frame of mind he had no chance of getting through the minefield that lay ahead. His approach to dealing with challenges and danger was born of his own hard-won experience, from having lived through danger and high adventure, from having survived and been the stronger for it. He was shattered but had to pull himself together.

Have no expectations, for they will certainly be delusions. Do not seek to hold on to anything material, for all material things are impostors. Have no plans that cannot be changed, and, ultimately, hold nothing so dear that you can't walk away from it, or else be prepared to die for it. Tread warily, exercise compassion, remain dispassionate, take as much time as is available to decide; but when you do decide on a course of action, act swiftly with a ruthless, even brutal, killer instinct in the full knowledge that you do so to determine truth and protect those whom you truly love.

Do nothing in haste; look well to each step; and from the beginning think what may be the end.

With these final cautionary words of the first ascensionist of the Matterhorn, Edward Whymper, completing his mental preparation, he turned his mind to the next few crucial hours.

***

There is often a singular point in time in a series of apparently chaotic events when participants and observers alike are unaware of a convergence of fates, of lives moving as if to a pre-determined outcome; the effect of which predicates success, failure, survival or death, which is obvious to all only in retrospect. This was such a moment.

As the police convoy headed down the Witney bypass to RAF Brize Norton in Thames House, London, two young women soldiers of the Special Reconnaissance Regiment were sitting in a briefing room, awaiting the details of their proposed mission with more than a little apprehension.

Celia Fanshawe entered the room with Major General Gibbs, who was dressed immaculately in a pin-striped suit. The two young soldiers, Captain Dhar and Corporal Murria, both stood as if to attention. The young officer looked askance at Gibbs before recognising the chiselled features from the photograph in Regimental Headquarters. 'Oh, sir, goodness me, I didn't realise it was you. Sorry... sir.' To the two soldiers, DSF was one rank down from God. They didn't know whether to stand to attention, salute (they couldn't, as they weren't in uniform), shake hands or just quake in their shoes. They did the latter. Gibbs, at his most charming, smiled and broke the ice. Quickly putting them at ease, he made the necessary introductions, then, with no more ado, explained succinctly that the mission on which they were about to be briefed was a matter of national security and international sensitivity.

Celia Fanshawe next proceeded to outline some, but not all, of the intelligence background to the women soldiers. Gibbs had already received a fuller brief with intelligence context. Still operating on a need-to-know basis, the security services compartmentalise information, even in this age of so-called inter-service co-operation. Dhar and Murria received just the right information to give them sufficient context for their mission, no more and no less.

Their mission was to follow the bag carriers from the bank in Pakistan to wherever they delivered the funds, and to report the destination accordingly. The UK, monitoring their communications through the British High Commission in Islamabad, would decide on any course of action from thereon in. They would have the back-up of a small team of watchers, two or three at the most. They would also have the support of a couple of members of 267 Signals Squadron – a Special Forces Support Squadron – also operating out of the High Commission. There was no other back-up, as it was considered just too dangerous as a 'black' operation on foreign soil, even if the foreign soil was, on balance, an ally in the fight against terrorism.

'I have a question, please, sir?' Captain Dhar looked at her military boss for permission.

'Go ahead, please.' It was Fanshawe, establishing the intelligence hierarchy.

'Well, ma'am, we're out on a limb here, so do the Pakistani authorities actually know we're operating a surveillance operation on their turf? And if not, may I ask why not?'

'Sounds like two questions to me,' replied Fanshawe, not unkindly. Secretly, she was rather envious of the opportunities for women in the military nowadays, and as a mark of respect for their forthcoming mission, she gave a fuller answer than she otherwise would have.

'The answer, for they are really one and the same question, is that the ultimate purpose of this money could be to wreak havoc on any continent, including within the UK and within the Indian subcontinent itself. If the latter is the case, then we need to have our facts clear before we start disseminating information that could upset regional stability. We don't wish to precipitate a regional nuclear stand-off, or worse, either through good intentions or, perhaps, misconstrued intelligence. But neither can we stand idly by. We have moral and political obligations to make our allies aware of intelligence that might affect their internal security.'

'Another question if I may, please ma'am.' It was Corporal Murria. 'How far do we follow the bag carriers and for how long?'

'The guiding imperative is that we need to know where the money is going. The 267 Squadron team will establish the boundary of their communications with you. Should you believe it operationally necessary to go out of communications range, well, you're out on your own. Just find the end delivery point. That's the key. All local decisions are up to the commanding officer on the ground, and that is you, Captain Dhar.'

Gibbs was not entirely satisfied himself. 'If they get into trouble, what back-up do they have and what's the plan for exfiltrating them from trouble?'

Fanshawe paused for a moment as though not wishing to contemplate the words 'trouble' and 'exfiltration'. She looked directly at the soldiers.

'You will understand that we can't afford for our whole intelligence-gathering operation to be blown apart; it's much wider than the important part you are playing. The scale of the potential or actual threat is enormous. Your fallback is the High Commission. You have, as a matter of course, multiple identities provided, and Elizabeth here will take you through the operational detail. But if you were to go, shall we say, "long range", the chances of getting you out of any trouble are almost non-existent. What we cannot afford is for British Forces to be involved in a fire-fight on Pakistani soil without the full co-operation of the Pakistani authorities and services. As for being captured, well, I'm, er, afraid we will have to deny any knowledge of your existence, should that occur.'

Gibbs levelled his eyes. He had suspected as much: a deniable operation. He tried not to sound patronising as he addressed the women.

'Do you understand what this means? If things go wrong, no one is coming to help you.' Both girls were silent and contemplative. 'With all that we have to do this evening, you have just fifteen minutes to consider if you wish to accept and volunteer for this mission. We can't make you go, but if you do, you do so in the full knowledge of the nature of your position over there. Is that clear?'

'Yes, sir,' they answered in tandem.

'Okay. Take a break. Fifteen minutes, let us know.'

But if Captain Dhar and Corporal Murria were feeling apprehensive at what lay ahead, their fears were nothing compared to those of Kate, who lay bound and gagged in the back of a travelling ex-military Land Rover. She was neatly wrapped up in a couple of old Army 'green maggot' sleeping bags, panic-stricken and utterly terrified.

***

After only five minutes, the women soldiers re-entered and Captain Dhar spoke for them. 'It's a "Go", sir, ma'am. It's what we joined up for.'

'Does that mean both of you?' It was Gibbs who posed the question.

'Yes, Boss,' they said in tandem again, slipping into the Special Forces form of address to their officers.

Gibbs simply nodded. Wishing them the best of luck, he shook their hands and left. He thought that in signing up to this they were either very courageous or foolhardy; only the outcome would determine that.

***

The convoy of vehicles turned off the Witney bypass and headed along the back roads to RAF Brize Norton. As they approached the airbase, they split into designated task teams and joined up with the detachments of RAF Regiment already deployed at key points around the six-mile-long perimeter. Beckwith, Commander Hoskins from Counter Terrorism Command, Freshfield, Lovat and Chief Inspector Robinson from S019 Tactical Firearms Unit headed towards the office of the Commandant RAF Brize Norton, Wing Commander Ed Law. Law was unimpressed. 'Commander, by what means did your intelligence suggest your man would enter this base and board a flight?'

'Er, uhm, it didn't. But from the intelligence pattern and Dunstan's trajectory it's pretty clear that he's going to attempt it somehow,' responded Hoskins.

Wing Commander Law did not reply but his thoughts were less than charitable.

A female Flight Lieutenant air traffic controller entered the office, saluted, and handed a slip of paper to the station commander.

'Well, gentlemen, we'll soon find out. The Al-Qurum flight is on its run-in to Brize for its refuelling stop.'

'How long should it take?' asked Lovat.

'As the refuelling teams are already primed, about one hour at the most, Miss Lovat.'

'Don't mind if we take a look round the base perimeter, do you?' asked Freshfield.

'Not at all, Mr Freshfield. Just make sure you are easily identifiable from a distance,' Law replied.

Freshfield smiled sardonically and nodded to all in the room. Then he went off with Rebecca Lovat to pursue his own agenda. Outside, he was in the process of placing his portable blue flashing light on the super-charged Ford when a loud droning sound came from the east. The Al-Qurum MC-130 Talon skimmed the fencing on the Bampton Road, glided to a perfect landing and taxied straight over to the refuelling tankers on the south side of the main runway. A hundred plus troops, police and related services went onto the highest state of alert. Freshfield eased his car out of the main gate and headed due west to the Filkins Road end of the two-mile-long runway.

It was Rebecca Lovat's turn to do her headmistress impression. 'Now, are you going to tell me what you're up to, or do I have to guess?'

'Just wait, Rebecca. It's all in the best tradition and interests of the service.'

'Don't patronise *me*,' replied Lovat, not amused. 'And where has our own team disappeared to?'

'Re-deployed,' said Freshfield with finality.

Chapter Eleven

Dunstan waited with The Monk in the woods above Bourton-on-the-Water, a short distance from the designated Forming Up Point that he and The Monk had chosen carefully. They estimated that they could cover the distance in ten minutes if required, allowing three minutes maximum to reach the final RV. They switched off the engine to reduce the heat signature, but the helicopter was still making passes overhead. They had to assume that the chopper was relaying their location to the police. This being the case, achieving their final RV without being intercepted was going to be hairy in the extreme; the next forty minutes were going to be long ones. Time to phone Faith.

'Faith, it's me... Yes, I know I shouldn't phone you from my mobile but in a way it doesn't matter anymore. Yes, I'm fine, darling. Now listen, please. A man called Redmond should be phoning you shortly. There's a possibility that you and the kids may be in danger. Redmond is sending a protection team in to look after you as soon as possible; please co-operate fully with him. And for God's sake don't start telling him or his team what to do; they'll know what to do, they're professionals, so please follow their instructions.' Faith Dunstan was not amused and made it more than clear to her husband. 'God, Philip! You said we would be safe here. What the hell has changed? I need to know, so don't try to pull the wool over my eyes!'

No point in that, thought Dunstan, *though one thing at a time. Best I should leave the house bit until later.*

'Faith darling, it's Kate. She's been abducted or kidnapped, and therefore the view from the police and security services is that you need protection – purely as a precaution.'

'My God! Kidnapped! It all sounds bloody ghastly, Philip! All I can say is that you had better be right that we won't need it! Where the hell are you now?'

'I'm still in the Cotswolds, but that may change shortly. Faith, listen, I must go, darling. Love you loads. Lots of love to the kids. And do as Redmond says, he's looking after both of us. Love you. Bye.' Dunstan hung up and stared into space.

'This "Redmond" character is looking after you?' The question from The Monk was both incredulous and rhetorical but he nevertheless answered it himself. 'Bollocks he is, Sherpa. He's the puppeteer and you're the puppet. He has his hand right up your arse, boyo, and he's playing with you.'

Dunstan delivered his next words deliberately, with an intensity and certainty that The Monk had not seen in his friend for many a year.

'Shortly, my dear Monk, the roles will be reversed.'

The Monk could have been wrong, but he thought he caught a manic look in his friend's eyes. *What the hell has he got up his sleeve?*

***

Freshfield parked up on the western perimeter of the Brize Norton airbase on the Filkins Road, next to an armoured reconnaissance vehicle of the RAF Regiment. They were parked at the southern geological point of the Cotswolds, where the limestone plateau fragments into long fingers, then disappears altogether into rich farmland. The runway to the east is slightly convex, so they couldn't see what was going on two miles away. It concerned Rebecca that they were away from any action.

'What are we doing here?' she quizzed.

Freshfield was extracting a piece of paper from his trouser pocket. 'Waiting, Rebecca, waiting. Not for long, I promise you. I just need to place a call to Dunstan's wife to let her know our protection team is on its way.'

Rebecca Lovat was no fool and she didn't like being treated like one. 'You've done a deal with him, haven't you? He isn't getting on this flight, is he? You've used the potential threat to his family to bring him in! I hope you know what you're doing, because there are going to be some pretty pissed-off policemen around when they find out you've gone freelance!'

'*If* they find out!' shot back a confident Freshfield. 'So what's the plan?'

'There is no actual plan: we have to await developments. I'll navigate, you drive.'

***

From the control tower of the airbase, the intercept team watched the refuelling of the Al-Qurum aircraft until it was complete. They had been receiving regular location reports from the helicopter and knew that Dunstan had been stationary for some time, but that he was now moving at speed, due south from Bourton-on-the-Water towards Brize Norton.

At 2138 hours, simultaneous events occurred that determined the fate of a lot of people.

The pilot requested clearance from the control tower to take off within the next fifteen minutes. As the Talon taxied to the east end of the runway and went through its final checks, at the other end of the runway Freshfield received the call he had been waiting for.

'Dunstan here. Move to grid reference 673272, a distance of 11.5 miles from your location. You have fifteen minutes maximum to complete your journey and RV with us or we're gone.' The line went dead. Freshfield located the RV on the OS map and pointing, showed Lovat. They both looked at each other in disbelief. 'Oh shit!' said Freshfield with feeling, as Lovat gunned the Ford northwards.

In the control tower at Brize, Beckwith received a live report from the West Mercia police force. He motioned for the room to be quiet. 'What do you mean he's stopped? Where?' He requested a pen. Wing Commander Ed Law moved up to his shoulder. The helicopter co-pilot relayed a grid reference and Law took down the co-ordinates. Moving to the large-scale OS map on the wall, Beckwith checked the co-ordinates. He began to swear, softly but with feeling. The pencil pointed to the southern end of Upper Rissington aerodrome, some twelve miles to the north-west of Brize, long disused but, for a Talon, still serviceable. 'They've fooled us. They're using a different airfield.'

'Stop that aircraft!' exclaimed Hoskins. A few of the RAF contingent looked down at their shoes and hid their smirks.

It was Law who responded. 'And cause a major diplomatic incident with one of our closest allies in the Middle East? I don't think so,

Commander Hoskins.' As he spoke, there was a roar of engines; a final request for take-off. The Flight Controller looked at Wing Commander Law, who simply nodded.

'Well, if you won't stop it, I bloody well will. Come on, Lowe.' Beckwith dashed for the door as though he were twenty years younger.

Hoskins and Chief Inspector Robinson of SO19 looked at each other and followed, not knowing whether they were doing so in order to intercept Dunstan or stop an international incident.

***

The Talon lifted off at the half-mile point of the Brize runway. The crew switched all lights off, put on night vision goggles, and turned on the terrain-following and terrain-avoidance radar. Instead of climbing to a cruising altitude the aircraft skimmed along at eighty feet above the runway. The commander of the armoured recce troop sitting atop his vehicle at the end of the runway didn't see the aircraft until it was full in his face. He later claimed he could see the rivets on the underbelly as it passed overhead, and he remained somewhat dazed for several days afterwards. The Talon treated the good people of the village of Kencot with similar contempt, rattling their windows before executing an aggressive banking manoeuvre, then making a couple of wide slow circles as if to gauge the precise time to begin its run north.

***

The small town of Burford had not seen such drama since the seventeenth century, when Charles II's entourage ravished the women of the small Cotswold market town during a royal tour. The police cars screamed down the hill at seventy miles an hour, almost taking off over the Windrush River Bridge before powering north.

However, if the peace of Burford had been disturbed, it was nothing as compared to what was about to happen at Rissington.

Beckwith, Hoskins and Robinson were now on a parallel road to that travelled by Freshfield and Lovat, but several miles apart. These roads converged about a mile north of Upper Rissington village. Upper Rissington's ex-RAF houses are now privately owned and there is a small estate of new houses. The old airbase buildings were converted to a business park and light industrial use after the MOD sold off all the housing stock. The disused runway is right next to the houses.

It was 2149 hours, and Dunstan was waiting on the south-west corner of the runway, lights out in the Land Rover.

'What now?' asked The Monk. 'We wait and pray.'

'Which God, Sherpa?'

'All of them, Monk, all of them!'

As he said that, the Talon made its final turn and headed north, overtaking Freshfield and Lovat in the Ford, which was now hitting ninety miles an hour on the long, straight Roman Road. The aircraft contoured over the ground at below two hundred feet and dipped into the Windrush valley, skimming the trees over the ancient Taynton quarries which had provided the stone for St Paul's Cathedral. The first anyone knew of its presence was a low throbbing from the four Alison turbo-prop engines that shook all the windows in Upper Rissington. Dunstan grinned at The Monk as the camouflaged hulk popped its nose out of the shallow valley and started its run in to the airfield. Even The Monk was impressed.

Freshfield was following its progress through binoculars. As the speeding car approached the designated RV at the south-west corner of the airfield, a brilliant halogen light suddenly blinded him. Similarly dazzled, Lovat fought to control the Ford before bringing it to a juddering halt.

As the Combat Talon slowed, Freshfield and Lovat caught up with Dunstan. Leaning out of the Range Rover, Dunstan shouted, 'Turn your lights out and follow me!' Behind him, the aircraft set down and taxied halfway down the length of the runway.

Flashing blue police lights appeared on the far side of the old aerodrome, followed at once by the wail of sirens. Lovat hesitated for a second and then slammed the Ford into gear. The Range Rover hit eighty miles an hour and accelerated along the runway with Freshfield and Lovat right on its tail. The Talon was now taxiing along the runway with the tailgate opening. Hoskins, Beckwith and SO19's Robinson in the lead police car burst onto the far end of the runway. Hoskins articulated their common thought. 'That's Freshfield's car. What the hell is he doing? Trying to catch Dunstan?' Almost as he finished the question, he realised that he couldn't have been more wrong. 'We've just got time to take out Dunstan's car!' Robinson volunteered.

But by the time he had finished speaking it was too late: the two cars were rapidly approaching the tailgate of the moving aircraft. Inside the Talon, the two loadmasters were swiftly checking the high impact netting set up to absorb the entry of Dunstan's vehicle into the load bay. They were not expecting two vehicles. Two Al-Qurum Scimitar Force Special Forces soldiers stood ready with Armalites on either side of the bay entrance. The loadmasters dropped the tailgate the last couple of feet. The Range Rover hit the strengthened tailgate at sixty miles an hour. It shot up the ramp into the load bay, almost taking out one of the soldiers, and then rammed into the high impact netting. A shudder went through the whole fuselage. Dunstan leapt straight out of the vehicle on a full adrenaline surge.

'Decision time, Rebecca!' Like Freshfield, Lovat had done the defensive and evasive driving course, but the prospect before them was not on the syllabus.

'Damn, I had a date tomorrow. First one in ages, too…let's do it!'

The Talon was starting to accelerate. On the ramp the two soldiers raised their rifles, fingers squeezing the triggers. 'Hold your fire!' Dunstan yelled. 'They're with us!' The loadmasters looked aghast as the Ford shot up the ramp, bounced wildly, and slammed into the back of the stationary Range Rover at a relative twenty miles per hour, with sufficient impact to set off its air bags.

On the apron, the police watched with a mixture of emotions as the Talon, still shuddering with the impact of the double crash inside its reinforced belly, clawed its way up into the night sky. Hoskins was spitting mad, Beckwith curiously phlegmatic. But all the others, especially the high-speed chase cops, were awestruck – utterly envious of the driving spectacle they had just witnessed. 'Wish it had been me,' Lowe muttered, speaking for many of them.

'What now?' said Hoskins, watching the Talon's dark silhouette fade and finally disappear into the night sky.

'I don't know about you,' replied Beckwith, 'but I have two serious crimes to solve and a kidnap victim to locate. Goodnight… sir.'

***

On board the Talon, the two Al-Qurum Special Forces soldiers were pointing their weapons at the occupants of the second car, whose faces were almost enveloped by the air bags which had gone off on impact. The Monk exchanged formal greetings with them in Arabic then moved over to the MI5 car, now embedded in the rear of the Range Rover. He checked Lovat then went round to the passenger seat. He drew his parang and placed the sharp edge close enough to the throat of Graham Freshfield to get his attention. He didn't get it. He pulled Freshfield's head back. The Head of UK Counter-Terrorism was dead, his chest ruptured by the impact of hitting the air bag at speed with no seat belt restraint. Lovat was fine, bruised and shocked, but aware enough to realise that this would take some explaining. And that perhaps at last, her moment had come.

As The Monk turned, he caught the eye of the two Al-Qurum Special Forces soldiers and said, 'Ehmel jothet al rejjal, lefha be kol hathar wa ehteram wa da'aho fe moa'akherat al sayyara.' *Move this man's body, wrap it with care and respect and lay him in the back of the car.*

They didn't know who he was, but he had just spoken to them in their local Arab dialect, and instinct told them that here was a man whose orders they should follow.

***

Oxfordshire, 2300 hours

Kate Cross stared out into the darkness. She was still bound and gagged in the back of the Land Rover. They were somewhere in the middle of woods near Oxford – she didn't know where. For a while now, she had heard her captors talking into a microphone or headset, as though receiving instructions. The language was one she had never heard before. Not African – Oriental but not Chinese, more Indian in intonation, she thought. The conversation finished and the rear flap opened. Her captors, three of them, sprung into the back of the vehicle with the lightness of cats. The razor point of a broad-bladed knife touched her throat, and the finger of the man holding it went to his lips in the universal signal for silence. He pulled the gag away from her face. The questioning was polite but insistent, and conducted in heavily accented English. All they wanted to know was the whereabouts of Dunstan and his family. As to the former, she answered truthfully that she did not know. As to Dunstan's family, her protests of ignorance lacked conviction even to her own ears. The blade went to her shoulder and cut through her clothing. It fell away, exposing her left breast. She didn't know how long she could be brave but as the cold steel pressed into her nipple with enough pressure to draw blood, she did know that it wouldn't be for long.

***

The Combat Talon flew south towards the English Channel and down towards the Bay of Biscay. Over Hampshire, it picked up a diplomatic escort of two Typhoons, which saw it out of British airspace before dipping their wings in salute as they peeled away. On board the MC-130, the crew had explicit instructions not to talk to their passengers other than to serve them some food and drink.

Lovat was now sitting in the back of the Range Rover on the baggage and weapons, with Dunstan and The Monk in the front. The adrenaline rush had subsided and they were all subdued. The Monk in particular was pensive, staring sightlessly through the windscreen. Lovat sought to drag her mind away from Freshfield's body in the other car just a few feet away. 'You must be the man they call The Monk?' She turned her violet eyes on the man in the front passenger seat.

The Monk turned and met them full on. In a voice that was hoarse and deliberate, he said, 'My name is Edwards, John Al-Buddaq Edwards. I have my grandfather's Maltese/Arabic name, although my father was English.'

Dunstan stared at his friend open-mouthed. The Monk smiled. 'So now you know my full name, Sherpa…I'm part Arab.'

'Sherpa?' Lovat was intrigued. 'What is it with you Special Forces guys and names?'

'Don't go there,' advised The Monk.

'So what do we do now?' Lovat enquired.

Dunstan turned to look at her. Even under pressure she was alluring, perhaps more so given the way she was dealing with it. 'We're going to do what every good soldier does at times like these.'

'What's that?'

'Sleep,' replied Dunstan emphatically.

***

In London, a thoughtful DSF was running back to his weekday *pied-a-terre* across London from Thames House, his 'civvies' neatly folded in his ruck-sack. A distance of some six miles, it would give him time to clear his mind. Gibbs had spent the last couple of hours with Celia Fanshawe while the SRR soldiers were receiving their operational briefing – ground, situation, multiple identities, fall-backs and communications methods – at the new MI5 facility near Heathrow. This was a recent addition to the security services' establishment, which allowed quicker deployment to the north and west of the UK and to Heathrow if required. The soldiers were now having a couple of hours' rest before catching a PIA flight direct to Islamabad. To all intents and purposes, they were already on their own.

He was thinking about this, and all the possible scenarios for a prize cock-up: how could he possibly provide ground support, especially if things went pear-shaped for the women during the reconnaissance? Then Gibbs remembered reading an internal bulletin to the effect that a troop of 59 Commando Squadron Royal Engineers were out in Pakistan-controlled Kashmir, helping the local population in mountain areas to rebuild their shattered lives after the recent catastrophic floods which had triggered many landslides. They were a military aid mission and most emphatically unarmed. *But then again...* he mused.

The UK has a long history of deploying Royal Engineers (Sappers) to far-flung outposts of the world, former dominions or countries friendly to the UK, to help rebuild local infrastructure after natural disasters, and the Regiment's Latin motto – *Ubique* – reflects this propensity to be 'Everywhere'. The Sappers have a number of special squadrons which include EOD (bomb disposal), a Parachute Squadron and Commando Squadron, part of a Commando Regiment. All members of Para and Commando do the full paratrooper and commando selection courses to earn their respective coloured berets. They are, above all, combat engineers as well as paratroopers and commando soldiers. A half-troop of 59 Commando Squadron under the command of a senior captain had been deployed in rotation at high-altitude locations in Kashmir to help the local population rebuild their destroyed homes. They were fit, acclimatised to altitude, and above all, commando trained. Gibbs made a mental note to ascertain their redeployment capability the following morning, via his own discrete channels.

***

Inside the Talon, Dunstan was lying in one of the slung hammocks, his old friend asleep in the one next to him. His mind was a tumult of thoughts, with a waterfall of events rushing through his brain and then circling back round again and again, like an Escher print. If he carried any baggage around with him in this world, it was a large sack full of guilt. He had a strong tendency to blame himself and he found it hard to forgive himself for his perceived mistakes. *Forgiveness! Now that's interesting. Who hasn't forgiven me? Or what have I done to someone, consciously or unconsciously, that is so painful that they can't forgive me and want to destroy me? That's what is at the heart of this: someone's inability, for whatever reason, to forgive.*

Chapter Twelve

Thursday, 26th April: London, 0600 hours; Al-Qurum, 0900 hours; Islamabad, 1100 hours

As the bright lights of the world's largest construction site, Dubai, glowed under the port wing, the MC-130 banked a few degrees to the south-west. The journey had been typical of all C-130 flights: noisy, smelly and long; ten hours of tedium. The crew had stayed out of the way of the passengers, other than the senior loadmaster who proffered a steady stream of non-alcoholic juice drinks and plates of quite delicious food. For the most part though, Dunstan and The Monk swung in their hammocks while Lovat, unexpected and therefore not provided for, stretched out in the Range Rover. The plane started to descend. The loadmaster asked that all passengers strap themselves into the bucket seats alongside the wall. Almost immediately they were on the final approach. With the sun already a huge disk, the MC-130 glided past a modern barracks bristling with satellite and microwave communications dishes before settling itself down on the military aerodrome's mile-long runway. It turned at the end and taxied towards the compound. The doors were opened and the arid desert heat hit them.

The Monk spoke in colloquial Arabic to the two soldiers, who began to reverse out the MI5 car with Freshfield's body in the back. 'Look after this fallen man. He did great service for his country.'

Lovat eased her bruised and aching body from the Range Rover and followed the others down the steps into the heat. Dunstan had been expecting a reception committee but there wasn't one. Instead, the loadmaster directed them across the pan to a desert-camouflaged Bell Jet Ranger 111 helicopter waiting, with engines running, some distance from the barracks.

They strapped themselves in. The Monk was sitting in the doorway of the helicopter with his face to the sun, soaking up his favourite environment, the desert. Scattered randomly across this arid landscape were huge circles of green crops, created through a sophisticated computerised irrigation system that combined water from the nearby *Jebel,* or mountains, with desalinated sea water. The chopper circled over the old harbour where dhows still plied their trade of material and human cargo, a centuries-old tradition but now with a sharper edge. Increasingly the smugglers used high-speed boats that could cross to Pakistan, deliver a cargo of illicit goods, take a fresh one in exchange and be back in the same night.

As they turned inland towards the capital, they could see just how much oil money had been invested in its infrastructure. The medieval souk still beat at its heart, for Sheikh Al-Qurum valued his cultural heritage, but beyond that were wide boulevards of villas, each with it its own irrigated 'oasis' – a grand corniche along the edge of the Gulf, with a small number of high-rise hotels and apartment blocks.

The chopper headed directly for the tallest building, its façade emblazoned with the words *National Bank of Al-Qurum.* Giant flared flutings, like upside-down flying buttresses, sprouted from either side of the top few stories. They approached the left-hand fluting, which they could now see incorporated a helicopter landing pad. The other fluting was home to a pair of Astroturf tennis courts and a dazzling blue swimming pool. Next to the landing pad could be seen a number of men wearing closed-neck *kameez* or, colloquially, 'dishdash' tunics under gold trimmed black *thawbs* (robes). Dunstan tried to spot his old friend but couldn't.

Welcoming strangers is a fundamental part of all desert cultures. The harsh realities of the arid and dangerous environment bind travellers and nomads in a sense of common generosity. For millennia this unconditional hospitality enabled inhabitants of the Arabian Peninsula to survive thirst, hunger and sudden attacks. This custom of showing courtesy and consideration to strangers is ingrained in the psyche of Arabia. To understand this, and to understand the Arab mind, you have to understand the harshness of desert life. Few westerners have ever really done so. Thesiger, Burton and Lawrence did and, having become part of it, found it almost impossible to assimilate back into western ways of life.

As they stepped onto the pad, they were greeted by the eldest of the three men: tall and angular with a hawk-like countenance, his shrewd black eyes noticed everything and missed nothing. If the three Arabs were offended by the sight of the dishevelled Englishmen, together with a white woman inappropriately dressed in a dark two-piece suit that left her head and her legs bare, they were polite enough not to show it.

Dunstan stepped forward and introduced himself. 'Philip Dunstan, sir.'

'*Salaam alaikum.* Welcome. Peace be with you. I am Abdul Thabet, First Minister of Al-Qurum and personal adviser to His Excellency Sheikh Suroor bin Mohammed Al-Qurum. We were notified that only two people would be arriving,' he added acerbically.

The Monk was discreetly weighing up Abdul Thabet. *Not an Emirates man with a name and looks like that. Yemeni; probably from a mountain tribe.*

Dunstan mirrored their host's formal, diplomatic approach. 'My sincerest apologies, First Minister. This is my friend Mr Edwards, and this is Miss Lovat. I am afraid she is a late invitee. However, I can personally vouch for her integrity and credentials. My party feel embarrassed that you should have to receive us in this state of unpreparedness, but our journey here has not been without its adventures and challenges.'

The First Minister's tone softened but his eyes, Dunstan noticed, did not. 'I have heard something of what you say, Mr Dunstan, and I look forward to learning the rest. His Excellency has requested that you attend a private audience with him directly upon your arrival. Your companions will be taken to a comfortable hotel where they can refresh themselves. Please, come this way. Come! His Excellency graciously awaits your presence.'

His manner was still forced, and Dunstan got the feeling that Thabet was not accustomed to being designated to receive guests of such an obviously low social status.

Dunstan nodded to his companions, as if it say *it'll be okay*, and then followed Thabet and one of his colleagues into the lift. As they stepped out of the lift into a vast atrium, the chill of the air conditioning hit him and for a moment he realised how tired he was. He felt conspicuous in his dishevelled state as the smartly dressed senior staff of the bank passed him, some in the traditional dishdash but most in Western business suits, their faces averted, but curious at this strange spectacle of the First Minister escorting a filthy individual with several days' growth of beard, bruised and with cuts and rents in his clothing.

They reached a huge set of hardwood doors guarded by two soldiers armed with Heckler & Koch MP5s. There was no covert close protection here. The sentries stepped aside for Abdul Thabet, but not without a hard look at Dunstan. The doors swung open from the inside and they were in a reception area as big as Dunstan's home, furnished with Islamic art and ceramics of historical importance. Beyond was an identical set of doors guarding the inner sanctum.

Thabet dismissed everyone else in the room and turned to Dunstan. His eyes narrowed to slits and his voice had the harshness and grittiness of wind-blown desert sand.

'I don't know why you are here, but the fact that His Excellency has blessed your arrival in such a way, that he has graciously granted you an audience at such short notice, and that he has agreed to see you in your *filthy* state, indicates to me that you have something valuable for him, information or something like that. For myself, I do not care what it is unless it affects most gravely the safety of His Excellency's person or the security of the State of Al-Qurum itself. You should therefore conduct your business in an efficient but deferential manner, and be prepared to leave with your friends at short notice. On entry, I will present you formally and you will incline your head and address His Excellency only after he has invited you to speak. You will address him as "Your Excellency" at all times and speak in answer only to direct questions. If there is a breach in protocol at any stage, I shall have you escorted under armed guard with your friends and placed on the next flight to Britain. Is that clear, Mr Dunstan?'

'Abundantly clear. Thank you for taking the time to brief me so thoroughly.' Dunstan knew that the English art of irony did not translate well across any language barrier.

'Good. Wait here!' The First Minister spoke into an intercom. 'Your Excellency, Mr Dunstan has arrived and most humbly requests that he may enter to receive the audience that you have so graciously granted to him.' After a short pause, a green light came to life on an LCD panel next to the door.

As they entered, Dunstan made out the vast bulk of a man rising from behind an enormous ornate desk. The size of Dreadnought caught Dunstan by surprise; clearly he was living up to the nickname he had given himself. If Dunstan was somewhat taken aback, it was as nothing compared to Thabet's amazement. What happened next was not in the First Minister's plans.

A deep baritone voice filled the office of the Chairman of the National Bank of Al-Qurum and bounced off the walls. 'Sherpa, where are you! Get in here, my man. Let me see you. Get out of the way Abdul Thabet! Let me see my old friend!'

The First Minister of Al-Qurum was bounced out of the way as His Excellency Sheikh Suroor bin Mohammed Al-Qurum deftly moved his substantial frame towards the doorway. The first thing Dunstan knew was that he was being enveloped in the swathes of a luxurious black and gold-embroidered thawb and crushed in an all-embracing bear hug. His immediate thought was *how on earth did I manage to carry him down a mountain*?

Abdul Thabet looked on aghast at the spectacle before him. There was no precedent for this. He had no point of reference to comprehend what he was seeing. In ten years of devoted service, he had seen nothing like it. *And with this stinking infidel at that!*

'Sherpa, Sherpa, let me look at you. In the name of the Prophet (peace be upon him), you stink!' A bellowing laugh emanated from deep within Al-Qurum's frame as Dunstan was hugged once again and then firmly escorted over to the seated area.

'Abdul Thabet!' Al-Qurum was still beaming. 'You look like a man who has swallowed a scorpion! Let me explain: to this man, I owe my life! Through his courage and physical prowess, he saved me from certain death in unfortunate and very uncomfortable circumstances.' Abdul Thabet felt as if he *had* swallowed a scorpion. He knew now that he was witness to a bond that could not be broken. He inclined his head towards Dunstan, still wondering why the man had come and what he wanted from his Emir. At a nod from Al-Qurum, he withdrew from the room backwards.

Sheikh Suroor Al-Qurum could see the anxiety etched in his old friend's face. 'Now, Sherpa, you have not come here to make small talk with your old friend. You look exhausted. Do you wish to rejoin your companions, take a rest, or get to the point and tell me why you're here?'

'I'd rather get to it, if that's okay by you? My first priority, though, is to arrange the repatriation of the body of one of our colleagues. A brave man, a warrior in the fight against international terrorism.'

'Ah, I see. This shall be done. Clearly you have a troubled mind. So do not spare me the details. You have my attention.'

A large pot of the finest Afghan green tea was brought in and put before them, and the two men settled into a long, intimate discourse.

***

The Cotswolds, 0730 hours; Al-Qurum, 1030 hours; Islamabad, 1230 hours

Kate Cross stirred from a deep sleep to the sound of the roar of a small multi-fuel stove and the smell of eggs on the simmer. The first thing of which she was conscious was that she no longer had a gag in her mouth, even though her legs and arms were still tied. The events of the previous evening came back to haunt her; her left nipple was very sore from the deep cut of the kukhri and served to remind her that she had given away the location of Dunstan's family all too quickly. She was still in the army sleeping bag, buffered from the hard, cold stone floor by a thick layer of straw. A single shaft of light penetrated the building and illuminated the small, stocky man dressed in camouflage clothing who was leaning over the stove. At the sound of her stirring, he looked across at her, put his finger to his lips and picked up his kukhri, drawing it across his throat in an explicit gesture which she could not fail to grasp. She looked around her and, though still petrified, tried to take stock of her surroundings. They were obviously in an old Cotswold barn with a set of doors some twenty feet high and with high, beamed ceilings. As this barn, unlike many others in the Cotswolds, had not been converted to a multi-million pound home, it was reasonable to assume it was still in use, and probably in the middle of a field.

As if reading her mind, the crouched figure looked up. 'No point shouting and screaming. This place very far from people.' His voice was very soft, giving a sense of natural good manners and consideration, which for Kate only served to heighten the surreal nature of her ordeal. She studied him carefully in the strong light that was shining full on his face. *He can't be any more than nineteen or in his early twenties*, she thought. 'Why are you doing this?' she asked at length.

'Eggs make very good breakfast. You eat. Stay strong.'

She looked across at him incredulously. 'I didn't mean the breakfast!' 'I know.' A spontaneous grin, then a pause and a more serious, melancholy, look. 'Orders,' he said, looking into the frying pan. 'What are you going to do with me?'

'I do not know.'

She felt tears welling up and struggled to maintain her composure. 'Who decides whether I live or die?'

'I cannot say. Not me.'

'The other men that were with you last night, do they decide?'

'You are alive now, so here, take some breakfast.' He passed his captive a British Army-issue mess tin containing bacon, eggs and two thick wedges of buttered bread. She was just going to ask him how she was going to eat it when he moved swiftly to where she lay and in a single, sweeping movement severed the bonds on her wrists with his kukhri. Kate was conscious of an almost feline agility and grace. *Like a mountain leopard*, she thought. *No point in trying to escape.*

As rough and ready as it was, breakfast had never tasted so good. As she was eating, her captor continued to cook. Another of her captors came in carrying a backpack radio transmitter. Older and much stockier than the first man, he also appeared much more taciturn and purposeful. He didn't acknowledge them, but connected the radio transmitter to a long whip aerial positioned at the barn door, then plugged the whole into the battery he had removed from the Land Rover. He seemed to spend an age setting the transmitter up and tuning it in.

Thoughts racing, Kate decided her best plan of action was to establish some empathy with the younger man. 'Are you in the British Army?' The older man looked up at her but said nothing.

'Yes and no,' the first replied. 'We are Nepalese.'

The older man was typing into a small keyboard plugged into the radio transceiver. The younger of the two looked across at him with obvious pride. 'He is my brother, was Sergeant in Gurkhas. Very strong! Good signaller!

Best with anti-tank weapon in British army! Me and my other brother, we are Nepalese guerrillas.'

The older brother silenced him with a look. It seemed as if he had established communication. The transceiver was a PRC319-01, a burst transmitter which can store messages for up to 500 hours before automatically transmitting them at a high data rate, making it many times more secure than conventional radios.

Older Brother put down the transceiver and spoke at length to his sibling in their native language. The latter nodded respectfully. Kate didn't like the tone and manner of the conversation. Trying not to panic, she asked, 'What is it? What did he say?' The younger man looked into her eyes.

'He says orders are that if we do not get what we want in next three days, you die.'

'Die? For God's sake, why?'

'You die if must. We all have a time to die.'

Kate slumped back into her sleeping bag. The whole thing was surreal, like the Pulp Fiction movie. It occurred to her she had forgotten to ask the obvious question.

'What is it that you want?'

Calmly and without emotion, the elder of her captors said, 'The life of your employer, Mister Dunstan.'

***

Al-Qurum, 1200 hours

Dunstan was finishing his conversation with his old friend. There was deep concern etched in the Emir's face. 'That's quite a story, Sherpa. I wish to help, of course, but I can't give you a blank cheque. I don't mean money, I mean that we have political sensitivities here in Al-Qurum to consider. There is a groundswell of fundamentalism which is threatening our social cohesion. Combine that with demands for a democratic constitution – which, by the way, I have a certain sympathy for – and you see that we tread a fine line between stability and total chaos, even the possibility of civil war. It's a delicate situation, and in such circumstances I cannot be seen to be entertaining British intelligence activity here on my own soil. And any activity that might be construed by Pakistan as an incursion into its sphere of operations is to be avoided at all costs. Anything we do, therefore, has to be carefully thought through with all diplomatic sensitivities taken into account.'

Dunstan said, 'Our key task is to track down the source of the money laundering operation, find the destination and purpose of the funds, and destroy those who are trying to wreck my life.'

Al-Qurum looked serious. 'This is between you and me alone. So for now, rejoin your friends. They are currently restricted to the one floor, but under your, ah, custody, they can stretch their legs around the hotel. As my personal guests, you will not, of course, be worried by such trivialities as expenses. Please advise your friends not to do anything that will put undue strain on our friendship and my ability to help. I will have my people make arrangements to repatriate the body of your fallen colleague. Now, take some rest. I shall consult with my advisors, Philip. Until this evening then, Salaam alaikum, my friend.'

***

Islamabad, 1400 hours

Across the Arabian Gulf, two new administrative assistants for the British High Commission were arriving in Pakistan. The immigration officer was impressed by their brand new diplomatic passports and their fluency in Urdu. They were fast-tracked through Immigration, the Customs inspection was uneventful and the High Commission driver was there to meet them on the other side of the barrier.

Chapter Thirteen

Dunstan had finished a long, hot bath when he was brought out of his reverie by a soft but insistent knock at the door. There was no security chain; he called out to hear a muffled female voice answer. Rebecca Lovat stood there clearly refreshed, dressed in a full length cream crepe abaya and scarf. 'Courtesy of our hosts,' she said as she glided into the room.

Startled for a moment at the elegant and fetching apparition before him, Dunstan recovered and put his fingers to his lips, signalling his concern at the possibility of the room being bugged. Rebecca gave him her best weary look. The problem with assuming a room is bugged is that the resultant dialogue seems contrived and faintly ridiculous. It's incredibly hard to be guarded and yet sound natural at the same time. 'I think I should phone mother, *Philip*.' The emphasis was quite deliberate and she obviously enjoyed making it. 'You know how she frets when we're away; safe arrival and all that.'

Lovat's mobile phone roamer picked up the local network. In Thames House, Elizabeth Hamilton had just sat down at her desk. She heard her encrypted mobile phone ring, picked it up and listened.

'Elizabeth, this is Rebecca. Could you let mother know we've arrived in Al-Qurum? Just booked into the hotel so we'll phone again later when we've had a chance to look around. Oh, could you tell mother that we *lost* Graham on the way? Permanently and irrevocably, I'm afraid, my dear!' 'Dear' was not in Lovat's lexicon and Hamilton knew it. Recognising the call for what it was, she immediately put in a call to 'mother'.

Down the hotel corridor, The Monk was happily playing I-spy, searching for listening devices. Satisfied there were none in the bathroom at least, he took the precaution of turning all the taps on full blast before placing a call back to the UK to an old colleague.

At 2000 hours, Dunstan received the call from the office of the First Minister. 'I am directed to inform you that His Excellency will receive you and your guests at ten o'clock tonight. Please be ready in reception at nine-forty to be picked up and escorted from your hotel.'

At 2140 hours precisely, their escorts arrived in the shape of two very large Arab men dressed in Armani suits. They were invited into the rear seats of a custom-made Mercedes 600 SEL, which, The Monk noted, was fully armour-plated. With escort vehicles front and rear, they were whisked through the busy streets of Al-Qurum in air-conditioned comfort, back to the bank. No one spoke, assuming that the car was wired.

At the bank, they were greeted respectfully but not enthusiastically by the male secretary to First Minister Thabet. For The Monk and Lovat, this would be their first chance to see this mythical friend of Dunstan's.

Seated in the opulent ante-room, they were served green tea and left to wait. The minutes ticked by, and then an hour. Even The Monk was beginning to fidget when finally, just before eleven o'clock, the door swung open and six men in full Arab regalia backed out of the inner room with a departing bow, then deftly swung round and glided past Dunstan and his team without acknowledgement. Finally, Abdul Thabet's secretary came out and gestured to Dunstan that he alone should enter the inner sanctum. The ornate hardwood doors closed behind him with a heavy *thunk*.

His Excellency, Sheikh Suroor Al-Qurum, was standing with his back to the door gazing out over his mini-kingdom. He turned and smiled at his friend. 'Sherpa! Come, my friend. Sit, please. You know, sometimes it is a source of great regret that I am not completely autocratic in my own Emirate! However, here we are affected by the politics of this region and indeed those of the wider world. By necessity, we have had long deliberations over your request and its wider political implications.'

Dunstan could see the tension in Al-Qurum's face. He could only assume that the discussions had been long and hard. He feared the worst. At the slightest of hand gestures, the role of speaker was handed over to Abdul Thabet who spoke with incisive authority.

'Mr Dunstan, I can tell you that in spite of the great friendship of our two countries and ongoing diplomatic co-operation, it was felt by some of His Excellency's advisors that for His Excellency to allow you to operate from here without having first gone through due diplomatic representation and appropriate clearances would be unwise. To sanction agents of a foreign nation to operate independently, and as it were, in a *freelance* capacity, could put His Excellency in a difficult position diplomatically. Furthermore, there is grave concern in most quarters that this situation in which you find yourself is concerned with the internal and international interests of a State with whom we have close diplomatic ties, namely Pakistan. You will understand, Mr Dunstan, that His Excellency cannot be put in a position which may compromise the delicate political and religious balance of his country.'

Al-Qurum had returned to looking out of the window. Thabet took the measure of the man in front of him. He was looking for any flaws in Dunstan's integrity, any slight chink that would suggest Dunstan was being disingenuous in his request for help.

After a long pause, he continued, 'His Excellency graciously acceded to give his advisors an account of the circumstances under which his life was saved over twenty years ago. This personal insight into His Excellency's time in the UK is, you will understand, unprecedented. It is clear that this country owes you a debt of gratitude for your actions in what were unimaginably difficult conditions. The Emirate of Al-Qurum will discharge that debt in full by helping you in your cause, although bounded by necessary political and practical constraints.'

Dunstan reflected that he had been naive to assume that his request for help to his old friend was nothing more than personal and unconditional. He was waking up fast to the diplomatically sensitive nature of his mission and its impact on pan-regional sensitivities.

'The Emirate of Al-Qurum will settle its debt to you as follows, no more and no less. You and your people will be given the use of one whole floor of this building, which will be sealed off from the rest of the bank. You will have separate computer and secure communications facilities – I believe *dedicated* is the correct terminology, is it not? You and your team will eat and work in these facilities and not move from the floor until your work is done. Is that acceptable to you?'

Dunstan felt as if he was standing with a begging bowl – but at least he was receiving some practical help. He nodded his assent and replied, 'It is.'

'There is just one other thing, Mr Dunstan. By virtue of our political constraints, communications in and out of your facility will be monitored. Any indiscretion that creates a potential embarrassment for the State of Al-

Qurum, or in particular, His Excellency personally, and your whole operation will be shut down immediately.'

Dunstan checked at this. 'With all due respect, First Minister, this whole affair has security implications for countries other than Al-Qurum. We are potentially looking at national and international security interests here. It would be most unfortunate if our sensitive information were to fall into the, ah, wrong hands.'

'Mr Dunstan. Those responsible for monitoring your communication will be trustworthy military personnel of this country, especially selected for the task by His Excellency's brother, the Chief of Al-Qurum Armed Forces.'

Dunstan saw that he had no option but to go along with the arrangement. 'The facilities will be ready for your use by tomorrow morning. As His Excellency commands, so it is done! Now, His Excellency has graciously indicated that he will meet with your colleagues.'

Sheikh Suroor Al-Qurum turned on his heel. His eyes settled on Dunstan, his face serious as though a mighty burden weighed heavily on his broad frame. Then a spark came into his eyes, and his whole face lit up. Smiling broadly, he declared, 'So, my friend, it is settled! My country is pleased to help. Now bring in your colleagues. I wish to meet them!'

The enigmatic smile on Dunstan's face told The Monk and Lovat there had been an outcome to his discussions behind closed doors. They followed Dunstan through the heavy, ornate entrance to the inner sanctum, to be greeted by a larger-than-life character whose presence filled the room. 'Welcome to my country. I am only sorry that you are here under such constrained circumstances. We will afford such help to you as we can give, and I am sure that under the inspired leadership of my old friend here, you will quickly get to the bottom of this whole affair. For now, I hope your accommodation is acceptable.'

He turned to Dunstan but extended his arm towards The Monk. 'Philip, I have been thinking about your friend here, Mr Monk! He has a strong interest and much experience in military matters of a *tactical* nature, is this not the case?'

The use of Dunstan's first name was not lost on the others in the room. 'Indeed he has, Your Excellency. Much *practical* experience,' Dunstan replied emphatically.

'Is he needed with you early tomorrow?' Al-Qurum gave The Monk the slightest of winks. 'First Minister!'

Abdul Thabet jumped to attention. 'Yes, Your Excellency?'

'I have decided to conduct a snap inspection of Scimitar Force tomorrow at 0600 hours. Operational inspection only, un-announced: no parades or formalities. If he is so willing, Mr Monk will accompany me to review our operational and training capabilities with the Chief of the Armed Forces. Please make the arrangements!'

'But Your Excellency... tomorrow is Friday!'

'That's rather the point. And we are not an Islamic State – yet! If you please, Abdul Thabet.' Al-Qurum's tone shifted ever so slightly to a harder edge. Abdul Thabet's blood rose. It wasn't just that this unexpected announcement fell outside his ability to control his Emir, he was also wondering why 'Mr Monk' was suddenly qualified to review his country's most secret and prestigious military unit.

'So that's settled!' Al-Qurum rose to signal that the meeting was over. He escorted them to the door to save them the embarrassment of observing royal protocol. Abdul Thabet stepped out to summon the head of Al-Qurum Armed Forces and put him on standby for the following day. As they exited into the ante-room, Sheikh Suroor Al-Qurum took hold of Dunstan's arm and eased him back into his office, closing the doors.

In the chairman's office, Al-Qurum led Dunstan by the arm and sat next to him on the sofa. He let out a huge sigh.

'Philip, I must apologise for these damned politicians and advisors. My father ruled as an autocrat and he made some terrible decisions, especially in giving away rights to our oil at ridiculous prices. I swore I would never do the same and so I hand-picked some of the best political and economic advisors that the Arab world has to offer, mostly Oxbridge or Harvard educated. They have accounted for themselves very well and served me and my people diligently. Without them, I could not have built such a modern economy and maintained political neutrality in respect of my neighbours around the Arabian Gulf.'

'You mean Pakistan?'

'Pakistan, of course; we have very close military training ties with their Special Forces. But also, I should let you know in confidence that we have cordial relationships with India.'

'If you've employed all these hotshots, then how did First Minister Thabet come to be where he is?'

'Ah, Abdul Thabet. He was in my father's Cabinet. He came as a young merchant from the Yemen some forty years ago. My father spotted his acumen and hired him as a commercial advisor. He also proved himself to be politically astute. For me, he is a useful bridge to the old school of Al-Qurumis. Every time I seek to modernise this country in some way, he translates my plans for the benefit of the traditionalists and religious fundamentalists. He is very good at smoothing the way.'

Suroor Al-Qurum's eyes were now sparkling again. 'I am looking forward to spending the day tomorrow in the company of one who served for over twenty years with – what do they call it now – "The Regiment"? It will be my honour! When all this is over, Philip, come back and we will spend some time together in the desert. Better than bloody cold mountains and far more beautiful, I assure you! My true friends are very few and I need all the true friendship I can get!'

Chapter Fourteen

Friday, 27th April: London, 0530 hours; Al-Qurum, 0830 hours; Islamabad, 1030 hours

Dunstan and Lovat were escorted in the armour-plated Mercedes from the hotel to the bank. Overnight, the floor had been miraculously converted into a fully-equipped operations centre by an army of contract workers: builders, to rearrange office partitions; electricians; network cabling specialists; communications and server engineers; computer, network and security experts; office layout and furnishing specialists. Mostly foreign contractors, it had been made clear to them that their continued presence in the Emirate was dependent on them completing the job by the morning.

Dunstan was in no mood for niceties. He had hardly slept and his usual courtesy deserted him. 'Let's get straight down to business, shall we?'

He was interrupted by raised voices from outside. Recognising a familiar voice, Dunstan went to the door and flung it open. A short, wiry, Lancastrian was remonstrating with the heavies on the threshold.

'Tysoe! What kept you?'

'Don't give me that shit, Philip. I've battled half-way round the world to get here, and now your goons won't let me in. Where's the coffee?'

'Nice to see you, too,' grinned Dunstan. 'Marc Tysoe, this is Rebecca Lovat, a friend of ours. Don't ask her what she does for a living. We'll probably find out in the next few hours.' Lovat shot him a glance which did not go unnoticed by Tysoe.

She addressed Tysoe. 'Now, Marc, I assume you haven't travelled here just for the coffee, so what have you brought with you?'

Tysoe grinned and with a distinct lack of ceremony threw a file of transaction log reports across the desk towards Lovat. 'I've profiled all the transactions and I reckon I've identified and recorded all, or most, of the fraudulent card transactions passed through CyberX. They break down into several specific blocks. What's more, they all have one very interesting characteristic. It looks as though the internet retailers used for the purchases are all false in themselves, spoof sites. They're all hosted by one of CyberX's licensed payment service providers in Eastern Europe and switched through our Prague settlement gateway.'

Tysoe looked across at Lovat who, he noticed with satisfaction, seemed more than comfortable with the terminology he was using.

'Shit, a closed loop!' exclaimed Dunstan. 'But why? Why not use the cards to purchase from any internet retailer?'

Tysoe gave him the answer. 'Because, Philip, they wanted cash, not goods; cash from the cardholder's account. The whole set-up was a simple mechanism that mimicked a normal cycle of payment card purchase, clearing and settlement. And it was made more legitimate by using the cover of an external clearing house, CyberX.'

Lovat nodded in agreement and outlined the scam to Dunstan. 'This was an automated computer operation. Stolen credit card details were automatically fed into false Internet merchants set up by the corrupt payment service provider, in collusion with a bank, and then processed through CyberX and out into the card scheme systems. The whole chain was corrupt. That's why it worked. It took a while for the cardholder or bank issuer to realise that the payment card had been used fraudulently, especially with the time difference across, say, the Atlantic or Pacific Time Zones. By that time, it was too late. Several transactions per card, small individual amounts in units of ten so they didn't attract too much attention, had already been processed through the system, and that card then ceased to be used for any further fraudulent transactions. Bingo.'

But Dunstan's mind was on how the fraud had continued to run at all. 'There must have been an acquiring bank for all of these spoof retailers. Who was that?'

Tysoe continued the logic. 'The very bank that appointed the payment bureau in the first place issued a block of legitimate online merchant IDs to legitimise the spoof retailer sites; a rogue bank, or more probably corrupt individuals within the bank. And don't forget the PSP was a fully licenced bureau, which meant that as soon as it was sub-licensed and issued with blocks of merchants it could act as its own payment acquirer; it didn't need a bank. To the outside world, it seemed a wholly legitimate operation. By using CyberX to clear and settle the payments, they remained one step removed from the operation. The stolen cards were mostly used one time only on the sites, before the fraudulent use was identified by the banks that had issued the cards in the first place. Any issuing banks around the world that didn't have the behavioural software in place to spot such a fraud may not have noticed at all. However, it's clear from the logs that certain card numbers continued to be used for days on end before they were pulled. It was an automated process – very creative, really.' Tysoe stopped with a self-satisfied grin.

'And CyberX provided all the international payment switching and settlement,' mused Dunstan aloud. 'Shit!' he said with feeling.

'Precisely!' responded Tysoe with equal feeling.

Lovat pressed her point. 'Until your man Idris Morgan switched off the processing part of the operation. Correct?'

'Correct,' confirmed Tysoe. 'I reckon, in his own peculiar way, Idris was protecting you, Philip.' He was about to mention that Dunstan had appointed the rogue PSP in the first place, but in a rare moment of diplomacy thought better of it.

Lovat sounded defeated as she continued, 'Which will make it almost impossible to trace the originating source of all the stolen card numbers. They're all long gone.'

Tysoe managed to keep the self-satisfaction out of his voice and the smirk off his face. 'Which is why I switched the processing back on in Bermuda.'

Lovat and Dunstan stared at him in anticipation. It was Lovat who blinked first. 'And?'

Tysoe allowed himself a grin. 'I had no idea whether or not they would start the fraud again, you would have thought they would be suspicious. But after six hours, there they were, in business again, switching transactions through CyberX. They may have been using someone else in the interim, or most likely they were using an automated process which kicked back in automatically, like. I just don't know. We should be able to get the latest profiles now, though.'

'You may have a job offer after this is all over,' replied Lovat with a degree of admiration.

Tysoe accessed one of the Bermuda servers and logged on securely to his financial controller's account at CyberX. Within a minute, they were viewing a steady trickle of payments derived from spoof web retailers switching across CyberX's networks.

'There we go. Fraud in action.' Tysoe pointed at the card numbers.

'Okay, so we can see them. But where are all these stolen cards from? How were they acquired – bought if you like – in the first place?' queried Dunstan.

'That's what we're going to see now,' smiled Lovat. 'You're about to find out how the black market in payment cards works!'

She typed a URL into the browser and a black screen with green writing came up. They were looking at an electronic black market in all things to do with card fraud, everything from cashpoint skimmers to chip and PIN readers. Lovat keyed in a customer number and password and was taken to another level of the site. There, buried deep within, were stolen credit and debit card numbers for sale.

'You've done this before, haven't you?' smiled Tysoe.

'Yes. It's what we do. Track financial fraud around the world for indications of terrorist-related activity and serious organised crime. Right, let's have some numbers. Let's see if there are any matches in bank identifiers or anything else. Quite often, one finds employees of banks offering legitimate card numbers up for sale in blocks.'

'Who runs these sites? Who are the market makers?' asked Dunstan.

'That's what we're trying to find out. Mostly organised crime syndicates: Russian, Bulgarian, Nigerian – no real pattern. We set ourselves up as trustworthy customers by making purchases from the sites in order to gain the criminals' trust and infiltrate deeper inside. We have quite a number of memberships.' It was clear that Lovat enjoyed her work.

Together they compared, correlated and cross-referenced. But there were no matches, let alone emerging patterns. Three hours later, with ten black-market sites trawled, they had got nowhere.

'Maybe they didn't purchase them from a known source?' volunteered Tysoe.

'That's a possibility. But this is a tightly controlled black market. You just don't get that volume of stolen card numbers being made available through a random newcomer. It takes years to set up the supply and distribution channels.' She paused, with a look as though a veil had been lifted.

'Oh, God, I wonder.' Lovat quickly typed "RedMarket" and was taken to another site.

'One you forgot about?' enquired Tysoe.

'In a way, yes. In this game of charades, all is not what it seems. This one is akin to an online broker, matching buyers with sellers. Now, give me the latest card number ranges!'

Tysoe and Lovat seemed to have entered a zone together, bound by a sense of common interest and purpose. Tysoe passed over the card range printout of the latest transactions.

Dunstan, meanwhile, seemed to be retreating into a mental zone of his own. Inside his mind, an insight was emerging and he didn't like where it was taking him – deep into his past.

'Wow! It's like bloody eBay!' exclaimed a gobsmacked Tysoe.

On the RedMarket site, they could all see instantly that the first four digits of the fraud card numbers matched those of certain ranges available for sale.

'Now let's see who purchased them in the first instance, shall we?'

The prospect of finding the source broke Dunstan's reverie. 'How the hell are you going to do that?' His eyes were now glued to the screen.

Lovat went to another screen and typed in a different user name and password.

Dunstan had now fully switched his brain into gear. 'Bloody hell! This is *your* site isn't it? You've spoofed the spoofers! You've created a card fraud site yourself, haven't you?'

'Not us, Philip, "friends" of ours across the water with whom we have a Special Relationship, capital S, capital R. And if you and Marc had the slightest doubt before, assume you are *now* covered by the Official Secrets Act. Period. Let's see if we can identify where these card details were stolen from in the first place, shall we?'

'How the hell do we do that?' enquired an incredulous Dunstan.

On her browser, Lovat typed in her username, password and a seventeen-digit number which synchronised with the site security server. The screen welcomed her, and she was in.

'Don't ask, because I won't tell you.' She pre-empted any awkward questions from Tysoe and Dunstan.

'Now give me some of those stolen card numbers!' She tapped them into the field in front of her and thousands of numbers ran across the screen as the high security super-computer at the heart of the system, deep underground somewhere in the environs of Cheltenham, cross-referenced her numbers. Within seconds, the term 'MATCH' appeared on the screen.

'Well, well. The plot thickens. The Lakeside Village fraud.'

'What's that?' asked Tysoe.

Lovat took a deep breath. 'About a year ago, a bunch of workmen in a Southern Utilities van, wearing bona-fide uniforms and ID badges, dug up the road outside one of the UK's biggest shopping malls and tapped into its main data communications pipe. Believe it or not, the credit and debit card transactions they captured were unencrypted. Tens of thousands of card details over a twelve-hour period were acquired before it was spotted. Audacious and extremely effective.'

'But surely if they were being brokered on this RedMarket site, you guys could have worked all this out a year ago?' an astute Tysoe observed, getting the hang of this murky world.

'You're right, of course. You've just witnessed a fundamental weakness in the global effort against terrorism: sharing of information between agencies still isn't comprehensive enough. We in the UK were not let onto the RedMarket site until six weeks ago, so cross-referencing has not been made with our UK fraud intelligence base. Furthermore, the agency which picked up the original laundering through CyberX is different to the one that created RedMarket. And so it goes on. Different boxes with separated compartments, unable or unwilling to communicate.'

Tysoe was finding this intriguing. 'So if one secret outfit had told another secret outfit what it knew, they could have worked out who was behind this in Eastern Europe ages ago and saved us all this grief?'

There was a considered pause from Lovat before she replied, 'Probably *not*, as a matter of fact. You see the destination of the card data redirected from the Lakeside Village fraud was nowhere near Eastern Europe. We know from the routing address discovered on the digital line tapper that the card details had all been redirected straight to *Pakistan*.' She paused for a moment and looked hard at Dunstan. 'It's as though the whole of the Eastern European operation was, and continues to be, a front for a Pakistani created and controlled fraud, which netted forty million plus. And if that was the case, then it seemed logical that CyberX had to be a fundamental part of the original master plan… embedded in its very fabric as the international switching and settlement service.'

She let her words hang as she reflected, *he wouldn't have created such a complicated front for his own nefarious purposes, let alone have his own secretary kidnapped as an elaborate cover up would he?… Would he?*

She buried the thought and continued on her line of deduction. 'And on that assumption, the reason for putting at least some of the stolen card numbers up for sale on RedMarket and buying them back utilising their *own* front operation was… what? For what purpose? To be discovered? Or not? It doesn't make sense.'

A sudden realisation hit her. *Perhaps at some point, the architects of this fraud wanted the Eastern European operation to be discovered. Or… they wanted CyberX to be discovered as being a key part of the fraud, or… set up to look like the perpetrator, as part of the original planning. That would make CyberX a target of this fraud from the outset, wouldn't it? But then why set up CyberX for a fall from the beginning? What's behind this? Who wanted CyberX to be destroyed? Or was it more personal than that? Was it Philip Dunstan himself they wished to destroy?*

Putting her deliberations aside for future reflection, Lovat navigated herself to the reports section of RedMarket. 'OK, let's see if we can run a sales report for some of these card details. Let's see if we can get a name for the end customer, the account holder, shall we?'

***

London, 0900 hours; Al-Qurum, 1200 hours; Islamabad, 1400 hours

The courier parked his red Toyota outside the Islamabad branch of the Commercial Bank of Pakistan, shook hands with the policeman on the door and slipped him sufficient rupees to ensure his car remained undisturbed. He looked right and left, opened the boot and took out two large and ancient saddlebags of a distinctive tribal design. After a final look around, he entered the building. Two young women dressed in full burkhas on the opposite side of the street to the bank observed his actions with well-disguised interest. After some forty minutes, he came out, thanked the policeman, put the saddlebags (now bulky and clearly a lot heavier) in the boot of the car, locked it and strode down the street to an electrical store. Twenty minutes later, he came back out, followed by a small boy carrying a large cardboard box. He himself carried a smaller box that was clearly heavier. The boxes went onto the back-seat and the courier drove off down the wide boulevard away from the centre of Islamabad.

Underneath the burkhas, the two young women were fully wired with micro headsets linked into transmitters strapped to their lower backs and connected to the 267 Squadron Signals Intelligence (SIGINT) team in the High Commission.

'It's Go, Go, Go. Tailing red Toyota saloon car heading north-east, repeat north-east, away from City Centre.'

The two jumped into their small, battered run-about and followed at a discreet distance. They could see the driver was checking for tails. He had obviously had some basic training. Very basic, as he saw nothing out of the ordinary. After a couple of miles, they entered a wide suburban boulevard and observed their target parked behind a newish Land Cruiser outside the drive of a smart suburban villa, which was concealed and protected by a stone wall and large, locked, wrought iron gates. The SRR team parked a few hundred metres down the road on the opposite side, at a sufficiently acute angle to see the courier step out of his car and be greeted by a tall handsome man emerging from the villa. *Probably in his mid-thirties*, Captain Dhar observed. The courier was deferential, indeed obsequious, towards the man, who was of uncommon bearing. With an air of authority, if not plain superiority, he indicated towards the boot of the courier's car before sliding his hand into his pocket to extract something.

If there is mystery surrounding the intelligence-gathering activities of 14 Int Company, 'the Det', and its parent unit, SRR, the next few moments were an example of the full application of their operational capability. The SRR soldiers knew this was their time to move, to apply all their training and operational experience into a single moment of calculated risk in order to grab the initiative.

Chattering animatedly to each other, they got out of their car. In the time it took for their target to pull his cellphone out of his pocket and place it to his ear, the two women were heading towards him, locked together in a babble of Urdu. As the pair passed the Toyota, Corporal Murria glanced at the back seat and clocked the contents: the larger of the two boxes had a white label on it, marked *Sony ICF-SW 12S Compact Travel World Band Receiver. Quantity 40*. It was still sealed.

Still with heads together and in animated conversation, shrouded in their full burkhas, Captain Dhar contrived to bump into the tall man. A swirl of confusion was created; Corporal Murria stumbled into the courier, triggering the hidden camera behind her veil as she did so. She got several full-face shots of both men. For a split second, Dhar found herself taken aback as she gazed into pale blue eyes and a long, handsome face capped with a mop of light brown, almost fair, hair. She covered her mouth and giggled before gathering herself to let the man move past her. As he did so, so she dropped her mobile phone on the ground at his feet. She swiftly bent down to pick it up, and in the blink of an eye, she had tagged a micro-thin listening device onto the hem of her target's shalwar. Simultaneously, Dhar pressed the toggle on her SIGINT mobile scanning device and captured the signal, and hence the number, of the Blackberry. There was an unseemly scrabble as her target, possessed of the natural good grace and manners of an impeccable upbringing, bent down to help her. In the middle of this distraction, Corporal Murria eased her back towards the Land Cruiser and slapped a magnetic tracking device under its rear nearside wheel arch. Less than ten seconds, job done.

For the urbane, handsome man, it was as close as he had got to female company in the last few months, and as he caught the slightest scent of perfume, he was knocked off balance for a moment. As the girls walked off giggling and chattering, he turned on his heels and, somewhat nonplussed, went inside to await his guests.

The SRR pair circled around the block, clocking and photographing villas and gardens to get a more complete understanding of the topography of the surrounding area. They completed a circular promenade and got back to their vehicle, heading off on a wide detour around Islamabad, all the while checking for a tail. Some thirty minutes later, Dhar decided to do a final sweep past the villa to see if anything had changed. As they sped along the suburban road with Murria behind the wheel, they observed a pick-up truck outside the house with two men unloading saddlebags. Murria eased her foot off the accelerator to a speed which still looked as though they were making reasonable progress. They noted the somewhat unusual tribal dress of the visitors and the fact that the saddlebags were of a similar design to the courier's. Dhar squeezed the high-speed shutter of the miniature camera inside her burkha several times, getting good shots of both the men in their distinctive tribal dress. The team then headed back towards the High Commission to send their report via the 267 SIGINT team to London. Captain Dhar drafted it as quickly as diligence and accuracy would allow and sent the encrypted document back to her two operational controllers, DSF and Celia Fanshawe.

***

Al-Qurum, 1230 hours

The Monk slid in silently, his black eyes taking everything in. Dressed in dust-covered desert combats with his remaining hair desert-blown he looked completely out of place in the hi-tech room. But he was a happy man; his dawn visit to Al-Qurum's Special Forces Scimitar Regiment had clearly been enjoyable and productive.

Dunstan, seeing the delight in his friend's face, laughed at this incongruous sight and made the introduction: 'Marc Tysoe, Finance Director, CyberX; The Monk, retired hairdresser,' said a grinning Dunstan. The two men shook hands, Tysoe feeling the hard, gnarled grip of the seasoned warrior.

The pleasantries of the introduction were broken by a beckoning Lovat. Her arm was waving, signalling them to come over to the screen. She peered intently, as if making sure the information before her was real.

'Here we go... account in the name of... well, what do you know, The Greater Himalayan Education Foundation. Sole mandate on the account: Ghol, Mr Anil Ghol.'

Her piercing violet eyes turned to Philip Dunstan at the window. 'Philip, does the name Ghol mean anything to you? Philip?... Philip?'

But she received no response. Dunstan was not with them. Although he appeared to be looking at the computer screen, he was a thousand miles and many years away, on a dusty, rocky mountainside in sub-zero temperatures, dug into a burrow, and camouflaged to make himself and his colleagues disappear. Or so they had assumed at the time.

Lovat searched Dunstan's face for clues; she found none, yet knew instinctively that for the first time in this investigation they were getting closer to the truth.

'No, I don't know an Anil Ghol,' replied Dunstan flatly, his thoughts still elsewhere, replaying scenes on an endless loop. His mind bounced around, trying to get a perspective and find the simple truth at the heart of this affair that would lead him to his tormentors.

He got a grip of himself and fired an apparently random question at Lovat. 'Is the protection still in place for my family?'

'As far as I know,' replied Lovat cautiously.

'Very reassuring,' Dunstan said, with more than a hint of sarcasm. 'I need it confirmed, ASAP. Can you do that?'

'On my next contact, I will confirm that for you, of course,' Lovat replied in a stilted fashion, concerned and curious at the change in Dunstan's mood. She wasn't the only one taken aback by the random nature of the question.

The Monk was direct. 'What is it?' he fired at Dunstan sharply, part concern, part interrogation.

But Dunstan didn't answer the question, he deflected it. 'We're missing something, Marc.'

'What?' asked Tysoe.

'*At least* fifteen million dollars, that's what we're missing! Probably more. This Greater Himalayan Education Foundation doesn't lead us to a financial end point, it's just a smokescreen. You said that forty million dollars had gone into this account. Abdul Shahid told me that by Idris' reckoning the total fraud was thirty-six million *pounds*. The median for the pound-to-dollar exchange rate over the last few years is at least one point six to the pound, probably higher, as it was nearly two dollars for part of the period. That's over fifty-five million dollars. So where's the rest? We're not at the source yet. We have no idea where the money is being directed to, and for what end. There have to be other clues here. Marc, we need a more comprehensive picture to get to the end destination. Let's find out what these bastards are really up to!'

The others didn't know it, but Dunstan was forcing practicalities to the front of his mind, creating his own smokescreen, until he could deal with the dark thoughts and memories stirring in his deepest recesses.

Chapter Fifteen

London, 1200 hours; Al-Qurum, 1500 hours; Islamabad, 1700 hours

Having sent their initial report back to the UK via 267 SIGINT team, the SRR soldiers had received new orders from the UK: they were to get as close in as possible to the villa, set up an Observation Post (OP) and maintain observation. They would send reports direct to the 267 team by Morse code via a series of 'clicks' on the pressel switch of their scramble transmitter. Wearing full black burkhas and carrying black cotton sacks under their voluminous clothing, they were dropped off three streets away and made their way to their proposed OP position via a circuitous route, all the while chattering to each other and turning their heads this way and that to make sure they were not being observed and that they didn't have a tail. They reached a road that ran parallel to the target villa, a full block away, and stood on the street for a while in animated conversation. Satisfied that the already quiet suburban street was fully clear, they calmly walked up the garden path of a house which they had spotted earlier that day on their previous recce, its shutters closed, with no sign of life. In the blink of an eye, they ducked into a large bougainvillea bush in the front garden. Covered by the bush and tucked in next to the high boundary wall, they pulled off their burkhas to reveal black combat overalls, black canvas jungle boots and camouflaged faces. Stashing their outer garments in the cotton sacks along with photographic equipment and handguns, they began a methodical crawl behind the bushes along the edge of the garden, stopping every four or five yards to control their breathing and listen intently. After some twenty minutes of slow, deliberate progress, they crossed over the rear boundary fence into the garden of a house diagonally opposite the villa.

Dhar and Murria settled in for what they assumed to be a long haul. They were perfectly at home; it was work they were used to – and highly skilled in – from their days of providing close observation support to Black Teams in Serbia and Bosnia Herzegovina: Special Forces teams who were tasked with hunting down and capturing Most Wanted war criminals. Deep inside a rhododendron bush, they set up their low-signature infrared cameras for night-time observation. Dhar was on camera duty observing the surroundings. Murria, the signals expert in the team, put on her headset to listen and record any communication relayed from the listening device attached to the tall man's shalwar.

***

London

Fanshawe had spent most of the night dealing with the aftermath of Freshfield's death, including personally organising diplomatic co-ordination for the repatriation of his body. Her challenge had been to keep it as 'low key' as possible, avoiding any media leakage from diplomatic circles, and she had needed to pull in quite a few favours in order to do so, on the promise of a full briefing in due course. She had spent the morning initiating an urgent selection process for a new Head of UK Counter-Terrorism, a post she herself was filling until a suitable candidate could be found. She was now awaiting the first reports from Lovat and SIGINT in Pakistan. The adrenaline that had carried her through the night had now subsided. With no tangible progress and the loss of a key man, a potential successor to her at that, Fanshawe was feeling, and looking, drawn and dispirited. The loss of her Head of Counter-Terrorism had rocked her and for the first time in her career she found herself questioning her own professional judgement. Her bloom had all but gone and stress and tiredness were etched in every heightened line and wrinkle on her face.

Fleming knocked and entered her office, holding a buff file containing the decrypted transcripts of Dhar's report. He could hardly contain his excitement; beneath the shaggy mop of hair, his face wore a crazed expression that exceeded even his normally eccentric look as he said, 'I think we're onto something!'

Fanshawe took the transcripts and scanned them. Her eyebrows lifted as did her morale, momentarily. From the first glance, she *knew* they were onto something, although she would need some specialist interpretation. She screwed up her face at a couple of passages, marking them up for questionable accuracy, and immediately called an analysts' meeting. Just as the reports landed on her desk in London, Detective Chief Inspector Beckwith and Detective Sergeant Lowe were attending the scene of a macabre murder in a field near Fifield on the Oxfordshire-Gloucestershire border.

Celia Fanshawe sat in silence for several minutes, uncharacteristically wavering on her next course of action. Decided, she sent a text from her encrypted mobile to Lovat: >>>*Plse be on standby for SITREP posted to your account at Thames Portal within hour.* >>> Within a minute, Fanshawe received the response: >>>*Acknowledged. Flash: authority name on G.H.E.F account is Ghol. Anil Ghol. Do we know him?* >>>

***

Room 768 in Thames House felt depleted without Freshfield and Lovat. A minute's silence was held for Graham Freshfield, followed by a long and reflective pause as refreshments were poured. His death had affected all of them. They conducted a full review of the content of the reports from Captain Dhar.

Elizabeth Hamilton still had her nose in the transcript, paying very close attention to the photographs, some of which were clear portrait shots of the men outside the villa, in particular the taller man who was now designated 'Target One'. She had ordered close-up images of the saddlebags, tribal dress and – of particular interest to her – Target One's features. While the others had been talking, she had made a couple of general searches on her web browser. Satisfied with her deliberations and conclusion, she went straight to her point.

'I think we've been barking up the wrong tree!'

Her outburst caused a momentary pause as the others looked at her in anticipation.

'Nothing would surprise me,' observed Fanshawe drily. '*Which* tree have we *not* been barking up?'

'I reckon this laundering operation has nothing to do with Al-Qaeda Core, or what we might call established Islamic terrorist movements.'

The other two stared at Hamilton. 'Explain,' Fanshawe commanded. 'There are several things at work here. Each one taken on its own merit doesn't mean much but, taken together, an interesting picture emerges. Firstly, the unusual saddlebags, made of rough goat hair and leather. Secondly, the distinctive appearance of Target One. Thirdly, the appearance of the men who visited what we assume to be Target One's house, especially the description of their relatively flamboyant tribal clothing. Lastly, the probable name of Target One: "Ghol".'

Fanshawe nodded. 'I was curious about Ghol's appearance – fairish hair and blue eyes. Either the SRR women are mistaken or he isn't Pakistani.'

'Oh, he's Pakistani all right, ma'am; he's one of Alexander's Children. A living product of an ancient myth.' Hamilton's voice was soft but assured. She stared almost absently into the pages of the report.

Fanshawe was beginning to lose patience. 'Elizabeth, you're talking in riddles. What on *earth* do you mean?'

Elizabeth Hamilton took a deep breath. 'In three-two-five BC, Alexander the Great's army passed through northern Pakistan on its way to India. The myth is that as a result of those, er, interactions, certain Northern Tribes have a significant percentage of their population with blue eyes and light, even positively fair hair. Two tribes in particular, the Kalash and the Balti, have significant numbers, but the characteristics have been observed in Hunza and also in sub-divisions of Chitral. The saddlebags here in the photos are of Chitrali design. And the photographs of Target One's visitors show them as Ismaili and Hunza. The name Ghol appears to be of Kashmiri origin, but of course there are many tribes within Kashmir. My strong submission is that we are dealing with money being directed to one or several of the Northern Tribes.'

'Which, according to your theory, have nothing to do with Al-Qaeda?' Fanshawe enquired.

'No, ma'am. Quite the contrary.'

'So for what purpose, then, are these funds being directed? What are these people up to?'

'My theory is that there's both a political and a practical purpose. To unravel what might be happening here, we have to understand the background and political standing of the northern territories of Pakistan, called the Northern Areas from the partition of India up to last year, when their name was changed to the Gilgit-Baltistan Region.

'Go on,' said Fanshawe. Although conscious of time, she was nevertheless intrigued.

Hamilton settled herself and pushed on. 'Politically, the Northern Tribes are in a no-man's land. This area, which borders on India, China and Afghanistan, is of enduring strategic concern to India, Pakistan, China and the US. India claims the whole region as Indian Territory, firstly, because it views the 1947 Pakistani occupation as illegal. Secondly, this area, particularly Baltistan, has close ethnic, religious and cultural links with the Ladakh region of *Indian* Jammu and Kashmir of which it used to be a part before the Pakistani occupation. Thirdly, the Shias and the Ismailis of the area, who constitute the majority, have close fraternal links with the Shias of the Kargil area of Ladakh, and look up to India and its Shias for moral support in their struggle against the Pakistani authorities.'

'What struggle?' Fanshawe had not wanted a lesson in regional politics but she was fascinated by Hamilton's reasoning. 'Fleming, get a regional map in here so we know where we are!?' Fanshawe had lightened her mood; her intuition told her they were onto something.

The map arrived and they gathered round it. 'Elizabeth, please go on.' Hamilton, standing in front of the map, continued: 'This area is strategically vital to Pakistan because the river waters that flow from it sustain agriculture in the Punjab, the bread basket of Pakistan. The Karakoram Highway from the Xinjiang province of China – constructed with Chinese help in the sixties and seventies – is of tremendous strategic significance, not least for the clandestine transport of nuclear and other military material, missiles and missile parts, from North Korea and China to Pakistan. The mountain heights in this area provide vantage points in any Pakistani attempt to cut off Ladakh from the rest of Jammu and Kashmir, and the Shias of this area have always proved to be a thorn in Pakistan's flesh.

'It's important to China because the Karakoram Highway helps maintain Pakistani military strength in its power struggle with India, which has always been an important Chinese strategic objective. The Chinese also want to monitor the potential impact of the growth of Wahabi extremism in this area on the Islamic Uighur nationalists and nascent jihadi terrorist groups in Xinjiang province. The USA keeps a close a watch on the Chinese nuclear establishment located in the province.

'Our "Friends" are also attempting to recruit local Northern Territory tribal leaders as ground-based assets in their attempts to have the remnants of Al-Qaeda and The Taliban leadership smoked out.

'And your conclusion...?' interrupted Fanshawe.

'It's the last point, I reckon, that could just give a clue to what all this is about. The Northern Tribes hate the Taliban. They've already imposed their medieval creed on South and North Waziristan, almost next to the Northern Areas. Boys are being butchered for refusing to join and the locals are now arming themselves to fight back against so-called Talibanisation.'

'What an awful word!' Fanshawe reacted badly to any 'bastardisation' of the English language. 'So, South Waziristan and the Swat Valley today, these Northern Areas tomorrow. Are you suggesting that this money is being directed to arm the Northern Tribes in a struggle against the Taliban and Al-Qaeda?'

'Er, no, not quite, ma'am. I think it's much bigger than that.'

'Bigger!' Fanshawe was by now wondering how much 'bigger' this could get. 'How, exactly?'

'My belief is that they could be looking to take matters into their own hands, create a *de facto* autonomous state. What will that mean in practice?' Hamilton answered her own question. 'Instability on a vast scale. At the moment, as far as major regional powers are concerned, a delicate but pragmatic balance exists. A push by the Northern Tribes for autonomy potentially creates a stand-off, or worse, between India, Pakistan and China. Even a limited regional war between three nuclear powers is an unattractive option in terms of where it might lead. It could be cataclysmic.'

'Not in the least bit attractive,' agreed Fanshawe, with a studied understatement that served to underline the seriousness of the emerging scenario. 'And not in the UK's long-term interests either. So if this is the likeliest scenario, we need to cut this venture off in its prime. Elizabeth, please prepare a synopsis of what we know, and your best assessment, for Lovat. And I need it within the hour.'

Fanshawe was keen to push on and rose to leave before stalling in mid-stride. 'I almost forgot! What do we make of these short-wave radios on the back seat of the courier's car? How many were there? Fleming?'

'Forty, according to the description. As to their use, I think the answer to that one is obvious, ma'am.'

'Don't be sanctimonious, Fleming!'

'But it *is* obvious, ma'am! At least, it *should* be, to us of all people; it must be a number station with forty recipients.'

Fanshawe looked at the ceiling in sudden realisation. 'Forty stations, forty tribal areas?' she surmised.

Fleming continued for Elizabeth Hamilton's benefit and the enjoyment of the sound of his own voice. 'Short-wave radio is a classic medium for transmitting coded messages. There are two well-tried-and-tested cryptological techniques. The first is the one-time pad system. In this system, both the sender and recipient have copies of a code pad. The code pad will have several columns of numbers entered at random. The received numbers are added or subtracted from the numbers on the sheet of the pad being used, and the results are compared to a master code key list. Each number block will usually represent a complete word or phrase, rather than a sequence of characters. After each page in a one-time pad is used, it's torn from the pad and destroyed. While the one-time method sounds crude, messages sent using it are unbreakable – so long as a copy of the current pad doesn't fall into enemy hands.

'The other system uses a book known only to the sender and recipient for encoding and decoding. The first three digits represent the page number, while the last two digits are the position of a certain word on the page, usually counting from the upper left corner of the page. This method has the advantage of eliminating the risk of delivering one-time pads to agents. The big disadvantage has traditionally been a lengthy, slow encoding process, although computers can now handle this easily and quickly. Instructions are simply sent over the radio "in clear" to be decoded by the recipient.'

'So what does all that mean as far as this threat goes?' asked Hamilton keenly.

Fanshawe smiled inwardly, seeing something of herself in this sharp young woman.

'The upshot,' said Fleming, 'is that it's impossible to intercept and penetrate the communications of this group without access to the book or code pad. Our only hope is for the SRR team to track them to their purpose or objective, whatever that might be.'

A pensive Celia Fanshawe thanked them, got up and went back to her office. As she played back over the meeting her initial reaction was one of relief; there was no prima-facie international terrorist threat to the UK. Beyond that? Her brow furrowed. The implications went far beyond her department and the remit of her service. She made a list of all the agencies and government departments that *should* receive copy of this and subsequent reports, including some very senior civil servants. She stopped when the list hit twenty.

Her pen trailed off. Hamilton entered her office, unannounced, carrying a folder. Fanshawe looked up, about to ask her to come back later, when she saw the look on her face. Whatever was in the envelope, it was clear that Hamilton was much affected by the contents.

'You need to see this, ma'am.' Her voice trembled as she slid a digitally enhanced photograph across the table.

'Good grief!' Even Fanshawe was shocked. She scanned her eyes over the photograph, taking in all the appalling details, then, keeping an even voice, she said, 'You'll need to add this to the report to Lovat. Please let me see the final draft before it goes, Elizabeth.'

Hamilton turned and left. Fanshawe put the contents of the envelope to the back of her mind and took stock. *The threat is demonstrably real and tangible but where is the hard intelligence, let alone any evidence? Is it only immediate action that will serve our purposes here? Can I even contemplate it? Do I have a choice? What's the alternative? Committee meetings will fudge the issues; too many vested interests, not enough time... I can't possibly let this go to the Inter-Service Committee.*

Having come to a decision, she looked at the list of names on the paper in front of her and put a fresh pencil line through each of them in turn. She then made out a new list of only three names.

Fanshawe's first telephone call was to Major General Gibbs.

'Celia Fanshawe here, General. I have to say your SRR team are doing a great job.'

DSF concurred: 'Having seen their report, I have to agree with you. It looks interesting, doesn't it? Any thoughts from your people as to what it all means?'

'You'll have our analysis in your inbox in the next few minutes. Meanwhile, is it possible to get a small team of your people, the armed variety, into Pakistan in the next twenty-four hours?'

'Officially? No chance!' Gibbs sounded emphatic but Fanshawe interpreted his direct response as being by no means unequivocal.

'And unofficially?'

'Unofficially, there is a small but useful military presence already on the ground, although engaged on purely humanitarian matters at the moment, and definitely unarmed.'

'General, I need to brief you as a matter of urgency. Sandwiches? Over here in my office? I gather the ham is particularly good today.'

It was an offer he couldn't refuse. Gibbs pushed his chair back and called for his driver.

Chapter Sixteen

Al-Qurum, 1500 hours

The Monk could see Dunstan was growing impatient. Tysoe had been trying to access the archived transaction reports in the CyberX Prague gateway for the past three hours without success. Ironically, for purposes of security, CyberX's archived transaction records were not held in a central location at HQ in Oxford but distributed across their computer network, like a mini worldwide web. Tysoe couldn't access the Prague gateway, where the fraudulent transactions had been processed, from his cloned system in Bermuda. He was locked out of his own system. Dunstan had stopped him contacting Prague, just in case there had been collusion from staff there. 'Look, Philip, I'm getting nowhere here. Why can't we just bloody well contact Miro and ask him to get access to these records?' Miro Marak was CyberX's general manager in Prague.

Dunstan thought of the risk. He looked at his watch – it was late morning there. Risk evaluated, decision made, he picked up Tysoe's mobile phone and dialled the Prague office himself.

'Philip Dunstan here. Marie, I need to speak to Miro, please... What? He's what?... When? How?... Christ! The police are there? Does Oxford know? I'll get a rep from Oxford over to you immediately...Henry Stanton's on his way? Okay, he's a solid pair of hands in a crisis. Tell him to engage the best local criminal lawyer and security advisers. Please convey my sincere condolences to his family. I'll be in touch with them, and my best wishes to all the staff...best wishes; and take care!'

'Jesus!' Dunstan was shaken.

'No need to guess what's happened,' volunteered The Monk. 'How did it happen, though?'

Dunstan replied, 'Two guys came to see Miro this morning. They threw him out of his bloody office window! Three floors up. Correction: *through* the window!'

'A bit extreme,' observed Lovat drily. 'Ah, that figures,' replied The Monk.

'What do you mean, "that figures"?' enquired Dunstan, wondering if The Monk had some inside knowledge.

'Defenestration: a form of ritual murder or execution used in Czech territories in medieval times to get rid of enemies and send a message to others. Your man Miro wasn't just murdered, he was fucking well executed! And somebody is sending a message to you, Sherpa. They're keeping up the psychological pressure on you, and you can bet it will continue.'

The Monk's words hung over the team. No one could think of anything to say. Dunstan simply stared out of the window with his back to everyone, wrestling, as if trying to slot this piece of the jigsaw into a non-existent picture. It was the ever-practical Tysoe who came to the rescue and pulled them together. 'Come to think of it, I'm sure Miro used our Melbourne archive servers to back up transactions. I thought I heard Idris mention it. We can get in through the back door. Philip, you've got the super-administrator passwords, haven't you?'

Dunstan forced upon himself a huge mental and emotional effort to recover from this latest blow. With an iron will, he focused his mind on the present, swivelling on his heels to face the others. 'Of course! You're right! We should be able to get in via the back door. I have the rights and privileges for Melbourne. Here, let me get you in!'

Dunstan pulled Tysoe away from his computer and within seconds was typing in a series of IP addresses and passwords. 'There we go, we're into the Melbourne data centre. Now all you need to do, Marc, is to fire the Prague back-up and find the missing bloody millions! Just make it quick!'

'Thanks, boss,' Tysoe grinned. Relishing the task ahead, he started running transaction reports.

The Monk winked at Lovat, put his arm around Dunstan's shoulders and forcefully eased him into the briefing room, a soundproof room behind a solid glass wall.

Once inside, The Monk looked strangely at his friend. He poured each of them a strong black Mocha coffee, imported direct from Mocha itself in neighbouring Yemen, and eyeballed his friend across the table, as though trying to access Dunstan's innermost thoughts.

'Look, Sherpa, I've put some contingency plans into place to cover the UK end. I managed to place a call to the UK to some old mates.'

'With what in mind?' asked Dunstan.

'To look after your family, of course! Because, frankly, I don't trust any of the other fuckers.'

Dunstan's shoulders tensed, then he visibly relaxed. *Know who your friends are*, Faith had said. Dunstan didn't enquire of The Monk which 'other fuckers' he meant; *he obviously meant all of them.*

The Monk filled him in. 'I remembered that when two of the lads retired from the Regiment they used their savings to set themselves up in business photographing electricity power lines from the air for possible defects and physical damage. All from the comfort of a chopper.'

'I'd often wondered what those helicopters were doing following power lines up and down the countryside,' responded a curious Dunstan.

'Well, now you know. Hopefully, by now, these guys will be diverting from their normal path to find that bastard ex-military Land Rover that upset our equi-fuckin'-librium.'

'Bit of a long shot, isn't it?'

'Look: those guys in the Land Rover are taking orders from someone. If they're the ones that have kidnapped your secretary, they're most likely to still be in or around Oxfordshire, hull-down in a wood or some old buildings somewhere. My guys have the capabilities to spot and photograph a mouse's arsehole from three thousand feet.'

'And when they do find them?'

'Depends if they still have Kate with them, doesn't it?' The Monk was staring into his coffee.

'How will we know that?'

'That also depends...' He let the notion hang in the air. 'Now, on an entirely different subject...' The Monk leaned conspiratorially across the desk. Pointing to imaginary hidden mics, he said in an almost inaudible whisper. 'My visit to your mate's Special Forces outfit, Scimitar Regiment, was more than useful. It wasn't just a bloody Cook's Tour; your old chum has put a whole bloody troop at your disposal along with a couple of Talons, support kit and, get this – a Spectre Gunship!' The Monk's eyes lit up as though he had spent the morning since dawn pressing his nose to the window of his favourite big boys' toy shop.

A sudden realisation came over Dunstan. 'But to get that lot organised for your dawn visit this morning, he must have started preparations *before* his meeting with his advisors last night and the so-called "final decision" to help us, isn't that right?' he whispered.

'Exactly.' The Monk's black eyes were shining. 'Switched-on cookie, your old mate. And I reckon that's why he didn't want that snake-in-the-grass Thabet or any of his staff on the trip this morning. And why he didn't fully brief Thabet before we arrived. Remember the old goat was clueless?' There was a shout of triumph from the main computer room. They looked out to see Tysoe on his feet with his thumbs up and Lovat peering intently at Tysoe's screen. Dunstan leapt out of the briefing room. 'What have you got, Marc?'

'A series of payments into two separate accounts, totalling over seven million dollars. The first, a total of three million dollars in four equal tranches, mandated from the PSP Bureau, settled on an account with a Lichtenstein bank. The second, of four million, paid in a load of ad hoc tranches on a similar mandate from the PSP into a London private bank, Cavendish and Company, one of the older independent ones, I believe.'

'Names?' asked Dunstan.

'Er, the first… is Ishfaq Mohammed Khan who got the three million; the other, Shafquat Iqbal Khan.'

'Brothers, cousins, unrelated?' asked Dunstan rhetorically. The question hung in the air.

Lovat, the investigator, was on a different tack.

'Why, I wonder, did the first guy get very specific tranches of money and the second didn't? It's like the first guy received his money as a result of a prior agreement or arrangement for services, and the second guy…?'

'Operational expenses, or big fuck-off reward for successful performance.' The Monk was already there, 'What's the betting this Shafquat Khan wallah is pulling the strings on making your life a misery, Philip? Not to mention blowing up my Welsh hidey-hole!'

No one in the room disagreed with The Monk's insight. Dunstan, though, wanted immediate tangible results.

'Rebecca, run these names through Google and see what you get.'

Lovat's fingers flew across the keyboard. 'Shafquat Iqbal Khan: Pakistani political journalist. That's it. Nothing else. The next one, what's his name…? Ishfaq Mohammed Khan. Well, you have a choice here: top Pakistani cricketer, a bit of a mean leg spinner; or the head of the Pakistan Institute of Nuclear Physics? Which one would you prefer?'

'Nuclear!' exclaimed Dunstan.

Lovat was just about to say something when her open laptop beeped and let her know audibly that she had a 'message on the dark side'.

'It should be "from the dark side",' said Tysoe, in geek mode.

'No, Marc. It's *on* the dark side. I have to travel there to pick it up. It'll be from mother.' Her eyes flashed as she grinned at him mischievously. Tysoe actually blushed.

She logged into the Thames Portal which took her through a series of passwords and questions before she reached another login sequence in the middle of a blank screen. She took out a small security token, punched in her password and proceeded to enter swiftly the seventeen-digit number sequence on the small screen, which was synchronised with the main security server in London. A 'welcome' sign with her name told her she was through. The message was encrypted and she had to run a decryption using a private client security key. Lovat scanned the email. The only emotion she registered was a series of rapid blinks.

'What is it?' Dunstan picked up the vibes.

She hesitated. Her body went rigid as she reread the message. She considered changing the order of the news that she knew clearly she had to deliver to Dunstan. She pondered for a moment and then realised that, given the nature of the news contained in the three points, the meticulous Celia Fanshawe would have given the order of precedence serious consideration. *How the hell was she going to deliver this news to Dunstan?* Her inner voice responded and commanded her: *professionally and with a straight bat.*

'There are three key points of, er, interest,' she started. 'First, from ground-based intelligence reports and photographs, the research analysts believe we are *not* dealing with Al-Qaeda Core, but something quite different. The nature of the intelligence indicates a *possible* drive for autonomy or independence by elements of the Northern Territories: it says here Chitral, Baltistan and possibly Hunza.'

'The old Kashmir,' interjected Dunstan. 'What are these guys up to?'

'We can speculate all we like, Sherpa, but that's not going to get us any closer to the target,' observed The Monk.

'True,' responded Lovat. 'We'll get the analysts in London working on these two Khan characters' backgrounds shortly. Our ground-based operations are, I understand, well placed to gather more intelligence.'

'And how are your *operations* going to glean this intelligence, short of *bugging* the target on Pakistani soil?' asked Dunstan, sarcastically.

Lovat's eyes burned. 'Out of all of us in this room, *you* should be best placed to know the capabilities of our operations team, Dunstan. They are, after all, members of one of your old units!' she shot back.

'Bloody hell! You've actually dropped a couple of Det guys in there? Who the hell gained the authority to do that?'

'Not guys – women, Dunstan. And though you don't know it yet, Mr Philip Dunstan, you have the remote support of a far-reaching mind with the power and influence to deploy such resources. Call it enlightened self-interest if you like, but that support is working behind the scenes to try and sort out what the hell is happening here. To our mutual benefit! Now look, Philip,' Lovat paused as her tone softened considerably, 'there's more in this email that you need to know.'

'And what might that be?'

There was no easy way for Lovat play it. *A straight bat.* 'It's your secretary, Kate Cross.' A pause. 'She's dead.'

Dunstan's hands gripped the back of the chair until his knuckles went white. He rocked slightly backwards and forwards for a while, not saying anything, absorbing the news. Then his voice rasped, 'How?'

'At the moment, we don't know *how* exactly. An autopsy has yet to be done.'

Waves of guilt and loss shook Dunstan. He stood without moving, rock rigid, staring into space. The Monk, concerned, eased himself towards Dunstan, watching him intently.

Lovat knew that she had to engage with Dunstan and press him. 'I have to ask you. Does the date 2001 mean anything to you?'

'No! Why the hell should it?' The veins in Dunstan's neck and forehead looked as if they were about to burst; his whole body was wire-taut, fists clenched, knuckles bared white almost popping through his skin.

'Because...' Lovat paused, but there was only one way to say it. 'The number, or date, "2001" had been carved on her chest.'

Nobody in the room could have predicted Dunstan's reaction to the news. With a primal scream of anger he picked up the chair he was gripping, swung it through a hundred-and-eighty degrees and launched it straight through the plate glass window of the briefing room behind him. The Monk, moving quickly to save Dunstan from himself, seized his friend in a vice-like grip from behind; Dunstan stood shaking with anger and hurt. The sentries came rushing in but just stood there, bemused at the scene in front of them. The Monk spoke to them harshly in Arabic and they quickly disappeared.

There was silence as the team watched and waited. Lovat broke it. In a soft voice she said, 'Philip. We have work to do. We have to find the source.' She took an intuitive leap. 'Philip, what is it? What is it about this man Ghol? You know him don't you?'

But still Dunstan didn't answer, he just continued to stare into space. For a full half-minute he was motionless, perspiration dripping from his forehead in spite of the air conditioning. Lovat's determination to get to the truth was tempered by the sight of Dunstan's efforts to come to terms with whatever he was struggling with in the recesses of his mind. 'Come on, Philip, it's now or never. This is personal isn't it? All this: Ghol, Kate Cross, the fraud, Idris Morgan... it's all linked back to you, isn't it? Am I right, or *am I right!?*'

The Monk eased his grip; he knew instinctively that Lovat was getting through to his friend.

The words when they came sounded painful for Dunstan to form. 'I know his name... but I don't know *him*.'

'This *is* personal then?'

'Yes, possibly *very* personal.' He paused again, still with his focus in the far distance. Part here, part not, part way-out-there.

He paused again and swallowed hard, his voice low and rasping, seemingly struggling with the consequences of past actions.

'Before I set up CyberX, I thought I would have one last military adventure. Nine-eleven had just happened. The intelligence services were struggling to get meaningful ground intelligence as they had no ground-based assets, just lots of satellites orbiting. But that doesn't replace hard won Intelligence from human assets buried deep in target organisations, in this case from within Al-Qaeda. Running informers deep within terrorist organisations went out of favour in the mid-Nineties. Huge mistake! The

US administration at the time had become pretty squeamish. They're not squeamish now, I can assure you! The next best thing then was to get ground-based intelligence from close-quarter observation. It had to be covert and probably deniable. There weren't many guys around who had sat for weeks on end in hedgerows and on mountains, observing comings and goings and gathering intelligence in a particular form of use to the security services.

'I was approached by an old friend of mine from the Det, by then employed by the Foreign Office. He was putting together a small team to conduct deep reconnaissance of possible Al-Qaeda strongholds and points-of-presence. It was a great opportunity to use old skills. And the pay was obscene.'

'Afghanistan,' The Monk said flatly.

'Yes, Monk, Afghanistan. We were in the south-east. Close to the Wakan Corridor, down near the Pakistani border. We were there for weeks, on hard rations, crapping into sealable bags, usual SOPs. Intelligence gathering, just observing local activity and sending short-burst encrypted reports back to the UK.'

'So what happened, Philip? Who did you upset?' Tysoe had found his voice at last. As Dunstan turned his face towards him, Tysoe saw a very different man to the one he had known as a close working colleague. What he saw unnerved him.

'Upset? Let me tell you the story and then see if "upset" is the right word.' Dunstan took a long draught of water, as though steadying himself. 'I infiltrated with two other guys over the border from Pakistan, if infiltrated is the right description. More like we wandered for a hundred or so miles at night-time in local garb over mountain tracks with a guide. We went hull-down during the day and moved fast at night. It was hard going as we struggled to get acclimatised over seventeen-thousand-foot passes. Eventually, we dug in on the side of a mountain, on the north side of a pass at about eight thousand feet, away from any tracks. Stunning views, stunning country. And we were pretty happy there. Until...' Again the thousand-mile stare.

'Until?' prompted Rebecca Lovat.

'Until, well, we were rumbled. Just like the Bravo Two Zero SAS patrol in the First Gulf War. Although this wasn't a young goat herd but three lads in their twenties, cousins as I later found out. Two Afghanis and a

Pakistani national, a Kashmiri in fact. They claimed to be on a hunting trip for mountain sheep and had left the network of paths to walk over the mountain behind us. They were only young lads really, armed with old Lee Enfield rifles, which in my mind at least supported their "out hunting" story.

'We were compromised and we had no choice but to disarm them and capture them. We ordered a quick exfil from a US Special Forces flight out of Pakistan. I thought we would let them go, but our American team had different orders and they were bundled onto the same flight with us.' Dunstan stopped and stared into space again before continuing 'The younger one thought they were fine because we had landed back in Islamabad, his own country. I'll never forget the look of bewilderment, fear and betrayal on his face as he was taken off-limits by the Americans. When we asked, he said his name Abdul Sher Ghol.

Dunstan exhaled sharply, reliving the memory that was forever burned into his mind.

'Then what happened?' Lovat pushed him on again.

'We came back to the UK and with the money I had saved, I started CyberX.'

'To the captives, not you!' The Monk was quite sharp, seeking the truth. 'I don't know. Not the whole story. That's what I've wondered on many occasions since.' He took a deep breath and exhaled before continuing. 'I learned about a year later from my Foreign Office recruiter that the three young lads had been er, rendered. Rendered all over the fucking place: Morocco, Rumania and God-knows-where. Rendered... eight letters representing so much suffering. Two of them were by that time in Guantanamo. They were the Afghanis. Made of tough stuff, I gather. The other, the young Kashmiri Abdul Ghol – nobody knew where he was. I asked my old Det friend to find out but either he couldn't or wouldn't; most likely he was disinclined to. I saw him in the Special Forces Club in Knightsbridge about a year later. He *advised* me not to pursue my own personal enquiries. That's all I know, period. No more, no less.' Dunstan sat down and slumped in a chair, visibly shaken by his own rendition.

The silence hung like a pall in the room. Eventually, Tysoe spoke. 'Philip, if this is retribution by the Ghol family, then, well, call me naive, but how did they know it was you?'

It was Rebecca Lovat who provided a possible answer. 'Probably the ISI. The Pakistani intelligence services. There are many factions within it who serve different masters. That's all you need to know, Marc.'

The Monk got to the point. 'On the basic assumption that this young lad you captured didn't survive the attentions of the US Government and its agencies, *you* seem to have got yourself into a blood feud with the guys that wrote the bastard manual on blood feuds! Bloody good effort, Sherpa!'

Silence. His words hung in the air before Tysoe, ever the logical pragmatist, again swept away the pall hanging over the room. Tysoe was still a man with a financial mission.

'Look, this guy Ghol; the living one, not the dead one. I reckon either he or someone in his organisation has some pretty sophisticated knowledge of financial markets, above and beyond just committing this fraud. I've been trying to work out why these guys have been holding cash in different currencies in different accounts, dollars and pounds. The money trace tells us that a multi-currency fraud took place out of Eastern Europe and all multi-currency funds were converted into pounds prior to transfer. Why didn't they just change all the fraud funds into dollars and ship them out? I reckon the answer to that is that someone was having a one-way bet on the pound increasing against the dollar over the period, which funnily enough, it did.' Tysoe was pointing at his screen; he had the attention of at least two others in the room. Dunstan and Lovat moved across to look where he was pointing, at a report of fraudulent funds transfers between accounts.

'Look, the fraudulent card payments are transferred from the PSP, the processor of the stolen cards, into a CyberX settlement account and instantly converted into pounds. And they sit there. Doing what? Awaiting instructions? They're certainly not earning any interest. We don't pay any! They accumulate as the fraud increases. They sit there, and then a series of apparently random transfers converted into *dollars* takes place: The Greater Himalaya Education Foundation account; Lichtenstein for Khan number one, and London for t'other Khan. Now that's no big deal, but I got to wondering why all the transfers are so random. I started checking and, what d'yer know, look here!'

Tysoe switched to a screen showing two graphs where he had charted the volatility of currency movements against the timings of the fraud funds transfers. His charts exactly mirrored the spikes of GB pound vs US dollar. 'What we have here is someone playing the currency markets. Over the past nine months, sterling has risen over 30% in value against the US dollar from its lows. The transfer dates are uncanny. *My* bet is that someone behind this laundering activity has *consciously* made a very astute one-way bet on the pound against the dollar, and by my calculations, they've made themselves approximately four million, two hundred thousand dollars *extra* over the last three months alone by not converting at the outset into dollars. And I reckon this was part of the master plan, if you like. That's my theory, that you've got a currency play here on top of everything else.'

Tysoe sat back but he was far too matter-of-fact to show any signs of self-satisfaction, or any other emotion for that matter.

Dunstan was impressed with the figures and Tysoe's insight. Even The Monk had come over to have a look at Tysoe's screen. The Monk was pretty quick on the uptake. 'What sort of person would factor this currency exchange gamble into their plan with this degree of, er, what the fuck's the word…anticipation?'

'For someone to be so *assured* in this matter, I would say this person has to be close to the financial markets: a broker, currency dealer or hedge fund specialist,' Tysoe responded flatly.

Dunstan had recovered from trawling memories and was now firing again. He turned his attention to Lovat. 'Rebecca, can your research analysts, or whatever the hell you call them, dig out something on this guy Ghol? As Tysoe here so astutely put it, the living one, not the dead one. Get round all the financial contacts you have in every major currency trading centre on the planet and find out if he worked in the industry. I need all the inside track I can get on my enemy and I need it quick!'

Lovat had been watching Dunstan closely and had become impressed with his apparent ability to absorb body blows, recover, bounce back within minutes and get on with the job. *Maybe that's real toughness: a potent mix of moral fibre, resilience and an uncanny ability to keep the long-term goal in focus*, she perceived.

Dunstan's thoughts were gaining momentum. 'Right, Monk, how much notice to move? Realistically, no bullshit!'

The Monk was now back in his comfort zone, seeing his old friend with his hackles up. He also knew what was in his mind. 'Four hours' standby. Realistically, let's say six with full checks. You'll need to make sure all contingencies are in place with His Excellency.'

Dunstan looked at his Breitling chronometer: three dials for three different time zones. 'Five hours. Okay, send out a six-hour warning order, pronto, Monk. Back to the hotel for a quick freshen up and repack our kit. You'd better get out to the desert and make sure final prep runs are okay. I'll do all the contingency with His Excellency.'

'Hang on a minute,' said Lovat. 'What's going on here?' She had been caught off guard by the pace of the conversation between the two men and the mutual empathy, almost telepathy, between them, which left the outside observer in the dark.

'The Monk and I are off over the water,' said Dunstan, adapting an old euphemism to his new theatre of operation. 'You and Tysoe are staying here to be the intelligence link between London and us. And of course to trace these Khan characters, find out what they're really up to.'

Lovat, uncharacteristically, was flustered by the turn of events. 'But… but I still have the third item on the report from London.' she protested.

However, Dunstan now knew what he had to do. 'It'll have to wait. Haven't got time now, Rebecca. Tell Monk, he can update me later. I'm off to find His Excellency.' With that he turned on his heels, slapped Tysoe on the back and said, 'Thanks chum, keep at it. Oh and give yourself a bonus of fifty grand from the Bermuda contingency pot. You deserve it!'

'Mad bastard,' responded Tysoe affectionately.

With what passed for a Lancastrian compliment ringing in his ears, Dunstan headed for the door, leaving a nonplussed Lovat with the image of his disappearing back burned on her retina.

Chapter Seventeen

London, 1300 hours; Al-Qurum, 1600 hours; Islamabad, 1800 hours

Isamabad, the modern capital of Pakistan, sits side-by-side with Rawalpindi, its older sister city, on the Pothohar plateau in the north-west corner of Pakistan. At an altitude of some 2,000 feet, it enjoys a warm micro-climate that is not shared with the colder provinces to the north. With its planned layout of straight, tidy boulevards, it's often said that the city is situated 'a few miles outside Pakistan'. Yet this is the political heart of a country struggling to balance opposing cultures and perspectives of East and West: between the promotion of its Islamic Nation status and the tolerance of an older religious heritage, between the opposing lifestyles and philosophies of mountain men and plains men, and between religious tolerance and a rising religious dogma.

The city also acts as the gateway to the Northern Territories of Pakistan, a barely-controlled land of harsh climates that breeds tough people, and where tribal law holds sway. Now, a group of men from these territories began converging on Ghol's house in the outlying D12 Sector of Islamabad, close to the Margalla Hills. Many had been travelling for days from their mountain strongholds. Their purpose was to implement the final pieces of a Great Plan that in its execution would give their people the power, influence and recognition they wished for in the face of continued outside pressure on their culture and way of life. They were from Chitral, Hunza, Gilgit, Skardu Baltistan and Pakistani Kashmir. They had been born into different religions and creeds: Shia Islam, the Ismaili sect, Buddhism in the case of the Dodar (thought to be the descendants of the aborigines of the region), and their own ancient animistic-based religions in the case of the non-Muslim fair-haired Kalash and itinerant Bhotias. Even so, although each had his own language – Burushaski of Hunza and Nagar,

Wakhi from the Gujal and Yasin valleys, Khowar of Chitral, and Balti, an ancient Tibetan language – they all had one thing in common: they were seasoned mountain men of the Greater Himalaya.

Ghol himself was Kashmiri, from an ancient family of landowners who had migrated from their original homelands in Baltistan, a country with a deep history and ancient culture. Its old winter capital, Skardu, lay south of the Baltoro Glacier, and it was from here that many expeditions over the past hundred and thirty years had set off to explore the Karakoram and to climb K2, "The Savage Mountain", using Balti porters to transport expedition equipment. But the traditional Balti homelands are now split between India and Pakistan and that political split runs like a festering wound through the Northern Tribes' culture: a political division that needs to be healed, a wound that needs to be cauterised.

Three years earlier, Anil Ghol had been summoned from his home in London to a meeting, chaired by his father Ali Sher Ghol, an imposing figure and the *de facto* tribal leader of all Balti people regardless of modern political boundaries. Present at the meeting were leaders and representatives of a wide number of different ethnic groups. Some he recognised: those from the northern areas of Pakistan and others from Azad Kashmir. In addition, there were representatives from other ethnic groups he did not recognise. However, he could see that they were all mountain men. At this meeting, his father outlined a grand scheme, a plan so ambitious in its concept and breadth that even these cynical and hardened men gasped at its audacity.

Up to that point, the funding for this Great Plan had been provided from a trust set up by a group of enlightened British political officers in 1945, prior to the partition of India in 1947. Its charter stated that its purpose was:... *to benefit all Greater Himalayan peoples so that through the education of their brightest, the remote tribes of the Himalaya and Karakoram will continue to thrive and maintain their ethnic identity and cultural independence... it shall be known as The Greater Himalayan Education Foundation.* The Foundation had served its intended beneficiaries well. It continued to do so even after Ghol Senior had become Chairman of the Board of Trustees and had persuaded his fellow trustees that 'maintenance of ethnic identity and cultural independence' could be interpreted to encompass a much wider remit than pure education, if only in the letter and not in the spirit, of the charter.

It had occurred to Ali Sher Ghol that when the Greater Himalaya Education Foundation account was set up in 1945, all the Himalayan tribes, from the North West Frontier Province on the border with Afghanistan in the west, across the Karakoram and Himalaya to Burma in the east two thousand miles away, were part of one territory: British India, part of a Greater Himalaya. Its remit and aims, therefore, had no regard to latter-day political boundaries, and indeed (reflected Ali Sher Ghol), it represented a model that with just the right political pressure points applied, together with the right amount of financial muscle, could once again become a political reality.

The most surprising thing about the Trust, though, was that it had survived through and beyond the political schism known as Partition, which had divided a large portion of northern India into West and East Pakistan (now Bangladesh) and which continued to exist to this day. In doing so, it had provided a thread of continuity, acting as a financial gossamer linking disparate nations and tribes, perhaps the only tangible thread between present-day Indian and Pakistani territories. Partition had left the State of Jammu and Kashmir as a disputed territory divided by the Line of Control, a negotiated peace boundary over which Pakistan and India fought a periodic and sometimes vicious high-altitude war at heights of up to 16,000 feet, with skirmishes even higher.

Through this redirecting of its funds to what Ghol Snr had called 'a greater purpose', loyalties had been secured, as had protection and influence at the highest levels, not least within the ISI. But at that point in time they had neither the financial nor practical means to execute their Great Plan. It would take at least two years to assemble the pieces of the jigsaw and find the means to finance the project through to its inception.

And this is where Anil Ghol was introduced into the frame. Through the munificence of the Foundation, Anil Ghol had received an education that was far superior to any enjoyed by the tribal leaders around him at the meeting. Now, he was entrusted with the role of financier, and chief distributor of, and signatory to, the withdrawals of all monies from the Educational Fund account held at the chief branch of the Commercial Bank of Pakistan in Islamabad. He was trustworthy and loyal to his tribal heritage and he was nobody's fool.

At the age of thirteen, Ghol had been sent to one of Pakistan's top boarding schools, Abbottabad Public School, popularly known as APS and modelled on the British public school system. Being a natural mathematician, he had graduated from the London School of Economics with a First Class Honours degree and had been offered employment with one of London's major hedge funds. Here he came to specialise in currency swaps. He was home on leave when his father had called him to the meeting of elders. The new role had presented Ghol with a huge personal dilemma: loyalty to his father and tribe or to his employer and his career. He had emailed his boss to ask for an extended sabbatical for 'family reasons'. This had been refused; he took it anyway, and used his financial acumen and mathematical brain to further his tribal cause.

However, Ali Sher Ghol was a tortured soul, and he had discussed with his son a hidden agenda to be financed from the funds raised. A very private agenda of a personal kind, a matter of family retribution, family honour and revenge of the highest order, a revenge which Ghol Senior would not live to see: a blood feud.

The last three years had seemed like an eternity to Ghol. His father's premature death – some said it was from a broken heart – and Ghol Jnr's subsequent rise to a position of unexpected, and indeed unsolicited, power, had weighed heavily on his young shoulders.

Anil Ghol's investigations had led him, via his contacts in the ISI, to a profound insight: that he could avenge the torture, pain and grief wrought on his family by directly targeting the harbinger – first ruining him financially, then proceeding to destroy him personally at leisure. The more he thought about it, the more plausible and complete it became; *his* revenge, *his* retribution, and only he had the means to do it! Over a period of three years, he used all his acquired financial acumen to identify, seek and destroy his target, Philip Dunstan, with the added bonus of raising millions of dollars in support of the cause.

With his love of mathematics, high finance, speculation and his unswerving family and tribal loyalty, Anil Ghol had found in playing this Great Game that he was indulging in the supreme application of all his talents.

***

The two surveyors and the staff-man had been working steadily around the suburban boulevards close to Ghol's house. What they were surveying was anybody's guess, but they took meticulous readings through their theodolites and made copious notes in their small, black, hardback notebooks. The elevations of the surrounding pavements were duly recorded, as were the comings and goings of all vehicles and people. The readings they took were enhanced by the digital images snapped by the long-range digital cameras built into the equipment. The images were compressed, encrypted and transmitted a short distance to their van for viewing and scrambling by the 267 signals officer, who relayed them back to the British High Commission for onward transmission to the UK. The staff-man, who was also a signaller, had a tiny radio transmitter stuck onto his skull, behind his ear. The small team could maintain only a peripheral watch on Ghol's house, but they were pretty sure that nobody had come in or out in the time they'd been there. They had about an hour before sunset and their handover to the listening skills of the SRR soldiers.

As the spring heat of the day gave way to the cool of the evening, and the sun began its descent behind the Karakoram Himalaya, those observing and listening became aware of something extraordinary happening. A convoy of four-wheel drive vehicles, mostly Toyota Land Cruisers, some new, some battered, turned into the road leading to Ghol's villa and decanted their occupants. Each wore their own tribal variation of the Pakistani shalwar kameez, the loose-fitting baggy trousers with long-tailed shirt, or the long, white woollen chogha. Even the casual observer could see that all were of a proud and noble bearing. Some embraced as though old friends; others were more reticent and held back, notably the Kalash from Nuristan, whose total ethnic population is probably no more than six thousand, and whose very existence is threatened. They had more to gain – or indeed lose – than anyone there. Some tribal leaders had retainers with distinctive saddlebags slung over their shoulders. And in the middle of them were men with quite different features: Bhotias, nomads from Western Tibet, and two Ladakhi Buddhists dressed in monk's robes of the Kagyu sect, the 'red hats' of Tibetan Buddhism. All the visitors were welcomed individually, and with great warmth, by Ghol. They were moving into the final phase of execution of the Great Plan.

Four large men patrolled up and down the road, their automatic weapons concealed beneath baggy clothes. Reaching the end of the road, they eyed the survey team suspiciously, who in turn reckoned they had done their job for the day and made a display of packing up their equipment and preparing to leave. There was to be no smooth handover to a new team.

Inside the villa, Ghol moved through the gathering. Relaxed and happy, he greeted each of the different groups in turn in their own language: *Ju~le!* to the Ladakhis; *Chi Khabar*, 'How are you?' to his Balti friends; *Chiz holi* in Wakhi; *Tu kicha assus* in Khowar – the language of Kho – to his old Chitrali friends. He spoke in Burushaski to those who had travelled from the more remote parts of Hunza, in Shina to those of Daimir, and so on around all the guests, welcoming each and every one individually and by name in their own language, and in many instances enquiring after their immediate family by name. What made his linguistic dexterity the more remarkable was that none of these languages are related to each other.

Eventually, he sat down on a *kelim*-covered camel saddle set so as to raise him very slightly above his seated audience, but not high enough to imply any degree of social or cultural superiority on his part. This was a meeting of equals, yet he had the undivided attention of the whole audience. He paused to compose himself and to appreciate the atmosphere of the moment. 'My friends,' he began, 'thank you all for coming; we have waited for this moment for more than fifty years. I am one of you, the people of the Greater Himalaya, the Karakoram – the Northern Peoples. To be with you here is an honour and a privilege. Your homelands straddle one of the most important and volatile regions of this earth. Geographically, it is where the two greatest land masses collide, causing havoc and tragedy as they grind up against each other, as we have seen in a series of natural disasters in recent years. Politically, the national interests of three great superpowers converge on your ancient tribal areas. Militarily, three nuclear powers point their weapons at each other across your fields and villages.'

At this last point, some shuddered and many looked at their feet and muttered imprecations to Allah.

'In your very own backyard is the highest battlefield in the world. And – closer to my heart – many of your children are not educated, but fed religious dogma in the accursed madrassas of the Taliban.'

A murmur of assent and anger rippled through the crowd. Many had relatives in the Swat Valley and Waziristan.

'Anil,' the man who spoke was one of the key representatives from the Baltistan Freedom Front, 'I put it to you that without power, *real armed power*, we will never influence Islamabad and gain self-determination. That is why we have been engaged in an armed struggle for the past thirty years!' There were murmurs of agreement from the room.

Ghol smiled and looked around the room. 'Our success will come soon. Before the sun sets twice more, I shall have the privilege, bestowed on me by my father, Ali Sher Ghol, to initiate a Great Event which will ensure the break-up of Pakistan as we know it and will give us, all of our peoples, the opportunity to claim freedom from this yoke! In the post-event chaos, we will make a Unilateral Declaration of Autonomy for Baltistan!'

A cheer came from elements of his audience, but some of the wiser grey-beards kept their feelings and counsel to themselves.

Ghol looked at the shrewd and expectant faces in front of him, absorbing the atmosphere.

'And this is just the start of our dream. One day the Greater Himalaya will be reunited under a single federation of mountain peoples, from your homelands a thousand miles across to Eastern Nepal, Bhutan and Sikkim. My people, our day has come! You will be given only six hours warning to prepare yourselves and your families. I shall say no more at this stage but the signal for the declaration of our freedom will reach you through secure communications. Which brings me to a practical matter: in order to co-ordinate our activities we are going to use secure, yet simple, communications. We will achieve this with short-wave radio using a code. Trained liaison staff will be dispatched in the next few days to each area to assist in this and give other practical support.

'More of this later, but for now, I can tell you that inclusive of tonight's donation, each tribe among you will have received the equivalent of five million dollars for immediate operational expenses from the Greater Himalaya Education Foundation. In addition, I can tell you that at least another twenty million dollars has been set aside for future purposes of autonomy. This has been used in part to retain a fully-armed contingent of up to two thousand hardened Nepalese guerrillas. Experienced officers are available to train and support your people in the transition to full autonomy and, where appropriate, provide specialist armed support. In conjunction with your own local militias, our Nepalese mercenaries – our fellow mountain men – will be deployed to resist any attempts at incursion into your homelands.'

It was time for Ghol to wrap up the meeting. 'Now, my friends, we must take our leave. It is time for you to head back to your tribal homelands and make preparations for the new dawn, for there is much that remains to be done in the next twenty-four hours!'

It was not in their culture to make a hasty exit; the tribal leaders lingered and chatted for about an hour and a half before meandering out of the house carrying the distinctive saddlebags, now heavy with dollars and rupees, together with their short-wave radios and master code keys. To a casual observer, it looked like the break-up of any small-sized religious or political meeting.

Outside, Dhar and Murria continued to monitor proceedings via the micro-thin bug tagged to the bottom of Ghol's trousers. They had no basis on which to make a pre-emptive move. Besides, they were completely outnumbered and outgunned by the tribal leaders and their guards. They reasoned, correctly, that their political masters would not want a bloodbath on the streets of Islamabad. The SRR team waited and watched Ghol and his aides go back into the villa. They settled down to wait for Ghol's next move or communication; it was what they did best.

***

Al-Qurum, 1830 hours; Islamabad, 2030 hours

At the same time as the tribal leaders were leaving the villa in Islamabad, His Excellency Sheikh Suroor Al-Qurum was entertaining Philip Dunstan alone in his private dining-room in the Royal Palace, an architectural confection of extended dhow sails and giant Bedouin tents, 'a brilliant fusion of classical and futuristic Arabia' to its supporters and, to its detractors, 'Sydney Opera House on Speed'.

Sheikh Suroor was relaxed and ebullient. His guest was the beneficiary of the sort of intimate gathering he himself rarely enjoyed, given the formal demands of state business and protocol. As the informal meal came to an end, he signalled that all servants should leave him and Dunstan alone.

'Philip! Efendi! Earlier today, I summoned the High Commissioner for Pakistan to announce to him that we wish to make a *substantial* financial and practical donation to assist those who suffered in the recent terrible floods and landslides, and who are even now trying to rebuild their lives.' He waved his hand magnanimously, then almost as an afterthought added, 'Plus, of course, other unspecified support in the interests of extending joint co-operation and fraternity between our two countries.' At this he laughed, feeling pleasure and pride at this opportunity to play on the international stage. 'Now, such an aid programme cannot be put into action without proper reconnaissance and preparation, and indeed an *operating base* within Pakistan for the programme.' There was a pause as Sheikh Suroor popped a succulent medjool date into his mouth and ate it. 'The bilateral agreement I have reached with Pakistan is that I shall be able to put certain elements of my military on twenty-four hours' notice to fly into Pakistani-controlled Azad Kashmir as a way of preparing for, and testing, my Forces' reaction to a hypothetical regional, er, *situation.* Of course, this is all in support of our Pakistani brothers! This includes the landing of transport aircraft in remote valleys, with prior notification and diplomatic clearance. It also encompasses in-flight refuelling and other *useful* exercises.'

Dunstan knew from The Monk that certain preparations had been made, but all this now laid before him was on a scale far greater than he had imagined.

'And how do your Pakistani brothers feel about all this?' Dunstan asked Sheikh Al-Qurum pointedly.

'They are delighted, of course! Wouldn't you be, with the offer of tens of millions of dollars in humanitarian and military support from a friend? Now, Sherpa, a riddle for you: what is the common factor in diplomacy, good relations between neighbours, and the waging of war?' He looked intently at Dunstan as though he had a big surprise up his sleeve and couldn't wait to present it.

A bemused Dunstan thought for a few seconds, then the fog lifted. 'Effective communications?'

'Exactly! You're going to need sophisticated, *high security* communications to conduct your search and other operations in the terrain you're going to find yourself in. Ground-to-air, satellite, radar, all that sort of thing,' His Excellency declared with a flourish. 'And so, Sherpa, it is arranged!'

'What's arranged?' asked Dunstan. 'An AWACS!'

His Excellency Sheikh Suroor bin Mohammed Al-Qurum observed with amusement his friend wrestling with the notion of having an Airborne Warning and Command System aircraft at his personal disposal.

'But you can't just park an AWACS over another country's airspace!' Dunstan protested.

Again, the expansive hand gesture from his friend. 'Agreed! Unless it is as part of a joint exercise between two allied countries to test mutually-supporting command and control systems! Look, Philip, I must tell you that we have two of the latest Boeing E3 AWACS here in Al-Qurum and I need to have them exercised and tested. Pakistan has recently acquired Saab AWACS aircraft. A joint exercise has been on the cards for a while. Our AWACS will provide, what would you call it? Top cover, as mothership to their AWACS. The aid deployment into the landslide zone gives a perfect opportunity for it. And the topping on the cake is that I personally insisted that our AWACS come with the Link-16 extra facility, which gives me ground-to-air and air-to-ground communications.'

Dunstan opened his mouth to speak but His Excellency had by no means finished.

'Plus GPRS positioning! There's no point in having Special Forces on the ground if they can't communicate with me and my commanders from anywhere in the world, is there? You see, I take a strong personal interest in such matters, as they affect the capability and performance of my Emirate. Also, with the aid of the capable, and the very lovely, Miss Rebecca Lovat, we will co-ordinate with London from here, Inshallah.' He waved his hand dismissively. 'There was some opposition from my advisors of course, but I have declared it!'

Dunstan's mind was reeling at the facilities that had been made available to him. A large and heart-felt exhalation was his only response.

Sheikh Al-Qurum continued, 'So, Philip, all is in place. You just have to turn up. With that in mind, my friend, I suggested to the Pakistani President that time is of the essence, and that I shall despatch a top team *immediately* to make preparations. This team is to consist of two military gentlemen who might be joined by a trusted female advisor or advisors fluent in Urdu and Kashmiri – '

'But what? *Who?*' interrupted Dunstan, agog at the preparations that his friend had put into place on his behalf in the last twenty-four hours. *Or am I perhaps naive in assuming this is solely on my behalf? And who is this woman*

'advisor'? He must mean the Det contingent. So we have Det women on the ground, do we? What really has been going on behind the scenes this last twenty-four hours?
'Plus a small team of military advisors who can look at the practical side of matters and plan the detail. All this under full Al-Qurum Diplomatic Protection, of course.' In a final flourish he continued, 'My friend! You have your diplomatic entry into Pakistan and the means, God willing, to achieve your objectives! I shall be monitoring proceedings with a close personal interest. Now, we have only a few hours to prepare. Before dawn tomorrow, it will be All Systems Go in Pakistan!'

Chapter Eighteen

Friday: Oxford, 1700 hours; Al-Qurum, 2000 hours; Islamabad, 2200 hours

Dr MacAllister's propensity for moving beyond the factual nature of his profession and trying to get into the killer's mind was inherent: 'The neck was broken very cleanly, in a single, swift action. To me it conveys a desire on the part of the killer not to cause unnecessary suffering.'

'Aren't we missing something?' Beckwith's attention was on the exposed cadaver in front of him that had once been Dunstan's Executive Assistant. 'What? You mean the numbers, or date, carved on the chest? Nothing to do with cause of death, Chief Inspector! They were cut *after* the event. Quite a bit later, as a matter of fact.'

'How much later?'

'I would estimate about two to three hours, probably just as the body was dumped. It has a hint of the ritualistic, doesn't it? Rather like the man in Boars Wood – Morgan, wasn't it? I'd say that the murderer's intention is to convey something, a message. But to whom?'

The thought came to Beckwith from nowhere: *Could it be that the killers weren't acting on their own, but that there was someone else controlling them? Dunstan himself, maybe?*

***

The Monk had returned from Scimitar Regiment in what was fast becoming his personal mode of transport around the Emirate, the Jet Ranger 111 helicopter. He was happy in his new-found role as a Major in Al-Qurum's Special Forces. A few obligatory bollockings directed in equal measure to the deserving and the undeserving alike had helped to get matters finalised to his satisfaction. None of his Scimitar Regiment contingent knew their actual mission, other than that they were offering military support to an 'aid programme' in a neighbouring State.

For the past hour, he had been briefing Dunstan in the hotel room, and together they had been planning actions-on once they were in Pakistan. The Monk did not seem surprised by Dunstan's revelation that they had the facility of some of the latest airborne communications technology.

Had it been The Monk's suggestion in the first place? wondered Dunstan. Having gone through various scenarios, they focused for a while on their ground-to-air communications capabilities and equipment. They knew the first link-up had to be with the ground-based operators to get the full intelligence picture. Co-ordination with the SRR soldiers on the ground was to be the first priority on landing.

Dunstan was pensive, seemingly torn between different courses of action. 'I was wondering…'

'Wondering is bad for you, doesn't get you anywhere!' interrupted his friend. 'What is it Sherpa?'

'I was wondering if I'm acting in the best way to protect my family. Shouldn't I be back in the UK, in Scotland, close to them?'

The Monk would have none of it. He gripped his friend. 'Listen to me. There *is* no going back, you know that. You know your enemy. Whatever they want from you as revenge, they'll chase you to the ends of the earth to get it. And anyway, the truth is they don't want anything *from* you, they just want to *destroy* you and all that you have. They're going to keep coming, Sherpa. It's time for you to stand and fight. More than that, it's time to take the fight to the enemy. If you don't, then you're dead. If you do, you might just survive. Let me look after your family through my own channels and my trusted friends. I want to get to these bastards and neutralise the threat as much as you do. As for me, well I'm never going back to live in the UK – there is nothing there for me, so I stand here and fight with you.'

Dunstan mulled things over for a moment, but he knew The Monk was right. Then he realised what his friend had just said at the end of his peroration. 'What do you mean, *never going back to the UK?*' Dunstan enquired.

The Monk moved closer to him, adopting his old secretive posture. 'When I went round your mate's Scimitar Force establishment today, I got a full capability briefing. Pretty impressive set-up. Certainly got all the toys, and the lads are pretty enthusiastic. They just need to make a few training and operational adjustments over the next, er, decade. So I made a few suggestions, didn't I, and, what do you know, His Excellency Sheikh Dreadnought was impressed enough to offer me a permanent job as Training

Major, advising his Scimitar Force, when I get back from our little jolly.' 'When did you decide you wanted to stay here?' asked Dunstan, already knowing the answer.

'When I saw the desert from the air, Sherpa!'

There was a comfortable silence between them, both deep in thought. Dunstan broke the spell. 'Look, Monk, going back to the safety of my family. Are you sure your mates in the chopper can eyeball this hit team from the air?'

It was the first time that Dunstan had used the phrase 'hit team' and it brought home in full what they were dealing with: a team of killers apparently contracted to kill his family.

'Don't worry, my guys will be able to spot whether these gadgies are flaccid or erect from a mile away.' The Monk's black eyes turned on Dunstan. 'Anyway, you can't go home because home doesn't exist!'

'True,' said Dunstan.

'So that makes us even, doesn't it? One house down for each of us!'

The Monk was grinning. He pulled out a soft package from his Bergen and threw it at Dunstan.

'What's this?' asked the bemused recipient.

'Combats; you're now a full colonel in His Excellency's Forces of Al-Qurum. Pretty quick promotion, eh? From a fucking civvy tosser to red tabs in the blink of eye! Get yourself sorted and packed, Sherpa. We leave for Scimitar Base at twenty-one thirty hours, dead. See you in reception.'

As Dunstan found himself alone with his thoughts in the surreal moment of easing on his brand new Al-Qurum Special Forces combats, he reflected on how far they had got during the day: far, but not far enough. It had been a long day. If only he could find and eliminate the cause of this vendetta against him and his family. His business was trashed, his hopes, dreams, ambitions and his home destroyed, and *still* he didn't have all the answers as to why. *But I'm getting much closer, and now I have the resources and the means to deploy them. All I need now is Providence and balls of steel.* With mixed feelings, he picked up the Sat phone to dial Faith. It took a few attempts to connect to the satellite service provider, then he had to dial Lynacraigie several times. He was just about to give up on the final call when a familiar female voice answered. 'Who the hell is this now?' 'Love you too, darling!' responded Dunstan, laughing.

'Philip! God! I thought it was another of those Home Office types telling me of yet another change to their threat status. Up, down and bloody sideways. They don't seem to know what on earth is going on!'

'What protection do you have in place?'

'There are eight guys on the hillside with big guns who take it in turns to come in for a cup of tea, and there are two blokes in the house with bulging jackets. Level with me, Philip. Is there a threat or not, and if so, what is it?' Their whole relationship was based on a deep mutual empathy and being straightforward with each other. By God, he admired her more than ever now, and he knew that the time to level with her was *now.*

'OK, Faith, this is the score: yes there is a threat. It's all to do with something I did, or rather *didn't* do, on that trip I made to Afghanistan. The money from that operation set us up in business, you might remember. I trusted some people that perhaps I shouldn't have and, indirectly, I was responsible for the death of a young man. He was Pakistani-Kashmiri. His family found out my connection and swore revenge. There's no easy way to say this, Faith, but I, *we,* and seemingly everyone dear to us, are targets of a blood feud. The guys that visited the house earlier in the week were probably the hit team.'

Faith had been listening intently until those two words came across the ether. She had heard enough. 'Hit team? Are you telling me that the kids and I – your precious family – are the target of an assassination squad or whatever, as a result of what you did on some goddam hillside up the bloody Khyber Pass?'

'Er, yes. Though we think they're still in Oxfordshire at the moment,' he replied lamely. He thought about the fact that their home had been blown to smithereens and thought better than to tell Faith about it now. Clearly her blood was up. 'Look, darling, you have protection in place and we'll know if and when these characters make a move.'

'Don't you bloody well "darling" me, Philip Dunstan! How will they know where we are? Has someone told them?' demanded Faith.

Dunstan took a deep breath. 'We have to assume that Kate did. Before they killed her, that is.'

There was a momentary silence. When she came back on the line, Faith's voice had changed out of all recognition; she was not the wife he knew. 'Oh my God. What have you done, you bastard? You have blood on your hands, Dunstan. Just make sure there isn't any more! I'll look after the kids here with the police, so don't bother flying back!'

With that, the line went dead and Dunstan was left standing holding the receiver in a numbed state.

He put down the receiver with a heavy heart. His conversation with Faith had been an emotional car crash but he could do no more. He was drained.

He showered, had a close shave to sharpen up, and spent the next half-hour running scenarios through his head so that – to the extent it was possible under the circumstances – he could quickly develop an operational plan shortly after landing in Pakistan.

There was a faint knock at the door. He was not expecting anyone. He crossed the room, curious and bemused. He looked through the spy hole warily, and saw a shapely female form. He opened the door on the chain, to see Rebecca Lovat standing on the threshold in a long silk robe.

'Are you going to let me in or are you going to stand there goggling like a teenager?' Dunstan took the first option, wondering what she wanted at this time of night. She glided through the door. 'I hope you don't mind, Philip. I just *had* to sort something out with you before you disappeared to Pakistan.'

It took a while for Dunstan to register her meaning. As the silk robe slipped from her shoulders and glided down her body to reveal a figure both athletic and curvaceous, his only and instant thought was: *Oh bugger! What do I do now?*

***

Friday: London, 1730 hours

At Thames House, Celia Fanshawe was briefing Director Special Forces on the latest intelligence assessment of the reports from Pakistan and Al-Qurum. They also compared notes on related activity in the UK.

'So what are the next steps, Celia?' They were on first name terms by now.

'I should like your SRR team to try and lift this Ghol chap, take him to a safe house and sweat him. It's the only way to qualify and quantify the threat.'

Gibbs was not only against it, he considered the whole operation was in danger of going rogue.

'Celia, SRR's job is intelligence gathering, not "lifting" targets. They have neither the planning nor the resources to execute such a task. Isn't this a job for the Pakistani Intelligence Services? Isn't it...' Gibbs searched for a word or phrase other than "bloody stupid", *'unwise* to keep them out of the loop?'

'And tell them what, General?' Fanshawe couldn't help reverting to formal address to make a strong point. 'There's nothing conclusive here. Involving Pakistan's ISI and maybe other Indian subcontinent agencies at this stage would mean the instant withdrawal of our people on the ground. We'd be out of it without having found the UK connection. Besides which, I'd much rather your chaps sweat this Ghol fellow than we hand him over to Pakistani intelligence inquisitors – he's more likely to make it out alive, and we get the information first hand. The ISI has a right to know, but it's a question of *timing*. When *we* know the truth – and we've decided *how* to act upon it, then – and only then, can we can bring our Pakistani allies up to speed. My primary concern is to find the UK connection and identify any threat, real or potential to this country which is International Counter-Terrorism's bailiwick and my responsibility. Information regarding any other category of foreign intelligence we pass on to "Friends" and "Relatives" as and when appropriate.'

DSF could see the logic but nevertheless he could not accede to Fanshawe's request.

'The safety of my two SRR soldiers in theatre is of paramount importance. They have full SIGINT capability in place. I strongly suggest that it would be far better to track and trace the target until we're in a position to make informed decisions before getting close up and personal.' He paused for effect, then pulled the ace out of his sleeve. 'Besides, Celia, we don't really want a Gibraltar type of incident, or worse, on the streets of Islamabad...do we?'

Fanshawe knew that he was referring to Operation Flavius when, in March 1988, three suspected Provisional IRA bombers were shot on the streets of Gibraltar by an SAS team, after having been trailed by 14 Int Company – the Det. The only problem was that the IRA team was not armed and their vehicle did not contain an explosive device. Although a car belonging to one of them was later found packed with explosives in Spain, it was considered a political disaster and had handed a propaganda coup to the IRA. The fallout was containable because it was on 'home territory' in Gibraltar; Islamabad would be quite different.

'I take your point,' Fanshawe conceded finally. 'Observation, track and trace only.'

***

The SRR team were having difficulty picking up the signals from the listening device embedded in Ghol's clothing. 'They must have moved into a basement or sealed room,' whispered Dhar.

There was a rustling sound, and Dhar and Murria both clearly heard Ghol speak the words 'So, to APS!' Murria looked at Dhar, whose expression was one of bemusement. Yet more rustling sounds came over the headset as though bags were being packed, then nothing.

A short time later, Ghol and three aides carrying several heavy saddlebags and personal belongings exited the villa and loaded their baggage into the back of the Land Cruiser. With a final look around, Ghol got into the passenger seat. The Land Cruiser reversed out of the drive and Ghol pointed the driver northwards. As Ghol left, Murria initiated the tracking device under the wheel arch of his vehicle by remote control. With a professional satisfaction she saw the GPS positioning signal come through strong and clear.

The SRR team reacted quickly, sending a quick SITREP to 267 SIGINT for onward transmission, including the phrase: >>>*Target One heading north from current location, possible destination, quote APS unquote, question*>>> There was no need to follow in hot pursuit; the strength of the signal from the tracking device allowed them the luxury of a methodical breakout from their surveillance position.

***

London, Friday 1930 hours; Al-Qurum, Friday, 2230 hours; Islamabad, Saturday, 0030 hours

In London Celia Fanshawe and her analyst, Elizabeth Hamilton, were glued to BBC News 24, which had replaced its lead item with a breaking-news report of mounting chaos in Lahore and Karachi. It appeared to be on a scale far greater than a couple of unco-ordinated suicide bombings; this was an orchestrated and finely-timed series of bombings aimed at key seats of government administration.

There was a knock at the door and DSF Gibbs was shown in. Fanshawe simply nodded, motioned Gibbs to a seat and then pointed to the events in Pakistan unfolding before them on the screen.

The BBC correspondent reported from a blacked-out hotel lobby in Lahore: *There are unconfirmed reports of simultaneous explosions at the Ministry of Interior, the main electricity distribution sub-station, police stations and mosques. The Taliban are the main suspects. However there are claims that other radical elements may be responsible, including terrorist organisations thought to have backing from India. There is looting in the streets and law and order is breaking down. People here are saying that such acts could only have been perpetrated with the assistance of, or collusion with, elements within the police, or military, or both...* The reporter's voice was drowned out by the sound of another massive explosion close by and the transmission was dropped.

'So it's started,' observed Elizabeth Hamilton.

Fanshawe was phlegmatic. 'What we are witnessing, my dear Elizabeth, is the start of the biggest diversionary tactic in the history of terrorism. This is a smokescreen to the main event, presumably the so-called "Great Event" referred to in the latest SIGINT report from the SRR team.' She paused to let this sink in. 'These Khan characters, Ishfaq Mohammed Khan, the one who got three million, and Shafquat Iqbal Khan: these people are key to understanding what's really going on. Have we got any more detail on Ishfaq Khan?'

Fanshawe's team had noticed that since Freshfield's death Fanshawe had become less formal, less acerbic, and on more intimate terms with her subordinates, especially with those on whom she relied. In turn, her team had become more relaxed in her presence.

'No, other than the singular fact that he is Head of the Pakistan Institute of Nuclear Physics. To the best of our knowledge he isn't on any of our own lists, or indeed our Friends' files as being anything other than a diligent nuclear physicist loyal to the interests of his country. Nor does he appear to have strayed from the path of loyalty and devotion, unlike his namesake, the so-called "Father" of Pakistan's nuclear bomb.'

'Until now perhaps...' Fanshawe lapsed into one of her silences before asking, 'Any professional or familial relationship between the two, or indeed to this man Ghol?'

'None, as far as we can tell. But then again, three million dollars in Pakistan can buy a lot of loyalty. And we can't find anything whatsoever on this other character, Shafquat Khan, other than that he is an inconspicuous political journalist for the Karachi Times newspaper.'

Fanshawe had an insight that the others present were not party to. 'He isn't; you won't find him in any newspaper office. This political journalist isn't our man. You won't discover Mr Shafquat Khan through normal channels. My own view is that our man resides not far from here. In all probability he's a foreign national residing in London under a respectable cover. He may even be known to us,' she added enigmatically.

'If there's a nuclear angle to this, where is it leading?' Hamilton posed the obvious rhetorical question.

'All seems a bit far-fetched, doesn't it?' Gibbs volunteered.

'In our world, fact is universally stranger than fiction. It's the nightmare scenario, nuclear capability in terrorist hands; a nuclear terrorist state,' replied Fanshawe. 'Such a scenario within Pakistan has the potential to wreak havoc on a regional and global scale. If it isn't stopped at the outset, it will come back to bite us here in the West very quickly. Now that *is* in our national interest!'

There was a silence wherein each reflected on the dramatic picture that Fanshawe had just painted. Gibbs used the impasse to make his point. 'So this guy, Philip Dunstan, is now deemed to be innocent and is going to save the day. Is that about the sum of it?'

'As to saving the day, we shall have to wait and see, won't we? At least he's freelance, more than just "arm's length", so we can deny all knowledge of his operations, can't we?'

'Just as long as my SRR team don't get dragged any further into this mire. Which prompts the thought that I'd better issue orders to that effect!'

Fanshawe ignored Gibbs' point. Privately, she felt that Dhar at least would wish to participate in this latter-day vignette of the Great Game now centred on her ancestral homeland – and that she might yet wish to interpret or ignore her orders to that end.

Gibbs continued, 'Earlier this evening, I had a word with the Brigade of Gurkhas and the Royal Military Police. It seems that the theft from the armoury was in all probability carried out by a Sergeant Prem Gurung after finishing his final guard duty at the end of fifteen years of loyal and exemplary service, but prior to his imminent honourable discharge from the Army. As the senior NCO on guard duty, Gurung would have been entrusted with the keys to the armoury.'

'Discharge? You mean redundancy?' interjected Fanshawe.

'His discharge was part of the latest redundancy programme in the interminable but inevitable wind-down of the Brigade of Ghurkas. He had been upset about leaving the Army, but the following day he was due to go to London to meet with his three younger brothers, who had flown over from Nepal to see him. Eyebrows have been raised as to how all of them could have afforded the cost of the flight over, business class at that.'

'Funded by the Greater Himalaya Education Foundation,' Fanshawe speculated, 'for *educational purposes* no doubt. Hardly innocents abroad; I think we'll find that they're connected to the Maoist guerrilla movement in Nepal and are all seasoned guerrilla fighters…'

'Trained Maoist guerrillas, you say?' Gibbs couldn't help but interject.

'Yes. There are nineteen thousand of them languishing in United Nations camps in Nepal, waiting to be integrated back into mainstream Nepalese society. All available for mercenary work.'

Gibbs was thinking what he could do with a force of trained Nepalese fighters. 'You could invade a small country with that force!'

'Precisely!' said Fanshawe in response to this statement of the obvious. Gibbs got up to leave when his PDA signalled an incoming report from the SRR team via the secure SIGINT link. As their direct commanding officer for this operation, Gibbs received the SIGINT reports first, marginally ahead of MI5. The precedence of the chain of command had to be maintained.

He plugged his private encryption key dongle into his PDA device and read the synopsis. 'Interesting; your man in Pakistan has moved. It says here *"Unverified Destination APS. Question Mark"*.'

'APS!' exclaimed Hamilton. Fanshawe and Gibbs looked at her uncomprehendingly; she looked at them with equal perplexity until she realised that they would not necessarily be wholly conversant with the names of top Pakistani schools. 'APS: Abbottabad Public School, a sort of Eton of Pakistan. Why on earth should Ghol be travelling there?'

'Let's not jump to conclusions until this is verified. The SRR team could have misheard; after all, they appear to be questioning their own intelligence.' Gibbs was exercising caution, but he knew his SRR team would not have sent the report unless they were confident of what they had heard. To Gibbs, the question mark was probably their way of conveying the same reaction as Hamilton's.

Fanshawe did not seem uncomfortable with the obfuscation. 'Well, one thing I am sure of is that all manner of things will unfold in the next twenty-four hours, almost all of which will be unanticipated and wholly unexpected. And in that vein, I am now going to take great pleasure in disturbing the senior partner of Cavendish Bank, Bankers to the Great and Good, in his club or wherever he is on this fine spring Friday evening, and instruct him to enlighten me on the financial dealings of one of his foreign-domiciled customers. It should ruin his weekend nicely!'

Chapter Nineteen

Saturday, 28th April: Oxford, 0500 hours; Al-Qurum, 0800 hours; Abbottabad, 80 Miles (120km) North of Islamabad, 1000 hours

In the morning sun, Dunstan strode out across the disused Pakistani military airbase which had been transformed into a fully operational Forward Operating Base (FOB) for the aid programme. He was accompanied by The Monk and his new acquaintance, an officer from his old regiment, Captain Hugo Laycock, Officer Commanding Condor Troop, 59 Commando Squadron RE.

Laycock was smaller and stockier than the other two; he was bronzed, very fit but above all, like the rest of his men, acclimatised to the rarefied air of high altitudes. Laycock had been in the hills of Azad Kashmir for some three months when the call to action came through. The briefing in the British High Commission an hour ago in Islamabad was not what he had been expecting. A secure satellite video link put him face-to-face with the Chief Royal Engineer and Director Special Forces. It seemed that even his squadron commander was not part of the briefing. He was asked if he wished to be seconded to Al-Qurum Special Forces under the command of a British-born colonel to take part in a live operation. He found it an unusual request, as he was more used to taking direct orders than being asked his opinion. He understood when it was explained to him by DSF in no uncertain terms that this operation was deniable, a 'black' operation. Only volunteers were required, and he was left in no doubt as to the potential consequences of failure. Laycock had no second thoughts for himself; he was more than up for it. He had quickly contacted his staff sergeant, waiting with his troop on standby, and asked him to select a pool of combat engineer commandos who might be 'interested'. When his troop heard that an unspecified 'live op' was on the cards, there were so many volunteers that he had to cull the numbers down to a small section of eight seasoned and multi-disciplined commando combat engineers.

Dunstan had spent the last couple of hours since his arrival from Al-Qurum devising a loose operational plan with some likely scenarios. It would be tightened up when he knew where his target was going to be. He had hardly slept, just a few nods on the flight over, but adrenaline and a greater sense of purpose were carrying him through. On arrival at the base near Abbottabad, he was surprised to find that a big logistical effort had been underway for some time. The aid equipment for Azad Kashmir was currently being loaded onto C-130 transport aircraft. Now, dressed in combats in the insignia of a full colonel in the Al-Qurum Armed Forces, he was heading to the ops room to receive the latest intelligence briefing from Captain Dhar, who had been directed to the base by her controllers in the UK.

The Monk and Laycock were marching alongside him stride for stride. 'For God's sake, slow down, Sherpa: you'll panic the troops!' Dunstan lengthened his stride. Laycock sensed there was a strong bond between these two men and that gave him a good feeling about this op. *Nothing worse than a divided leadership,* he thought.

Laycock turned to watch with interest as three modified C-130s landed on the airstrip to join the aid programme aircraft. *Bloody hell! That looks like an AC-130 Spectre Gunship with a couple of Talons.* His adrenaline was pumping, wondering where this strange outfit was leading him.

***

Dhar and Murria had diverted to the base near Abbottabad, having received orders from the office of Director Special Forces UK to give assistance to Special Forces Al-Qurum, under the command of a British officer. They were now bringing their new Commanding Officer up to speed.

'Ladakh!' Dunstan was gobsmacked. 'Are you sure?'

Captain Dhar was very clear. '"To Kargil" is exactly what we heard. And Kargil is in Ladakh. And Ladakh is in Indian Kashmir. It might not be what you want to hear, and Ladakh might not be his real destination, but that is precisely what we *both* heard.' She looked across at Corporal Murria, who nodded vigorously.

'Where is Ghol, now? Do we have a trace?' asked Dunstan.

Corporal Murria looked at her GPRS trace of the bugged Land Cruiser. 'His *vehicle* is still parked at its previous location, sir. We tracked him and staked him out. It looked like a school. According to Google Maps, it's a school called APS.'

'You just wandered in and staked them out?' interjected an incredulous Laycock. He knew the depth of planning normally required in inserting a team into close-quarter covert observation.

Dhar looked at him scathingly and Laycock shifted uneasily. 'Covert observation is our job,' she responded acerbically. 'Now, while we *observed*, Ghol got out of his vehicle and was met by a dapper-looking man, smaller than Ghol, with a neatly trimmed beard, wearing a starched white shirt and a blue, Western-style suit. He had with him an assistant carrying a sealed wooden box, who with great care, carried the box to a helicopter waiting in the grounds – on the cricket pitch in front of the main buildings to be precise. Ghol and the visitor embraced, exchanged a few words, then the visitor left in the helicopter together with said assistant and wooden package.'

Dunstan kept his thoughts to himself but he had a number of Pakistani military friends who had attended Staff College with him, a few of whom had been to APS. He knew of at least one who had gone on to take up a senior position in military intelligence. *Abbottabad Public School, APS! Greater Himalayan Education Foundation... I wonder if APS is the spiritual home to this Game?*

Now, however, instead of a clearer picture emerging, he was seeing more and more barriers coming up, presenting him with the prospect of his quarry outstripping him – over the hills and far away. Literally in this case.

'Which direction did the helicopter go in, Captain Dhar?' he asked.

'Hard to say; generally south. Of course that doesn't mean very much. Ghol went into the main building of the college. We maintained observation for two hours. Then we saw the helicopter land again, no passengers this time. Ghol didn't come out to greet it. We then got the order to break out and RV with you.'

Dunstan thought aloud. 'A two-hour round trip to drop off a sealed container. Hmm...'

Dhar still had some surprises up her sleeve. 'By the way, Corporal Murria got some good long-range shots of all the players before they took off in the chopper. We squirted them off to Headshed for analysis.'

'Good work. And we don't know where Ghol himself is right now, and we can't trace him?'

'Unless he switches his mobile phone on,' responded Dhar. 'We've captured his mobile number. You can try ringing him if you want!'

She made this offer not altogether tongue-in-cheek. After all, she had arranged for such calls to take place to warlords on several occasions in the Balkans, to offer them deals to come in from the cold, or simply to let them know they had a sell-by date on their life.

'It was a pity he changed his trousers, as we lost the bug we planted in the hem,' she added nonchalantly.

Dunstan was both incredulous and admiring. He knew they must have got very close up and personal to Ghol, and wondered how they had done it without blowing their cover. The Monk grinned and Laycock knew then that he would have enough stories from this to stand several nights in the Squadron Mess when he returned home – if he was allowed to say anything at all post-Operation.

The Monk had been holding the receiver of the secure Sat phone link for some time. Now he thrust it at Dunstan. 'Rebecca Lovat for you. She says it's urgent.'

'Dunstan, it's Lovat.' She sounded remote and stand-offish, perhaps overtly so. The ice maiden was back to her professional self. 'I've been doing some research on this nuclear physicist, Iqbal Khan. Mostly circumstantial stuff, nothing specific, but I have found something in the FO portal: a report from the Pakistani equivalent of the Audit Commission, citing a discrepancy of point eight of a kg of weapons grade plutonium unaccounted for in the annual nuclear facilities audit. One of our Foreign Service guys on the ground in Pakistan must have got hold of it. Iqbal Khan was quizzed by a secret committee of MPs but he was unable, he claimed, to throw any light on the matter and it was put down to "wastage". I've cross-referenced dates with Tysoe. The date on which this so-called discrepancy occurred was shortly *before* any transfers of funds into Khan's Lichtenstein account. Although it's only circumstantial evidence, it does make the possibility of a nuclear dimension more likely!'

'Thanks, Rebecca. The only way we're going to find out is to trace and track Ghol right to his end game, wherever and whatever that might be. Any more on the UK threat?'

Lovat knew exactly what he meant: 'No further developments. Wide area protection is in place. Rest assured, I'll keep you informed of any developments. Now, I have a personal message to you from your friend, His Excellency. The message reads as follows, quote: >>>*Top Cover as promised is now in place and airspace has been cleared at the highest levels. Communications will be relayed direct from Call Sign Top Cover to you via Al-Qurum and London to your secure Sat link. UK communications people have the connections. May God go with you, exclamation*>>>. Message ends. His aide who delivered the message said you would understand what it meant. Do you?'

'Indeed, I do. Hopefully it means we can track non-commercial flights. Thanks, Rebecca. The Monk will keep channels open to you. Out for now.'

Dunstan put down the receiver and looked across at the 267 Signals Squadron warrant officer who had been seconded to the team. 'Do you have the incantations to set us up with uplink and downlink to Call Sign Top Cover?'

'Yes, sir. The co-ordinates came though from London about thirty minutes ago. It's a satellite uplink but I don't know what the downlink is; a surveillance satellite, I presume.'

'Something like that,' replied Dunstan. He wasn't about to explain to this general audience that his whole surveillance operation was to be directed from an Al-Qurum Air Force AWACS flying overhead in Pakistani airspace.

'How do we actually establish communications?' Dunstan asked.

'It's a bit like the Internet, sir. We ping it, wake it up if you like, and send the equivalent of an email wrapped up securely in an encrypted electronic address.'

Which is received by a human being, orbiting overhead, not a satellite.

Dunstan kept the thought to himself.

Murria was peering intently at what looked like a heavily modified, ruggedised iPad. 'We'd better get on and do it quickly then, sir,' said Murria. 'Our target's switched on his phone. I have a position: he's still at the school but he's on the move.' She was getting a new GPRS position through every five seconds. 'In fact, I reckon it's too late to intercept. At the rate he's moving, he must be airborne, sir!'

Dunstan was quick off the mark. 'Get the last three co-ordinates through to Call Sign Top Cover before we lose Ghol's mobile phone signal in the hills. Quick! That should be enough to get an initial bearing, then we can track him. Rough direction, Corporal Murria?'

She made a quick plot from the last three GPRS points. 'Looks like east-south-east, sir.'

The 267 Squadron warrant officer had become animated. 'Sir, I've received a positive response from Call Sign Top Cover. We're linked up. But... erm, sorry to state the bleeding obvious, sir, but we're only capable of tracing Target One based on his communications signals. His mobile phone will go off-signal at some stage. Without being able to latch onto Target One's aircraft communications signature we're stuffed, sir. The only way is to pick up a physical trace and track him by radar.'

Dunstan's response was an enigmatic smile. As reality dawned on the signals specialist, his eyes opened wide but his mouth stayed shut.

Whilst this discourse was taking place, The Monk had been pensive. He indicated that he and Dunstan should ease over to a quiet spot.

'This place, Kargil,' said The Monk softly. 'What about it?' responded Dunstan.

'It's where the world's highest battle took place.'

'What? I thought that was supposed to be the Siachen Glacier?'

'Nah. It was nineteen-ninety-nine. Pakistani Special Forces penetrated into Indian Kashmiri territory along the Line of Control and dug themselves into high positions, some of them on tops of hills at eighteen thousand feet around Kargil. The Indians took them out by pointing their Bofors howitzers at them, using them line-of-sight like an anti-tank weapon. They blasted most of the Pakistanis out of their positions. But some enemy pickets on the tops they had to take out by direct assault, right on top of the fucking mountains. Caused a real international stink as well. Surprised you don't know about it?'

'I remember a nuclear stand-off between Pakistan and India at the end of the Nineties but not much more. How do you know so much about this, Monk?' enquired Dunstan.

The Monk leaned closer to Dunstan and in his secretive, conspiratorial fashion, whispered, 'Because it's my fucking hobby!'

Enlightened by his friend, Dunstan turned to the others. 'Right, whilst our target is still airborne, let's get onto the Internet and see if we can get more detail on Kargil.'

The search produced immediate results. Dunstan scanned several sources and paraphrased for the others.

'OK, here we go: *prior to Partition in nineteen forty-seven, Kargil was part of Baltistan, a sparsely populated region with diverse linguistic, ethnic and religious groups, living in isolated valleys separated by some of the world's highest mountains...* Well, we know that much. *The first Kashmir War of forty-seven to forty-eight concluded with the Line of Control being established, dividing Baltistan in the process, with the town of Kargil on the Indian side of the LOC, in Indian Ladakh... After Pakistan was defeated in the Indo-Pakistani War of seventy-one, the two nations signed the Simla Agreement which redefined the Line of Control and in doing so both promised not to engage in armed conflict across the LOC. The area shot into the spotlight in spring of nineteen ninety-nine when, under a covert plan, armed infiltrators from Pakistan, aided by the Pakistani army, occupied vacant high posts belonging to India in the Kargil region. The result was a limited-scale conflict – the Kargil War – between both nuclear-equipped nations which ended with India regaining the Kargil region through military power and diplomatic pressure. Kargil is just a hundred and eight miles from the Pakistani-controlled town of Skardu, which was capable of providing logistical and artillery support to Pakistani combatants...* And I can tell you all from personal knowledge that Skardu is one of the two key towns in the Northern Area's Gilgit-Baltistan Region,' finished Dunstan.

'So why is our man heading into Indian Kashmir?' asked The Monk.

It was Dhar who provided a possible answer. 'Perhaps he wants to reunite his homeland, Baltistan. After all, Kargil *District*, as defined within *historic* Baltistan, actually straddles the LOC.'

'You're suggesting he's trying to carve out a new homeland from territory currently held by both Pakistan and India? How the hell is he going to do that?' asked The Monk.

'Yes, I'm suggesting just that, together with all the profound danger that it poses for the whole region,' responded Dhar with gravitas.

The Monk summed up the situation succinctly. 'Well, let's hope we can track the bastard down before he causes a first-rate global fuck-up, then.'

Hearing this, Dunstan knew he needed to inject a fresh sense of urgency. 'Right, what's everybody waiting for? Let's prepare to get airborne. Hugo, how long does your team need to get tooled up?'

'We're here on peace-keeping duties only. Weapons and ammunition haven't as yet been issued. Other than that, the boys are ready to go, sir.'

'Good. Monk will issue instructions to get you sorted out with your weapons of choice. Monk, is your Scimitar Troop ready?'

'Sat on their packs, Boss, waiting for the word,' replied The Monk. 'Well, you've got it. Right, let's get kitted up and go. Mission Orders will be given when we get a clearer idea of our objective, wherever and whenever that might be. Captain Dhar, as far as I am aware, you and Corporal Murria haven't officially been seconded to us, have you?'

'No sir, we've reached the limit of our brief by delivering this information to you,' Dhar responded.

'Understood. However, put it this way: do you have any *specific* orders that would prevent you from accompanying us?'

'We have clear orders not to get involved in any military action, sir. In answer to your question, it depends on where we're going, *specifically*, sir. And of course, for what reason,' she replied cautiously.

'At this stage, I can only hazard a guess as to Ghol's destination. What we've learnt from your admirable intelligence-gathering efforts hasn't enabled us to verify his end game and destination, so our information isn't yet definitive. I have no idea *precisely* where we're going but our mission comes under the cover of the Al-Qurum Aid Programme and so has to remain within Pakistani territory.'

'In that case, I don't have any direct orders preventing me from going to any such unknown destination under the auspices of an aid programme, sir,' Dhar replied carefully. Corporal Murria opened her mouth to interject but then thought better of it.

'Welcome on board, then!' Dunstan knew he was being disingenuous but his interest lay in Dhar's Kashmiri background, together with her cultural insight, rather than her military skills.

As they all headed out of the door to finalise preparations, The Monk's satellite phone rang; the pylon survey helicopter in the UK was logging in. The Monk heard the ribald greeting. He said nothing but merely signalled to Dunstan that he would be along shortly after the call.

'Monk, it's Digger. Do you know how much it costs to phone a friggin' maritime SAT phone from a mobile? Twenty-four quid a bloody minute, mate, but that's fuck-all compared to keeping this chopper in the air.'

The Monk had been expecting such a tirade and had squared the answer off with Tysoe before departure from Al-Qurum. 'I don't know what you're gum-bumping about, you'll get your reward in hell...think of all those virgins lined up. Look Digger, more than enough money to keep you in wine gums for a lifetime is heading into your bank account. No worries, mate. You're more than catered for.'

To Digger, The Monk's idiosyncratic way of informing him that he would receive more than adequate compensation for his efforts was as much as he needed. 'Good effort, Monk. Now look, we've got 'em: decamming and reloading kit, edge of woods near Ascot-under-Wychwood.'

'You sure?'

'Of course I'm bloody sure! Been over them several times. Looks like three up, loads of equipment being restacked in the back, including a couple of GPMGs and some long metal boxes that look like surface-to-air to me. Don't want to do any more overpasses in case they get spooked.'

The Monk wasn't exactly surprised at the fruits of Digger's observations but they didn't make him any happier. 'OK, Digger, good effort! Now, keep a track on these gadgies, and if and when they make a move, track their trajectory. Then telephone this Beckwith bloke at Thames Valley Polizei and give him the full gen. Next, phone your old troopy, Gibbs, in London Headshed. Correction, he *is* the fucking Headshed, he should already know about this.'

'Monk, it's early Saturday morning! Headshed in London will be on civvy time!'

'Don't worry. My int says they're all working overtime to cover our collective arses. I'll talk to our spooks at this end to get his number from *their* Headshed and I'll ping it over to you.'

'OK, will do, mate.'

'I owe you one, Digger!'

'You fucking well owe me lots! Oh, by the way, Monk!' 'What?'

'You're still a tosser!'

The Monk laughed out loud as he killed the call. Then he fell very still, his black eyes far away. He made a few operational notes then picked up the handset and called Lovat in Al-Qurum. He needed contingency – a shedload of it.

***

An excited 267 signals specialist entered the makeshift armoury, and ran over to Dunstan, who heard what he had to say and called The Monk and Captain Dhar on the local area net (established to co-ordinate the logistics of the aid programme), then ran full tilt back over to the make-shift ops room taking Captain Laycock with him. Target One had landed.

'What? Where?' Dunstan questioned the 267 team, who pointed to a location a few miles inside the Line of Control in Azad Kashmir, in what was ancient Baltistan, the old District of Kargil. Dunstan grabbed his laptop, logged onto Google Earth and typed in the co-ordinates. It took a while for the digital image to resolve itself. When it had, they could all see clearly a semi-ruined ancient fortress located in wild and arid country, atop a stony pinnacle.

'Doesn't look like the centre of a smart operation,' The Monk commented. Dunstan pointed to the bottom of the screen. '*Satellite image date: 2007.*

It could have changed considerably since then, especially with the resources these guys have.'

Dunstan turned to his intelligence expert. 'Well, Captain Dhar, if this *is* Ghol's final destination, your local insight and intuition will have proved correct. At least it gives us an objective *within* the LOC. I really didn't fancy a cross-border incursion into India, no matter how well-intentioned. I'll deliver a preliminary mission briefing in thirty minutes' time in the main hangar, based on what we know, which is by no means perfect. All operational hands to attend. I don't want to mess about with hierarchy briefings, I need to look every man and woman in the eye and make sure they're up for it!'

***

Oxfordshire–Warwickshire border, 0800 hours

The chopper landed in a field close to some suspect pylons. Digger Cole got out to make a couple of calls.

'Thames Valley Police, how can I help you?'

By getting off your shiny arses and putting more criminal scum behind bars. 'By putting me through to Detective Chief Inspector Beckwith, please,' Cole said with an unnaturally polite intonation.

'May I say who is calling?'

'Yes. Tell him it's a bloke with information that will save the rest of his career and ensure him a nice fat pension.'

'Oh. Right. Er, I'll see if I can put you through,' the receptionist said awkwardly.

'Detective Sergeant Lowe speaking.'

'I was trying to get through to a bloke called Beckwith with a higher rank than you,' Digger said flatly.

Lowe did a good job at remaining unruffled. 'I work for DCI Beckwith. What do you want?'

'Are you involved in this CyberX case?'

'I couldn't possibly comment.'

'I'll take that as "yes", then. Look, cutting through the crap, I'm told that you're looking for a military Land Rover in connection with a kidnap and other matters such as blowing up a few houses. Well, I've found the little bastard.'

'What! Where? Who are you? How did you get this information?'

'Too many questions at once there, Detective Sergeant. Be careful now. There's a way of dealing with anonymous tip-offs, isn't there? You must have done the course. B3400 north-bound to Stratford, obboed from helicopter.'

'"Obboed"? Helicopter?'

'Observed. Whirly Bird. Rotors. Goes up and down, you know the sort of thing. Look, are you interested or not?'

'Indeed I am, er, we are!'

'Then be a good lad and stay by the line while we pick him up again and give you a grid reference and bearing. What's your direct line?'

Lowe gave it to Digger. *Either this guy is insane, or he's the breakthrough we need*, he thought.

The next call was more difficult and Digger was relying on The Monk's judgement being spot-on. *The chances of DSF taking an unsolicited call at his office or anywhere else are remote*, thought Digger. He decided to call someone he knew, who was in close proximity to DSF, and would be in his office early on a Saturday morning: DSF's hyperactive Chief Clerk.

'Hi Dave, it's Digger Cole here. I've got some gold dust info for DSF. No time for pleasantries – I need to speak to him pronto.'

'And he hasn't the time to waste, Digger. It had better be bloody good.'

'The Monk said he would want to know this gen, Dave.'

'Odd. That's twice in the last couple of days I've heard that name. He's just landed at base – DSF, that is. I'll try and get him for you. Be careful what you say, Digger, you're on an open mobile network.'

'Of course I am – it's me making the bloody call with the mobile!' Digger shouted down the line.

'Just covering my arse, Digger. Hold on to yours...'

A cultured voice came on the line. 'Sergeant-Major Cole! How are you? Haven't heard from you in years!' Gibbs was always genuinely pleased to hear from his old Regiment contacts, especially the likes of ex-troopers from his first SAS troop command.

Even as a civilian, and as chipper as Cole might be, his inclination was to show his ex-commanding officer all due deference, especially as he had now made it to the pinnacle of Special Forces rank. *As The Monk said, he is the fucking Headshed,* mused Digger.

'Good morning, sir. No time for chit-chat on this call I'm afraid, Boss. If this works you can buy me a pint at the Club. The Monk said you would want to know the location and bearing of a civilianised military Land Rover.'

'Indeed, we might, Digger,' Gibbs replied cautiously.

'That being the case, Boss, we're airborne in a chopper – my new civvy job. On a tip-off from The Monk, we spotted the target twenty minutes ago near Stratford-on-Avon, heading north. If you give me a mobile number I'll text you grid references, road, bearing, etc.'

'Digger, that would be most useful. Chief – I need your mobile number!'

'It's not secure, sir!'

'I bloody well know that. Just give it to me!'

***

Thames Valley Police Headquarters, Kidlington, Oxfordshire

'Anonymous?' queried DCI Beckwith. 'And he'll get back with an update later? We've been looking all over the county for this Land Rover and some bloke rings up as though he's giving a bloody running commentary on its whereabouts!'

'Yes, sir. He wouldn't give his name or location, or how he had come to be tracking the Land Rover. He said he would ring back with an update on the direct line, sir.'

'Am I missing something here, Lowe?'

'Helicopter, sir. You're missing the helicopter. I didn't get to that bit.'

'So who the hell pays for a helicopter to stay in the air for and on behalf of Her Majesty's Constabulary of Police, tracking a possible fugitive vehicle? Who's paying for this? Sounds bloody odd to me.' Beckwith's natural cynicism was growing the more he heard. 'Any other odd things about this call, Lowe?'

'Only that he asked for you by name, sir.'

'Listen, Lowe. My experience tells me you've got a crank here. Forget it. If he does phone back be polite, but get rid of him, pronto. We've better things to do than entertain…'

The phone interrupted Beckwith. Lowe grabbed it.

'Detective Sergeant Lowe… Oh, hello.' Lowe mouthed '*It's him!*'

'A new location… one minute, please, I have Detective Chief Inspector Beckwith with me, I'm putting you on speaker phone.'

'DCI Beckwith here. Who am I speaking to?'

'Hi there,' said Digger, sociably. 'You the bloke who wants to track this poxy old military Land Rover then?'

'I could be,' replied Beckwith, bridling at being dismissed as a "bloke".

'Don't be obtuse, son,' shot back Digger. Beckwith hadn't been called 'son' in a couple of decades; he had *never* been called obtuse. Lowe turned away to stifle a grin. 'Now pin your conch-like back and listen in: B3400 north-bound, currently stationary in a lay-by three miles south of Stratford-on-Avon. That's outside your manor. If I were you, old son, I'd get yer inter-force alerts out now to keep tabs on these little buggers. And no bloody heroics from over-ambitious constables! From what I hear and see, these guys are well tooled-up and professional with it. The last thing you want is a full-scale firefight with high velocity weapons and missiles on an English motorway – or anywhere near a populated area for that matter. These guys are death-on-a-stick according to The Monk.'

'Who?' queried Beckwith.

'Somebody whose opinion and judgement I respect, and you would be wise to as well. Now at some stage you might well get a call from my old Headshed offering some help and useful back-up. If that happens, take it. Grab it with both sweaty hands – for your own good!'

Beckwith and Lowe looked at each other, not understanding. 'We didn't get that last bit about "help" and "head" something. Can you explain?' asked Beckwith.

'Headshed. And no explanation,' said Digger flatly. 'You'll know when the call comes.'

'Er, registration number?' asked Lowe, trying to ask something useful. 'From five hundred feet it's a bit unclear, son,' replied Digger with more than a hint of sarcasm.

'What's your name?' asked Beckwith again.

'Digger, my name is Digger,' replied Digger, helpfully. 'That's my bit done, guys. At the risk of sounding impatient, I suggest you get your arses into gear, like pronto.' With that Digger Cole terminated the call.

Lowe looked at Beckwith, unsure of his boss's reaction. He soon got it. 'Well don't just stand there, Lowe! Do as the man said! Get your arse into gear and get an inter-force alert out with a "track and report only" order. Emphasise: *under no circumstances to be approached*. Until we know more. Off you go!'

'How did you decide he was genuine, sir?' Lowe asked tentatively. 'The voice of authority, Lowe. He spoke to me like I was a young copper and didn't waffle. And he wouldn't give his name. Nutters always give a name. He has to be genuine.'

Lowe went away muttering to himself, *and I thought this Digger bloke said "arses", plural and collective!*

***

Aid Programme Ops Base, 1100 hours

Preparations over, all flight and military operational personnel were assembled in the hangar awaiting Dunstan's operational briefing.

A focused Dunstan picked up a long wooden pointer and went straight into his briefing session.

'*Situation:* this is Pakistani, or Azad, Kashmir. And this – Indian Kashmir.'

'Between India and Azad Kashmir runs the so-called Line of Control, or LOC: two nuclear superpowers facing off against each other over a negotiated notional line, a barely agreed border. To the north of the LOC is Gilgit-Baltistan, formerly called the Northern Areas until 2009 when it was awarded a higher degree of autonomy by Pakistan. India still has claims on this area as part of its total claim on Jammu and Kashmir. This is one of the most politically volatile borders in the world, with continual skirmishes occurring between Indian and Pakistani troops stationed on the high vantage points up to 20,000 feet. It's sometimes referred to as the highest battleground in the world.'

He had already got every single person's undivided attention. He pointed into Gilgit-Baltistan, to a particular location within a few kilometres of the Line of Control.

'Intelligence indicates this is a key location, possibly headquarters, for the planning of terrorist insurgency operations across the LOC, possibly with the aim of securing self-determination for Gilgit-Baltistan. This has the potential to lead to pan-regional unrest. We have been tasked by local powers who do not wish to be seen to be deploying troops to a strategically sensitive area right on the Line of Control. In short, this is a containment exercise preventing an escalation in tensions between India and Pakistan. Geographically, it is one of the highest valleys in the world at 3,500m and it straddles one of the most sensitive border areas in the world, between India, China and Pakistan.' He paused, then stated with deliberation,

'*Mission*: to seek out and, if practical, remove this threat to pan-regional stability.'

Dunstan repeated the mission statement. There were gasps of surprise in the room when they heard this. The atmosphere notched up a rung. Laycock understood now why it was deniable.

'*Nature of Threat*: intelligence is not specific. It could be anywhere between a few key people to a welcoming committee of several hundred Nepalese mercenaries. For planning purposes, we must assume the latter. That's why we have significant firepower with us.

'*Resources*: Two MC-13 Combat Talons, one DC-10 in-flight refuelling tanker, plus one AC-130 Spectre gunship to provide air support; one mobility troop from Scimitar Regiment plus one section of a British Army Commando Troop.

'*Plan*: General outline: the force will move to the region under cover of an aid mission to the landslide zone in Azad Kashmir. The aid programme flight will drop off aid and return to base, whilst the remainder will continue east along the LOC.

'*Phase 1*: 1300 hours to 1400 hours local time. Move together with aid mission flight.

'*Phase 2*: 1400 hours to 1500 hours local time: as the Aid Mission flights deploy to their air drop zones, our force will continue flying due east approximately 250 miles, heading along the Line of Control close to Indian Kashmiri air space. If there is a moment designed for a cock-up then it is at this point...' Dunstan looked hard into the eyes of each and every soldier. He turned and pointed at the map:

'From Google Earth, it seems there is a suitable landing zone on a broad alluvial plain some three miles due west of the objective. This is the "Forming Up Point". The Spectre gunship will remain airborne, together with the fuel tanker on stand-off, to provide air support if needed.

'*Phase 3*: Reconnaissance: qualify and quantify target. We need to get as close in as we can, but quickly. As we all know, time for reconnaissance is seldom available and there will be precious little time in this operation. We have manned aerial vehicle capability with thermal imaging.

'*Phase 4*: Target objective. Take out the threat. Complete mission.

'*Tasking*:....'

As he proceeded to give his orders, all in the room, even The Monk, were impressed by the boldness of the plan.

At the end, Dunstan asked for questions. There were a few queries on the co-ordinating instructions which were easily dealt with.

Laycock spoke up. 'The mission contains the phrase "if practical". For the sake of all present, could you clarify what that actually means, sir, and what limitations might apply?'

'Good question, Hugo. The simple answer is that should our reconnaissance assessment show overwhelming odds, we'll make a very quick tactical withdrawal. I assure you, this is *not* a suicide mission!' Dunstan used all due emphasis to make his point.

With that unequivocal statement, orders were over. The final check was to ensure that those who were not already acclimatised had taken their Diamox tablets to offset the effects of altitude sickness. Acetazolamide, or Diamox, is the most tried-and-tested drug for preventing this condition. Taking full doses was allowing the non-acclimatised soldiers to adapt and operate more effectively in the rarefied air.

As Dunstan walked out across the airbase to the aircraft, it dawned on him that his life to this point had consisted of a series of rehearsals for a play in which he now found himself taking the leading role. It was like sliding on an old and familiar glove; he felt more comfortable in his own skin than he had for many years.

Chapter Twenty

Saturday: London, 0830 hours; Al-Qurum, 1130 hours; Abbottabad, 1330 hours

Celia Fanshawe had managed only three hours' fitful sleep in the arm-chair in her office. She had been at her desk since 5 a.m. reviewing all the material in front of her and she was now wondering how long she could wait before she felt compelled to call her Chief, and then the Permanent Under-Secretary at the Ministry of Defence in charge of inter-service intelligence co-ordination.

Major General Gibbs had come over from his Regents Park office and joined her for a working breakfast. The safe return of his SRR soldiers was uppermost in his mind, yet if he had known that Captain Dhar was even then putting herself far beyond a reasonable margin of safety he would have been doubly worried.

Scenes emerging on BBC News 24 interrupted their deliberations:

'All commentators now appear to agree that Pakistan is in crisis: parts of the country are in the hands of local warlords and the Taliban has extended its control across large parts of the Swat Valley and North and South Waziristan. Emergency services are reported to be struggling and cannot cope with the dead and wounded in Lahore and Karachi and there are reports of the unrest spreading to other major cities... in a worrying development, sources close to the Pentagon believe that one or more Pakistani nuclear weapons facilities near Wah, just west of Rawalpindi, may have been infiltrated by terrorists. The Pakistani government strenuously denies this. The BBC Security Editor, Frank Beswick, has said that such a takeover of highly-guarded facilities would require 'internal collusion'... breaking news: The United Nations is to convene an emergency meeting of the Security Council to discuss, quote >>>the growing threat to regional stability>>>unquote'.

The place is very clearly on the edge of chaos, thought Fanshawe. She now realised that she could no longer viably keep matters under wraps. She was reaching for the phone resignedly to call her Chief when it rang. It was her secretary asking if she would take a call from Commander Counter Terrorism Command. With an audible grunt, she agreed. Hoskins had not been the harbinger of good news recently, and she assumed this call would be no different. She was right.

'Good morning, Celia, Jim Hoskins here. I thought I would find you at your desk early this Saturday!'

'Please get to the point, Jim.' She was in no mood for platitudes.

'Okay, the point is: have you any *hard evidence* of a UK terrorist threat arising out of this CyberX fiasco?'

What can I say to him except the truth? 'No, Jim. Nothing whatsoever at this moment.'

'So nothing quantifiable, then?' Hoskins persisted.

'No, I said so, Jim,' she responded, irritably. 'Why do you ask?'

Hoskins continued as though he had not heard his Home Service counterpart. 'Which leaves us where, Celia? I'm afraid that *unknown, unquantifiable and unrelated to terrorism* is not deserving of a dedicated Counter Terrorism Command anti-terrorist protection squad. I'm sure you'll agree?'

'Now hang on a minute! There may not as yet be a specific threat to Dunstan's family, but there is the matter of the murders of Idris Morgan and Dunstan's secretary. And the latest is that CyberX's manager in Prague has been, er, done away with. We believe the perpetrators are likely to target Dunstan's family, and they are known to be moving north from Oxfordshire at the moment.'

'So no *proven* threat within the UK then, Celia?'

'Nothing definitive, I would have to agree.' With so many joint Counter Terrorism Command and MI5 surveillance and protection tasks running concurrently, Fanshawe knew she couldn't afford to cry wolf on this one.

'Well, I see no reason for Counter Terrorism Command to expend this level of precious resources on maintaining a comprehensive wide area presence in the middle of the Scottish Highlands. Do you realise what it takes to protect a twenty-thousand-acre estate, or whatever obscene size it is? I apologise, of course you do! Look, you more than anyone know how thinly we're stretched. I'm downgrading the cover to close quarter protection only, with immediate effect, Celia.'

'That's your call, Jim. But all the indicators are there for this being a personal vendetta against Dunstan, which in my mind puts his family in real and possibly imminent danger!' She realised her voice had risen half an octave; she knew she was in danger of sounding shrill and checked herself.

'Look, Celia, I've spoken with the local Assistant Chief Constable and he's agreed to supplement my team with a couple of his firearms officers. My resources are at full stretch as it is. You know that we have over seventy potential terrorist threats running concurrently, a number of which require close protection of identified targets based on *real* intelligence.' Fanshawe knew she had no response to that; she remained silent.

'The wide area cordon is coming out, Celia. If anything changes, I'm sure you'll let me know.' With that, Hoskins rang off.

Fanshawe stared at the phone, checking her emotions.

Gibbs had got the gist. Now on home ground instead of the murky world of intelligence and obfuscation, he thought for a moment, then said, 'Given the armed capabilities of these mercenaries – for let's be absolutely clear that's *exactly* what they are – the police have very few tactical options open to them. If they're travelling on major arterial roads, there's no way the police can risk apprehending them, it's simply too dangerous. *Theoretically,* we could wait until they're on a remote road and take them out with, say, Hellfire missiles launched from an Apache, but that would be politically unpalatable; in fact, it would probably cause a real stink. So, in summary, in order to avoid endangering the public, it would be best to contain them in an out-of-the-way area before we can deal with them. And that means the remote Highlands.'

'General, do I take it that you're suggesting using Dunstan's family as bait, and Special Forces to apprehend and make an arrest?' Fanshawe couched her question carefully.

DSF let the unformed thought hang in the air. Each knew what the other was thinking, but could not bring themselves to say it: Special Forces could only be deployed on the UK mainland in support of the civil authorities, and then only at the request of the Prime Minister or a sitting COBRA (Cabinet Office Briefing Room) committee. A shoot-to-kill policy was out of the question unless there was a real and immediate threat to life.

But then again, each knew that an arrest would open a whole can of worms that would in the end raise more questions than it answered.

Gibbs concentrated on immediate practical matters: 'The Monk's friends seem to think these men are using a UK Special Forces HF radio with a long-range aerial. HF means long-distance, probably short-burst and probably Morse code. Could our friends at GCHQ intercept their transmissions?'

'Now that *is* interesting. I'll get someone onto it straight away,' Fanshawe responded, without articulating *why* it was interesting. But for her it was another missing piece in her fast-emerging intelligence jigsaw.

She now knew that the time for deliberation had passed, it was time for action. She paused for a moment, evaluating her next step. The 'full and frank' dialogue with the senior partner at Cavendish Bank last night had proved illuminating and had served to confirm her suspicions. She was now as sure as she could be that she knew who was directing the vendetta against Dunstan and his family from within the UK. The surveillance she had put in place a couple of hours ago would hopefully pay dividends. Now she had decided to make her move.

She turned to Gibbs. 'Christopher, I have to introduce the Joint Intelligence Committee, Home Office and Foreign Office into this matter, but that's been inevitable for some time now.'

'That's your call, of course.'

Fanshawe continued, 'First though, it's time to take the initiative within our own territory and arrest a foreign diplomat on British soil. To do this, we need a policeman with a strong interest in this case in order to level charges of murder, and conspiracy to murder, at a certain Mr Shafquat Khan, the Security Services Liaison Officer at the Pakistani High Commission. The mandarins might decide to put him on trial here, but I very much doubt it; most likely they'll determine that it's better to keep a lid on these matters. Such are the expedients of international diplomacy. Our Pakistani friends at the High Commission will be suitably embarrassed of course. No doubt they will prefer that we keep it all very quiet. After all, Christopher, we don't want to heap opprobrium on them, do we?'

She looked at Gibbs for approval. He merely nodded in agreement, trying to imagine large piles of opprobrium being heaped upon the Pakistani High Commission.

Fanshawe was in full stride. 'Now, given the substantial downgrade of protection by Hoskins, we also need to keep track of this hit team who are presumed to be threatening Dunstan's family. I agree with you that it's a matter of national security that we find these mercenaries as soon as possible and deal with them in a time, manner and location of our choosing. Clearly only COBRA can make the call to deploy Special Forces in the UK mainland in support of the civil authorities. However, if that *were* to occur, it would be helpful to your planning to have some prior intelligence, wouldn't it, Christopher?'

'Indeed it would,' responded an attentive Director Special Forces.

'Good. We're agreed then. Let's now place a call to this Detective Chief Inspector at Thames Valley Constabulary, whose misfortune it has been to chase ghosts…and hopefully we can get to Mr Khan before he issues any more orders over his HF set to his team of, er, executioners.'

They were interrupted by Hamilton, who knocked and entered without pausing to be invited in. Her news more than justified the interruption. 'Excuse me ma'am, but Rebecca Lovat has found some key information regarding a quantity of weapons grade plutonium going missing in Pakistan.'

'How much, Elizabeth?' Fanshawe enquired.

'Point eight of a kilo. More than enough to make a compact-sized nuclear device, ma'am.'

'Now that *is* interesting, Elizabeth – worrying information, but useless intelligence unless we're able to tie Ghol to it. Have we done that?'

'Not yet, ma'am.'

'Keep at it. Let me know if and when you have a tie-up.' Fanshawe turned to DSF and in doing so effectively sent Hamilton on her way to push on with her alchemy of turning data into intelligence. Fanshawe hesitated for a moment, seemingly juggling priorities. *I need to make the calls to my superiors and we need to bring in the FO and the appropriate Whitehall mandarins. Then there's a call to GCHQ to get them to prioritise intercepts of HF calls for analysis… No, I'll phone Thames Valley first and push on along that front, we need to get to Shafquat Khan before he causes any more mayhem… Anyway, the watchers and lift team are already in place. The Whitehall hierarchy can wait for an hour.*

'Right, Christopher, let's get on to Thames Valley Police; and remember both of us are from the security service. I'm sure you want your organisation to remain under the radar!'

***

<u>Oxford, 0930 hours</u>

At Kidlington Police Headquarters, DCI Beckwith had been interrupted in pursuit of his quarry to take an urgent call that had come in to his boss, an ambitious Detective Superintendent who had been brought up in the new regime of achieving crime-solving targets and prosecutions within tight timescales. The DS was not a happy man. As yet, he had had no result out of DCI Beckwith and his team for an execution-style murder; a kidnap, possible torture and murder; an international card fraud run from within his patch; and the destruction of a smart Cotswold house in a large explosion – not forgetting the extraordinary disappearance of the chief suspect by air. He was under pressure, working over the weekend, and this call coming through on a Saturday from the office of the Chief Constable, Thames Valley Police, had added to it. He was not best pleased, and on the basis that 'shit flows downhill', he took some small pleasure in knowing that Beckwith was about to get dumped on.

Beckwith entered the DS's office with his defences up. The look he received said it all.

The DS was holding the line waiting for Beckwith. He covered the receiver, 'Whatever you do, Beckwith, play it straight with these people. Don't screw up! I don't know who they are, other than that they're senior intelligence officers. They'll introduce themselves.'

He uncovered the receiver and spoke in respectful tones. 'Sir, ma'am. DCI Beckwith is with us now.'

The cultured male voice at the end of the phone was authoritative and exuded self-assurance; however, both men noted that it had a clipped, sharp, edge to it. 'Good afternoon, DCI Beckwith, my name is Gibbs and I have with me Miss Fanshawe. Both of us are concerned with national security and in particular the fallout from the CyberX case.'

Fanshawe came in on the call. 'Good afternoon, gentlemen. Now that Mr Gibbs has made the introductions, we can press on with business directly.' If Gibbs' voice and intonation engendered instant respect, the female voice at the end of the phone instilled instant professional terror into anyone foolish enough to be of a sloppy-minded disposition. Both senior policemen involuntarily straightened their backs and switched their minds into a higher gear as she continued, 'We haven't much time here, so we'll get to the point. Have you found your murderer or murderers yet?' Fanshawe knew it was a somewhat disingenuous question, but she wanted to know where Beckwith had got to in his investigations.

Beckwith knew he could not hedge with this woman. 'Miss Fanshawe, this is DCI Beckwith here. Our chief suspect, a Mr Philip Dunstan, the assumed brains behind these, er, atrocities, has skipped the country and we have no other suspects except the actual hit team. He's covered his tracks by apparently arranging for the kidnap and murder of his secretary, and destroying key evidence by having his house blown up in his absence. As a result of intelligence from, er, sources, we've put out an all-forces alert to track the suspected perpetrators of these atrocities, who are believed to be travelling in an old military Land Rover, somehow acting on orders from Dunstan.'

'I shall take that as "No" then,' responded Fanshawe. Beckwith's boss looked at him as if to say, *I told you, don't screw this up.*

Major General Gibbs picked up on Beckwith's emphasis on two words. 'DCI Beckwith, did your *intelligence sources* mention that you might receive a call in connection with this matter?'

There was a momentary silence, then the veil lifted for Beckwith as two pieces of the jigsaw puzzle clunked together in his mind: *The Headshed. The man Digger had said to expect a call from 'the Headshed'.*

'Ah, are you the Headshed then?' he enquired chirpily.

The DS looked sharply at Beckwith in rebuke for his insubordination. Besides, he himself was obviously not up to speed on the latest developments, which annoyed him intensely. Beckwith was in for a serious grilling, post-call.

Unexpectedly, a warm chuckle came down the line from Gibbs. It was a light moment in the middle of a bloody affair. 'Yes, you could say we're the *Headshed*, Chief Inspector.'

The DS heard the words 'Headshed' and suddenly realised where he had heard Gibbs' name before.

'Do you know where Dunstan is, then?' responded Beckwith, making a quantum mental leap.

Fanshawe replied, 'The question of Mr Philip Dunstan's whereabouts, Detective Chief Inspector, is pertinent but ultimately irrelevant. I can tell you that he is currently in Pakistan. However, before you book your Club Class flight to Islamabad at taxpayers' expense, I assure you that far from being the perpetrator, Dunstan is actually the victim of a long-standing blood feud, dating from 2001 to be precise. I'm sure you recognise the date, Detective Chief Inspector?' Fanshawe was punctilious in using correct titles; she knew how much hard work was involved to get them in the first place. And she didn't ordinarily use acronyms.

'Yes, indeed I do, Miss Fanshawe.' Curiously, Beckwith felt as though a burden had been lifted. He knew at that moment that someone else knew a lot more than he did. It felt strangely comforting.

Fanshawe enlightened her listeners. 'Our interest here is to protect Dunstan's family. This is not necessarily personal to Dunstan, but is part of a broader picture of national security. Do you have an update on the movements of the military Land Rover currently on its way to Scotland?'

'Is it on its way to Scotland?'

'We have reason to think that it might be.'

'Oh. Well. I'm sorry, I don't. It has, er, disappeared... for the moment, that is.' Beckwith added confidently. He looked at his boss who was turning puce.

'Disappeared?' responded Gibbs.

'Yes, Mr Gibbs. Officially, there is an all-constabularies alert out: *extreme caution, do not approach, report location only*, but unofficially we've lost them and we don't know where to start looking.' Beckwith thought it was no time to apportion blame and point fingers, but then he didn't want the fat finger of blame pointing at him, either. 'Our fellow officers in a constabulary north of here have lost track of it.' Then, thinking of Digger, as an afterthought Beckwith added, 'Any help or information you can give would be useful.'

'Is that an official request?' elicited Fanshawe.

'I don't know who to make the official request out to, so officially, it's an unofficial request.'

The DS buried his head in his hands, but the Iron Lady was not so ferrous after all. 'I think we can do better than that, gentlemen. I should like to request, Detective Superintendent, that Detective Chief Inspector Beckwith diverts his efforts and comes down immediately to London to participate in the interrogation of a man whom we have strong evidence to suspect as the main orchestrator of these murders. It's Detective Chief Inspector Beckwith's case, and he can have the privilege of laying his charges before our suspect. He'll be lifted before you get here.'

Bloody hell! On a plate! thought Beckwith.

The DS now knew without a shadow of doubt that they were a small part of a very big game. He was no fool, and he was astute enough to know that this offer was to divert attention away from the hit squad heading north. He kept that insight to himself. 'Well, that being the case, Miss Fanshawe, when do you want DCI Beckwith to come down to London to attend this arrest?' 'Within the hour. He'll have to come down by helicopter. Immediately.'

Beckwith looked at his boss, who had no choice but to say, 'He's on his way, Miss Fanshawe.'

But Beckwith was not quite finished. 'Excuse me, Miss Fanshawe, Mr Gibbs. After we've made this arrest, where do we interview the suspect? A Metropolitan Police station for example – or here in Kidlington?'

A good point, thought the DS, and grunted as much. Neither policeman wanted their new chief suspect interrogated in a Metropolitan Police station. Fanshawe had anticipated this one and had her answer prepared. 'Neither of those options, gentlemen. He will be taken into our jurisdiction and interviewed in comfortable surroundings, rather like the first interview with Dunstan, Detective Chief Inspector, which you attended less than a week ago. There are diplomatic considerations here and, besides which, we don't want him in a dungeon.'

Something didn't fit and Beckwith knew it. 'That being the case, Miss Fanshawe, why have I got to come all the way down to London if there's a good chance this new suspect is going to be quietly shipped out of the country under a blanket?'

'Because, my dear Detective Chief Inspector, it allows us to formally close your case files, which clears Mr Philip Dunstan of any wrongdoing and allows him back into the country with a clean sheet. You're not alone in this matter. We have a similar exercise to go through with a police force in mid-Wales. We simply wish for you to lay serious charges against Mr Khan before we read him his horoscope, so to speak.'

Beckwith had by now realised who he was dealing with, but just to verify he said, 'And how *is* Mr Freshfield, Miss Fanshawe?'

'He's dead, Detective Chief Inspector. Operational, in the field,' came the matter-of-fact response.

Beckwith rocked on his heels. It wasn't exactly the answer he was expecting. 'I'm sorry to hear that, Miss Fanshawe. He was a top operator. A good man.'

'Indeed he was, a first-class operator, sorely missed. There will be a reception team awaiting your arrival at Battersea heliport, DCI Beckwith. Goodbye, gentlemen.' With that, the call ended abruptly.

The DS looked at Beckwith with an uncharacteristic degree of compassion. 'Tread carefully, Beckwith. You're travelling into the company of some unusually high-powered people here. That man Gibbs isn't a civilian, he's a serving army officer. He was guest speaker one night on the Strategic Defence Course I attended at Shrivenham. He was most interesting and *very* impressive.'

'Sir,' replied Beckwith, with uncharacteristic deference, taking in what the DS was trying to say to him. 'Sounds like a fairly young bloke. Which bit of the army is he in, then?'

His boss gave him a withering look. 'The *Special* bit; he's Director Special Forces.'

'What, *all* of them?'

'Yes. Every "S" you can think of. And as far as I'm aware, Headmistress Fanshawe could well be the next Director-General of Security Services. You keep distinguished company, Beckwith. Tread lightly and assume at all times they know a lot more than we do. We're bit players in this game, Beckwith.'

***

Gibbs was born with a natural optimism which was tempered by a hard-won pragmatism gained on numerous tough operations. He looked at Fanshawe challengingly.

'The hit team have gone off-radar, so on the principle of turning a weakness into an advantage that means no one will miss them if they disappear completely.'

Fanshawe was thoughtful. She did not want to be implicitly responsible for ordering a cold-blooded execution. 'I would rather they were captured alive. After all, it's clear now that this hit team, as you call them, are not operating on their own initiative.' She knew it sounded holier-than-thou.

Gibbs had his response. 'Of course, but you must agree the greater tragedy would be the killing of one or more members of Dunstan's family. And the political and media fallout would be enormous. You couldn't possibly put a lid on it.'

Fanshawe sighed. 'Yes, I have to agree, Christopher. I'll increase the priority on HF and other monitoring to trace and track this team. Let's squeeze Shafquat Khan when we get hold of him, and see where we get to. In the meantime, you might wish to put your own team on standby.'

'I already have,' Gibbs replied emphatically.

***

And on such delicate weighing of outcomes and determination of priorities do events turn. Fanshawe was not to know until some forty-eight hours later that the very moment she had placed the call to Thames Valley Constabulary, one of the GCHQ receiving stations at Chicksands in Bedfordshire had picked up an HF Morse code transmission that appeared to emanate from the environs of Knightsbridge, London, and was being transmitted to an unknown recipient at a location triangulated to be somewhere in the north of England. Deep under the limestone escarpment near Cheltenham, the item was duly logged by the Cray computers as a possible transmission-of-interest for the GCHQ analysts to process. Transcribed, it read: >>>*Clear to finish job in your time and by your own means stop signal when task complete and final stop funds will then be transferred as promised stop*>>>. It was Shafquat Khan's final transmission prior to his departure to a warmer climate and, as it happened, it was allocated a low analysis priority by GCHQ. Fanshawe had missed the boat by minutes.

***

The watchers, who had been repainting the high gloss iron railings in Knightsbridge Square from early morning, had done their job. Their tag-team covering the rear of the Pakistani High Commission radioed through that Target was on the move: Shafquat Khan, Cultural Attaché, yet secretly Head of Liaison between Pakistani ISI and British SIS, was leaving the building in a relaxed manner with a couple of flight bags. It was now time for the watchers to hand over to the lift team.

Chapter Twenty-One

Saturday: Pakistan, 1600 hours

Dunstan and The Monk, together with half of the Scimitar contingent, were in the leading Talon; Laycock and his Commandos, Dhar and the remaining Scimitar soldiers in the other. A portion of the front hold of each Talon was taken up with a specially designed, almost soundproof operations cell. In their cell, Dunstan and The Monk were looking at Google Earth, analysing the terrain around their target from multiple angles. They could distinguish the broad alluvial plain below the old fortress but it was difficult to assess the steepness and nature of the terrain leading up to the building itself. There was a tap at the door and the First Officer came in with the transcript of a signal with 'Most Secret' at the top. The Monk took it. It was from Lovat, and it was brief.

>>>*S Khan verified as controller stop lifted and caged stop refuses to speak except to Target One stop Comms channels are open for when you take Target One stop*>>>

'So why the hell do we need to open up comms between this Khan bloke and Target One?' questioned The Monk.

Dunstan was silent. He was rereading the signal and he shivered involuntarily. He was deadly serious. 'Because, Monk, you were right; this is a blood feud and Ghol is the only one who can call off the hit team.'

The aircraft landed on the broad alluvial plain at the pre-designated Forming Up Point some three miles down from their objective, the fortress. Dunstan split his troops into three units: Scimitar Troop under The Monk, and another section comprised of mainly combat engineer commandos under Laycock, were designated to move down either flank at a slightly higher elevation. Dunstan's unit, with Captain Dhar, set off in a wide arrowhead formation down the centre of the plain.

The border area between Gilgit-Baltistan and the Ladakh region of Indian Kashmir is a frozen wasteland for eight months of the year. Even in late April, it was cold out of the sun, and the perspiration on the backs of the soldiers was starting to chill as the peaks of shattered granite rose up on either side and cast their long shadows over them. Dunstan wanted to keep everyone moving. Laycock's acclimatised team led the way, hugging the side of the valley. Dunstan followed with his large assault team, all feeling very exposed on the broad, featureless, alluvial plain.

Dunstan was warming to his new companion, 'Right, Hugo, get a GPMG and anti-tank team of your fittest blokes up onto the southern ridgeline to cover us when we go in. They should have a clear view from there to lay down covering fire if necessary. Any significant fire from the enemy positions on the west ridge and we'll blast them. If you meet with insurmountable odds, transmit the word "Spectre" and we'll call in the gunship; last resort, though! And double check your comms: we don't want any friendly-fire cock-ups. I don't want to have to explain it to your mothers, especially as you're not even officially here!'

'Sir!' said a grinning Captain Laycock.

They all noticed the effects of the altitude, although the acclimatised Commandos felt it much less so. Two miles and one-and-a-half hours of tactical movement later, they could see their objective about a mile away: an ancient Balti fortress perched atop a thousand-foot pinnacle of frost-shattered granite. Dunstan peered through his binoculars to see a wall of solar panels stretching across the mountain behind the fortress, backed up by several wind turbines. In the still, crystal-clear, pure atmosphere they could hear the deep throb of a large generator. *So that's how they power this place, a mixture of eco and diesel*, thought Dunstan.

High above them the Spectre gunship circled like a Nazgul over the plains of Middle Earth. They prepared to make an aerial reconnaissance. The troops deployed into positions on either side of the valley as a Scimitar Regiment NCO pulled a black case out of his pack and rapidly assembled a drone, with a powerful camera mounted underneath in the centre. Another man set up the drone's video link receiver. When they were ready, they launched the craft into the still bright sky.

Dunstan was keen not to incur any casualties if humanly possible, not least because exfiltration at this altitude would be very difficult. The drone was their best chance of gaining some idea of the enemy's strength and disposition.

'What are you expecting?' enquired Laycock.

'The unexpected,' replied Dunstan. 'My main interest at the moment is finding out how to get up to the base and to get into the place!'

'Target acquisition made,' announced the video link operator.

The Monk moved over to the high definition screen and interpreted while the other officers gathered around. 'No sign of activity. No obvious troop dispositions around the objective. What do you make of that, Boss?'

Dunstan was not surprised. 'That's exactly what I expected. Any movement of troops along the LOC are going to be picked up by cross-border reconnaissance which means that we've got to get in and out quickly.'

The Monk continued with his virtual recce. 'Fortress-like structure atop a pinnacle with no visible entry points; fully separated from mountain behind – looks like a narrow but deep chasm, probably only thirty feet wide, separates the fortress from the more accessible ground on the east side. The other three sides look to be almost vertical drops; looks like a three-sixty drop all round. Large Sat dish on the roof with a couple of smaller ones. How do they get in and out?'

That's what Dunstan wanted to know. 'Can you zoom in so we can get a closer look at the structure of the building?' he asked. The operator reacted, and immediately a clear colour image of the fortress structure appeared on the HD screen as the drone did its high-level tour around the target.

Hugo Laycock, the Royal Engineer, ran the commentary. 'Look at how it's built! It looks like it's made out of water-worn river boulders, with a dry stone construction and a layer of flat through-stones every five metres to bind it together. The whole building is slightly tapered. The windows are small and high; not one in the first fifty feet of wall. Small windows all round above that height. Window frames made of a local red wood, possibly cedar or deodar. Looks like the walls are made of progressively smaller stones the higher you go. Higher up they've used mortar to bind the stones. Looks to be in good order, no cracks. Okay... high on the north elevation a large balcony with a small derrick hanging over the edge, presumably to winch up stores and possibly people. The Monk's right, no obvious entry point in the superstructure… Wait! Look there! On the east elevation, it looks like they've walled up the main entrance and taken down what was probably an old drawbridge across the chasm… *360 turn please operator…* Okay. There appears to be the remains of an old roadway winding its way up the other side of the gorge on much less steep ground… no other visible way of getting inside the fortress other than the derrick. No sign of human activity either.'

'Let's get a bird's-eye view!' demanded Dunstan.

The drone shot up above the fortress. As it rose, they could see the inner courtyard. Its size, sophistication and architecture suggested it was a historic building of regional importance, with a complex of rooms arranged around an inner courtyard. The lime-washed walls, painted in motifs clearly Bon in origin (the ancient religion of the area before Islam became pre-eminent) indicated its age and provenance. More rooms could be seen to be accessed from an inner, elevated open gallery, itself reached by a winding wooden staircase and framed with intricately carved wooden fretwork. All this was key operational information for an assault, but it did not immediately grab their collective attention. What did grab it was the elevated H pad within the main courtyard and a small Bell helicopter perched upon it.

'Well, that's how Target One gets in and out,' observed The Monk, for once uncharacteristically stating the blindingly obvious, 'but how the hell are we going to get in without blasting our way in through eight-feet thick walls?' With the Spectre's immense firepower available to them, they could blast the place apart and neutralise the inhabitants, but for Dunstan getting into the fortress was merely the first step. A lot of questions needed answering and he wasn't about to be gung-ho and risk losing his precious family. Besides, there was a wider implied threat to consider, for which he now felt a moral responsibility. His objective was therefore not to kill Ghol, but to capture him and his operation intact; he just had to find a means of penetrating the redoubt by stealth. For The Monk, and no doubt for the others, it was just 'Target One' in that building; for Dunstan it was a lot more personal. From the moment he saw the detailed structure of the building, Dunstan knew there was only one way, and he answered The Monk's question: 'Climb the walls, of course!'

The Monk was suitably underwhelmed. He took Dunstan to one side, as he always did when unimpressed with his friend's thinking. 'OK, Sherpa, so you do your rock ape act, and we all sit around at the bottom giving you points for fucking style. What happens then?'

Laycock had also anticipated the problem and provided a solution, 'Er, excuse me, sir. We've brought the chasm-crossing kit. We've been using it to ferry loads at difficult access points across the Nelum gorge to save miles of walking down to the next bridge.'

'So how does that work?' asked a sceptical Monk.

Laycock was enthused even if The Monk wasn't. 'Well, if Colonel Dunstan and I could establish a bridgehead in the form of a couple of bolt anchors in the stonework high on the east elevation of the fortress, we could attach a lightweight SWR – sorry, steel wire rope – and anchor the other end on the other side of the gorge at a slightly higher elevation, construct a Tyrolean traverse and get an assault party across.'

A Tyrolean traverse is a roped means of crossing a void between two high points, mostly used in climbing and caving.

'You're mad,' said The Monk flatly, and there was general agreement from those around the drone screen.

'Brilliant!' exclaimed Dhar and her enthusiasm clinched it for Dunstan, who looked at Laycock's crazed grin and made his decision. It sounded mad, but with no other way of penetrating the redoubt and getting an assault party within the fortress walls, it had to be a 'Go'. The Sappers have always managed to accommodate a lunatic fringe in their officers, men such as the WWII Chindit leader, Brigadier 'Mad Mike' Calvert, and General Gordon of Khartoum, and Dunstan was more than convinced that Laycock was a fully paid-up member of that select club.

'And you've brought all this gear with you, I suppose?' asked a somewhat incredulous Monk.

'That, and lots of other potentially useful kit,' grinned Laycock, 'including several long climbing ropes and a full rack of climbing gear.'

Dunstan had been thinking through the detail of the assault on the fortress. 'A couple of things, Hugo. First off, using the SWR might be good in controlled conditions but it's going to be too heavy for an assault environment, especially at this altitude. What other options do we have?'

Laycock already had the answer. 'If we can get the end of the rope anchored high up the far chasm walls and tension it off enough, the assault party should be able to death-slide across the gap onto the top of fortress walls. I can do some quick calculations to see what height differential we need so that we don't get guys smashing into the fortress walls at high speed.'

Dunstan knew as an ex-military engineer himself that such on-the-fly calculations would be second nature to Laycock, and knew the operation was in safe hands, especially with Laycock's highly experienced senior NCOs on hand to execute the task.

'Second point: how on earth are we going to get the bolts into the masonry on the fortress walls?'

'We've got a lightweight hammer drill with us, very quick, though they are pretty noisy.'

Dunstan knew all about these drills: they made a racket, which would be even louder in the pure air.

'Too noisy; it's not an option.' Dunstan could feel the mounting tension in his small team. There were a few mutterings around him and he could feel The Monk's eyes boring into him. He needed a solution urgently but he didn't want to have to use overkill in the assault. 'Hugo, you said you had a full rack of climbing gear?'

'A full set plus extras,' responded Laycock.

'Rocks *and* cams?' Dunstan asked for confirmation. 'Yes, Boss'

It was just what Dunstan wanted to hear. 'Rocks' and 'cams' are types of temporary climbing protection which can be removed after the ascent. Rocks are blocks of metal of varying sizes and shapes forged on to a loop of high tensile wire; they are used by wedging them into narrowing cracks in the rock. A 'cam' is a spring-loaded device consisting of four curved lightweight metal 'clam-shells' mounted on a common axle. The device is set by pulling on the 'trigger' – a small handle – so the metal clam-shells contract, then inserting it into a crack or pocket in the rock and releasing the trigger, allowing the clams to expand again. Because of the massive forces which are exerted via outward pressure onto the rock when a cam is fallen on, it is very important that they are placed in solid, strong rock. Dunstan was well aware of this.

'Monk! I need to get a close-up view of the parapet, specifically the capping stones on top of the fortress walls. Can the drone get close up and personal without disturbing the residents?'

'Shouldn't be a problem.' The Monk nodded toward the Scimitar Troop operator, who zoomed onto the capping stones of the fort walls with the drone's high-powered camera.

Dunstan peered closely at the video link display. 'Look, Hugo, what do you think?'

Laycock did the analysis. 'Massive granite capping stones, some heavily eroded; gaps of about an inch between them where the mortar has weathered out, but look solid.'

'That's what we'll go for, and this is how we'll do it.' Dunstan gave a quick set of orders in which he emphasised the need for stealth and silence. He ordered the Spectre to stay high and five miles away, until and unless needed, and ordered that the virtually silent drone should stay monitoring. By way of emphasis, The Monk informed all hands that he would personally shoot anyone who broke silence or dislodged any rocks. No one presumed he was joking.

***

The acclimatised Commando Engineer team quickly pulled away in front and made their way up the hill on the opposite side of the chasm, to the east elevation of the fort. The GPMG and anti-tank team sprang higher up the same slope like mountain goats, then settled into position to give covering fire; the remainder followed at a more tactical pace. All soldiers were in a high state of alert, muscles taut, eyes and ears ready to pick up the slightest response from inside the fort.

Dunstan and Laycock set off to climb the north-east spur of the pinnacle to reach the base of the fortress itself. Although exposed, the going was technically easy for the two experienced climbers – just steep scrambling – but the rocks were shattered and loose due to the repetitive freezing and thawing action of frost and ice over millennia. The effects of altitude were exacerbated by the weight of their rucksacks, which slowed them down, especially the older and unacclimatised Dunstan; it took them over an hour to get to the base foundation stones of the fortress.

Laycock spotted the faint red signal on the other side of the chasm that he had been looking for. He took a thin lightweight climbing rope from his sack, uncoiled about a quarter of it, and threw the remainder outwards and downwards across the chasm to the other side. It snaked open in mid-air, and the Royal Engineer corporal on the other side caught it first time and proceeded to climb upwards on the far side of the chasm to a higher elevation. This rope would serve as the slave-rope to tow the traverse ropes across.

Whilst this was happening, Dunstan had been putting on his climbing harness and sticky rubber-soled climbing shoes. Laycock moved over to belay Dunstan: no climbing calls, just hand signals, told Dunstan that Laycock had him secured through the belay device on his harness and that he was clear to climb when he felt ready. Dunstan gave a thumbs-up and set off in the shadows up the lower reaches of the fortress. The scramble had warmed his muscles and, as his fingers curled around the first large stone, he felt his climbing flow return. He quickly realised that the base of the fort was less steep than he had thought, but as he gained height rapidly, the steepness of the walls increased as he headed towards the vertical top third. He stopped to place his first protection at twenty feet and clipped his rope through the karabiner, whilst Laycock below channelled all his concentration into paying out the rope smoothly and efficiently.

Dunstan got to the vertical headwall of mortared granite at sixty feet, a spectacular position. As he explored the headwall for a secure resting place, he found that the cement mortar between the large granite blocks was insufficiently weathered to allow for deep finger holds, and the granite itself was smooth. Instinctively, he decided to traverse out right to the north-east edge. He pushed on up and out to the edge. As he progressed to the right, he became more aware of the increasing exposure until, with a two-seventy degree drop all around him and the plain far below him, he was poised on the sharp edged arête of the tower. He made some tentative explorations and found that his instinct was right. Here on this knife-edged arête the mortar was more weathered and he found he could sink his finger-ends up to the first knuckle between the granite blocks on each side of the fortress edge.

He took stock and, as he did so, he looked at his rope looping out to the left. It was going to be a big swing if he came off, with painful consequences; he just hoped he could place some protection on the arête itself. As he looked around, the precarious nature of his position hit him and his fingers began to sweat. Every climber experiences this if they are pushing against their limits and the sensation is called 'being gripped'. Dunstan, if not wholly gripped, was well on his way to that point and he forced himself to focus on the task in hand, on the few inches in front of his nose. He dipped his hands into the chalk bag which almost every modern climber carries, the action itself a psychological comfort. He made the first tentative moves, his mind and body unwilling to commit to this last thirty feet of wall. A flash thought of his family was a jolt sufficient to force him on, squeezing the toes of his sticky-soled climbing shoes onto the minute edges.

He looked round the corner onto the north wall of the fortress to see if he could access the high windows on that side, but he couldn't see any along the plane of the wall. As he eased back round, the exposure now hit him in full, and in his isolation out on that edge he felt as though he was on the margins of space itself. He groped his way upwards. He found a three-finger-sized slot for his left hand and, in this seemingly minute action, he passed through an invisible barrier, a portal to another dimension. It was now harder to reverse the moves he had just made than to carry on upwards; he was now committed. And as so often happens in climbing, once committed, his flow returned, the adrenaline pumped through his veins and, with mind, spirit and body all operating in unison, peripheral concerns fell away and progress became a certainty.

He was cruising now, in rhythmic control, a synthesis of effort and precision. Below, Laycock could just hear the suppressed grunts and whispered curses. Eventually, Dunstan placed the smallest cam in a much too shallow crack. His forearms were now burning with the effort and his fingers were in danger of simply uncurling from the holds. Digging deep into his mental and physical resources, he pressed on until he was six feet from the capping stones at the top of the wall. He looked up; he felt around, curiously at first, then more frantically. So near yet so far: he had run out of holds.

***

On the opposite side of the chasm, The Monk was getting increasingly concerned at the delay. He got out his high-powered field glasses and zoomed in on Dunstan perched on the knife edge. *What the fuck's he doing?* He muttered with more than his normal level of concern and bewilderment at his friend's actions, or in this case, manifest inaction.

BANG! The reverberations echoed around the courtyard walls of the fortress.

Everyone froze. Hearts raced, then relaxed. It wasn't a sound anybody had anticipated; a door slamming inside the fort. With his friend stuck on the fort walls and the assault force impotent on the other side of the chasm, The Monk grabbed the drone video link operator. Whispering harshly into his ear, he directed him to zoom into the courtyard. Via the link, he could see a figure dressed in coveralls walking across the inner courtyard towards the helicopter: the pilot.

Let's hope it's a routine check, thought The Monk. But he was going to be disappointed.

***

High up on the fortress walls, Philip Dunstan had heard the noise but his concentration was such that it made little impact on him. Indeed, at that moment he was trying to avoid another form of impact, his own onto the ground far below. He had given up trying to find holds on the arête and had eased himself back into the centre of the wall. He shifted his feet uncomfortably on the tiny edges that served as his footholds, moving his centre of gravity higher to give his burning fingers and forearms a short rest. In such a position a climber's mind does a series of rapid calculations.

If he came off now, the small cam below him would almost certainly rip out and he would have to rely on the more substantial protection below that. His problem was that his climbing rope was brand new and designed to stretch up to forty percent to absorb the shock of a lead climber falling. By his rough calculations, he knew he was looking at a probable ground fall if he was to fall off now. If he didn't hit the ground, he would certainly break his legs on the slabby base of the fortress. Neither prospect was appetising. He simply had to complete the climb. He tried again to go for the capping stones but they were beyond his reach, let alone his grasp, nor could he find any interim holds on the face of the wall. *Ah, but a man's reach should exceed his grasp or what's a heaven for? Well screw you, Robert Browning!* The random, uncharitable, thought flew through his mind.

Hardly daring to breathe, maintaining his tenuous hold on the face, he snaked his right hand upward and curled the tip around the corner of a large capping stone: extreme standard climbing with no meaningful protection at twelve thousand feet. The fingertip hold was enough; one more stretch and a nudge and he was pulling for his life over the top of the fortress wall, buffeted by the wind. He lay momentarily on top of the capping stones, heart pumping in the rarefied atmosphere, gulping lungfuls of air and trying to resolve in his mind the sight of the helicopter with its rotor blades turning slowly.

***

As Dunstan tried to regain his composure, he became aware of a door opening on the galleried first floor landing and three figures emerging: two guys, small in stature, but broad shouldered – close protection – and a tall, elegant man looking rather impressive in Chitrali formal dress, a long, white, handmade woollen chogha overcoat with a woollen hat (a pakol) which sported a magnificent black and white falcon plume. He thought of drawing his weapon but realised he had given it to Laycock before his ascent of the fortress wall.

He eased himself back off the top of the capstone and started stuffing protection devices into the cracks on either side of it to create a secure belay. A couple of tugs on the rope told Laycock it was time to move. He started quickly but soon slowed down and Dunstan, desperate not to lose the initiative, urged him upwards with insistent tugs on the rope; on the upper section Laycock had to have a tight rope to make the final moves. He reached Dunstan, panting with the effort, who silenced him with the two-finger-to-the-eyeballs sign and pointing. Both men pulled themselves upwards. Laycock eased his Browning 9mm out of its holster but Dunstan cautioned him. They watched the unfolding scene below.

The helicopter revs increased, the scream of the rotors turning faster. Ghol and his minders emerged from the bottom of the winding staircase and paused. Dunstan pointed at the pilot and Laycock took aim, but before he could take him out the three passengers started their crouched run to the chopper, spoiling Laycock's line of sight to the pilot. Dunstan pushed down Laycock's weapon. He was on the horns of a dilemma. He couldn't afford to risk killing Ghol, nor could he possibly let him escape. In that moment of pull-back, Ghol had completed his traverse of the courtyard and jumped into the back of the chopper.

Across the chasm, The Monk had also seen these events unfolding on the video link. He swore under his breath, feeling impotent to prevent what was obviously happening: Ghol was about to slip through the net. He needed to prevent the helicopter taking off, yet without killing Ghol. He looked at the video link monitor and he knew he had the solution in his hands.

On top of the fortress walls, Dunstan knew he was running out of options. The chopper was reaching maximum revs and the pilot tilted the collective, put in his left pedal and adjusted the cyclic. The helicopter lifted off the ground into the hover.

There was no choice. Dunstan was left with only one option. 'Shoot the pilot!' he ordered Laycock who, lying flat on top of the massive capstone, held his handgun with both hands, bringing it down into the firing position. As he did so, Dunstan caught sight of a black object diving down towards the helicopter and, more from instinctive reaction than rational thought, grabbed his companion and launched himself backwards off the parapet into space, taking Laycock with him as his weapon discharged skywards. Within the fortress walls, there was a tortured mechanical scream of shattered rotor blades hitting the interior walls as the drone, controlled by The Monk, dived terminally straight into the helicopter's rotors.

It was all over in an instant as the helicopter crashed back down to the launch pad from a height of some five metres, shaking the occupants. Outside the walls, The Monk looked at his blank video link with a professional detachment, whilst Dunstan and a nonplussed Laycock hung in space from the belay. They hauled themselves back up onto the parapet and surveyed the scene of devastation, just in time to see Ghol being whisked away through a door by his close protection team.

Across the other side of the chasm, The Monk was already making preparations and giving orders. A team of three Scimitar troopers, under the direction of a Sapper corporal, was hastily establishing the anchors for the Tyrolean traverse around four large granite blocks.

The Monk had been thinking about the next phase for some time, and planning for an assault.

'Right! GPMG and anti-tank team get your arses high up this hill behind us to a point where you can see down into the fortress courtyard. Then start giving covering fire – just enough to keep their heads down, no more. Very short burst only and don't hit the buildings; keep it overhead! Check comms before you start. The rest stay on sharp standby for tasking. Now go!'

The Sapper team picked up its weaponry and made rapid upward progress to a dominant position.

He turned to the others. 'Now, who's had recent CQB operational experience or training? And I don't mean playing on fucking computers!'

Four Royal Engineers, six Scimitar Regiment soldiers and one Special Reconnaissance Regiment officer signalled they were up to speed in close quarter battle, or FIBUA – fighting in built-up areas.

'Good,' said The Monk, pleased but not wholly satisfied. Out of all of them, he was sure that Asha Dhar was the most experienced. 'You guys make up the two assault teams – the door kickers and room clearers: two teams of five. Captain Dhar here will lead one team, I'll lead the other. We have limited knowledge of the layout so we need to keep things straightforward. Two simple objectives:

'Objective One: find Target One and secure him. That's my team's task – Team Lima.' *I've had enough of fucking Alphas and Bravos to last a lifetime,* thought The Monk.

'Objective Two: Dhar, I want your team – Team Kilo – to locate and take the central operations zone and secure it. My team will lift Target One and get him into there, then the Boss follows. I don't want him reaching Target One before we find the bastard and secure him! Understood?'

'Yes, sir,' they all acknowledged in unison.

'Speed and aggression is the key – so no need to set about clearing every nook and cranny and musty old prayer room. We don't know the enemy's strength and capability, but from what I've seen on the video link-up, I'm assuming a few highly trained ex-soldiers. Can't say any more than that, so prepare for surprises. Each team will maintain rear-guard cover at all times to protect our flanks and arses.

'Now in case any of you are a bit rusty at this game, the SOP we use is as follows.

'First off, we alternate point-men to ease pressure and mistakes. Point-man will go through the door and head to the nearside left corner, clear and secure corner, then turn and provide supporting fire to the other team members. Right behind him and almost up his arse, Number Two enters and clears and secures the nearside right corner, the most likely ambush point unless we have an awkward left-handed bastard in there. There can be no gap between Point Man and Number Two. Okay! Number Three is the Team Leader and will head for the far left corner. Number Four will head for the far right corner. Number five DOES NOT enter the room, but handles rear security.

'Start positions: One and Three will take up start positions on the right side of a door, and the "evens" on the left. Stick to that and you won't look like the Keystone Cops. If a team is forced to retreat, it does so in reverse numerical order. Everyone got that?'

Everyone got it and The Monk continued his briefing.

'We start with rooms off the gallery, one team from each end. Clear that floor. Then if we haven't found the centre of ops and/or Target One, Lima moves up and Kilo down. And no fucking spray-away firing. If I hear or see any more than double-tap shots, I'll personally lob the culprit from the roof. Accuracy, precision, execution. Understood?'

'Yes, Boss.' Again, common acknowledgement. The Monk turned to the remainder of the squad.

'Right, the rest of you will form the crossing and support fire teams. First man across takes his support weapon and ammo and lays down covering fire. Second and third men across take extra ropes, anchors and abseil gear so we can get a multiple drop-in down the walls. I want a battlefield medic in that team to treat any men down, and I want the support team to form a casevac plan to get any wounded out of the fortress and over the walls. All clear so far?'

Heads nodded vigorously.

'Right! The assault teams follow the support teams across the chasm. They ab down the walls, cross the courtyard and get into that building like greased weasel shit. Any questions? No? Get yourselves sorted now and across the chasm as soon as the crossing line is up. And make sure your harnesses are done up properly!'

He finished his orders session just as the first short bursts from the GPMG team whizzed overhead.

***

From a hanging belay position on top of the outside wall of the fortress, Dunstan and Laycock had been getting organised for the crossing. Using a small three-to-one ratio pulley system, they quickly hauled in the slave rope, followed by the main traverse rope, tensioning and securing the latter with friction hitch knots into the many belay points embedded between the capstones.

As the first man on the other side of the chasm prepared himself to slide, Dunstan popped his head over the parapet in order to confirm the best abseil points. His initiative was met by a hail of well-directed semi-automatic fire from a room within the galleried area. For the second time within half an hour, he flung himself back over the outer wall to dangle on the belay, sweating with cumulative effort and fear.

'Shit! That was close, Hugo! We need to suppress that fire...' He stopped as he caught Laycock staring at him, 'What is it?' It was then that he felt the warm stream of blood flowing over his right ear and gingerly touched a substantial flap of skin hanging off his scalp.

"You'll need to get that seen to but we've got to get off here first!" observed Laycock, drily.

Dunstan, his adrenaline still flowing, shouted across the chasm from his perch high on the wall. 'Monk!' He got his friend's attention. 'It's time for the heavy horse! Just enough to frighten the inhabitants. We need to keep this place and ourselves intact!'

I know that, you pillock! thought The Monk, but he kept the thought to himself.

'Sure, Boss! On its way,' he shouted.

A quick predefined message to Callsign Top Cover and the AC-130H Spectre gunship manoeuvred its bulk, dipping its wings and turning for the run into the fortress from a distance of four miles, taking care to remain well within Pakistani airspace. The tasking from The Monk to the Spectre gunship was to strafe the west side of the fortress, close enough to create noise and confusion sufficient to frighten and disorientate the inhabitants, but not close enough to cause structural and collateral human damage, including that of Dunstan and his team. Even so, the cacophony of the four 20mm six-barrelled Vulcan Gatling cannon, firing at 6,600 rounds per minute, sounded like the arrival of the Four Horsemen of the Apocalypse. Even the seasoned warriors in Dunstan's team had never heard such an ear-splitting sound of rock shattering as large swathes of the granite hillside were reduced to rubble. Against this backdrop, the GPMG cover from the other side of the chasm sounded oddly ineffectual, though it kept up a steady rate of short-burst fire.

Under cover of this mayhem, the support party crossed the chasm and set up four extra abseil points for the assault teams, followed shortly by The Monk and Dhar.

The Monk could now see the blood that was soaking Dunstan's shirt. Making no comment, he put his face close up to Dunstan and shouted above the racket. '*You* are the target for your enemy, so for God's sake wait until we secure the place before you come over the wall! Pretty fucking embarrassing if you get killed or taken hostage!'

The assault team members clipped their abseil descenders into their ropes and abseiled rapidly followed by the rest of the squad, comprised of combat engineer commandos and Scimitar Regiment troopers. Weapons at the ready, safety catches off, The Monk led his team hard-targeting across the inner courtyard to the red cedar staircase leading up to the first-floor gallery. As they did so, the large central doorway on the gallery, covered in paintings of demon figures, opened marginally. A burst of semi-automatic fire from within brought down one of the Scimitar troopers in The Monk's team, a severe wound to the shoulder. His cries of pain rent the air as, simultaneously, the GPMG team brought the full firepower of their weapon to bear on the ancient door, blasting it to pieces. Screams from within the building joined those of the trooper in the courtyard, then silence.

Up on the wall, Dunstan and Laycock had adopted a support role, laying down fire. The casualty in the courtyard was now being treated by a medic under the protection of their supporting fire. The team under Captain Asha Dhar had by now ascended to the far end of the gallery by climbing the wooden lattice work and both assault teams started to clear from their respective ends the eight rooms leading off the gallery, working towards the middle. They were all empty. Room clearing is an intense, high-pressured activity, and the tension and adrenaline were mounting as they moved toward the shattered middle doors, meeting The Monk's team coming the other way. The Monk signalled a wait-out; he wasn't happy, and an inner sense of danger stopped him entering. He looked around the door frame and saw a length of para-cord stretched around it: booby trap. What to do?

The Monk had to make a quick decision. *The enemy wouldn't booby-trap their main centre of operations would they? Must be there to slow us down. The operations centre must be beyond. Only one thing for it – overkill: blast it.*

He signalled a quick withdrawal of the assault teams along the gallery as he tasked the Javelin Anti-Tank team with a quick series of taps on his radio pressel switch.

'Cover your ears!' he screamed, seconds before the 2.74kg high explosive warhead smashed through the door at a downward angle of fifty degrees from the hillside above, triggering the grenade necklace booby trap beyond before exploding with deafening violence somewhere in the depths of the building, causing a virtual collapse in the structure the assault teams were standing on.

Fucking evens now; one house each, mused a satisfied Monk.

He led his teams through fallen masonry and shattered wooden joists, stepping over the remains of two of the enemy who had been ready to ambush and 'mop up' the assault teams after the booby trap had detonated. Dunstan, meanwhile, had had enough of sitting up on the wall and joined the action, grabbing a field dressing off the medic to staunch the flow of blood. He followed The Monk and Captain Dhar through an inner stone entrance hall into what looked like a large prayer room, although it had ceased to have anything to do with prayer some time ago. Dunstan indicated that Dhar should stick with him whilst The Monk and his men should spread out to secure the floor they were on and capture Target One.

Chapter Twenty-Two

Dunstan and Dhar took in the sight before them: the room was bedecked with modern technology. There were several clusters of stylish desks with three or four computer screens arranged in an arc on each station, displaying fluctuating prices for multiple 'markets'. The dealers, terrified at the array of weaponry pointed directly at them, cowered beneath their desk cluster.

Dhar looked at Dunstan quizzically, as if to say, *What on earth is all this?*

'A dealing room, Asha. A top class one by the looks of it. Let's see what these guys are dealing in, shall we?'

Dunstan walked round the room peering at the screens. Without intimate knowledge, he didn't know exactly what and how they were trading, but he could make an educated guess.

'Looks like Forex: Foreign Currency Exchange Swaps; European Equities; Emerging Market Debt; Bond or Fixed Income; maybe Derivatives markets. The whole bloody gamut by the looks of it! So this is what the fraud is being used for, is it?' The question was rhetorical; he knew he wouldn't get any sense out of the dealers in front of him. They were just specialists operating in their own worlds.

As Dunstan viewed the charts and fluctuating prices on the screens he felt he was about to explode. With an effort, he capped it, resisting the overwhelming temptation to blast all the dealers and their dealing screens into a different universe. Instead, in a controlled and deliberate voice, he said, 'But you dealers don't call the shots, do you? So where is the man that does? Where is Ghol?' To a man, they all stared back, wobbling their heads. As if in answer to his question, The Monk and two of his Scimitar soldiers appeared and beckoned Dunstan and Dhar into an adjoining room wherein several large television monitors showed rolling satellite news feeds, the ubiquitous 'Breaking News'. The Monk pointed to a control. A

Scimitar Troop NCO got the message and turned off the screens. Into the room were frog-marched two men at gunpoint. Dunstan instantly registered the contrast of style and substance between them: one a small, geeky type in denim jeans, sandals, wire-framed spectacles and T-shirt, who had clearly wet himself; the other the tall, imperious Ghol, displaying no fear, just pure contempt. He was still wearing his formal national dress which served to accentuate his height and breeding.

The edges of Ghol's mouth turned down and his eyes drilled into Dunstan as though he were viewing something that had crawled out from under a stone. If Dunstan had never before in his life felt what it was like to be the object of uncompromising hatred, he did now.

He was surprised by Ghol's urbane calmness – or was it insouciance – but he didn't react to it. He tried to make sense of his surroundings. He was in the heart of the operation that had destroyed his life, yet none of this stacked up as the centre of a pan-regional government–in-waiting. He cast his gaze around the room as if to make full sense of the scale of this operation, settling his eyes back on his enemy.

Something dark started to build up inside Philip Dunstan. All the torment of the past week, and perhaps beyond, welled up inside him, an internal eruption rising to the surface. *It's only a week, but it feels like a lifetime.* Spread out in front of him in this room was the source of his misery and anguish at the death of his friends, the real and present threat to his family, and the trashing of his professional life. He felt the throbbing in his hands, the tautness in his muscles and the damp stickiness of the blood on his head and his shirt. With his mind in turmoil and his thoughts becoming more and more irrational, he fought to contain the rising anger. He failed. Something inside him snapped. His vision blurred and all rational thought left him. Before anyone had time to realise what was happening, Ghol was going backwards across the operations room with Dunstan's vice-like single-handed grip around his throat. All present were taken by surprise, even The Monk.

Dunstan screamed into Ghol's face, '*Why*, you bastard? In the name of God, *why?*' But Ghol could not even form a reply as the grip tightened around his larynx. Both men's anguish and anger met face-to-face, less than an inch away from each other. Ghol was struggling to breathe, his colour changing to purple, his slate-blue eyes bulging, looking if they were about to be expelled from their sockets.

In one impressively swift movement, with his other hand, Dunstan drew his kukhri out of its sheath and placed the razor sharp edge directly underneath Ghol's eye.

'Is this the type of weapon that was used to kill Idris Morgan and torture my secretary? Is it? What does it feel like close up, eh, Ghol?'

Dhar looked at The Monk with a mixture of pleading and terror. She knew full well the chaotic consequences of Ghol dying now. She made a silent but instinctive move but The Monk checked her; he knew that only he could reach through his friend's madness.

The Monk's gnarled hand gently gripped Dunstan's arm, then squeezed harder. His tone was all the more effective for being subdued yet insistent. 'Sherpa!... Sherpa! Sherpa! Ease your grip, set him down. If you kill him, you'll lose your family. And even if they survive, the blood feud will continue. Leave him be! Philip! Leave... Him... Be. Let him down.'

The muscles in Dunstan's hand were bulging. They tensed one more time and a strangled, gurgling sound came from Ghol. Then Dunstan turned his head away from Ghol's face and with a blank expression looked at The Monk. The Monk had never seen his friend like this before. Maybe for the first time he really appreciated what Philip Dunstan was capable of in his wildest psychopathic moments. The Monk thought Ghol was on his way out.

Suddenly, Dunstan eased his grip, stood back and looked at The Monk. Then he threw his kukhri, just missing Ghol's left ear, straight into a large LCD screen just behind Ghol's head. The smell of burning electronics and acrid fumes filled the air.

Ghol, who had been on the verge of passing out, was holding his throat, gasping for air. Even in his moment of distress though, he managed to maintain an air of moral superiority. He turned to Dunstan with a look of undiluted hatred.

Dunstan was raging. 'Look, if you don't start talking soon, the next target will be human. Understand?'

When the words eventually came from Ghol's lips they were brittle, harsh. 'For someone who is responsible for the horrible death of an innocent human being, you do not bear your responsibilities very well, do you, Mr Dunstan? In fact you seem to be in total denial of them.'

It was as though Dunstan needed this verification to finally accept the link between the man in front of him and a younger, innocent man on a hillside far away in another life. 'So you *are* the brother of Abdul Ghol!'

Ghol's voice was as cold as a Karakoram glacial stream in winter. 'I am! And you are responsible for his death and that of my father, who never recovered from the blow of losing his youngest son, especially in such degrading and inhuman circumstances!'

'I didn't kill him, Ghol.' The others noticed the shift in Dunstan. The Monk was watching carefully; Dhar and Laycock, who had now joined them from the wall, had not a clue as to what all this meant.

'You did! You captured him and handed him over to the Americans!' Ghol was becoming more animated, anger growing in his voice.

Dunstan's tone conveyed his exasperation, 'For God's sake, I thought he was going to be sent home immediately, to Kashmir! That's where he said he was from. We were in Pakistan and we had no reason to doubt otherwise!'

Ghol's voice rose in his anguish, almost screaming at Dunstan, 'He was my father's life, his beautiful son and our little brother. And they skinned him alive! Bit by bit, in Kabul prison. They took him to Kabul so no one could hear his screams. He took four days to die and the bastards videoed it! He wouldn't tell them what they wanted because he didn't know anything, did he? The bloody bastards videoed it and then they sent it to the Pakistani ISI. For fun! Like Saturday night entertainment. My beautiful brother, butchered and skinned!'

'Oh fuck! Someone got carried away,' said The Monk with feeling, as Dhar drew a deep breath and moved over to the window to get some air. One or two of the soldiers present turned to face the wall.

Dunstan visibly reeled, emotionally pole-axed. There was nothing he could say that would make any difference. With some difficulty he recovered, but his temper had lost its edge.

'And it was you who had my secretary killed... and the date carved on her chest... never mind Idris and Miro in Prague.' Dunstan's voice was oddly disconnected. The Monk was eyeing him, willing him not to do anything rash yet again. 'So you found out from your friends in ISI that I was the one who captured your brother and you decided to destroy me and mine. Full tribal retribution, eh, Ghol? And you blame *me* for others' actions?'

'Yes! It is total and final! Nemesis. The law of retribution is personal and extends to all members of the offender's family and his friends. There is no half-way house in a blood feud!'

Dunstan was torn. He was trying desperately to reconcile his situation with that of Ghol's. He couldn't do it: there was no moral equivalence. 'Look, I'm sorry if my actions led indirectly to your brother's death but your extreme response is over the top. Moreover, you're in a position to do something about it. So you are now going to issue orders from here – right now – to stop your mercenaries from targeting my family. Stop this blood feud now. Do you understand, Ghol?'

'I can't stop it, Dunstan, even if I wanted to. You can skin me alive here and now, like my brother, but I can't stop it.'

'Bullshit! What do you mean? You started it and you seem to be in charge of it. Period.'

'You can't stop a blood feud once initiated, Dunstan!' came the harsh response.

Dunstan's mouth dropped, he had no answer. He turned to The Monk who looked back at his friend. 'You can't stop it like this, he doesn't care,' he said resignedly. 'This is a matter of honour; with the loss of Abdul and his father the only thing he can do is to discharge his responsibilities to honour their memories. And if we kill him, other family members will take his place, for generations. Isn't that right, Ghol?'

Ghol simply stared at the object of his hate and the target of his retribution, and nodded imperceptibly.

Asha Dhar had been quietly observing proceedings, on the horns of her own personal dilemma. As this improbable impasse was reached, she now knew that by virtue of her origins she was the only who could bring about a resolution. She decided it was time for direct action to break the stalemate – cool and calculated action. She stepped forward and almost nonchalantly emptied two 9mm rounds into the right knee of the geek. As he collapsed into a heap, his howls rent the air and echoed off the stone walls. A few dealers from the dealing room ran through then turned quickly, one of them vomiting on the way out.

'What the hell was that for?' enquired The Monk, nonplussed but nevertheless impressed with the ruthlessness of the action he had just witnessed.

The purpose of Asha Dhar's action was to get some attention; it had the desired effect. Everyone looked at her, appalled and baffled.

Dhar ignored them, her whole attention on her fellow Kashmiri. 'Now listen to me, Ghol. This feud *does* stop. Now!' Ghol opened his mouth but through her immediate and violent action Dhar had gained a psychological edge, and she knew it.

'Shut up and listen. If you refuse to call it off, two things will happen. The first is that *I* will shoot your little friend here bit by bit, and then I will start on you. I will find your nearest living relatives and kill them, and *I* will have started a many-generation Kashmiri blood feud. That makes two blood feuds simultaneously. Think hard, Ghol! You said it just now: there's no half-way house in a blood feud. Fancy that for your heirs and successors? Consider it to be a blood feud trade. One debt cancelling out another; it seems like it should be something you would understand.' She needed to raise her voice above the racket emanating from a painfully injured Geek. 'Oh, for God's sake! Someone get him out of here!' The dynamic had changed; she was in charge. The Monk had by now fallen for her completely. Two Scimitar Regiment medics picked up the Geek and dragged him out.

Dhar could see Ghol was having difficulty processing what was going on. Then it suddenly occurred to her that with her received English accent, Ghol would have no idea as to her ethnic background or familial links to her homeland. He had not made the connection. So just to make sure he got it she repeated it in Kashmiri, which threw him even more. A Kashmiri woman capable of maiming and killing without apparent compunction was outside the scope of his personal experience or knowledge. He stood slack-jawed, momentarily unable to speak.

Dunstan stepped into the frame again. 'Now, Ghol, you're going to call off your mercenaries from targeting my family.'

'I can't! Orders have already been given. It's out of my hands. It's all too late!'

'Just do it!' Dhar barked at him with her least lady-like demeanour, levelling her Glock at the charismatic Kashmiri in front of her, and yet inwardly fighting to control tears of frustration.

Dunstan had read the situation though, and had his response. 'Well we could kill you here and now but I realise that would be crude and ineffectual. So how about we start by throwing Mr Shafquat Khan to the dogs, eh?'

The air rushed out of Ghol's lungs. 'How do you know of Shafquat? You can't know where Shafquat is! Even if you did, how do you presume to hold his life in your hands?'

'He's been picked up by UK intelligence and certain other enforcement agencies. I gather he's been formally charged with murder and conspiracy to murder. Alternatively, I'm sure the Pakistani authorities would like to get hold of him. In short, your right-hand man and chief planner is screwed, Ghol. Whether or not we protect him or hand him over to the ISI to finish his days screaming in one of their torture chambers, or use him as bargaining chip, is now wholly dependent on you and on your answer.'

'You're bluffing, Dunstan!'

'With my family's well-being at stake, I assure you I am not bluffing!'

The Monk was now back in his comfort zone. He picked up the SAT phone receiver and dialled Top Cover, who patched him through to Lovat in Al-Qurum. He proffered the handset to Ghol, who accepted it gingerly as though it would bite him. The Monk pressed the loudspeaker button so everyone could hear. They heard a woman's voice on the end of the line: 'One moment please, Mr Ghol,' intoned Rebecca Lovat. 'We will patch you through now.'

'Anil! It is me, Shafquat!' The voice on the end of the line was barely recognisable as the once self-assured, urbane, intelligence officer. Apart from feeling decidedly wary and self-conscious in the presence of Celia Fanshawe and his other inquisitors, he was acutely aware that whatever he did or said, his future was bleak.

'Shafquat! Have they harmed you, Shafquat? Are you okay?'

'No, they have not harmed me. The British are too subtle for that. They have given me a list of destinations where I could potentially end up if I don't co-operate, where I should certainly be harmed in a variety of exquisite ways.'

Ghol looked at Dhar, who had her Glock firmly and squarely aimed at his most sensitive parts. He drew a deep breath. He spoke quietly and with resignation. 'Shafquat. Call off the team. Pull them back!'

'Why? What has happened?'

'The blood feud is over. An honourable and, er, equitable, deal has been done. Just send the signal to pull back the team. It's over in the UK, but here our greater cause shall endure!' With that, Dunstan grabbed the handset; he wasn't going to have any grand-standing from Ghol.

Ghol looked at Dunstan defiantly. 'So, you've got what you wanted, but there's one thing you can't stop and that is the reunification of my homelands. Look!'

Ghol picked up the remote controls and one by one started switching on the television screens surrounding them. The first was BBC World News with more 'Breaking News':...*the latest from the region is that a hitherto unknown organisation calling itself 'New Baltistan' is claiming responsibility for the widespread disorder and bombings in Pakistan. No one has heard of this organisation before but certain sources say it could be a new front for Kashmiri liberationists.*

Ignoring the array of weaponry aimed at him, Ghol turned around to switch on a large LCD screen. As it came into life, a detailed map of Northern Pakistan and Kashmir emerged: Gilgit-Baltistan, Azad and Indian Kashmir. Scattered across the map was a series of lights, mostly green, some red. Clusters of lights appeared in locations Dunstan knew to be the provincial capitals of the Northern Areas. It was plain for all to see that, according to the dispositions in front of them, most of the Northern Areas were under control of Ghol's forces. However, away from the northern clusters, in other areas of Pakistan, were two other lights.

'What are these?' asked The Monk, pointing to them.

'Those are two of Pakistan's key nuclear facilities: the main uranium enrichment plant and the nuclear warhead storage facility at Wah. Ultimately they will be under our control. Control these and we control Pakistan.'

Dunstan was outraged by Ghol's hubris. 'Bullshit. That's simply not possible. Your ambition exceeds your means. These are highly guarded facilities with specialist support from the US!'

Ghol was unfazed, and rather pleased that Dunstan had given him an opportunity to demonstrate his and his father's depth of strategic planning and foresight.

'*Quis custodiet ipsos custodes?* Who will guard the guardians, eh, Dunstan? That age-old problem of ultimate power. Just as CERN was infiltrated by French scientists of North African origin whose loyalty was to Al-Qaeda, so we have sown our own people into the fabric of our country's nuclear facilities: nuclear physicists, nuclear engineers and army officers loyal to our cause. I believe you used to call them "sleepers" during your Cold War? Well, my sleepers are emerging from a deep slumber!'

Dunstan thought it was time to demonstrate his insight. 'And that's how you've obtained the means to create a nuclear threat is it, eh? Is that what the package was all about? The one flown out from APS in the helicopter by your nuclear physicist friend; was that it? Was that the arming mechanism? Is this what the so-called "Great Event" is all about?'

Ghol was staggered for a moment at Dunstan's knowledge of his affairs. But something else had been troubling Ghol for some time, or more precisely, troubling his olfactory senses. As he stood in front of Dhar, he had caught the slightest hint of a scent he could only now place. No matter how this disturbed him, he could not help expressing his admiration, albeit sardonically.

'You're good, Dunstan, very good. Or is it this young lady officer here who is your surveillance expert? But you can't stop us. Everything is ready. The time has come to rectify a historical injustice. There's nothing you can do to prevent reunification of Kashmir. Historically, India never understood the pivotal strategic importance of the Northern Areas. But you British did, didn't you? That's why you played the Great Game for so long. For a fleeting moment, we *had* total Kashmiri autonomy; at the precise moment of Partition, India ceded Jammu and Kashmir. They had left ex-British Army officers in charge of the Jammu and Kashmir military. Independence was within our grasp! My father said they could all *feel* it. Then with your heavy, bloody boots, you messed it up like you did so much of the world! In a single act, you British destroyed the opportunity for all the Northern Tribes to unify under a new Kashmir!'

'What on earth are you talking about?' asked a bemused Dunstan. No one else in the room had a clue what he was talking about either, and an outraged Ghol sensed it. They had not come for a history lecture but they got it anyway.

'You have no idea, do you? A huge part of colonial history and you have no damned idea! Well, the commander of the Gilgit Scouts, British Army Major William Brown, took over the core administrative centre in Gilgit. Then, without a by-your-bloody-leave to any of the Northern Tribes, Brown summarily raised the new *Pakistan* flag over Gilgit! Can you believe it! In that single stupid act, they annexed the key Northern Areas to Pakistan without any prior consultation or constitutional mandate! Once that chunk of territory had been grabbed for Pakistan, the remainder went to Indian Kashmir by default. And we have had a bloody war ever since! Now there will be Unity.'

'Unity!' Dunstan shot back. 'You're talking about many disparate peoples, religions, not to mention existing political boundaries. There is no unity now, and there can't be in the future.'

'Ah, but you're wrong!' replied Ghol. 'We are united by our environment and ancient common cultures. As for topography, as you call it, we are united by the same band of limestone at eight thousand metres that crosses the Greater Himalaya for two thousand miles. The Himalayan peoples are all cast from the same mould – from the same ancient ocean floor.'

'You're crazy, Ghol!' spat back Dunstan.

Ghol's response was a self-righteous smirk. Then, suddenly, he turned on his heels. 'Follow me. I'll show you how crazy we are.' Dunstan shrugged and they all followed Ghol down several corridors lit by low-level lighting until they came to another chamber with no lights, but equipped as an operations room. Clearly the computer screens were monitoring something, but what?

The screens showed a murky image which was difficult to make out. The Monk wandered over and peered closely at one of them. 'Looks like a black suitcase.'

'A compact nuclear device, I presume,' said Dunstan wearily. 'Is it armed?'

'Of course it's armed!' responded Ghol, scathingly. 'All this orchestrated chaos we have unleashed around us in Pakistan is just the preliminary, a sideshow if you like, to the Great Event when we will finally sever the yoke. As dusk descends, the film showing the arming of our nuclear bomb will be dispatched to all news agencies. Then we will make our demands for independence. Then, hour by hour, we will increase the pressure until the government accedes to our demands – or not as the case may be.' He shrugged his shoulders almost philosophically, as though it didn't matter.

The Monk and Laycock were inspecting the image on the screen. 'It looks like it's in a cave, surrounded by high rock walls,' observed The Monk. 'Where the hell is it?'

'It looks like it's in the entrance of a rock tunnel,' added Laycock.

'And you are indeed right!' Ghol was mocking them now, which had started to irritate The Monk considerably. Ghol continued, 'And in case you think this is complete fantasy, we got the idea from the Chinese.'

'The Chinese? Where the hell do they come into this?' The Monk was exasperated.

'In 2000, at the end of a two-year study, the Chinese Academy of Engineering Physics issued a report recommending the use of nuclear devices to blast massive hydroelectric tunnels through the 7,000m mountain chain that separates Tibet from India, in order to divert water from the Tsangpo gorge. The Tsangpo is the world's deepest gorge, in which the world's biggest ever earthquake occurred in 1950, the same year as the Chinese invasion of Tibet. The proposed project caused an outcry. Indian geologists pointed out that the use of such devices would cause a devastating earthquake along the Tsangpo gorge, within the collision zone that divides South Asia from the high mountain plateau of Tibet. My father, Ali Sher Ghol, God bless his memory, had the vision of turning this Chinese proposal on its head and deliberately *causing* such a catastrophe, in the same collision zone between the Indian and Eurasian tectonic plates, but two thousand miles west of the Tsangpo gorge. The device is fully armed and there is nothing you can do to stop it!' Ghol's eyes burned with an intensity that both unnerved and annoyed his audience.

Laycock had spotted some co-ordinates on another screen. He memorised them easily and then moved over to the operations map on the wall. One glance was enough. He turned to Ghol, his face blood red and the veins in his neck bulging. For Laycock, it had just become close up and personal.

'You bastard! You've placed the nuke up the Nelum River gorge. Just where the major landslide was, and where we've been re-building the lives of the mountain people for the last four months. Hundreds of thousands will be killed, including all our friends. You've placed it right on the fault line!' Ghol was unapologetic: 'One line on the map drawn by British Administrators in 1947 caused the deaths of two million people in six months!' 'How did you get it down there?' asked The Monk, already thinking of operational detail.

'A track existed, which has just been blown.' Ghol shrugged.

'It *must* be capable of being disarmed,' Dunstan voiced aloud his thoughts.

Ghol merely laughed. 'Even if I tell you, it will not do you or anyone else any good. The arming mechanism is a PAL. It cannot be disarmed.'

'A what?'

'A Permissive Action Link. It's a one-time electronic combination lock: a multiple code, twelve-digit switch comprising two combinations of six digits, each held by two different people.'

'And they are where?'

'Not here,' said Ghol, flatly.

Dunstan could see The Monk was losing patience. He could see his trigger finger twitching and knew at that moment that he had to keep a lid on things. But he also knew he had to bring matters to a conclusion. He lifted his hand very slightly towards The Monk and addressed Ghol.

'You're prepared to kill thousands and precipitate a regional nuclear war between Pakistan, India and probably China, just so you can play Lawrence of Kashmir? By your overreaching ambition and arrogance, you will almost certainly precipitate a nuclear confrontation with India. It's the biggest and most dangerous stand-off in history. Is that what you call "stability"?'

'There will be no stand-off. We will achieve stability. It is guaranteed!' Ghol exclaimed, full of certainty and conviction.

There was a heavy atmosphere in the room as Dunstan processed this. He could feel all eyes upon him, willing him to put an end to the situation. His mind flashed to the shocked dealers at the screens in the dealing room. *Rocking heads. It's an Indian characteristic. Hindus wobble heads. Indians rock their heads, Pakistanis don't rock their heads.*

It came to him in a flash. 'You've done some sort of deal with India, haven't you?' Not so much of a question, more a statement.

Ghol was quiet for a moment. Then a smile came across his face. He seemed to relax, safe in a greater knowledge and wisdom. 'It's more than a deal. Within a few hours from now Gilgit-Baltistan will be accepted as a *de facto* independent state by the international community.'

'And then what? Do tell us, please. Just put us out of our collective misery,' said Dunstan with heavy sarcasm, now thoroughly irritated with Ghol's self-righteous posturing.

'Well, then naturally all the Northern Provinces will become a protectorate of India. What you British used to call a Dominion, I believe.

By default, a Greater Jammu and Kashmir will be established as an independent entity under India's protection.'

A pause to absorb the implications of the redrawn national boundaries, Dunstan realising that he was out of his depth as a potential arbiter of regional politics; The Monk wondering why life got so bloody complicated when in the presence of one Philip Dunstan; Laycock realising that the front line against international terrorism had been redrawn, or more likely now totally obfuscated; and Asha Dhar feeling the emergence of split loyalties and emotions.

Dunstan knew what had to be done and that – come the moment, come the man – he was the only one with both the opportunity and the means at his disposal. The Monk, as if reading his friend's mind, grasped the moment and used the impasse to initiate a call to Lovat.

'Well screw you, Ghol. We'll remove the threat and your biggest bargaining chip.' Dunstan pointed at him. 'I'm going to defuse your device. We know where it is and we're going in there to disarm it.'

The Monk had moved to corner of the room and was talking in a low voice to Lovat, 'Rebecca, get London to get all the info: plans and diagrams on nukes, and especially any Int you have on disarming them... Yes, that's what I said, "nuclear devices". We need to disarm a small improvised nuclear device – plutonium ... yes, I know it's insane, just get everything you can for us will you? Did the abort message from this Shere Khan bloke get through to the hit team?... What do you mean, nobody knows? What the hell does that mean? *Preset times to communicate, no acknowledgment from hit team yet.* Bloody brilliant. Is the protection still in...?... What...!"

Dunstan eased over and picked up the latter part of the conversation. His jaw set. There was a long, steel-hard look between the two friends.

'I'll keep bugging them for a response,' was all The Monk could say. What he didn't say was that at the end of the call, Lovat had informed him that the wide area cordon had been removed. He thought it best that his friend didn't know. He would factor that into his contingency plans, which he had just started to formulate.

Dunstan thought of the screens and what he knew of Ghol's background from Rebecca Lovat's intelligence report, and he took an intuitive leap. 'So what have you *leveraged* here? Ten to one on the original forty million plus? Four hundred million, eh? Or are you north of that now?

Closed a few of the original positions have we, and releveraged up to, what, six hundred, eight hundred million? With your background in currency trading and derivatives, I can't imagine you being happy with just the original principal amount from the card fraud!'

To all of Dunstan's companions, the language was from another planet. No one knew what on earth he was talking about. The Monk caught Dunstan's eye again.

'Gambling, Monk, money shuffling on a vast scale,' Dunstan enlightened his team, who still had not got a clue. He was not finished. 'Now, Ghol. There's something you're going to do to make good the ruin you've brought on my life. You will transfer immediately the principal sum you gained through your fraud against my company into an ESCROW account in Bermuda, where it will lie waiting for a good cause to come along, not the least of which will be paying back the card-issuing banks for a starter.'

'Is that all?' sneered Ghol.

'Not quite. Add interest of, let's say, 20%. Yes, I know it's usury. That will go to re-building my business and compensating my shareholders. Finally, another five which will create a pension fund for these good people here whom you have caused to put their lives at risk.' Dunstan looked around at his team, 'I make that a nice round sixty.'

Ghol still had the guile to play the wounded animal. 'But if our principal fund goes, we lose our collateral. We're then holding open our financial positions illegally!'

'You still have the temerity to talk of legalities when you're screwing up the known universe? You're bonkers, Ghol!' He motioned Ghol towards the banks of computers, handing him a slip of paper with the Bermuda account details. Ghol opened up his secure financial portal and, with a gun at his head and Dunstan checking over his shoulder, he executed the electronic funds transfer into the Bermuda account in less than a minute.

Dunstan looked at the transfer going through. 'Good. That at least gives me some satisfaction. Nothing more can be achieved here, so we'll now leave you to declare your precious independence. Our paramedics will extract your sidekick here, otherwise he'll bleed or fester to death. God help you and your country, Ghol. You think you've been smart! I *know* you've created the biggest recipe for world chaos imaginable. You've let loose the dogs of nuclear conflict and you won't get them back in their kennels. Oh, and if you ever think of resurrecting your blood feud, as some of my old Irish friends would say, *I know where you and yours live*! And by God, I will hunt you down to the ends of the earth and find you! Good night, *Mr Ghol!*'

They all turned to go, but Asha Dhar did not move. Dunstan gently motioned to her, but she stood as though in a trance.

'I'm not going. I'm staying here. For a while, at least.' Gesturing towards Ghol she said, 'I need to make sure that he's true to his word. And that for your sake, the funds actually hit your account. Besides which, we don't want him detonating the nuke while you're sat on top of it, do we? I'll make sure he doesn't. It's OK, I'll be safe.'

Dunstan looked at her and then back to Ghol. As he observed the torn loyalties, he understood for the first time what it meant to have your nation taken away from you, and to have to fight for generations to get it back. And he knew the funds had already hit his account. He simply smiled ruefully and nodded his assent, communicating an admiration and heartfelt thanks to the brave young Special Forces officer, which in turn was reciprocated by Dhar.

With that, Dunstan headed out of the fortress without looking back. As they were leaving, Laycock turned to Dunstan. 'Those figures you were bandying around with Ghol, "sixty" something, what did they mean?'

'Millions of dollars, Hugo. They should have been pounds. For some reason I chose to let him off lightly. Rest assured, he's accumulated a lot more than that in his dealings. Call it sympathy for the devil.'

***

Out in the courtyard, Dunstan assembled his full team and addressed them informally. 'We now have an unforeseen challenge that necessitates a change of plan: to disarm a nuclear threat. An improvised nuclear device has been planted in the Nelum Gorge. I believe the Sapper Commando guys here know the area well. If it's detonated, the fall-out will bring untold misery and suffering to thousands, if not millions, of innocent people in the immediate vicinity and downstream. I fully recognise that this nuclear option was not part of the initial deal when we came here. In order to reach the device, we're going to have to parachute onto the terraced fields above the gorge, probably abseil in, and defuse this thing. Captain Laycock, The

Monk and I will be the disarming team. We'll need a team to set up and secure the Dropping Zone and descent route, and a wide area cordon to guard us. Anyone not wanting to jump in with us can stay on the aircraft. This is a volunteer-only mission. I just want to know how many of you are with me for the whole trip.'

'What, and miss the party afterwards? We'll have top blaggers' rights for years if we pull this one off!' shouted one of Laycock's NCOs.

There was subdued and somewhat nervous laughter all round. He didn't need to mention the alternative to not pulling it off. Enough said; they moved out, crossing back over to the chasm and descending quickly down to the plain to the waiting aircraft. The sun was beginning its descent behind the mountains as the Talons took off and joined their sister aircraft circling overhead.

Chapter Twenty-Three

Lovat had made action notes from The Monk's call. As she heard the words 'improvised nuclear device' she realised the implied threat to regional stability had mushroomed. She also knew she needed to get acknowledgement from the UK that the threat to Dunstan's family had been removed.

She let out a very loud and unladylike expletive. She didn't know where to start, so her initial port of call was the Scimitar Force officer in charge of command co-ordination in Al-Qurum, Major Al-Menali.

He listened to the requirements with growing interest. 'Miss Lovat, Al-Qurum has a highly secret, though small, nuclear emergency unit that was trained by NEST. I happen to have attended the course as an observer.'

'NEST?' asked Lovat.

'Yes. The USA's Nuclear Emergency Search Teams. I gather it comprises about one thousand highly expert individuals who are trained to defuse nuclear devices – terrorist and the like. I submit that if we could x-ray the device and transmit the details to our friends at NEST in Nevada via our telemetry communications on board the Talon, we could devise a disabling procedure on the spot. The objective would be to disarm the triggering mechanism only, not a complete defusing, which needs to be done under controlled conditions by nuclear experts. These experienced civilian teams would stand a better chance of knowing how to disarm the triggering mechanisms on Pakistani weapons without causing the bomb to go off.'

Lovat was not convinced of the practicality. 'I'm sure this NEST organisation has an overseas role to play in certain situations, but for practical and political purposes, this is *not* one of them. We need someone with immediate and intimate knowledge on the ground, next to the bomb. We have to make some assumptions here: we know it's a plutonium device and the signal mentioned an electronic combination lock. How does that work and how on earth can Dunstan and his team get through it without setting off the device?'

'Good point, Miss Lovat. From recollection that will probably be a Permissive Action Link,' replied Major Al-Menali. 'It's a one-time electronic combination lock, two combinations of six digits held by two different people. It's not possible to arm such a device without those two halves of the combination.'

'So how do they *disarm* it once it has been armed?'

'That's not my area of expertise. I'll get all possible plans and diagrams that we have ready for electronic transmission to the aircraft.'

'Thank you. And I'll get onto Aldermaston in the UK and see what they can produce.'

***

Above the Border between Indian and Azad Kashmir, near Muzaffarabad, 2100 hours local time

The Talons had made fair speed westwards along the LOC on the southern edge of Gilgit-Baltistan towards Azad Kashmir and the Fault Line, the collision zone created by the constant pushing and grinding of the Indian subcontinent tectonic plate against the Eurasian plate, the very thing that had created the Himalaya in the first place. There had been no time for rest or reflection; a sense of urgency and mission infused the team and drove them on through fatigue. Secure communications to Lovat in Al-Qurum via Top Cover, the AWACS still on patrol, ensured a continual stream of encrypted data concerning the probable nature of the nuclear device. For an hour, Dunstan and Laycock, hulled down in the tiny sound-proofed 'ops room' behind the cockpit, had their eyes glued to the onboard computer screens, poring over diagrams sent by Lovat and firing questions back to her.

Now, as they approached their objective, they were not exactly ecstatic, but they felt professionally satisfied that they had a better understanding of the threat and the options for disarming it. The Monk gave orders for deployment over the DZ – Dropping Zone – and now the squad were waiting for the tailgate to drop: a mixture of 59 Commando, Scimitar

Regiment, and of course Dunstan and The Monk. Each of them had heavy packs and extra duffle sacks slung from a harness on their waist, packed with a variety of equipment and weaponry. Laycock, dropping first, had a specially devised chest harness complete with Global Positioning, flares and comms. The Talon made one more pass over its IP – Initiation Point – near Muzarrafabad, then dropped low to fly over the Nelum Gorge.

As far as the Pakistani Air Force knew, it was all above board: an allied Gulf state had been given sanction to practice night drops in mountainous terrain. The AWACS circling above gave Dunstan and his team continual GPS positioning. Down and down the Talon went, until the gorge walls could be seen ahead. Cold air streamed into the aircraft as the tailgate dropped. Over the DZ the jump lights went on and the Scimitar Regiment loadmaster signalled five seconds. The Monk and Laycock went first to establish the DZ, the latter frantically trying to use the GPS strapped to his chest harness to target a specific location which he had selected from his local knowledge. They opened their canopies at five hundred feet and Laycock tracked towards the high terrace field they had selected as the drop, The Monk following close behind. A smooth, flared, landing and then they immediately let off a signal. As the Talon came round a second time over the side wall of the gorge at a thousand feet, the remainder of the team, still airborne, waited momentarily for the loadmaster to give them 'Go'; they streamed out of the load bay down towards Laycock's marker, Dunstan revelling in the adrenaline coursing through his veins.

The Royal Engineer Commandos were now on their adopted home turf. They stashed their parachutes and picked up their loads, heading off immediately to the edge of the gorge. Dunstan and the others, suitably impressed with their efficiency and speed, had to work hard to keep up. Laycock, leading the way and benefiting from his months at altitude and natural feel for steep terrain, picked his way steadily and methodically down through the juniper and gorse, every so often stopping to check his GPS. On one of these occasions, Dunstan moved up to his side and saw in the young officer's taut face a resolve and steel that had previously not been in evidence. Struggling to keep up were two Scimitar Troop sergeants carrying a black suitcase between them. The pace was relentless and the going brutal, but still they headed down and down. Men cursed in the dark as they tore their flesh on thorn bushes or twisted an ankle in the numerous marmot holes. On they went until they hit a tangle of rhododendron, which slowed them up considerably, as they had to circumvent it. The climb down was interminable and all were sweating profusely. The heavy packs altered their natural centre of gravity and with each step they struggled to maintain balance.

After a short distance, Laycock stopped suddenly near a very large boulder and referenced his GPS. The roar of the Nelum River could be heard in the gorge below. 'I reckon this will do. We should be less than two hundred feet above the river bed and directly above the hydroelectric tunnel entrance. We'll abseil off this boulder. Let's get four of the guys to try and push it off the hill. If it holds with that push it shouldn't trundle off into space when we abseil off it.'

The solidity of the boulder having been tested, an abseil was quickly rigged using two climbing ropes. Knots were tied at the bottom ends to stop the abseiler sliding off into oblivion in the dark, and then the ropes were thrown into space. Laycock went to clip on first when Dunstan checked him.

'You've done a great job leading us here, but this is my risk, Hugo. I go down first. As soon as the tension comes off the ropes at the bottom, come down yourself with The Monk. If no tension comes off, it means I've blown it and I'm swinging in space. In that case I'll have to ascend back up the rope. I've got jumar-ascenders with me.'

Dunstan pushed the double ropes through his descending device, clipped the ropes into his locking karabiner and snapped the "krab" into his harness. He took a length of 3mm rope and with it formed a back-up safety link between his harness belay loop and the abseil ropes by use of a prusik knot. He moved down towards the edge of the rock walls of the gorge. As he did so, he noticed that the double ropes had tensioned over a sharp edge of rock. 'One of you guys put some padding between the rope and that rock so it doesn't abrade on the edge.' A simple instruction, born of years of climbing experience, that was to save his life.

Dunstan looked at his watch: 2200 hours. Switching on his head torch, he took off into the depths of the gorge, the rope coming into tension with his full weight on it. It doesn't take long to abseil a couple of hundred feet – four minutes of controlled descent at the most. As he descended, he quickly moved into space as the walls of the gorge became vertical. With every ten feet, the roar from the water below became louder and angrier. He knew he was getting close to the bottom as droplets sprayed him. He stopped. Below was a foaming torrent, and he had about twenty feet of rope left. He couldn't see the tunnel entrance. It was certainly not below him. *Where the hell is it?* He fought to control panic at the prospect of having to abort and ascend back up the rope. Then in the beam of his torch he saw what he thought was a faint red glow. *The nuke: is it armed?* As his eyes adjusted to the gloom, he saw the outline of the tunnel entrance about forty feet over to his left.

Fuck, I'm going to have to pendulum.

He braced his feet against the retaining walls of the gorge and started to bounce off them, creating some momentum. On the fifth bounce he committed, and started to run his feet across the wall to the left, then back over to the right, all the time increasing the swing of the pendulum and the height gained on each swing. Up above, The Monk saw the distinctive left-to-right movement of the rope as it brushed back and forth across the padding. Without the protection in place the rope would have quickly abraded through on the sharp edge of the rock.

'He's off for a pendulum across the gorge. The tunnel must be off to one side,' observed Laycock.

The Monk tried to stuff more padding under the rope but with the tension coming from below there was no chance. They all watched the left-to-right movement with morbid fascination, all praying that the padding would not wear through with the friction on the edge of rock.

Below, Dunstan was desperately trying to gain more momentum. Even if he did reach the entrance his problems were only just beginning, as he had to be able to grab some sort of protrusion and anchor himself on the wall in order to get into the tunnel itself.

As he bounced off the walls and swung left again, his fingers found a sharp layaway hold a few feet short of the entrance to the tunnel. His timing was off, so he missed. On his next pendulum he grasped too hard, and ripped off flesh on the tip of his middle finger. He cried out, more in frustration than pain, but the noise of roaring waters feet below took away his cry. Again, he swung in and this time curled his fingers around the sharp, leftward-facing hold. His strong climber's grip hung on to the wet hold, but his position was precarious, his body spread across the wall and held in tension between his grip on the rock and the tight abseil rope. He struggled to maintain position for what seemed like an age then eased the tension on the rope, carefully, so as to maintain balance and equilibrium.

As the tension came off, he knew he had one chance. He pulled as hard as he could on the left layaway hold. In the dry and in daylight it would have been a tricky climbing move; in the dark and in the wet it was technically desperate. As the weight came onto his left hand he slapped his right hand up and found a minute edge that could barely accommodate two fingers. With his feet scrabbling for friction, he transferred his centre of gravity leftwards, fighting the tension in the abseil rope pulling him off balance. He committed himself and with a final lunge born of desperation hooked his left heel around the right edge of the tunnel wall, and, with all the strength left in him, hauled himself round into the tunnel entrance itself – only to have his efforts mocked by a single, red, pulsing light. He eased the remaining tension on the abseil rope and, for the second time that day, momentarily collapsed in a heap, drained.

Looking up, he saw a series of anchors banged into the wall and clipped into them. He lay back down on the floor of the tunnel, exhausted by his efforts, taking further stock of his surroundings. Above him, attached to an anchor point, he spotted the web cam with a cable attached, leading up left and out of the tunnel entrance. His first action was to grab a rock and smash it.

At the abseil point, the experienced climbers had already surmised what had happened and were rigging up two more abseil ropes. One of them was a rope specially designed for mountain rescue that had a communications cable running the length of the central core.

The Monk and Laycock prepared to follow Dunstan. Laycock's combat engineer commandos prepared to lower the bomb disposal kit. As he groped his way down into the void, Laycock privately wondered if it would be any use at all. He abseiled quickly, tensioning diagonally into the cave along Dunstan's anchored rope. He pulled the other ropes into the cave, anchoring them in turn. The Monk abseiled in to join them, followed at a much slower descent rate by two of Laycock's men guiding down the bomb disposal kit which was being lowered from the top.

Dunstan had to raise his voice above the noise of the river. 'So, Hugo! Is this thing live or what?'

'No idea!'

'What?'

'The presence of a light doesn't necessarily mean it's armed!' Laycock shouted.

Dunstan looked around the cave. 'We're about to try and defuse an improvised nuclear device with limited knowledge and no prior experience, and we don't know if the electronic arming circuitry may or may not be activated? Great! So what *do* we know, Hugo?'

As an EOD-trained (Explosive Ordnance Disposal) Royal Engineer, Laycock had soaked up all the available information on arming mechanisms for nuclear devices on the flight. 'According to the stuff we received from NEST and Aldermaston, this should be a standard plutonium bomb that consists of a core of plutonium surrounded by a high-explosive lens, which creates a spherical shockwave which in turn compresses the core with enough downward pressure to trigger an unstable chain reaction. The HE lens *has* to be triggered with precision, so there's a net of detonators around it which is triggered by the PAL interlock device.'

Dunstan knew that this was no time for deliberation. 'How in the name of God do we disarm this thing?'

Laycock sounded professionally sanguine. 'According to the topology we received on the plane, if we were to disable any one of the leads to the HE lens, the detonator explosion would be limited to the extent that it couldn't produce the prerequisite spherical shockwave to initiate the chain reaction. In other words, it would be disarmed, but not defused. Having cut and disabled one or more leads to the HE lens, we would then have to remove each of the detonators to fully defuse it.'

'So if we manage to disable just one detonator, it won't explode, right? So what's the downside?' asked Dunstan sceptically.

'At any given stage, we might set off any of the detonators. If that happens then we'll have an almighty mess as plutonium is released and sprayed around. We'll all be dead and there may be a limited explosion – effectively a "dirty bomb". I just don't know, but at least it won't produce mega-ton levels of energy release.'

Dunstan looked at his watch. 'Sod it. Let's go for the single cut disarming and the Pakistanis can mop up the rest later. That will also minimise the risk of radioactive leakage. So, how do we get into this device?'

'As with any other bomb: with the drill rig. Al-Qurum seemed to think of everything when they equipped you guys,' replied Laycock.

Drilling into a bomb is a lot like brain surgery; the skull encasing the part of the brain to be operated on has to be removed by drilling into it without damaging the brain itself, a delicate procedure utilising high-speed drilling equipment.

Laycock instructed his two men who had brought down the drilling rig to ascend back up to the top of the gorge, and suggested The Monk might wish to do the same. However, The Monk, in his inimitable way, made it clear to Laycock that he wasn't going to be left out of the action. Together, the three men set up the rig above the target area. It looked like a large tripod with a downward pointing diamond-headed drill. This high-speed drill was state-of-the-art, with a running speed of over a hundred thousand revolutions per minute. The only problem was that, at these revs, the battery pack used to power it had only sufficient juice for some twenty minutes. As the most experienced bomb disposal officer, Laycock was the surgeon. He may as well have been wearing full surgeon's garb, such was the mask of concentration on his face. The thought of all those innocents that would be wiped out in the world above if the bomb went off focused his mind.

Fortunately for the drill operators, the outer casing of the device was made of a hard plastic. It was in essence a sophisticated IED. It had to be as light as possible for it to have been carried down into the gorge.

In spite of the cold, dank, atmosphere all three men were dripping with perspiration. The diamond-headed drill made light work of the casing as Laycock the surgeon drilled a circle of conjoining holes about 30cm in diameter. That done, the team held their breath as he carefully removed the drilled circle of casing. Underneath was a titanium dome with what appeared to be a very large percussion cap in the centre. Up to now, the prospective disarming had been merely academic discussion. With instant vaporisation a foregone conclusion if anything went wrong, their professional curiosity had overcome nerves.

Laycock took out his toolset and removed the Allen bolts securing the dome. Once it was removed, they could all see the titanium and lead-encased central plutonium core surrounded by the ring of detonators. Each detonator was housed in its own titanium casing to maximise stability, and each was connected to the core by a 2mm thick wire. Laycock put his face within a few centimetres of the heart of the nuclear device. It was too late to be worried by the prospect of any leakage. His sharp, hardened wire cutters hovered over the detonator ring, as though deciding which one to go for. A deep, slow, intake of breath to steady his hand, then, in one swift movement, Laycock cut two detonator wires and promptly sat back, looking at the others.

The Monk was baffled. 'Is that it? No fucking clock ticking down to zero. No booby traps, red wires, blue wires and all that shit? It's as simple as that?'

'Simple' wasn't the word Hugo Laycock would have chosen; he nodded, 'That's it!'

'Nothing else to do?' asked a sceptical Dunstan.

'No. It's disarmed, if not yet fully defused. There's quite a distinction between the two states. If you don't mind, I'd like to get out of here.' The adrenaline was already starting to subside and Laycock was feeling washed out by the intensity of his operation.

'That's easier said than done,' observed Dunstan. 'After we've knackered ourselves ascending back up the ropes out of this hellhole, we'll have to tab back down the ridge on the other side onto the plain where the Talons can pick us up. It's going to take hours of grinding effort!'

'We don't need to tab back down to the plain.' It was The Monk who spoke. 'We can be picked up from the fields on the ridge line without the planes actually landing.'

'How?' asked Dunstan.

'Skyhook. The Talons are equipped with an upgraded multiple-lift Fulton Skyhook. That's the big scissor affair on the nose.' The other two looked at him as though he were insane. 'Trust me; it's an exfil device that's been used for decades, since the fifties. It'll be adventurous, but it sounds as if we have no option. Two lifts of six men per lift. Take it from me, it's a piece-o-piss.'

'OK, Monk, you're on. As Hugo says, we need to move. It's going to take a couple of hours of sweat and toil for the whole team with all the gear to get back out of this gorge onto the terrace. Everyone ready? Let's go!'

Dunstan checked his watch; it was just after midnight. Exhausted, drained and chock full of confused emotions, he was wondering, with five hours' time difference, if it was too much to hope that he could be having lunch with his family later in the day.

***

The lead Talon made its first pass along the broad crest of the ridge above the Nelum Gorge, a practice run flying on heads-up night vision. A second pass, and a large rubberised cylinder dropped from the tailgate at a height of sub-100 feet and bounced. The other Talon came in shortly behind and followed suit with a second package. Two Commando Sappers sprinted across the fields and opened the cylinders to release what looked like inflatable circular capsules with an aluminium-strengthened base and a storm cover. Pressurised helium inflated a large helium balloon on each capsule, which at once soared skyward towing the 500-foot line of fluorescent nylon rope.

'Go!' shouted Laycock. The first of the pre-designated teams dashed for the dinghy and jumped in just as the second Talon was making its practice pass. The men in the lead capsule clipped themselves in and braced themselves for pickup. The first of the Talons flew low again, this time deploying the specially reinforced Fulton Skyhook scissors attached to the nose of the aircraft. As it approached, the scissors gripped the nylon rope, snatching the first capsule from the ground. Before they knew it the occupants were flying through the air at two hundred and fifty miles per hour.

Slowly, the line was reeled in until it could be hooked by the loadmasters, who attached it to a winch, which hauled the whole capsule and its occupants into the load bay. The other Talon with the second team, including Dunstan and Laycock, followed five minutes behind.

Being towed through a starry night sky and slowly hauled into the belly of the mothership was a surreal adventure that, if only in retrospect, was one that none of them would have missed. Even by the time the Talons landed back at the aid programme airfield near Abbottabad, their adrenaline was still pumping. In spite of the exertions of the past twelve hours, all but one of the team was on a high. The exception was Hugo Laycock who, even as everyone disembarked, was in the deepest of slumbers, wrapped up in several sleeping bags – green maggots – on the floor of the Talon. Even a mischievous kick from The Monk, who had spent the whole of the flight communicating with Rebecca Lovat to make onward arrangements, failed to make an impression on the comatose Laycock.

Dunstan turned to The Monk as they walked across to the makeshift Ops room.

'Let's get these guys fed: they've all done amazingly well. What's next, Monk?'

There was a lot in that question, and The Monk knew it. 'Right, Sherpa: Rebecca Lovat is scheduled to land here shortly on one of His Excellency's private jets. She'll organise the diplomatic bit via the British High Commission. I don't envy her the job. Laycock will get all the credit and probably a well-deserved non-public and unattributed medal. You and I will make ourselves scarce. I'm off back to Al-Qurum to take up my new job.'

The Monk paused and Dunstan could feel the black eyes looking at him through the gloom. He voice was flat and subdued. 'Sorry, Sherpa, but the word is that you're going to have to find a new country to live in.'

'What?' Dunstan was apoplectic. He tried to rationalise what this meant.

He ranted until he felt a large, gnarled hand on his shoulder.

'It's OK, I'm only joking!' The Monk laughed out loud. 'You and I, Sherpa, have some transport arriving to get us back to the UK via Al-Qurum and Malta re-fuelling stops. We're on the private jet out of here. You're an embarrassment to the Pakistanis so you are *straight* out of here.'

'You bastard!' said Dunstan with feeling.

'Don't question. Just do. We stop in Al-Qurum to pick up Tysoe and then straight on to RAF Lossiemouth, Scotland.'

***

By the time Dunstan opened his eyes, they were landing at Al-Qurum. His Excellency Sheikh Suroor Al-Qurum, looking resplendent in the uniform of Air Marshall of the Royal Al-Qurum Air Force, greeted him and the rest of his flight. Dunstan spotted Rebecca Lovat smiling at him. He waved and returned the smile: his own salute to experience shared, and a professional bond formed.

Sheikh Al-Qurum saw the deflation in Dunstan's eyes. They strolled together across the runway, out of earshot.

'Listen to me, Sherpa! You did a brilliant job under challenging circumstances. In the name of Allah, Peace be upon Him, I wish it had been me! I have received running reports from Rebecca Lovat...' his voice was conspiratorial for a moment, 'quite a woman, eh my friend?' before straightening his spine and continuing his peroration with gravitas. 'There is still a lot of chaos to play out in the region. The old orders are disappearing fast. The whole region is on the brink of civil war. I hope that internal squabbles can be resolved and national cohesion maintained. I fear though, that it is already too late for that; the geo-political landscape has changed and will continue to change.' He threw up his arms in exasperation. 'Who knows where it will end? I have my forces on full alert to counter both external and internal threats. I have instructed my cabinet to draw up plans for a democratic constitution. You can imagine how they took that, especially Thabet! Also, for your knowledge only, I have allocated a billion dollars, a nice round sum I thought, for the purposes of dealing with *external* threats beyond our borders in the future!'

Dunstan got his drift but he was too tired to register the implications of Al-Qurum financing cross-border incursions and the like across the Gulf.

'So, Sherpa, my friend, God speed back to your family. I trust you will find them safe and in good health. Get some rest. Rebuild your life. I gather you might have expropriated enough to get you going again, eh!' Sheikh Al-Qurum's frame shook as he laughed, 'Go with the blessing of Allah, Peace be upon Him.'

'Thank you. By the way,' it was Dunstan's turn to lower his voice, 'can we please now stop this "Sherpa" and "Dreadnought" business?'

He thought his friend would laugh; on the contrary he looked serious, indeed grave. Sheikh Suroor Al-Qurum paused for a while, then said, 'No, Sherpa. We cannot. We shall not. We do not know under what future circumstances we will need these names – guard them, cherish them, my friend!' He paused and then beamed. 'Next stop for you: Scotland!'

Chapter Twenty-Four

<u>Sunday, 29th April: RAF Lossiemouth, Scotland, 0530 hours; Islamabad, 1030 hours</u>

Dawn had brought large-scale rioting onto the streets of Karachi, Islamabad, Lahore and Rawalpindi. Now the world was holding its breath in anticipation of the fall of the government and the outbreak of full-scale civil war in Pakistan. The Northern Tribes stood ready to claim their independence. With civil chaos acting as a smokescreen, a newly armed Baltistan Liberation Front had taken over all local political and administrative facilities in Gilgit, Skardu and other provincial centres in Gilgit-Baltistan. Few in the Pakistani Government either noticed or cared. Those that did cried out in a wilderness of empty corridors. With the chaos getting worse with every hour, the tribal leaders waited for the siren call that would trigger their longed-for independence.

The Bombardier, personal jet of His Excellency Sheikh Mohammed Al-Qurum, asked the control tower at RAF Lossiemouth for clearance to land. On board was a select brotherhood: Dunstan, The Monk and Tysoe. After a quick shower and change of combat dress, the first two had crashed into a dreamless sleep as soon as the aircraft had taken off from Al-Qurum; the latter had spent the eight-hour flight crunching numbers, working out how best to use the funds Dunstan had liberated. The Bombardier was scheduled to take Tysoe onwards to Kidlington airfield in Oxfordshire, where he would head back to the office and sort out what was left of CyberX.

As they disembarked in the misty dawn, The Monk was pensive, his thousand-mile stare in place.

'What's the matter, Monk?' asked Dunstan. He assumed his friend would be upbeat now it was all over and they could get on with their lives.

'Nothing, Sherpa, nothing at all. Nothing that can't be sorted out, that is.' The Monk's tone was flat; even he sounded weary of this Great Game.

Dunstan assumed that The Monk was coming down to earth after the hectic time they had just shared, and that he, also, wanted to get on and rebuild his life. 'Understood, my friend,' he said with compassion. Yet Dunstan's thoughts, forgivably selfish, were with his family and their reunion. He had a lot of making-up to do with Faith. 'So how do we get to Lynacraigie, Monk?' Dunstan couldn't wait to see his family and wanted to get going. He assumed The Monk had sorted out the transport. He need not have feared, at least on that count.

'In that thing!' responded The Monk, as he pointed across the tarmac to an Al-Qurum C-130 which had obviously landed some time earlier.

As Dunstan peered across the airfield, he saw the familiar sight of the Overfinch Range Rover being driven down the ramp, looking in somewhat better condition than when it made the outward journey.

'His Excellency had the Land Rover dealership in Al-Qurum work on it round the clock. Apparently, it's the dog's bollocks again.' The Monk managed a slight grin.

Dunstan was too bone-weary to respond. The Monk walked round to the Bombardier's cargo hold and helped the crew unload the packs and some new, large, heavy wooden cases.

'What's that lot, Monk?'

'Contingency planning,' responded The Monk without looking up from his task.

Curious, Dunstan looked at them more closely. His eyebrows lifted at the 7.62mm ammo boxes, then his eyes rested on something altogether quite different: a case containing .50 inch calibre rounds. He twisted his head to look at the manufacturer on the large box: MacMillan Brothers, Phoenix, Arizona. He turned to face the sea and took a deep draught of the fresh sea air blowing in from the North Sea, 'You *are* joking, aren't you, Monk?' was all he could think of saying at that moment. 'What do we need this lot for, except to fill up your armoury?'

The Monk did not respond. Instead, he pulled out a long case, unpacked it, and assembled the contents to make up a rifle of uncommon size.

Dunstan picked up on it immediately. He spoke softly and with resignation. 'Do the authorities in the UK know where the hit team is?'

'According to Lovat, no they don't, Sherpa. She was a bit evasive on the subject. Which was odd in itself. I even had Digger Cole flying around at your expense but he's found nothing either. Given their tactical awareness, he reckoned they might be travelling straight north on a compass bearing, not even using main routes. With their natural fieldcraft they could be holed up in the slightest contour, invisible to a chopper flying overhead.'

'But the hit team was called off! By Khan on the HF transmitter!' protested Dunstan.

The black orbs levelled with him. 'Sherpa, you're just too fucking trusting sometimes. Think about it! Would the powers-that-be, your so-called friends, allow a tooled-up team of professional mercenaries to roam around the UK at leisure until challenged by an unarmed Mr Plod in a patrol car? Would they hell! I don't believe the Order ever went out. What I reckon is that they're allowing them to continue to their objective. Let them move into a wilderness area, corner them, let them get set up, then send in a task team, assault choppers, the Lads – and mop them up on their own terms.'

'They're using my family as bait!' exclaimed Dunstan, privately reflecting that, yet again, Faith's instincts had been right.

'I've been working on that assumption for the past twenty-four hours, Sherpa!'

Dunstan looked around him and grabbed a heavy jacket. He was shivering and it wasn't just from the cold. As he put it on he said to The Monk, 'I don't suppose you know if a task team has been dispatched, do you?'

The Monk held up his hands in an expression of submission. 'I don't fucking know, Sherpa. Best to be self-reliant and carry your own insurance policy, eh?' he said, patting the fibreglass butt of the weapon. 'Give me a hand getting this lot into your monster over there.'

Dunstan felt sick to the pit of his stomach. It was the biggest damper imaginable to the longed-for reunion with his family.

***

Lynacraigie, 0600 hours

Lynacraigie Lodge stood south-facing, proud in its granite splendour, in a broad glacial valley dominated by three Munros (Scottish mountains over 3,000 feet in height). These provided the stalking grounds for red deer, the main income and means of managing this shooting estate, although it was now outside the stalking season. A few hundred feet in front of the Lodge lay the remains of an old airstrip, constructed in the Second World War when the estate had been requisitioned by the War Office as a centre to train Special Operations Executive teams in clandestine warfare behind enemy lines.

Nearly seventy years later, clandestine warfare of sorts had again come to Lynacraigie, but this was no exercise. The Nepalese were hidden in a small defile, highly camouflaged, on the shoulder of Meall Dearg (Gaelic for 'Red Hill'), a 950m mountain overlooking their target. In spite of the sub-zero overnight temperature, not uncommon in the Highlands in spring, and the cold army compo rations for their only meal, the brothers had made their position professionally comfortable. They had camouflaged themselves with cam-nets interwoven with bracken and settled down to wait. Defensively, anything that came within 1,000m could be obliterated in the cross-fire of their weaponry, arranged with overlapping arcs of fire to give three kill-zones. Older Brother had calculated distances and angles to certain key features with his clinometer. There was still a layer of mist below them at 200m; they would wait until it lifted for a target opportunity.

***

Inside Lynacraigie Lodge itself, Faith Dunstan was in the process of getting the house up and about. She and the close protection team had been up most of the night. They had caught occasional snatches of sleep in the large, battered, but exquisitely comfortable leather armchairs in front of the log fire with its red-hot glowing embers. Covered in tartan rugs, they waited anxiously. She had been up to the old servants' quarters to give the kids their first wake-up call and had thrown Pull-Through under the boys' blankets to encourage them to rise. The litany of curses that ensued caused them to receive their first maternal rocketing of the day.

Faith looked out of the big sitting-room windows and knew there was something wrong – something not quite right out there in the hills. She knew this because she hadn't seen any deer; they came down into the valley every night to within a couple of hundred yards of the house, and moved back up into the mountains shortly after dawn. She had been looking for them before dawn with the naked eye and through binoculars – field glasses in stalking terms – and they were most definitely not out there. *If they're not there, then who is?* She tried to push the thought away but it stayed with her. In spite of her misgivings, she also knew that Dunstan was now on his way back and that gave her a warm feeling. In spite of all he had put her through, she couldn't wait to see him, to hold him close, on her own with no kids around. But she was going to give him hell first. The close protection team of three policemen would just be on changeover from their six hours on, six off routine. She would get the kettle on for morning tea. Then something made her change her mind: instinct, the caring instinct of a mother protecting her offspring? Whatever it was, instead of going into the kitchen, she headed to the gun room where she removed two Sakko Finnlight stalking rifles – light enough for her and the boys to use – and a considerable amount of .30 ammunition. She carried them into the sitting-room to lay them on the large table in front of the big window. Then she added an extra pair of field glasses and a stalker's scope to the collection. Satisfied, she headed off to the kitchen to make tea.

Faith Dunstan was leaning on the Aga stove when Sergeant Danny Tinsley came in from his tour outside. 'Nothing happening out there, ma'am. All quiet,' he reported in his soft Highland brogue.

'I know; that's precisely what's wrong, Sergeant.'

'Do you *really* think there's a threat out there, Mrs Dunstan?' asked Tinsley.

Faith answered the question with a question. 'What did your briefing say about the nature of any potential threat?' she asked him.

'Nothing specific, ma'am, I have to admit. Given that the wide area cordon was pulled out early, surely that means the powers-that-be don't believe a threat really exists?'

'Sergeant Tinsley, my husband's operations director, one of his closest friends, had his head chopped off near Oxford; Philip himself has been shot at with uncommonly powerful weaponry and just managed to escape his pursuers by fleeing overseas; his company has been attacked by fraudsters and his life's work lies in ruins…and if all that wasn't enough, Philip's secretary was kidnapped and ritually murdered, probably to find out where *we* are. So no real threat at all, what!?'

'Phew, I see. That background wasn't part of our brief.' An enlightened Tinsley was subdued and not a little miffed that his superiors hadn't thought to give him the full intelligence picture. 'Anyway, I'd better do another tour outside before handover to MacDonald.' With that, he put on his flak jacket and headed for the door.

'Be careful,' was her heartfelt advice to a closing kitchen door.

***

It was 0645 hours by now. At that moment, Dunstan and The Monk were on the long, single-track tarmacadam estate road. Philip had thought about trying to call his wife but then changed his mind; he wanted to clear his head first. As they came over the final rise with a view down into the valley, Dunstan asked The Monk to stop just below the skyline for much the same reasons as he had stopped above the Evenlode valley the night after Idris Morgan had died: to leave the bad world behind before seeing his family. A weak sun had yet to rise above the majesty of the surrounding Caledonian mountains, but the thin mist below them was dissipating, helped by the cold north-easterly wind.

The Monk viewed the tranquil scene below him with a professional appreciation. His eyes scanned the mountains; nothing was moving out there. All was peaceful. There was only one problem in his mind and in his heart: it wasn't the desert.

Unbeknown to them, they had just got in ahead of the police putting into place a very wide area protective cordon around the estate, covering all minor roads leading out of Lynacraigie Estate and at the ends of all key exit valleys. The forecast was for a fine, bright Highland morning. Major General Gibbs had deemed it wise to wait until his two units of four-man SBS teams – from the anti-terrorist oil rig protection unit at Arbroath – could move in with the sun low on the horizon, directly behind them.

The choices had been difficult, and the subject of much heated debate between Gibbs, Fanshawe and Counter Terrorism Command before they took the plan jointly to COBRA. Whichever way they looked at it, this outfit had the capacity to run rings round them, to escape and evade for weeks, and any move to arrest such a fully-armed and dangerous team would put the public at risk. Gibbs' view had won the day. They needed containment in a wilderness area and they already had one of those: Lynacraigie.

The set-up of the operation had been challenging, and it relied upon the dialogue established between Shafquat Khan and his hit team during the former's interrogation. Gibbs knew that to search proactively for this particular enemy in this terrain would be a non-starter, like looking for a needle in a haystack. He had an Apache assault helicopter available to him with night-time heat signature recognition capability. However, this capability relies on differential heat between target and environment. As the air cools at night, the target may lose or emit heat at a lower rate than the surrounding environment. At some point, the emission of heat from both the target and the surrounding environment may be equal, which makes target detection and acquisition difficult to impossible. This is called infra-red crossover and it occurs most often when the environment is wet; like on a dreech night in the Scottish mountains for example.

The whole operation was, therefore, dependent first on his enemy giving away their position, then on the assault team together with the Apache and back-up armed police marksmen from Counter Terrorism Command reacting collectively like greased lightning.

He just hoped and prayed they could get in there before any member of Dunstan's family was killed.

Chapter Twenty-Five

The Monk was just about to get back in the Overfinch and drive his friend down to the Lodge to see his family when his keen eyes observed a figure coming round the corner of the house. At that distance it was impossible to see who it was with the naked eye.

'Hang on, Sherpa, I'll get the binos.' The Monk headed to the car.

Philip Dunstan soaked up the beauty and momentarily relaxed, for a second daring to believe it was all over. It was premature: as he switched his scan back towards the Lodge, the figure at the front of the house reeled back, hit the front door and slumped to the ground.

The Monk was already at his side with the powerful binos.

THUMP! The travelled sound of the high velocity round leaving the barrel of the shooter's weapon caught up with the target. They both heard it and intuitively noted the gap between the policeman going down and the thump of the round.

'Fuck! Armed policeman down!' shouted The Monk.

'No crack!' shouted Dunstan, referring to the absence of the sound of bullet breaking the sound barrier.

'We're outside the shock wave cone of the round, we wouldn't hear it. Besides which, they're probably too far away to generate a crack,' replied a ballistics-experienced Monk.

They both felt horribly impotent as the body in front of the Lodge jumped with the impact as another round hit it. Instinct and training kicked in. The Monk and Dunstan counted the seconds.

One second... two seconds... three seconds... four seconds... THUMP!

'Four seconds! The bastard is four thousand, four hundred feet away. Nearly a mile!' The Monk was impressed.

The speed of sound is roughly one thousand, one hundred feet per second. By counting the seconds, The Monk, experienced in many hard firefights, instantly computed the distance between shooter and target.

The front door to the Lodge opened slightly and Faith Dunstan looked around and down.

Dunstan, his eyes to the field glasses, was gripped with terror, 'No! Faith! Get back in!' he screamed, but the wind took away his words.

As though she had heard him from over a mile away, Faith quickly disappeared back into the house just as another THUMP! echoed around the valley and a round embedded itself in the thick oak door, shattering it. Then the sound of rifle fire came from the house itself. Steady, rhythmic fire.

Dunstan stood petrified for a second, then his mind cleared. Fatigue was replaced by fear and resolve. 'Monk! Come on! Get in! I'll drive, I know where I'm going! Get in!!' he screamed.

Several miles away, a Royal Marines Apache AH1 helicopter, followed by a Lynx carrying the two SBS teams, together with two Eurocopter EC175s full of armed police, were tracking towards the estate. They were about to land at their designated FUP, where the Lynx would go forward to drop off the SBS squad. The Apache AH1, complete with its battery of sixteen Hellfire missiles, would provide overhead cover. As the teams disembarked, they heard the distant gunfire: the party had already started and they were late.

Dunstan reversed the Range Rover away from the Lodge back down the hill and charged straight south along a bumpy drovers' track, hitting over seventy miles per hour. After about half a mile, he stopped momentarily to electronically reduce the tyre pressure in all four of the 21-inch tyres and to raise the suspension. It seemed to take forever. Around the corner, they hit a fold in the hills with a tributary river running down it, fed by mountain streams. Dunstan forded the river and sped along a small winding track regularly used by Argocats, the main transport for a stalker and his party in this wilderness. He then cut right and west up a track which wound precipitously up the hillside. Still gunning the engine, he contoured round the ridgeline and stopped momentarily below a steep subsidiary valley.

'OK, Monk. If those bastards are in line-of-sight to the house but nearly a mile away, they can only be on the north-east slopes of Meall Dearg, and we're now located south-east and to their rear. Now we cut up this valley as high as we can get, then we have a hell of a stalk north-west up a stream bed to lead us out onto a shoulder opposite them. That means we'll be shooting west-north-west with a north-easterly wind coming in over our right shoulder. Let's hope the team in the house, whoever they are, can keep our targets' heads down. Let's go!'

As the sharp valley tightened and closed in, the stalkers' track ran out. Dunstan dropped the gears into low ratio and gunned the Overfinch over the steep boggy ground, its deflated tyres spreading the weight. It took them high up into a basin below the head of the valley from where several ice-cold streams fed into the main tributary. Dunstan stopped and dived out of the door into the chill wind.

The wind cut into them but they were by now inured to it. They headed up a steep side-stream strewn with boulders, tracking for the position Dunstan knew would give them line-of-sight to the target area. In spite of the cold, they started to sweat. They could see the head of the stream but the steep sides forced them into the stream bed. The stream was waist deep and the fresh cold Highland water of early spring numbed their bodies, shrinking their testicles. The boulders scrubbed their knees and elbows; if either felt discomfort it did not show, their bodies forced on by willpower and fear for the safety of Dunstan's family. They held their weapons slightly out of the water, a strenuous position to maintain with every mental and physical faculty working fully. The saddle they were heading for, from which Dunstan knew that they would be in line-of-sight to their enemy, was now close.

They stopped, listened, ears and eyes searching for sound and movement: The stalk was on: they found the old stalkers' scoop Dunstan knew was there from his days of stalking a different prey. Shooter and spotter settled in.

The shooter clipped in the bi-pod and settled his shoulder into the butt of the MacMillan; he did not underestimate the challenge. The distance was no problem for the weapon in ideal conditions, but these were far from ideal. In a perfect shoot, he should have been looking down at his target; instead he was at the same level. The wind was now turning to the north and blowing at least ten knots, for which he would have to compensate his aim. Wisps of early morning Highland mist were scudding over the hills, occasionally blurring his view. There had been a late spring frost in the night and even now the temperature was still in single-digit Celsius figures. He blew hot air onto his trigger finger.

His spotter, his eye searching the ground of Meall Dearg across the valley, directed him to a movement on the shoulder. All the sniper could see was a head appearing marginally over the edge of the dug-out. He was patient; he had to wait until timing and conditions were optimum. He waited, not wanting the adrenaline to subside. Controlling his breathing, he shifted his body position slightly, bringing his right leg a bit higher to give him a more stable platform. His clothing was soaked through but his focused mind blocked out the wet chill. He relaxed his cheek muscles on the butt of the rifle and consciously eased his trigger finger; any tension in his body, however slight, would transmit as a tremor down through his weapon, forcing a snatched shot. He settled again.

He was aware of rifle fire coming from the Lodge one thousand five hundred feet below him, and that fire was being returned sporadically from the well dug-in hit team. He shut it out of his mind, concentrating on the target area, maintaining position and posture, steadying his breathing, relaxing, waiting for the target on the hill a mile across the valley to show himself.

He was patient as he waited... waited... waited for his opportunity.

At that moment, over a mile to their south-west, the SBS units were being dropped off in dead ground by the Lynx, about half a mile away and a thousand feet lower than the hit team, who could hear the sound of the two helicopters but could not see them. The Apache was still airborne and giving cover to the drop-off, when the navigator spotted a small group of red deer hinds startle and flee, apparently away from something high on the mountain straight north. The spotter on the mountain opposite saw the same flight.

Up on Meall Dearg, the Nepalese still couldn't pinpoint the choppers due to the combination of the north-easterly wind and the dead ground. But they could hear them as they prepared for action.

It was as though the whole wilderness had tensed itself. The wind dropped momentarily. An odd stillness descended on the mountains but it was a fleeting moment of time standing still, as though it were a harbinger, for a lot of action was about to be compressed into a very short period of time.

As the Apache crested the rise, the pilot saw the Javelin targeting him from a well-camouflaged scoop in the ground. A wild banking manoeuvre was too little, too late. As the Apache banked away, the missile hit the underbelly and several million pounds worth of airborne fighting machine, with two highly experienced and valuable crew members, went down on the mountainside.

The supremely fit SBS teams were now powering up the flanks of Meall Dearg. They had seen the Apache go down and they knew now that, whatever their strength and disposition, their enemy clearly had a lethal capability. They were closing in and the officer in charge, a seasoned non-commissioned officer who had attacked enemy positions on similar but more arid ground at Tora Bora, was just wondering why they hadn't yet been on the end of incoming fire when he spotted, less than five hundred feet above him, three men standing, exposed, facing north away from them and towards the Lodge. One of them shouldered the Javelin missile launcher in the firing position; the other two were off to one side and slightly forward to avoid the back-blast primary danger area. He took a quick look through his field glasses, just in time to see the Javelin launch its deadly payload northwards.

The missile hit the front of Lynacraigie Lodge some twenty feet right of the front door and enveloped the building in a huge, deafening, explosion. The thick granite walls of the Victorian Lodge absorbed most of the force of the impact but that wing of the house was wrecked.

'Fire at will!' shouted the SBS leader.

In his peripheral vision, the shooter hunkered down in the old stalker's scoop, was aware of smoke billowing from the Lodge a thousand feet below. He shut it out of his mind, concentrating on the area of the target. He couldn't see the damage from the Javelin missile, but he could imagine it. He took careful aim. CRACK! The .50 round leaving the muzzle of his rifle made a savage report as the shock wave bounced off the mountains.

For a split second only, the SBS men froze, checking the direction of the incoming shot before starting to lay down withering fire uphill and onto the enemy position. Their officer however, concentrated on the view through his binos, registering the seconds before the THUMP! When it came, the young mercenary simply broke apart before his eyes in a slow motion display of gratuitous carnage, his shattered body fragmenting as the .50 inch round hit his torso with devastating and spectacular effect. In the same instant, the launch tube of the Javelin he was holding went up in the air, firing off its deadly charge into the Highland sky. *The SBS leader knew it was not one of his trooper's weapons that had caused such havoc.* His admiration for the shooter's killing ability, whoever he was, was left unstated. The two remaining mercenaries' instantaneous revulsion and anger at having been splattered by the blood, guts and organs of their young brother spurred them into immediate action.

'NOW!' The SBS squad pressed their attack uphill. As they launched themselves up the steep ridgeline, the middle brother, veteran of many a battle in the hills of Nepal as a Communist fighter, laid down a hail of fire from the GPMG, whilst elder brother fed the ammunition belt. Pinned down, and at a height disadvantage, the SBS found themselves losing ground. CRACK! Another .50 round flew between the two remaining mercenaries narrowly missing them. The wind had gusted, causing the round to be off-target. The shooter had missed his target but it was enough to deflect the concentration of the enemy and the assault party took advantage, laying down a barrage of fire. Three rounds fired, only two left. The shooter knew he had to make them count.

Then, as if in the final act of a play where the audience already knows the outcome, yet are on the edge of their seats with tension and anticipation as the finale plays out, the remaining two mercenaries stood up, firing the GPMG downhill.

He had them! The action of a skilled practitioner is always smooth and the squeezing of the trigger was more like a caress, a gentle, tender stroke of the hair, which was in complete contrast to the mayhem he was about to unleash.

CRACK! The machine gunner and his weapon were blown backwards by the kinetic energy of the rifle round, somersaulting man and weapon through the air.

Instinctively, the SBS team to a man mentally counted the seconds: one second ... two seconds ... three seconds. 'Three-quarters of a mile away,' shouted one of them.

Elder brother, ex-Sergeant Prem Gurung, sensed it was all over.

He called out several times. He was shouting, his voice trailing on the wind. 'Jai Mahakali, Aayo Gorkhali, Jai Mahakali, Aayo Gorkhali,' he cried out several times.

Mountains and men stood stock still in awe of this plaintive yet glorious sound.

Slowly, Prem Gurung stood up against the skyline; his right hand rose to the sky, the morning sun glinting off his kukhri. Then, seemingly in slow motion, he started to run towards his attackers, screaming, 'Jai Mahakali, Aayo Gorkhali', *Glory be to the Goddess of War, here come the Gurkhas!* The SBS team, sensing there was no danger, stopped transfixed at the sound of the battle cry and this final act of a warrior. They knew he was no immediate threat. They waited.

The shooter didn't.

CRACK! Sergeant Prem Gurung's body was almost severed at the waist by the devastating energy of the round. An instant death. A warrior's death. The SBS team fired and manoeuvred through and beyond their objective but they knew there was no opposition left. They inspected the mess on the hillside with mixed sentiments.

The Senior NCO bent down to pick up a damaged half-inch round. 'Radio silence!' he ordered. He rolled the round between his fingers, thoughtfully. 'Let's find the other three slugs if we can, lads. We don't want these presented to a Coroner's Inquest if, God forbid, there is one, do we? A half-inch sniper rifle doesn't exist in the UK, does it? And whoever the shooter was on the end of it doesn't fuckin' exist either! Everyone got that?'

The others merely nodded in agreement.

On the opposite mountainside, Philip Dunstan put down the sniper rifle and, without any visible emotion, looked at his spotter.

'It's fucking over now!' said The Monk with finality.

***

The gratuitous death of a noble warrior flashed into his mind – from his own beloved Brigade of Gurkhas, and by his own hand, no less. *How could Sergeant Prem Gurung do it, how could he betray years of loyal service, all that mutual devotion, loyalty and history since 1815?*

But Philip Dunstan knew the answer to his own question: Prem Gurung had sworn allegiance to this country, to the British Crown. And through the instrument of its politicians, this country had betrayed that unswerving loyalty.

Looking down on the mountains of ancient Caledonia, he could not help thinking of a struggle taking place nearly five thousand miles away in another mountainous country where, unbeknown to him, full independence of Gilgit-Baltistan had been declared, together with the announcement of a new Protectorate Alliance with India. And between a continual stream of phone calls to tribal elders, administrators and the press, Anil Ghol was paying more than passing attention to his new female volunteer assistant.

Chapter Twenty-Six

Exhausted, Dunstan and The Monk slowly descended down towards the Lodge. Each man was lost in his own thoughts, each absorbed in dealing with his own personal demons, both knowing that this was not the end of the affair.

Worn down by a life of danger and uncertainty, The Monk was reflecting that yet again he was cast adrift by events, this time ejected from the only solidity and security he had known in his Welsh mountain home, now all but destroyed, into a new world of unknowns. When you are young in mind and body, he reflected, such uncertainty is a prelude to adventure. The Monk now realised that his battered body and depleted spirit would no longer see him through any more "adventures". He could no longer treat triumph and disaster as equal imposters. His reserves gone, his gammy leg paining him, he limped slowly down the hillside, not broken, just bruised and bowed – a man old before his time.

If Dunstan's body was in better overall shape, his mind wasn't. Yes, he was alive and, more importantly, so were his family. But at what cost? He knew that it would take a long time for his flashbacks and nightmares to abate and recede; if ever they did. And had he destroyed the fabric of his marriage and family, the very thing he held dearest? Words from Oscar Wilde's Ballad of Reading Gaol... *Yet each man kills the thing he loves...* filled his mind as he supported The Monk over a particularly rough piece of ground. In their different ways, both men had been bankrupted and denuded by the past few days.

Dunstan didn't know what to expect as they approached the Lodge. As they headed down the mountain, a group came out onto the drive, looking up at the mountainside. Dunstan easily identified the rangy figure of his wife, but the others were not clearly visible.

The Monk looked through his scope and helped out, 'One woman with binoculars ... two armed policemen, weapons drawn ... and two young lads, the bigger one with a rifle and scope over his shoulder, the younger with a pair of binos as big as him round his scrawny little neck ... two small girls standing behind in the doorway ... small boy now looking through binos, looks like he is reporting his findings to the woman ... woman now taking binos and looking ... policeman now easing the rifle from larger boy's shoulders and unloading it...'

The Monk passed the scope to his friend with a wry smile on his face.

Dunstan's reaction was one of instant and overwhelming relief, then confusion. Perhaps he thought Faith and the kids, having recognised them, would run out to meet them descending. They didn't. They stood stock still, watching the painfully slow progress of the two men, Faith now pulling the two girls tightly to her. Finally, as the ground evened out, the policemen and two boys headed up the Glen to meet them and help them in.

Eventually, the two parties met. The boys seemed to sense the moment. After a brief hug, they took a hand each and walked Philip down the Glen. The policemen stayed close. They had orders to "contain" but not arrest or question The Monk and Dunstan: some senior types were on their way from London with questions of their own.

The last few hundred yards to the house were interminable for both men. The crepitus in The Monk's knee was getting worse as the cartilage ground against bone; for Dunstan, it was a mental anguish as he approached the Lodge. They could see the damage to the fabric of the house from high velocity weapons and his heart sank, imagining what he had put his family through, the impact of his actions now laid bare before him.

Dunstan looked at his wife and took a step towards her and the girls. 'Don't! Don't come near me! Just bloody well stay where you are and just tell me the truth. The worst of it.' The words hit Dunstan like the barb of a stingray in his chest. Silent tears flowed down Faith's cheeks. As he stood facing her, he knew this wasn't the end of the matter, yet how could he begin to tell Faith the truth? That their life as they had known it now lay in tatters. That they had nothing left: and, as far as he knew, he was still suspected of murder and money laundering?

Even The Monk recognised an emotional pressure valve was about to explode and moved quickly to ease the children inside the house, followed by the policemen. Dunstan tried to frame his thoughts and form his words, but Faith was ahead of him:

'So, Philip, what *is* the score, do we have any sort of future or have you destroyed our life together completely? Just tell me what we have left, if anything!'

'The business is gone...'

'I don't care about your *fucking* business! I am talking about *us*, what do we have left of our lives?'

'I don't know, Faith. I really don't know. Uhmm...I don't know how to tell you this, but I am afraid the house has gone, burned out. Sorry to tell you like this...And I think I am still a suspect in Idris's murder...Darling, look...'

But Dunstan was about to be on the receiving end of both barrels of Faith's unbridled anger: 'The what! What do you mean our home has burned down?! How and when?! And don't you bloody well "Darling" me!! You have swung a bloody great wrecking ball through our lives and all you can say is "sorry"!! ...You bastard!!'

Dunstan was suddenly spared the full force of his wife's vitriol as her voice was dissipated by the rotor blades of a Puma helicopter coming in low over the nearest hill. The policemen ran out followed by a limping Monk, who signalled back to the kids to stay inside. The chopper banked sharply and just before it touched down, six fully-armed soldiers with no insignia jumped out and formed a thirty-metre protective cordon around the chopper. The blades slowed and came to rest. There was a momentary pause and a Close Protection police officer jumped out, looked around, then looked back and offered his hand to the female Assistant Chief Constable of Police Scotland, followed by the stolid figure of Celia Fanshawe. It was perfectly clear who was in charge.

'Mr. Dunstan, Celia Fanshawe. Rebecca Lovat said that upon meeting you, I should mention the ridiculous sobriquet Fairy Godmother. I can't imagine why. And you must be Mrs Dunstan?' she said, turning to a perplexed and still fuming Faith. 'Well I think it is fair to say your husband has left quite a trail of destruction from Wales to Kashmir. Let's go inside and talk through the fall-out, shall we?'

The Monk was hiding half in and half out of the doorway. As they approached, he eased out of the shadows. As he did so, he stopped Celia Fanshawe dead in her tracks. She was momentarily at a loss, and Faith Dunstan later swore she saw Fanshawe blush.

'Good God! John?'

The Monk was more prepared than she, 'Celia: long-time-no-see. Looks like you are running the show now.' A statement of fact rather than a question.

'God, you look... er...'

'Old?' queried The Monk.

'I was thinking "battle-scarred" was a more appropriate epithet. So you *are* The Monk. I surmised as much from Lovat's report referring to *John Edwards*. She omitted your middle name otherwise I would have been sure.'

The Monk had a bashful look on his face that Dunstan had never seen before. Philip nearly opened his mouth to ask the obvious and then thought better of it. Whatever interaction had taken place in the past between these two it was a long time ago and was never going to be aired in public.

'Well, you *have* been in good hands, Mr. Dunstan. As I once was,' she volunteered enigmatically, her gaze still on The Monk. She recovered her internal composure, 'Come, Dunstan, John, we need to talk. Mrs Dunstan, please join us. I think it will be better than your husband trying to explain the inexplicable. I am sure the local police can entertain the children. In fact, Assistant Chief Constable, please direct all police to stay outside. We don't need them in here.'

Chapter Twenty-Seven

They withdrew to the drawing room, Celia Fanshawe consciously taking the high-back chair so as to maintain her authority, although her mere presence was authority enough. The Monk slumped in an old sofa as battered as he was; Dunstan and Faith sat on different chair arms, a suitable distance apart. The body language was not lost on Fanshawe.

From the outset, Celia Fanshawe made it clear she wasn't here for a social chat. 'For the avoidance of doubt, everyone in this room is by default subject to the Official Secrets Act. You too, Mrs Dunstan.' Faith nodded imperceptibly, wondering what was coming. Whoever this woman was, she clearly commanded and demanded respect.

'So, let's have a look at your life balance sheet shall we, Mr Dunstan? And yours as well, John!' The Monk shifted uncomfortably in the deep sofa. 'On the plus side, you have broken an international fraud and money laundering ring set up to finance terrorist activity on one of the most sensitive geographic and political fault lines on the planet: India and Pakistan. Furthermore, as a direct consequence of your actions, there are unsubstantiated reports that a specific terror threat that could have led to all-out nuclear war – and, by the way, might well have brought China into the fray – has been neutralised. Of course, this is merely speculation and rumour which is currently being strenuously denied by all parties in the region. That's the plus side; though in terms of world peace, I admit it is a very big plus.'

Faith looked at Dunstan, wide-eyed. His attention though was on the woman who held his fate in her hands, who looked as though she was weighing his future and was as yet undecided.

'On the negative side, then. Kashmir and Greater Baltistan – the Northern Territories – are in complete turmoil, having made a Declaration of Independence without much to back it up other than a widely orchestrated campaign of terror and public disorder, all financed through the fraud that took place via your payments company. Unbelievably, India has declared it a Protectorate. Interesting to see how that plays out. Pakistan has responded by strengthening its troop presence on the border, as has India. We currently have a three-way stand-off and the United Nations has called an emergency meeting of the Security Council. The jury is out on what will happen but it all looks a bit messy. Closer to home, we have the unexplained murder of Idris Morgan and the kidnap and murder of your secretary, Miss Kate Cross...' Fanshawe's discourse was interrupted by a stifled scream from Faith Dunstan, who slumped into her chair. Fanshawe shot her a compassionate look but nevertheless continued dispassionately, 'Then we have the unexplained death of a number of ex-Ghurkha soldiers, each with a hitherto impeccable service record, on a Scottish mountainside: according to a situation report received in the helicopter on the way here, by means of a high calibre round fired from a high velocity weapon usually used by American Forces combat snipers.' Dunstan clenched his jaw but otherwise outwardly remained unmoved. Inside he was in turmoil, wondering where this was leading. 'Then we have the small matter of a full-scale battle and the destruction of a house on a Welsh hill owned by a shell company based offshore in Gib...' she stopped abruptly and looked at The Monk with a sudden realisation, 'John, it was your place wasn't it?'

'Yes, Celia, it *was* my place.'

'Well you certainly *have* caused mayhem. The Welsh police are after at least two men of unknown identity for terrorist offences and stockpiling large amounts of illegally held weapons, rocket launchers, explosive devices and ammunition. That's a life sentence in itself, should the perpetrators be identified and caught and convicted of course, which on the *prima facie* evidence seems highly likely...Thames Valley police are after you, Dunstan, for escaping from custody and assaulting one of their police officers. Then the Financial Conduct Authority is also after you for misleading investors and the stock markets in general, and the Serious Fraud Office are at this moment preparing a case against you for running a public company as a front for fraud and money laundering activities. That in itself is several years behind bars and barred for life from being a company director. And a huge fine.'

Dunstan opened his mouth to speak but before the words were fully formed, Fanshawe cut him off. 'I have not finished yet. Now, to the thing that really upsets me, and for which I hold you personally responsible: the death of my best counter-terrorism agent in that outrageous aircraft stunt. The Foreign Office have carpeted Al-Qurum's High Commissioner and asked him to explain. He stated that the pilot unfortunately got the wrong airfield, that he personally knew nothing of any high speed vehicle ingress, and that the pilot has been appropriately reprimanded. Which in diplomatic speak means awarded a medal and fat pension. Diplomatically, there the matter rests. Officially, Graham Freshfield died in the course of operational duty and I personally hold you two responsible for his death.'

The Monk was stirred into defence, 'Rebecca Lovat lived, Freshfield died. He was unlucky. It was an accident. Shit happens. Celia.'

'Yes it does, doesn't it, John?" she replied without further expansion. She was quiet, dwelling for a moment on Freshfield's untimely, and in her view wholly unnecessary, death. Ultimately though, she reflected, Freshfield was responsible for his own actions on that day. She forced herself to move on, 'So, Mr Dunstan, how would you assess your balance sheet?'

'Pretty negative by the looks of it. I should have stayed in Al-Qurum,' a deflated and defeated Dunstan reflected, glancing briefly at Faith but unable to hold her gaze. If he thought he might have a warm welcome back in the UK, he was clearly wrong. He again looked at Faith but she was not about to let him off the hook, yet neither was she going to sit back and be a victim of circumstance. Besides which, she was shrewd enough to know how the world really worked.

'You forgot to mention the loss of our home, Miss Fanshawe, and all the danger and grief he has put his family through for the sake of some thoughtless action years ago, which he failed to mention to me in all the years of our marriage. Looks like you are in deep shit all round, Philip.' But Faith wasn't finished, 'So, Celia, if I may call you that, it seems to me that my husband has done all the dirty work for you, for which he has received no acknowledgement. I don't know the ins and outs of your organisation's activities, and I don't wish to know, but if any part of this tangled web came to light, the Press would have a field day unravelling it, Official Secrets Act or not. You would have investigative journalists crawling all over the place, joining up the dots and creating a picture of Security

Services, Armed Services, and Police incompetence. And this is how it would probably play out: in spite of an official line of not commenting on security matters, my guess is that your organisation and others involved would have to explain themselves to Parliamentary Select Committees, including Home Affairs, Foreign Affairs and probably Defence Committees, not to mention the Intelligence and Security Committee. In short, at some level, some of the story would leak into the public domain. Which in turn would sour certain international relations. A damage limitation exercise would follow. The Mandarins at the Foreign Office would be seriously bent out of shape and want some form of retribution. In other words, a major shake-up would follow. Heads would roll and responsibilities would be *reallocated* across the Security Services. And to cap it all, some nice cuddly Ghurkhas kidnapping and killing people because the British Army has treated them badly would be a nice sideshow for tabloid journalists and certain celebrities. And the Army would have some explaining to do, including how an ex-soldier managed to accumulate so much weaponry. So the upshot is, what are *you* going to do about all this?'

Fanshawe actually laughed out loud. 'Not a bad synopsis, but one which doesn't even scratch the surface of the potential fall-out. Mr Dunstan, your wife seems to have a better grasp of *real politik* than you do. You are more or less right of course, Faith, but we have work to do to contain this, so let's start here and now: Assistant Chief Constable, have any crimes been reported in the vicinity of this Lodge?'

'No, not as yet.'

'Well, that's a start. I can deal with the Army and Thames Valley Police. The Welsh see themselves as independent and they have the bit between their teeth. I will need to call in some favours, blame it on the re-emergence of an active cell of Welsh nationalists or some such. But it won't be easy. There will be a cost in political capital.'

Fanshawe looked at The Monk intensely for a moment. She didn't see the battered old warrior before her, just a young SAS trooper on his first job on the counter-terrorism team, his olive skin, a shock of black hair and sharp looks that stole her heart on her first real job in MI5 as a counter-terrorism liaison officer to the Army. Her heart skipped a beat as she looked at him and said,

'However you, John, need to disappear.'

'Shouldn't be difficult, Celia. I have a one-way ticket to Al-Qurum.'

'Good, keep your head down there for as long as necessary. And don't ever go back to Wales until you're a very old man!'

'Not long to wait then,' replied The Monk, drily.

Dunstan still had problems of his own, 'What about the Fraud Office and Financial Conduct Authority; and I still have responsibilities as a director of a listed company, not to mention employees and customers, if there are any left. And what should we say to the markets that won't arouse suspicion of what actually went on…'

Fanshawe held up her hand: she already had some answers. 'Bottom line is that you are down but not totally out. Yesterday, we held a series of preliminary meetings between the Security Services, Director of Public Prosecutions and The London Stock Exchange, and the usual collection of Whitehall mandarins. The outcome was somewhat encouraging. The DPP will shelve all charges but keep them on file, pending continuing investigations and wholly dependent on your absolute co-operation. The Stock Exchange made it clear that as the market could not be fully and fairly informed, and the shares are as you know almost worthless, they had no option but to suspend the company from its stock exchange listing…' at this news, Dunstan groaned but Fanshawe was unsympathetic, 'Well, what on earth did you think would happen? That doesn't mean that you can't continue to trade and sort out the mess. You have a lot do. That's it for the moment. I must get back to London.'

Fanshawe moved a couple of steps towards the door, 'This place is quarantined for the next forty-eight hours until the mess on the hillside is cleared up and in order to make sure the overall threat has been neutralised. There is a cordon around the whole estate, and no-one enters or leaves during that time. If you need provisions the police will bring them in….' she looked intently for a moment at Philip and Faith, 'Now, you two – far be it from me to interfere in your personal lives, but I suggest you spend the next few days getting to know each other again and building some bridges. You have more to live for than you know. Each of you are blessed to have the other and your kids: cherish what you have. Oh, and Faith, in spite of all the mayhem caused, your husband is nevertheless a *very* brave man.' She paused to let this sink in. 'By the way, Dunstan, do you know anything about cryptocurrencies?'

Dunstan was thrown for a moment, 'Er, like Bitcoin?'

'That is one form of cryptocurrency, yes. I suggest that you spend some of your time over the next few months learning as much as you can about them, the way they work and their potential applications. Then, if our damage limitation exercise is successful and the world hasn't gone mad, or into meltdown, we will meet to talk about it. Goodbye.'

She turned and as she passed The Monk she said, 'John, walk with me to the helicopter; we need to talk.'

The Monk eased his weary body out of the sofa and followed her. They walked in silence until out of the house, the rest following at a discreet distance.

The Monk broke the silence first. 'How long do I need to disappear for, Celia?'

'A couple of years would do it. We will let you know. I never thought I would see you again, but I never forgot you.'

'You knew where I was, you could have found me through your channels.'

'I know, but well, maybe I knew it wouldn't have worked out. We were from different backgrounds – and we had different paths.' Her voice had suddenly softened with a hint of melancholy.

They were nearly at the helicopter. Fanshawe reached into her pocket and handed The Monk a card. 'Don't lose it. Call me if you ever need me. Call me even if you don't. I am too old to care what people think anymore. Then she did something that surprised both The Monk and herself: she stood on her tiptoes and kissed him on the cheek. 'Now get out of the country whilst *I* sort out *your* mess.' At that she turned and headed into the helicopter, leaving The Monk staring at her back.

Back in the house, Dunstan was eyeing his wife warily, half expecting another tongue lashing and wondering how he was ever going to bridge the divide. Luckily, he didn't need to:

'So where does that leave us? Apart from all this shit you are in, what have we got left?'

Dunstan wondered how much to tell Faith, then decided that full disclosure was the best course of action – well almost full: he thought it wise to underplay the tens of millions which he had forced Ghol to transfer when he was in Kashmir; he didn't know when he might need it, or even if he might have to pay it back, though sorting out where and to whom would take years.

'The good news is I cloned our operations in Bermuda as the shit was hitting the fan. We still have an international business operational and making money. Even though CyberX has been suspended from the stock exchange, it can still trade, although the UK business is a dead duck as most of our clients have left us. And I put over a million quid of company money down there to cover operational expenses. Oh, and I stashed some other money offshore that will keep us going for a while, not a lot but it will keep us alive.'

'Enough to buy us a large tent and feed the kids?' Faith responded.

'Yes, more than enough for that.' For the first time in a while, Dunstan managed to force a smile.

'Well, you seem to have an ally there, Philip.'

'Who, Celia Fanshawe? That's what worries me, Faith. Nothing is ever what it seems where these people are concerned. I don't think I am out of the woods yet…'

Just as Faith was feeling a little more optimistic, she suddenly felt deflated and anxious.

Chapter Twenty-Eight

Six Months Later

The Monk was by now settled in his new role as Training Major with Al-Qurum Special Forces, still with part of his mind – and with quite a bit more of his heart – in the Elan Valley in Wales. Occasionally he thought of Celia Fanshawe, not as she was now – the newly-promoted Deputy Director General of MI5 – but as the young twenty-something operative he had known, sharing an attic together on a six-week stake-out of a PIRA bomb-making factory in Birmingham, though mostly his heart beat with a different rhythm, that of desert life, made stronger by the affinity he had with his fellow soldiers. In short, he was in his element. In consultation with the Sheikh, he had revamped the training to reflect and respond to the new and emerging political reality in the region: he had established and started to train a troop for ultra-long range desert patrols. A new fleet of armoured supercharged four-wheel drive vehicles was only part of it: he had them leading camel patrols deep into the desert and then dismounting to patrol for weeks on foot, establishing observation posts on the outer reaches of Al-Qurum's inhospitable borders. Al-Qurum had not yet been drawn into the Gulf conflict centred on Yemen and The Monk was determined to play his part in securing his host country's borders against any potential incursion or terrorist threat.

***

Asha Dhar had quite unexpectedly and impulsively fallen in love with Anil Ghol; and the feeling was clearly fully reciprocated. She returned back to the UK via Al-Qurum feeling thoroughly distracted. On arrival, she was taken by car for a detailed operational debrief by Director Special Forces, followed by a long interview with members of the Security Services, focusing oddly (in her opinion) on her views on the emerging political situation within Kashmir. This latter session proved particularly taxing as she now knew where her allegiances lay and she made it clear that, in her view, Kashmir's continuing drive for Independence should be supported by the British political establishment, not only to understand – and where possible influence – a new political reality, but also in her mind to be part of the solution in righting a historical wrong on the part of the British. She was asked point blank if there would be any circumstances under which she would return to Kashmir in a non-military capacity. Her heart leapt but she maintained her cool exterior and replied guardedly that it might be possible but it *would* have to be in a civilian capacity. Her audience nodded sagely and the conversation then proceeded to Awards. After a long-winded preamble wherein it was meticulously explained that she could not of course receive a military award as the operation did not officially exist; nor could it be a UK civilian award because it took place overseas, they informed her that they had therefore settled for a CMG (Companion of the Order of St Michael and St George) for exemplary overseas service. Corporal Murria would receive a General Officer Commanding's Commendation and would be promoted. Dhar gained the sense that more intellectual firepower and energy had been expended on selecting this award than on the analysis of the operation itself. She was also somewhat baffled by this national recognition. She looked at the mandarins and senior spies arranged before her and drew a deep breath:

'Excuse me, but what does receiving this award actually *mean?*'

'Well,' said the senior Foreign Office civil servant, 'I suppose it means, Captain Dhar, that you are *one of us,*' followed by congratulations and indulgent smiles all round.

She didn't know it then but a whole new life of adventure was just starting. Within three weeks, she had by mutual agreement resigned her Army Commission and officially retired from the army. After packing her bags and saying a long goodbye to her parents, she took the next plane to Delhi, before travelling north under armed escort to join Ghol as a personal advisor.

***

Rebecca Lovat's star was in the ascendancy. On the back of her work "cracking" the CyberX card fraud, she had been promoted and appointed to a newly formed role as Head of Digital Counter-Terrorism. This new department had a very loose follow-the-money remit. In that respect, nothing had changed since the days of the Gunpowder Plot, which was discovered primarily through the monitoring of large movements of cash required to fund the act. What has changed over the centuries is the sophistication and the means available to terrorists and organised crime to transfer electronic money around the world under strong encryption within the Dark Web. Now a new layer of complexity has been added: electronic cash can be transferred directly between funders, terrorists and criminals without ever going through a third party financial institution. Furthermore, the sender and recipient, or the buyer and seller in the case of arms, explosives, or enriched uranium could do this through strong encryption; and do it anonymously unless they wish to reveal their identities, which on the whole they don't. The effect of this is to make it almost impossible to track and trace such transfers.

Rebecca Lovat's newly-founded department – working with its US counterparts – had been charged with developing strategies for countering the funding of terrorism through cyber-crime. Five months into the job and she was stuck: her department knew such crime was taking place but simply couldn't penetrate the networks. Working with GCHQ, she had attacked known digital crime networks but all they got was a series of encrypted keys which hid the real identities of the perpetrators. All they could do was to try DoS attacks – Denial of Service – but they merely served to slow things down for a while. Lovat knew that she had to be creative and devise some other means. She had to start thinking laterally and for that she needed the permission of Fanshawe and the co-operation of other Security Services.

Chapter Twenty-Nine

Dunstan had spent the last six months trying to rebuild his life. CyberX was still suspended from the London Stock Exchange AIM market, pending ongoing Serious Fraud Office Investigations and Philip still had the spectre of criminal charges hanging over him. He had nagging doubts about how the future would work out but he forced himself to focus, taking solace in spending more time with his family and planning the rebuild of the family home with Faith.

He had down-sized operations in the UK in favour of Bermuda, where he had cloned the CyberX transaction processing operations, and from where Tysoe was running the show. Dunstan had used some of the money he transferred from Ghol to make generous severance payments to some his staff, though one person he did retain was Abdul Shahid. Dunstan liked Shahid – after all it was he who had discovered the fraud – and had tasked him with researching cryptocurrencies, especially the encrypted processing platform that facilitated some of them: the so-called *Blockchain*.

Blockchain is a technology which, using public-private key encryption, facilitates direct transfer of funds and assets between parties without having to go through an intermediary. That is why it's called "peer-to-peer". The concept of a peer-to-peer electronic cash system was proposed in 2009, by a man calling himself "Satoshi Nakamoto": he called it Bitcoin.

***

Under the circumstances, the day-to-day business of international payment processing was doing quite well under Marc Tysoe's new management. He had taken the initiative, spun out a new company in Bermuda, hired some sales guys and secured new customers in the Caribbean and Central and South America.

This left Dunstan space and time to reflect and recover, plan for the future, and try to penetrate the somewhat impenetrable world of the Blockchain. The more he found out about it, the more in awe he was not only of the concept but more especially of its implications. It was the next electronic revolution. Forget the Worldwide Web, this was the Worldwide Ledger and its implications were, he concluded, revolutionary.

Dunstan was now out in Bermuda, checking on the day to day-to-day operations, but also broaching the subject of peer-to-peer electronic cash with Tysoe, who was exercising his usual healthy cynicism.

'So we can get rid of the banks, then?' said Tysoe. 'For transactions using digital money, yes.'

'Which can then be converted to real money.'

'Yep: there is already an international market for digital currency conversion.'

'How is an audit trail kept, then?'

'Every transaction is recorded across the Blockchain. It's just like double-entry bookkeeping, both dispatch and receipt of funds is recorded and time-stamped so the same money cannot be spent twice. It's like a Worldwide Ledger. Just like a big electronic cash book, really.'

'So, where does this Blockchain thing reside then?'

'Everywhere and anywhere: the information is fragmented and scattered across computers all over the world... like our own CyberX nodes but tens of thousands of them all forming the platform for the Blockchain. It's called Distributed Networking and it's the future. Instead of data being concentrated within a few major banks or big international technology companies, it's distributed and people can control their own data and transact with each other anonymously... brilliant.'

Tysoe was quick off the mark, but without prior knowledge even he was having difficulty keeping up, 'So, er, what you are saying is that all transactions can be seen on this so-called Worldwide Ledger – just like all information is visible on the Net, but you cannot see the people behind the transactions? They remain anonymous.'

'Correct. Individuals and companies alike are represented by their personal private encryption key only – a long winded set of numbers and figures. Then for every transaction the private key – plus information on the payment, transaction timings and so forth – is all wrapped up and encrypted with a public key, then routed out over the Blockchain. Even if

GCHQ, the NSA or the Russians broke the encryption, they would see only part of the transaction detail and not the identity of the sender or recipient.' Tysoe was quiet for a second then his expression changed to one of amazement as he realised the full implications of this, 'Shit: that's a recipe for global money laundering and fraud on a huge scale!'

'Exactly!' agreed Dunstan. 'Can *we* make money out it?'

'Theoretically, yes, by providing peer-to-peer services. We would take a small amount of digital money from each transaction – we are talking micro money – but it would all add up. There are existing Blockchain platforms out there, like Etherical that we could use to facilitate such a service. In our agreements with customers we agree our small fee for each amount transferred and include it as a small component of every encrypted transaction, which is then deducted from the total amount after the transfer is made. We could also create an electronic wallet service for people to hold their digital money securely and offer a service for verifying identities or even the validity of assets.'

'So, say some bloke is buying a second-hand yacht, we could verify ownership and that the thing actually exists without going through, say, a yacht broker, and sort of facilitate the contract.'

'Yes. All electronically. They are called Smart Contracts. Every broker and bank you can think of can – theoretically at least – be taken out of the loop: *disintermediated* is the jargon.'

'Bugger me!' said Tysoe, with feeling. 'That's huge!'

'We need to get going on this. Establish a new company offshore here for a start.' Dunstan, for his own reasons, was in a rush.

'With what? We are a bit strapped for cash,' replied Tysoe.

Dunstan slid a piece of paper across the desk, 'Here are the account details, username and passwords for an account here at the Bank of Bermuda. There is more than enough – take a look,' said Dunstan with an enigmatic smile.

Tysoe logged into the account and looked at the available funds. 'Bloody 'ell!' he exclaimed, 'Where the heck did all that come from?'

'Transferred by Ghol in Kashmir: he wasn't very happy about it but then he didn't have much choice in the matter. Besides which, I reckon if his derivatives trading has been as successful as I think it has, he will have a lot more than that tucked away.'

Tysoe ruminated for a while, 'We could do a lot with this Philip, but is it really ours to play with?'

Dunstan was equally reflective, 'I have thought about this and the answer is that although these funds are the proceeds of crime, we don't actually know who they belong to. It could take years to unravel the fraud, if ever. And which country, agency or police force has an interest in doing that? My guess is none. Tell you what, let's *loan* the new company the money to get started from these funds. Or we could do it as an investment – operate it like an investment fund.'

'Looks like we have a new adventure then, Philip!' grinned Tysoe.

'I reckon we do, Marc. I think we should get going on this today. Abdul has come a long way with his research and we can use existing infrastructure that's already out there on the Blockchain. We could be up and running pretty quickly, with funding courtesy of Mr Ghol.'

Dunstan's urgency and enthusiasm were infectious. If only Tysoe knew Dunstan's real reason for his sense of urgency, he wouldn't have been so enthusiastic. And if Tysoe had had the chance to look closer at the "Ghol account" as Dunstan was now referring to it, he would have seen that considerable sums had already left it. Dunstan was once more looking over the horizon and making contingency plans. Or rather, he had already started taking contingency action and, at that very moment, Abdul and his small "research team" were further along the curve than even Dunstan could have hoped for.

Chapter Thirty

Philip Dunstan returned direct to the UK from Bermuda, arriving at London Gatwick on a Sunday morning in November in a relaxed state of mind and looking forward to seeing Faith and the kids. He had a car waiting for him to take him back to Oxfordshire, but what he didn't know was that the car would not be needed and his destination was not Oxfordshire, but rather the City of London.

As he passed through customs, two men in plain clothes stepped out from behind the screen, introduced themselves as senior detectives from the City of London Police and informed him that he was under arrest and would be formally charged in connection with fraud, money laundering and other matters. Not for the first time, he felt like fleeing: doing some serious damage to the two men in front of him and running. Instead, he steeled himself, groaned inwardly and followed instructions like a good soldier. He was driven to Bishopsgate Police Station within the walls of the City of London. There, in the presence of representatives from the Serious Fraud Office and the Crown Prosecution Service, he was formally charged with a raft of financial crimes and misdemeanours including fraud, misleading investors and false reporting to stock markets, and also international money laundering which, taken in aggregate, could, he was reliably informed, mean fifteen to twenty years behind bars.

Dunstan scanned the charges. He knew many of them would not stand up in court due to lack of evidence, and that others were spurious – presented as if to bulk out the charge sheet. His only comment was, 'This is rubbish,' and he declined to answer any further questions or indeed to call a solicitor. Oddly, for someone in his apparent predicament, he was not unduly worried: he knew that the events leading up to the denouement in Kashmir were too politically charged and diplomatically sensitive to be aired in open court. Faith's initial reaction had been right, he thought. *So why bring all these charges, then? And that being the case, why hasn't Celia Fanshawe been able to deliver on her promise to clear the decks? Where is this pressure actually coming from?* He thought he knew why but not from where or from whom and had for some time been preparing himself for something like this. Certain agencies, he had deduced, needed something, and he had the keys to the cupboard. He would wait to see what happened next.

***

In the event, he did not have long to wait. The assembled enforcement officers appeared unimpressed by his refusal to answer their questions but in spite of their threats and imprecations he just sat there in silence. Eventually, they seemed to get bored and left, although he had a sense that the whole thing was an act ... perhaps the final Act. He sat alone going through scenarios and possible outcomes, trying to put his family to the back of his mind for the moment. After some thirty minutes, the door to the interview room opened and he was informed he was going to be taken to another location for further questioning.

Dunstan had had enough of these games, 'Either formally charge me or let me go but I am not answering any questions,' he demanded.

At that, Dunstan was handcuffed and bundled into the back of a waiting car which sped across London from The City, along The Embankment into Whitehall, and onto New Scotland Yard. He was led into the building under tight escort into a room with a large oval table and seating for twelve. Handcuffs were removed and he was seated in one of the middle chairs – and left there. He assumed that he was being watched, so he exercised his right to visit Planet Dunstan.

Some ten minutes later, the door opened and a group of two men and two women entered. To his genuine surprise, the police were not amongst them. Two men in their mid to late forties, dressed (he thought) awkwardly in pin-stripe suites, were followed into the room by two women: one the woman from the Crown Prosecution Service carrying a bundle of papers – which he assumed to be his charge sheets – and finally a woman in a familiar well-tailored suit: Rebecca Lovat.

'Good afternoon, Dunstan. How are you keeping?' she was back to her formal self but Philip perceived a less self-assured woman than when they had first met.

'Overall, very well Rebecca. I have been in worse scrapes – I think,' he ventured, looking across at the group now seated opposite.

'Let me make some introductions: Sir Richard Oakham from the Foreign Office, Brian Fenton from Home Office; and Eilidh McIntyre from the Crown Prosecution Service.' Lovat got to the point, 'These charges are very serious, Philip – could mean up to twenty years, or so I'm informed.' She looked at the CPS representative, who nodded in agreement.

Dunstan wasn't going to remain on the back foot. Her, problem, he perceived, was not just one of seeking out and neutralising the bad guys. *It is wider than that, otherwise these other characters wouldn't be around the table.*

'Which means *you* have a very big problem, Rebecca. Otherwise you wouldn't be here.'

'Rather presumptuous of someone in your position, don't yer think, Mr Dunstan?' interjected Oakham in a drawl which irritated Dunstan:

'Don't treat me like an idiot, whoever the hell you are!' Dunstan shot back, and looked around the table, 'I have played enough games with you people to last a life time. In fact, by now, I am probably as good at this Game as you are: collectively, you have a problem and you reckon that I have the means to help you. We wouldn't all be sitting here if that wasn't the case. It concerns cryptocurrencies based on the Blockchain and your ability – or lack of it – to crack them. Am I right; or am I right?' Dunstan asked rhetorically. 'All these charges and my *arrest* at Heathrow are a simply an attempt to put the thumb screws on me. In fact, I don't know why you dragged this poor woman from the CPS all the way here unless you are feeling generous with overtime. Now, I suggest we cut the crap and get down to business.'

Oakham, visibly annoyed, moved to respond but Rebecca cut him short, 'You are partially right of course, Philip.' She turned to the woman at the end of the table, Eilidh, I think the Crown Prosecution Service have done their bit for the day, thank you.' Eilidh did not hesitate and she left her papers on the desk, which only served to confirm in Dunstan's mind that she was primed to leave anyway.

As the door closed, Lovat continued, 'Yes, we have a significant challenge in monitoring the use of cryptocurrencies for criminal and terrorist related activities. Even if we were able to deploy all our resources to gather data and to crack the encryption, we still wouldn't know *who* is doing what with *whom*. Anyway, attempting to monitor every cryptocurrency would be futile.'

Dunstan articulated the problem for what was now *his* audience. 'Your real challenge is distinguishing between good honest transactions on the Blockchain and those that might be money laundering or funding crime and terrorism, isn't it?'

Lovat looked at Sir Robert Oakham, who nodded very slightly, 'Yes,' admitted Lovat, 'we need a hunter to create a trap that will entice the bad guys. A Blockchain-based service where the criminals and terrorists can be identified and movement of funds can be traced.'

'That's not going to happen unless it is in an environment that criminals can trust…like the the so-called Dark Web.'

'Exactly.' responded Lovat, emphatically.

'So, why don't you create another RedMarket, but based on the Blockchain, then?'

Oakham and Penton shifted awkwardly in their chairs and looked accusingly at Lovat. There was an uncomfortable silence.

Dunstan suddenly realised that they had already done it: that the UK Security Services were part and parcel of at least one other Dark Web sting operation, probably in cahoots with Friends. He decided, wisely, not to go down that road, so instead he took another line, 'Ah, you want an arms-length Operation, don't you? So that you have full deniability. All the benefits with no accountability, eh? Well, no change there then. So, let me try and work this one out: you want me to set up a Blockchain based operation, invite in every evil bastard in the known universe to transact over it, get them all to trust it and then make all the transaction details and identities known to you, and presumably your Friends in SIS and GCHQ, represented here by Sir Richard Oakham and Mr Penton – or whatever their real names are. Now why on earth would I want to do that?'

'To stop you rotting in jail,' responded Oakham.

Dunstan feigned surprise, 'Ah, so that's the deal. I set this thing up and that pile of paper at the end of the table disappears for ever?'

'Something like that,' responded Lovat.

The door opened and Celia Fanshawe stepped into the room, 'We all have to sell our soul to someone, Philip!'

'But, it's always good to know to whom you are selling your soul, don't you agree Ms Fanshawe?' Dunstan was unfazed by her entry; indeed, he would have been disappointed and concerned if she hadn't appeared. At least he now knew with whom he was to cut a deal with and that whatever the outcome, it would have her seal of approval.

'In this case, Philip, it is your Country to whom you are selling your soul. You have done it before and so it is no different this time – just different Masters.'

'It's going to cost several millions just to set it up.' responded Dunstan. Lovat smiled, 'We know you have the funds to set it up: we debriefed Asha Dhar and she told us about the funds which were transferred into one of your accounts by Ghol.'

Shit, thought Dunstan. He had missed that one...*So that's how they formulated this – on the back of that small piece of intelligence; and now they don't even have to spend any of their own funds or resources. Ah, maybe that's their real problem...*The realisation that this was as much about an inter-departmental wrangle over finance and resources as operational deniability put Dunstan in a much better mood. He turned to Fanshawe,

'I will need guarantees: all current charges irrevocably dropped and immunity from any further charges being brought. In writing of course, lodged with my solicitors. That should be straightforward enough for you; what won't be straightforward is clearing my name and re-establishing the trust in CyberX. I need to re-establish my company's reputation, and therefore my own, and with all these fraud and market manipulation charges creating suspicion I can't see that happening. Bottom line is, I still need to clear my name and be able to run a legitimate business.'

'Well I think we can help there, Philip,' responded Fanshawe, 'As you might imagine, we have already been giving all these matters some thought.' She placed two sheets of A4 paper in front of her, 'We have drafted a Press Release which states that your company has been hacked and is a victim of an international fraud, whereby your systems were taken over by foreign agents without your knowledge. Incompetence on your part, yes – criminality, no. Without mentioning any specific foreign agency, everyone will speculate that it's North Korea and, with any luck, Press and Public alike will have infinite sympathy for your predicament and bad luck. That's the way of the world.' She slid the two sheets across the desk. 'The Press Release, and a letter informing you that the CPS have insufficient evidence to continue with a prosecution and all charges have been dropped. They shall of course remain on file.'

'Hardly a full exoneration is it? The implication being that you might find *sufficient* evidence at some stage in the future. Selling my soul indeed – this sounds like a Faustian Pact.'

'You will appreciate that we have to future-proof this.' Fanshawe responded.

Dunstan had one outstanding concern, which in his mind was a ball-breaker '*I* can live with that. But this is beyond me: it has a long term impact on my family. I can't possibly agree to this without gaining the full consent of Faith. Any suggestions for how I should manage that domestic challenge, Miss Fanshawe?'

'It has already been managed on your behalf, Philip. Your wife and I had lunch in London earlier this week, under terms and conditions of utmost secrecy of course. I was most impressed with her perceptive and succinct analysis of your situation in Scotland, so it came as no surprise to me that she not only grasped the matter fully and quickly – and readily agreed to the terms under which you will be bound – but she seemed to think it was a very good way to put some boundaries around your activities. In other words, she is fully supportive and signed up to this, in all senses.'

Dunstan allowed himself a moment to reflect that once again he had been ambushed, before trying to give himself some wriggle room.

'I cannot, and will not, offer any guarantees that this will work – that we will attract and capture data from criminal and terrorist activity, let alone find the perpetrators.'

Lovat was now back on home turf, 'No, but it opens up new channels and possibilities. The key issue is for you to get it up and running. How many months will it take…ballpark time to get going?'

Before he could answer, Dunstan's phone vibrated in his pocket with a distinctive rhythm. He knew it was Abdul. Much to the visible irritation of those in the room, he extracted it slowly, taking a moment to glance at it before answering deliberately,

'Well, Rebecca, in terms of how long our peer-to-peer black market will take to get going, it is already up and running on the Dark Web. In fact, the first version was launched just before I left Bermuda…' he replied, much to the amazement and further discomfort of his audience. He took a moment for the full implications of this to sink in, then he looked at his phone and logged into his new brand new service securely. Even he was surprised at the message and report, 'And by the look of it, we have already attracted our first customers.' He slid the phone across the table to Lovat where she could see anonymous blocks of encrypted transactions summarised in an electronic ledger, 'Welcome to the *Black*Chain, Rebecca.' Fanshawe and her fellow Security Services colleagues peered over Lovat's shoulder. They were suitably impressed.

Fanshawe exhaled, but she did have one final question, "Do you have the identities of the people behind these private keys on this ledger by any chance?'

Dunstan allowed himself a very slight triumphant smile, "We might have," he replied non-committally.